A S

"SHAPIN'S FIRST NOVEL is dense and eventful.... Recommended."
— *Historical Novel Society Review Online*

"A SWEEPING PICTURE of a woman's life, one that is at times heartbreaking and funny, ordinary and amazing..."
— *Estella's Revenge, a 'Zine about Books!*

A Desire Path

"POLITICS IS POWER and power always attracts. 'A Desire Path' is a novel of romance and politics set amongst the aftermath of World War II, with the frost of the Cold War coalescing. An affair between a union leader and a lawyer's wife leads to cruel intentions, as well as a woman driven to defect to the Soviet Union. A riveting novel with much romance and intrigue, 'A Desire Path' is well worth considering, not to be missed."
— *Midwest Book Review*

"I JUMPED AT THE CHANCE to review this book. Pretty quickly I realized I was over my head, but in a pretty wonderful way... I love when books push me to learn and grow."
— *Tiffany's Bookshelf Blog*

"A GENUINE STORY WITH HEART and possibly a message about the human spirit."
— *Lavish Bookshelf Blog*

"SHAPIN'S PROSE IS RICH in historical details about the Great Depression, World War II, the early years of the Cold War and communism. She paints a factually exhaustive portrait of the political culture at the time of these three characters' lives."
— *Kirkus Reviews*

"AUTHOR SHAPIN HAS REALLY DONE her research not just about the individuals but about the institutions, the secular churches of the 1930s and Cold War years.... I loved it."
— *Newsletter of the Pacific Northwest Labor History Association*, Ross K. Rieder, President

"SHAPIN'S WRITING is...spare and elegant."
— Melissa Fox, *Book Nut Blog*

"A REMARKABLE PIECE OF WORK....Shapin's novel captures the messy politics and passions of three exceptional people at a time when deep emotions were often stultified and repressed as worker rights and Communist orthodoxy took center stage in the lives of many thoughtful Americans. It reads like the best of E.L. Doctorow and Thomas Mallon."
— Paula Duffy, former publisher, *The Free Press,* a division of Simon & Schuster

A SNUG LIFE SOMEWHERE

by Jan Shapin

Cambridge Books

an imprint of
WriteWords, Inc.
CAMBRIDGE, MD 21613

𝕮𝖆𝖒𝖇𝖗𝖎𝖉𝖌𝖊 𝕭𝖔𝖔𝖐𝖘 is a subsidiary of:

Write Words, Inc.
2934 Old Route 50
Cambridge, MD 21613

ISBN 978-1-61386-231-5

Fax: 410-221-7510

Bowker Standard Address Number: 254-0304

Dedication

For my mother,
LuVerne Heger Conway

Part One

CHAPTER 1

My brother died on November 5, 1916. I found out one cold afternoon in Seattle, while waiting for a ferryboat that had steamed away that morning to Everett with a load of college students and union protesters who had gone to demonstrate support for a strike the world has now forgotten. Those of us waiting on the dock knew there had been passengers injured or killed. I remember the newsboys with their late editions, reporting on a massacre, how sheriff's deputies in Everett had fired on the *Verona* as it docked, passengers rushing away from the gunfire, pitching the boat so that those by the rail were pushed into the bay.

A cheer went up from men crowding against the gate. Far up Puget Sound I could make out the outline of the *Verona*. I remember clutching my coat tight around me, my favorite coat, a checked brown Harris Tweed, something my father bought me in an exuberant moment, the only thing I owned that made me feel stylish. I had worn it in a vain attempt to improve my mood, to gain my brother's attention upon his return. I remember wind-whipped tears, hope caught in my throat as I watched the ferry shudder its painful way into the slip, as the laboring engines cut off. We were herded back to make way for the wounded. Stretchers carried a procession to waiting ambulances, but my brother was not among them. Then the able-bodied poured off, a hundred, maybe two hundred men, not celebrating exactly, more dazed, frightened, but buoyant in their step, I noticed, grateful to be alive. The crowd surged around, bestowing hugs, fingers raised in victory salutes, as if they were soldiers returning from war. I watched this exuberant welcome, all the while repeating under my breath, maybe the newspapers are wrong. Crewmen went into the hold to bring up the last of the passengers, carried them out on stretchers down the gangplank and onto a single makeshift bier, until five bodies rested in a row. My brother Horace was second in line.

I stood there suspended, no feeling except for the wet wind seeping through the lapels of my coat. The captain arranged himself by their side, glanced at a scrap of paper, then turned to a deckhand, motioning for him to bring up something to cover the bodies. I looked at Horace, second in line, wondering if he were cold. Finally, the captain cleared his throat, straightened his shoulders. His voice seemed clogged, but strengthened as he went on, reciting first the details, the unexpected gunfire, the rush of passengers to the far rail, absolving himself, it seemed to me, of any blame. That done, he moved on to express concern for the families, noting the presence of Seattle's uniformed police, expressing confidence that, "We will get to the bottom of this."

Once again he turned his attention to his notes. "Three hundred and eighteen passengers boarded this morning," he said, but cautioned that was only an estimate, the ship had been chartered, the company had not kept a ticket register or roster of names. But, he added, looking pleased at this scrap of good news, he did have a firm count of the men returning. "Two hundred and sixty-six able-bodied passengers left this ship," he announced with a galling touch of pride. "Thirty-one wounded, including two crewmen, are going to hospital." Once again his eyes buried themselves in his paper. "And there are five dead." This last he dropped inaudibly, as if he didn't want to dwell on a destination. The morgue, I thought, Horace is going to the morgue.

Just then a crewman appeared with what looked like rough canvas, and proceeded to drape all five bodies to

6

shield them from view. Once more I wondered if Horace were cold, whether he liked having canvas dropped over his head. The captain consulted his notes one last time and added that an unconfirmed number of passengers had been washed overboard, their whereabouts unknown. Summing up, he looked out at us hopefully, apologizing again for the tragedy, for not knowing the names, especially the names of the five men who lay beside him, as well as the names of those missing in Port Gardiner Bay.

* * *

My brother Horace was the apple of my mother's eye. On that day, November 5, 1916, I was twenty-four and he had just turned nineteen. Horace was a name chosen by my mother from a book about Egyptian gods. The Egyptian Horace was brother to the goddess Isis, himself a god who had the honor (and burden) of being his sister's consort and twin. Thus Egypt's Horace was born into triple responsibilities, as was my brother, in a way. By birth, our Horace was my mother's consolation. And mine. And, in a way, my pa's. Our Horace carried a huge weight of family expectation upon his graceful frame. Then destiny took him to places we didn't expect. I never knew my brother. I thought I did, but I didn't. I doubt Horace ever knew himself. Nineteen when he died.

My naming was different. I was not the apple of my mother's eye. I was punished at birth for my uncanny resemblance to my pa and my propensity to puke. Fighting Joe Copper had red hair and crowed like a barnyard rooster. He was the one who christened me Penny Joe, a name destined to incite this schoolyard jeer:

> *A Penny, a Copper,*
> *Like father, like daughter,*
> *A mere cent from start to finish!*

My father thought this a huge compliment, one he liked to repeat over and over to his cronies in the many taverns he liked to frequent. My father was a shingle cutter, a good one, with a fierce pride in his craft, and three missing fingers to prove it. He was also a drinker, but they were all drinkers in Everett in those days, when the only sure way to make a living was by sawing fir and weaving it through furious mechanical blades to make shingles. How else but through drink could a man warm himself after a twelve hour day, tormented as he was by salt damp that never left his woolens, by black mold that slimed his drainpipes or bloomed overnight on his wife's cutting board? Everett's was a climate that required sustenance. Jesus wept, my father assured his fellows. He would slap a hand on the rounded edge of the bar and then go one better. "And, if I read my Bible correctly, he also drank!" A cheer would go up, the crowd toasting to the health of Jesus. Unlike Jesus, though, we who lived in Everett also cursed and fought. And organized into labor unions that did not turn the other cheek. Which, in time, culminated in an event known as the Everett Massacre.

* * *

I live quietly now, an old lady in Snoqualmie, on a sunny patch of land that stretches from the Cascades toward Lake Washington. Here, no Douglas fir blots my sunlight or drips on my shingles. My front yard has a picket fence and my back acre is an open meadow where I grow prairie flowers, to harvest and sell their seed. Indian hyacinth, pearly everlasting, bleeding heart, colt's foot, deer's foot, red clintonia. Almost seventy species in all. Plus fruit bearing bushes and flowering shrubs. A small living, but a peaceful life after a tumultuous one. Something, in a way, my pa also achieved. He got himself locked up in jail before he drank himself to death and was known far and wide in his last years as a martyr. An altogether satisfying end for a died-in-the-wool union man. After he left Everett for the hoosegow, in December, 1915, my mother and I took stock and decided to get out of each other's hair.

I left on the Interurban on February 29, 1916, leap year's day, the day after one of my many uncelebrated birthdays. Seven weeks after my pa had been taken in chains to the Eastern Washington State Penitentiary. He was not, on that day nor on any day that followed, a penitent man. He had been tried for the murder of a night watchman, a poor soul caught in a fire set in a tool shed that spread to the factory floor. On the basis of muddy boots and oil soaked rags in our cellar, my father was charged with murder. Later the charge was reduced to arson and manslaughter. His case was promptly taken up by the local band of progressive lawyers skilled at emptying the coffers of union defense funds. Except as an adjunct to the subsequent Everett Massacre, my pa's cause never would have amounted to much, and, in truth, my father was a far sight better off in prison. There he had the sympathetic ear of guards who had not heard his many stories, fellow inmates who were also, they claimed, unjustly imprisoned, a library full of books, three squares a day, two blankets and a cot. With his prison wages he could buy tobacco and held court to a steady stream of visitors. It was a life absent my mother, which must have seemed to him the greatest blessing of all.

At any rate, by the beginning of 1916, my father was in the hoosegow and proud of it. Proud of a reputation for rabble rousing that had merited him eighteen-point headlines. Falsely convicted, that's what the union newspapers said of him. "Fighting Joe Copper, the falsely convicted union organizer." He was always good for a quote and had quite a following among newspaper reporters. He wrote home regularly if not at length. Occasionally he would ask for some article of clothing, a set of long johns, a deck of cards. He was garrulous, made friends easily, with the jailers as well as the jailed. Had he had less of a taste for drink and a smoother disposition, he might have gone far. A pleasanter wife would have helped. Those leadership qualities so garbled in my father found full expression in Horace, in the same way my pa's red hair found expression in me. Horace, as they used to say, was an outstanding young man. A fellow going places. But he lacked my father's gift for hyperbole, a form of humor I've tried to cultivate, though in my case it comes out crossed with my mother's vinegary temperament.

My decision to go to Seattle in early 1916 came, in part, because of my father's departure. Without him to haul back from the saloons, without a need to mediate the ensuing fracas, I was left without vocation. The canning factory didn't occupy my spirit. Also, there was the lure of Horace, who, that previous fall, had escaped Everett through a scholarship to the University of Washington. Even though it was only ninety minutes away by train, Everett was a world away from Seattle. Horace did not return even once during my father's trial. Some might find that curious, but neither my mother nor I thought it remarkable at the time. I suppose we both judged Horace wise not to associate with such events. I am not criticizing the behavior of the union lawyers *per se*, nor in any way upholding the timber barons or their paid judges. I am simply remarking that the proceedings were tawdry. It was a rigged trial and everyone knew it. And the rigging suited both sides. It was a game, an old one where everyone knew their parts, an endless shoving match that, like everything else in Everett, crushed you in the end and left you no way out.

But Horace was another matter. He had escaped. Five years my junior, dark haired, broad shouldered and full faced, whereas I was lean and tight-lipped and freckled. He of the cupid's lip and sable eyes was a valiant, a beautiful boy growing into a beautiful man. My father never understood him, his calm indifference in the face of endless family outrage my father mostly provoked. Horace just set his countenance, even as a child, to the horizon. He was leaving Everett, that much was clear to every teacher and settlement house lady who ever crossed his path. The do-gooder's favorite child, he sailed through youth untouched by scorn and self-doubt. Horace had my mother's bedrock determination and my father's abundant self-confidence. Even in his infancy, as I toted him around on my hip, I used him as a shield. Diaper wet, sticky fingered, he was my protector, the central love and enigma of my life. Why had he been granted this placid disposition, this charmed destiny? Why did I get the other end of the stick?

As I said, destiny granted him a scholarship to the University of Washington. Once he was gone, I was bereft. Twenty-four years old, a factory worker, single, no future in sight. All though that fall of 1915 I mourned, and on into early winter, through my father's trial and imprisonment, waiting, waiting for word from Horace, waiting until leap year's day, the last date I had set in my mind for leaving. I had hoped he would write, ask me to join him in his new life, but, after watching my father led away in chains, I resolved to join Horace even if uninvited, join him in his destiny, whatever that was, as best I could, however he would let me.

I knew nothing about his new life in Seattle, his life at the university, nothing about Seattle's own cauldron of political activity that so mirrored Everett's endless skirmishes. Horace had gone away and so had my father. That was all I knew. Of the two paths open to me, to stay and shrivel into a life of no sustenance, or to garner some comfort alongside Horace, I could see no choice. I didn't write, trusting, as a smitten lover does, that my arrival would be welcomed. I had a lot to learn. It was my terrible need more than any hopeful dreams that gave me courage. To get away. To join Horace. That was as far, on that leap year day when I boarded the Interurban train, as my imagining went.

CHAPTER 2

I left my mother over an argument. I rarely argued with my mother, it wasn't worth the way I felt after. It wasn't that my mother overwhelmed me by her vehemence or logic, although she sometimes did. It was more that, in the heat of it, I would see her regarding me as spoils, a creature that, by my very act of disagreeing, she felt entitled to claim. There was also my sense of being ashamed. Of her, her narrowness of spirit. I felt pity that a human being could hold so little in reserve, all that anger coming out of a tiny molten pit. That was what made me shrink into a speck of my normal self. Any argument with her, regardless of the outcome, deflated whatever optimism I was able to bring to the day.

I chastised myself for not being more of a fighter. But in truth, there wasn't much to fight for. Except Horace, I wanted to fight for him. Nothing else seemed good enough, true enough. Nothing worth trying to stake a claim. After Horace left I had dreams that I, too, could soar above the earth. I would lift away, float, dive, then drift up again on the current. The earth would contract, rotate, ripple. Nothing else existed in those dreams, just me and the earth and the air. Once, years later, I went up in a glider and it was exactly as I had felt in those dreams. Detached, muffled from the earth's clamor. I've often wondered how I'd been able to sense so clearly what it was like, because no one I knew had ever been in a glider much less an airplane. To my best recollection I'd never even seen a newsreel of such a thing. The war footage in those days was choppy and blurred, nothing like the floating sensations in my dreams, so where had that knowledge come from?

A petty argument made me leave Everett. Something about potatoes, that I'd not wiped out the bin before putting in new ones and they'd begun to rot. It was the tiredness of this complaint, the grain of truth in it—I *had* been impatient, *had* resented the millionth time I'd wiped out threads of black mold clinging to the basket—something about the whole thing, the way we lived, my dismal situation, made me snap. I'd go. My mother would be better off without me, she deserved to be without me, she should feel the sting of my absence. Of course, not once in the next forty years did she ever so much as hint that she'd missed me, that the day I walked out was anything other than an event fully expected, overdue, a chick fledged from its nest. Even Horace, whom she adored, never seemed missed in those first months he was gone. In his death he was missed, but more in the way President Roosevelt felt missed, a huge hole left by a giant figure cut down. That was how my mother felt about the loss of her son. Of course, I am only guessing. Perhaps my mother didn't feel a thing, wasn't cut out to feel, wasn't much of a mother at all. Like a mother animal, maybe she was driven by instinct to nurture for a time and then returned to her natural state.

When I abandoned Everett I hadn't known what I was going to do. No plans except to go to Seattle to be near Horace. I'd done an inventory of my belongings and decided to take only two dresses, plus my good houndstooth coat, a pewter brooch my father had bought me, a sewing box with a secret compartment that Horace had fashioned in woodworking class and my life savings which amounted to twelve dollars and change. A one-way ticket on the Interurban cost me one dollar because I decided to splurge and ride in the club car. I took my lunch, in Pa's old lunch pail, and figured if I was careful I could make the corned beef last until the next day. By then I was sure I'd have a place to live and, if I were lucky, a job. What job didn't matter, I'd done as much scullery work as the next girl. I looked young, younger than twenty-four, and I figured this to be an advantage. If I had a plan it was to get a place to live, a job to support me, then find out what tests I had to take, what do-gooders I had to snoot up to, lie about my age, say I was eighteen and just out of high school, and talk my way into the university.

It was a good plan, and might have worked, if I hadn't gotten sideswiped by the Everett Massacre. My plan, such as it was, was to get off the train, take the trolley to the university district and start looking around. Walk the streets, find just the right rooming house, a neat "For Rent" sign in the window, a dry room, under eaves, cheap, warm, and decorated with cherry striped wallpaper, or maybe painted a tasteful blue and cream. The way I saw it, the landlady would need help, because there would be boarders, handsome male boarders, who ate like dray horses, so lots of potatoes would need peeling and lots of cabbage chopped. And the landlady would know a shop down the street that sold flowers and other knickknacks to wives of professors, and I would get a job there and meet the wife of the Dean of Faculty. (Was there even such a thing, a Dean of Faculty? I didn't know.) Anyway, the next thing you knew, lickety-split, I would be enrolled in the university, in some as yet unknown field I'd turn out to have great aptitude for. Things didn't turn out that way, I never did find the wife of the Dean of Faculty, never did discover that one special field I had an astonishing aptitude for. Unless you count the knack I discovered late in life for raising prairie flowers. But that was hardly the kind of talent I had in mind when I rode toward Seattle on the Interurban, that leap year day, February 29, 1916.

In some ways I was wise about life and in some ways I was wet behind the ears. I knew enough to stay away from certain kinds of men. And not to trust most women. My experience was such that my avenues of avoidance were rather wide. I felt safer being alone. If I'd worked in a circus I could have made friends with the elephants, but I didn't have an appetite for that line of work. Maybe that's why I came up with the harebrained notion of becoming a biologist. The idea that I could spend all day feeding rabbits. I thought that was what biologists did. When it came out that it had more to do with cutting up frogs I decided not to expose my ignorance and took the lesser road of studying plants.

But that was later. After Gabe Rabinowitz. I never knew what my brother saw in him. If he saw anything. I'm not sure how well my brother even knew Gabe Rabinowitz. He could have made the whole thing up, about knowing my brother. I knew very little about what Horace did, even after I got to Seattle, during those months after my arrival. My dream of fitting in, of being someone, of having purpose, some inner intention that was mine and mine alone, seems like an ordinary enough ambition in retrospect. I suppose many young people feel that way. But I didn't know that then. I thought that I was the only living person who awoke each morning battered by loneliness, sick at the thought of my own cosmic insignificance. Later in life I would know to call it feeling abandoned by God. But in those days I had no words to encompass it. And my brother, when I found him, was not pleased to see me.

As I said, I never did find out what Horace was up to, never did get a handle on the people he was associating with or the tasks they were all so wrapped up in. They could have been building bombs for all I knew. Except that Horace, who always wore an ironed shirt and freshly brushed suit coat, was an unlikely bomb-thrower. He could have stayed in Everett for that. Gabe, when I pressed him, was always vague about what Horace had been up to, but later, towards the end of our association, told me that Horace had been a Bolshevik. I've chewed on that cud, done some reading, researched in the library, and come to the conclusion that that is wrong. For one thing, there were no American Bolsheviks in 1916, no Communist Party. There hadn't even been a Russian revolution. Lenin was still in Switzerland writing propaganda tracts. Or rather Krupskaya, his wife, was writing tracts and Lenin was putting his name to them. That's my thought, anyhow.

So Horace was up to something else, in my mind, something big, something important, something he wanted to keep from me, in order to protect me, just as my mother and I felt safer that Horace kept himself away from Everett during my father's trial. We Coppers were an odd lot, partitioning off our lives, telling each other it was for their own good.

When I got to Seattle that last day of February, I took the trolley up to University Heights. Walked past the storefronts along 15th Avenue looking for rooms to rent. I went into one unlocked doorway. The stairs were dark and smelled of rot. I got no farther than the landing when I heard someone swear, a glass shatter. I turned and walked back down. And resolved, in spite of the spitting down rain, to walk for a full hour before I went into another building with a "For Rent" sign. Clutching my Gladstone bag, shielding my head with a newspaper, I walked up and down dozens of side streets. I walked between 41st and 45th Street, then over to the construction site for the new men's gymnasium, finally, exhausted, I ducked into the library, and it was there that my heart lifted. Dripping rain on the terrazzo floor (Terrazzo was a new concept to me, a floor that wasn't chewed up into splinters, or covered with sawdust.) I looked around the huge entry hall, at the marble staircase that led up to the balcony, drifted into the main reading room with its massive oak circulation desk, peered at the long row of card catalogs that I thought, at the time, must hold carpentry screws. "I'm going to work here," I decided. "I'm going to work here even if I have to clean toilets first."

I didn't clean toilets. I got a job, two days later, at the university laundry. But my dream to be one of those girls behind the circulation desk, a worker in the library's cathedral-like space, was not to be. I'd never been in a cathedral, but I'd read about them, read enough of my pa's dog-eared copies of Alexander Dumas and Victor Hugo to know what a cathedral felt like. It felt hushed, intimate in its vaulted space, and safe, full of not-quite-expressed purpose. Open, yet hidden, like an event off to the edge of your vision, and it smelled of wax. Suzzulo Library had all that going for it, and books, too, thousands and thousands of books, more books than my father could ever have dreamed of, and I fell for it like a ton of bricks.

But I found out, soon enough, that jobs at the circulation desk were reserved for girls enrolled in Library Sciences. With clean fingernails, the head librarian's face made clear. After examining me standing in my dripping clothes before him, he suggested I try the university laundry. I suddenly perceived the social chasm I was attempting to cross. Cowed by this insight, I nodded, and asked where the laundry might be. Beneath the biology lab, he informed me. That seemed fitting, tubs of steaming linens connecting in my mind with pickled creatures floating in jars in the name of science above.

Soon thereafter, and much to my surprise, a young man entered my life as well. His name was Marcel Freid and he was Jewish. Half-Jewish. His mother was French, at least she said she was. French Canadian, I believe, the sort my mother always said was three-quarters wild Indian. Marcel and his mother lived in a ground floor apartment in a large house on Queen Anne Hill. In a nice part of town, near enough to the university so that Marcel could take the trolley to his music lessons. Marcel was seventeen when I first laid eyes on him, small, dark, with fingers that seemed longer than his body could accommodate. You might have thought he hadn't finished growing, but that wasn't true. He had some kind of hereditary disease, a spinal problem that shortened and twisted his torso ever so slightly, so that he always seemed to be turning to catch some fleeting event taking place off in the distance. I liked that about him, that ghost event that always seemed just outside his vision. I believe his music was about that, the knowledge that the real business of life is always just outside your ken.

Marcel was a violinist, a prodigy. He later became modestly famous. We broke each other's hearts in the way that young people do. If I had paid better attention, nurtured what was between us, instead of getting myself plucked up by Gabriel Rabinowitz, maybe life would have rewarded us with long years of mutual happiness. Alas, happiness is rarely so easily coaxed forth.

When I got to Seattle, after getting settled, I resolved to set about penetrating my brother's world. I had a postcard from him, dated four months earlier, indicating that he was rooming in a house on 48th Street. On my first day off from the laundry, I found the house. But the landlady said my brother had moved out weeks before, and that he was behind on his rent.

I knew there was some way a university would keep track of its students, but I was too timid to set about asking, and so persuaded myself that it would be better to get settled in my job and become somebody who wouldn't be a drain on him before I set out to surprise and delight Horace with my sudden appearance.

But to get back to Marcel. I met him that April, at my newly taken second job at a diner, one Wednesday night when I was slinging hash. Actually, I was a waitress and had on a floppy green cap, part of the uniform the owner, Mr. Panopolous, insisted upon. It made me feel like a greenhouse plant. I kept trying to push it back, so it wouldn't flop over my eyes, and Marcel must have sensed my irritation, because he looked up from his soup and said, "Leave it alone. It looks nice."

"Maid Marion," I said, then felt a blush rise.

"Maid Marion," he agreed. As if that were my name.

"That's not my name." I blushed harder, feeling that I was implying something, I didn't know what.

I wanted to take back those words, but he held them. Held on, and looked at me as if that were the most intelligent thing a person could say. Looked thoughtful, thereby softening the shame, drawing out the sting. He had a level gaze, open and soft, eyes that took in hard things and dissolved them. "I'm sure you have a nice name," he agreed. Then went back to his soup.

He couldn't have been more different from Gabe. Gabe's eyes held you, but in a different way. Bored into you. Wanting, expecting something. When I first met Gabe, before they carried out my brother's body, I was in a state where I needed to latch on to something. Even something bad, something I was later bound to be ashamed of. That day in November, as I stood on the dock, I was so sure that Marcel's gentle eyes were an oasis I could not reach. Gabe's eyes offered no such complication. His eyes had a plan, a use for me, and, without fully knowing I had done it, without even knowing what Gabe's plan was, I signed on.

CHAPTER 3

I had been staring at leaves, deciding whether to buy chestnuts from a blind vendor's oven, when I first saw Gabe. My mouth was dry, I remember that, and the thought of eating chestnuts made my stomach hurt, but I bought some anyway, for something to do, for a way to distract myself from other thoughts. I remember opening the bag and staring down at the brown steaming mass, wishing life had delivered me somewhere else. I was not thinking of my brother then, or at least not entirely. I was thinking about Marcel, his slender body, the silky hair that covered his forearms, the coarser hair that grew below. That longing felt shameful to me and I wondered whether I was, indeed, the monster Marcel's mother had accused me of being. Just the day before she had sent me a letter, threatening to expose me to the child welfare authorities.

Those were my thoughts when I first saw Gabe, a young man of at least my age, with a bushy moustache that curved around his mouth, hunched shoulders, a crop of matted hair that lifted in the wind. A body used to hard labor, I could see, balanced in a way that looked like he was ready to launch a punch. I had known men like this, they had filled the many taverns favored by my father. But this fellow seemed different, his clothing more like a student's than a timber cutter. I could see intelligence in his eyes, a focused will. He was waiting for something, or someone. A fellow dangerous to be near, a cloud of mayhem about him. How I sensed all this, glancing up from my chestnuts, I do not know. But I felt, somehow, he was waiting for me.

Seattle, in those days, was in ferment. Fellows like Gabe, angry ones, were on every corner. The city's economy was booming. Saw mills making munitions boxes, later to be converted into coffins. Woolen mills turning out olive drab twill for blankets and uniforms. Apples and cherries, oysters and salmon, all harvested in their time, then stewed to be transported in giant cans east for shipment to the front. Not yet at war, Seattle had the best of both worlds. Wages high, mills running full. Greed prompted a truce between labor and industry. Progressives, socialists, the Chamber of Commerce could agree, foreign war made good business. But President Wilson was making speeches that fall about bringing us in. All of a sudden, patriotism, which had coexisted with peace marches, now became narrow and exacting. An alphabet soup of war agencies sprang forth, and, for good measure, government-sponsored vigilante groups to make sure everyone was in total support. Everything else, every nuance, every ambiguity, had to move to the side.

In 1914, the war split the European socialists wide open. It was about to do the same in Seattle. Before Wilson declared us in, the women's clubs and progressives opposed it. Seattle's business leaders and a fair amount of union members were in favor. That summer, before we entered, Seattle was awash in parades and rallies, for and against, petitions and counter petitions. Then, in the fall of 1916, a drumbeat of preparedness as our government got us ready to go in. Now the socialists and progressives began to split internally over the issue, as did the unions. Fellows like Gabe, naturally given to grievance, breathed in that polarized atmosphere and drew from it strength.

The looming entry of the United States into the war made Everett a testing ground for those larger political issues. The men who boarded the *Verona*, according to Everett's business council, were political soldiers, not *bona fide* union men. Drifters recruited in Seattle's saloons, homegrown militants that some called anarchists and some called communists. Egged on by students like my brother, antiwar activists, dangerous meddlers in a cause not their own. And behind the scene, the fearsome Industrial Workers of the World, the so-called Wobblies. So ran the headlines in Everett. The men on the *Verona*, the ones the sheriff felt constrained to shoot, were nothing but bomb-throwers, foreigners, hooligans.

But that day on the docks it was the hands of my young violinist that filled my thoughts. Marcel Freid had no political views, only a gift for music and a dreamy way about him. His mother, Josephine, a thin woman with a grim mouth, was a lapsed Catholic whose greatest regret seemed to be that her second husband had died before she was able to arrange Marcel's adoption, and thus relieve him of his unfortunate German (and Jewish) last name.

Josephine was a milliner. She lived on the ground floor of the house at the foot of Queen Anne Hill that her second husband had left her, and ran her millinery business out of the front parlor. Marcel's real father had been a tailor, and, in his early years, Marcel had lived south of Seattle's "deadline," in the zone where police were notorious for turning a blind eye to gambling and what was then called the "social vice." The family lived in a pair of rooms behind the father's store. One day, Marcel told me, a customer came in who was a bank vice-president, taking his tailoring, I surmised, to that part of town in order to partake of either the gambling or the social vice. At any rate, the banker heard Marcel practicing. He said something to the father, Josephine intervened. The bank vice-president was so taken with the boy's talent that he offered patronage. Marcel's mother took him up on that. A tutor was selected, an audition arranged. Thereafter Marcel's formal education, such as it was, was taken on the fly between music lessons and recitals. The bank vice-president and Marcel's mother spent a lot of time managing Marcel's career and, I suspect, other things. I never voiced this assumption to Marcel, but when I told him once he was lucky to have missed so much school, he gave me a strange look, then lost interest as I tried to describe the sad, damp rooms of my own school years, the dull boys and anxious girls, the precipitous drop in attendance at age fourteen, when the boys went into the mills and the girls got pregnant, with hasty marriages arranged so that the next round of whiskey drinking and wife beating could begin.

Most of the time I didn't talk to Marcel about my life in Everett, just listened as he ate his raspberry cobbler, nodded as I poured him more coffee, sat opposite him when the last customers left and the owner went upstairs to count the till. All that damp spring and summer of 1916 I listened each Wednesday to his lonely plaints, about having no friends, the loss of his father, his mother's sudden remarriage to an accountant in that helpful banker's employ, a baby sister who died at birth. Then the stepfather's death, just the year before. I remember thinking how lucky they were, Marcel and his mother, alone together in the deceased accountant's newly bought house. I envied them their snug life, so wrapped in each other, bound by his mother's carefully planned journey for her only son to a land of riches and fame. A world that left no room for me. A waitress in a floppy green hat, scratching out a meager existence, hoping to fashion my own snug life somewhere.

Marcel came every Wednesday after musicology class, all through April and May. The owner must have seen what was going on but didn't want to discourage a faithful customer. One night, after scraping up the last of his cobbler, Marcel asked if he could walk me home. He blushed and stammered through this, and at first I thought it was because he was unsure of what he was asking me, but on the way through the door I realized his embarrassment had as much to do with his limp as it did with any new found-boldness toward me. He had a steer-and-correct style of walking that followed the leftward cast of his eyes. I smiled to tell him I liked the way he walked, wrapped my coat tightly around me, took his arm and nudged him along the four blocks to my room. I walked in a daze, thinking, as young girls do, that maybe a year from then I'd be touring the concert halls of Europe. (I had forgotten there were no concerts being held that year in Europe.) At my door we stopped, he unsure what to do next. Without hesitation I opened the door, not thinking, although I can see now that he might have taken this as an implied invitation. But, as I climbed the stairs with him in tow, I was thinking only about my room, wanting him to see it, my new blue bedspread I'd spent a whole dollar on at the Bon Marche. Wedgwood blue the clerk told me, with tassels at each corner that matched the cream color I'd painted the walls. I'd been saving for lace curtains to cover my rain streaked windows, had picked out the fabric just the day before.

So I was anxious to show all this off to my new friend, my first friend in Seattle. I hadn't begun yet to think of him as a beau, though I could sense he was taken with me. Marcel was not the kind of fellow I usually attracted. The hand-on-the-bosom kind of fellows my pa's friends often were. Or the younger ones, their schoolboy invitations to behind the woodshed. This one was different. In his face I could detect desire, but not so much furtive as furled. Music not yet composed. I can still see him standing in that doorway, looking up the stair, then at me, seeking reassurance, alert to some call, some scent or signal from me, and I was flattered, deeply drawn. I felt myself lovely for the first time, and I was darned if I was going to let propriety stand in the way of getting Marcel to see my tasseled bedspread.

We sat on my Wedgwood bedcover and played cat's cradle. Then, when I leaned forward to untangle a knot, he kissed me. That was enough, a pact of some sort. Then he jumped up, muttering about getting back to his mother. I can still hear the sound of his steps down the hallway—

thump *Thump*, thump *Thump*. My heart in my mouth, a wild sureness swelling up in me.

The next day, I set out to look for my brother Horace. Where he'd been, the places he'd been seen, the classes he'd enrolled in, visited once or twice and then stopped coming to. I saw, and signed, a copy of a petition he had drafted and put his name to. It had to do with protests against the university president, who was chairman of the statewide preparedness board that was collecting names of undesirables to be rounded up, jailed and deported in the event the United States declared war. Those lists came in handy, later, when rounding up and jailing and deporting became the order of the day, but we only guessed, then, that something like that would happen. I remember signing the petition and thinking how proud my father would be, how infuriated my mother, if she only knew how her son was wasting his education.

My own feelings were somewhere in the middle. Frustration that Horace was eluding me, jealousy he was besting me in my father's eyes. Pride also that he was the author of this radical petition. Sadness, in the recognition that our reunion would be, for him, a distraction at best. Still I plunged on. It was probably during that time that I first ran into Gabe. He claimed he saw me first from a socialist speakers' platform, an event held every Friday night under a tent behind the student co-op, technically off campus and thus exempt from the university's ban on political speakers. If I saw him there I don't remember it. I went there often hoping to catch sight of Horace. But I do remember Gabe being one of six or seven fellows standing with Horace on the day I finally did come upon my brother, by accident, outside the Labor Temple. It was July, hot as blazes, and I was heading to the Bon Marche to buy wool for a scarf I was knitting for Marcel. Typical of me to be knitting wool in the middle of Hades. Anyways, the group on the sidewalk was engaged in a confrontation with an older man whom I later found out to be Harry Ault, the editor of the *Union Record*, Seattle's labor newspaper.

Horace had his back to me, but when I saw the way his head jerked, how his left shoulder rose, I knew it was him. It was my pa's signal that a fight was about to ensue, and I was struck by two things. First, that I'd finally found him, and, second, a realization that Horace had inherited my pa's pugnacious streak. I went cold, a premonition maybe, but I passed it off as fear that he'd not want to see me in the middle of whatever business he was up to. And then a paralyzing shyness that maybe he'd not want to see me at all.

One of the men turned, Gabe later claimed it was he, and stared. I suppose because I was staring at them. With a flick of his head he motioned me to be on my way, but then Horace turned, and saw me, and flushed, I was never quite sure why. My brother straightened his shoulders and composed his face. With an almost courtly manner, he stepped forward, took my arm, and brought me into the group, introduced me all around. I didn't remember any of the names, they all seemed older than Horace, in their thirties or even forties, but I did take notice of Harry Ault, because of his fine-lined face and clear blue eyes. He shook my hand and said he knew my father, that he'd just visited him in the penitentiary and was writing an article based on that interview. He asked if I'd like to come by the newspaper office and read the proofs. When I declined, I don't know for what reason, he nevertheless wished me well and asked me to remember him to my mother.

But to get back to Marcel. All that summer we continued to see each other Wednesday nights at the diner and then later on in my room. Soon I'd saved up for lace curtains and started knitting his red muffler. I was never much of a knitter, but my heart was so full it needed expression in some way, and socks seemed too mundane while sweaters were beyond my capacity, and required too much yarn. Anyway, by mid-summer I was halfway through Marcel's muffler and, during our time sitting on my bed together, Marcel's beautiful violinist's hands had advanced down my torso, the front as well as the back, which is how things like that usually progress. Anyway, one night we were startled by a knock at the door. I had forgotten to lock it. The door flung open and a pie-faced man holding a dusty bowler took in what we were doing. He gulped, then recited a set speech warning me I was about to be arrested for contributing to the delinquency of a minor. It was a Pinkerton Marcel's mother had hired to track us down, to surprise me in the act of corrupting her youth. Fortunately my dress was mostly in place and I suppose we could have talked our way out of any technicalities. But Marcel, to my sorrow, made a legalistic defense that he hadn't been corrupted as yet. It was then I learned he had just turned seventeen and he found out I was half way to twenty-five.

Those twin revelations set us both back. Through our long nuzzling conversations on my bed I had never thought to ask. I knew Marcel was young, but I attributed his youthful appearance to his disability, whatever that was. All this seemed too complicated to voice with the Pinkerton standing there, Marcel flushed purple and avoiding my eyes. Besides, I wasn't sure who I was to explain this to—Marcel? His mother? Surely not the Pinkerton. At any rate the pie-faced man told Marcel he was taking him back to his mother, Marcel consented, and I listened to their retreat down my hall—thump *Thump*, thump *Thump*, a clatter for all the neighbors to hear. When the sound faded away I was left on my still-virginal bed ready to weep bitter tears. Of frustration, mostly.

Notwithstanding this setback, not much time passed before Marcel again made his way to the diner for raspberry cobbler and we found ourselves plotting more overtly innocuous ways to spend time in each other's company.

In September I signed up for the biology club, to collect frog specimens in the marshlands off Lake Washington. By that time I was auditing a freshman biology class in the room directly above the laundry. Love made me bold, and I wanted so to belong to this university world of learning and accomplishment, that I gathered my courage along with some newly ironed lab aprons and asked the professor in the room above to let me sit in on his class. He was only a lowly instructor but agreed, and even offered to let me take tests and grade my papers, and it was thus that I got the first beginnings of a college education through a teacher who valued freshly ironed lab aprons above the starchy rules of university admissions.

I realize now, in my old age, that I have been blessed all my life with a good luck that generally took the form of an older man seeing some quality in me that I myself did not. Marcel may have sensed that same quality but didn't know how to credit it, didn't have the wisdom or the experience to place it for what it was. I certainly was of no help, prattling on about lace curtains and how big the checks on his muffler should be, or what kind of frogs we would be catching, that lovely autumn, as we stood shoulder to shoulder in high rubber waders, in the late afternoon sunsets, knee deep in Lake Washington muck.

It was about this time that I met his mother. Or rather was confronted by her at the intermission of a recital at the Moore Theatre. Marcel had invited me. She must have been angry that he gave away one of his precious tickets to me, and of course it was evidence that her plan to break things up between us had failed. So she had on quite a head of steam when she chugged over to me, arms like pistons, fire in her eyes. I was sure it was Josephine, even though I'd never laid eyes on her, and felt caught between the impulse to flee and a desire to laugh. I was thankful I had worn the better of my two dresses even though it was out of season.

I held to this thought as Josephine put on the brakes and stuck her nose in my face and told me in her harsh voice to stay away from her son. She said a lot of other things, loud enough to attract nearby concertgoers and maybe even the police at the precinct house a block away. Marcel, of course, was back stage and heard none of this. Anyway, after the first surprise, the first onslaught, I looked her level in the face, even though she was half a head taller, and said, with a calm that came from I don't know where, that her son was my friend, and that if he didn't want to see me he would tell me so. I implied that her ordering me to leave him alone wasn't good enough. Then the bell for the curtain sounded, so I took the moment to do a stage bow, turned and marched back to my seat. But she had managed to rattle me, in spite of how I carried it off. There was enough of my mother in Josephine that she raised a certain kind of conflict in me. A desire to stay out of her way but not to take any guff.

It may have been in retaliation for this encounter, to show her, that I signed Marcel up for a weekend of hut building and wildflower gathering at Snoqualmie Falls. Marcel, of course, protested, said he couldn't climb mountains, that he had violin practice, that his mother had other plans. I was adamant. "You've got to do something for yourself," I told him, implying that everything else he did was for his mother, implying that doing something for himself involved doing something with me.

And do something was what we managed to do, at that camp at Snoqualmie Falls, late at night, under a full moon, in musty sleeping bags snapped together in a way expressly forbidden by Biology Club rules.

CHAPTER 4

On May Day, 1916, Everett's shingle weavers went out on strike. They had been on strike before, of course, sometimes winning, oft times losing, then starting afresh. This was one of those afresh times. What with the war effort taking all the roofing tin, the price for shingles was strong. So the craft unions, the ones belonging to the American Federation of Labor, decided to charter a new union, to be called the International Shingle Weavers of America. This irritated the rival union, the Wobblies, to no end. Shingle weaving had never been considered a craft. It was hard unskilled labor performed by immigrants and native-born men down on their luck. Brutal work that killed or maimed you, one way or the other—if not by the saw blade, then through coughing your guts out from cedar asthma. You might ask why the craft unions—the aristocrats of labor, we called them— would bother with such riffraff. Well, the American Federation of Labor was then headed by a man named Samuel Gompers. Gompers liked hobnobbing with the Washington politicians. Since America was heading into war, Gompers wanted to prove his patriotism by organizing the war industries before the Wobblies got to them. In those days there were no industrial unions, no protections for auto, steel or miners. Oh, efforts were made, but they didn't last. The Pinkertons and the National Guard took care of that. The only industrial union with any staying power was the International Workers of the World, the IWW, the Wobblies, and they were not just a union, they were a political force.

Their political philosophy was in their name. One union, worldwide, workers everywhere organized under the Wobblies' red banner. Not anarchists, exactly, not Bolshevik, the IWW was first and foremost a union, located mostly in the Pacific Northwest, and drawing its strength from the mining and lumbering camps. It was rawboned and radical in the way the craft unions were not. The Wobblies were about solidarity, dignity for the world's oppressed. A grand idea that always brought my pa to tears.

> *Up from your knees, ye cringing serfmen!*
> *What have ye gained by whines and tears?*

He always sang that before ordering the last round, just before the fighting began. In Everett you were either one or the other, AFL or Wobblie, and in any drinking establishment there were always a good measure of each. So, what was going on up in Everett that summer was part of a long running feud, a contest to see which side could forge allegiance with the shingle weavers, the sorriest bunch of three fingered roustabouts there ever was. The AFL, by jumping the gun and chartering their union, tried to position itself in control of the strike. But by October, with winter setting in and no offer on the table, conditions were getting grim. That's when the Wobblie organizers started coming to town.

I had seen my brother twice since July. Then, just after the first of October, he came into Mr. Panopolous's diner and asked if I wanted to go up to Everett for a day. "What for?" I asked.

"To see Ma," he said. I took him at his word, or at least pretended to. He met me the next morning at the freight yards where we hitched a ride in the caboose with an off-duty engineer. We played pinochle. Or rather, the engineer and I played pinochle while Horace sat with his back to us, hunched over, looking at the departing rails.

"You feeling okay?" I asked. Something made me feel he wasn't. I wasn't feeling so hot myself, the thought of seeing

31

my mother making my stomach turn. "Did you write her we were coming?"

"No," he said, then looked at me, his eyes giving off some hesitation, almost embarrassment. "I guess I should have, huh?" Then I knew he had no intention of going to see Ma, he was going up for some other reason and I was just part of the stage dressing.

"Guess you'll want to look around some first." I laid this out smoothly, delivering what I guessed were the right lines. The engineer looked at me with amusement, still shuffling his deck.

"Yeah, I guess so," Horace said, yawning, taking on a look of studied distraction as he turned back again to examine the rails. I could see tension in his shoulders, ropes standing out at the sides of his neck. I turned back to the engineer who pushed the deck my way.

"Cut," he said, and I did.

* * *

Horace did stop in to see my mother first, and she looked appropriately surprised and gratified, removing her apron, checking both sides of her son's face before giving him a short hug. I stood at the door watching this, wondering when was the last time I'd gotten a hug, even this poor excuse for one, and realized it was before my father had been arrested, that what I missed most about him was his abundant if unsteady affection. I handed my mother the tin box of Canadian toffee I'd brought, her favorite kind. She gave me a polite smile, running her tongue up into the side of her mouth, to the place where the toffee always got stuck and later gave her a headache. She started to thank me, then gave me a short nod instead and turned back to the kitchen to put on some water for tea. That was as much of a welcome as I got but it was better than usual. Seven months absence appeared to have done some good.

"Glad you two are seeing each other," she said as she returned from the kitchen, handing us each a mug.

"Have you heard anything from Pa?" Horace asked.

"The usual," my mother answered. "Scribbled rants about his shingle cutting buddies. The new union, how it's going to fix everything."

"Maybe it will," Horace said.

My mother gave him a sharp look. "Don't you get mixed up in this," she said. But I knew he already had.

We took a walk later, down to the wharf, then through town to the speakers' corner. This being a Sunday, the Salvation Army and the Pentecostals were drawing their usual crowds, each competing against the other to see who could shout louder. During the rest of the week the corner of Hewitt and Wetmore was reserved for political evangelism.

I could see the town was tense. Barbed wire had been erected around the factory gates, the better to funnel through the few scabs that dared enter. Snipers, Pinkertons or the local militia, were positioned on top of the strike-emptied mill buildings and along the rooftops that bordered the intersection of Hewitt and Wetmore. The militia had been organized and financed by the Commercial Club and then detailed over to the police. The sheriff, a man named McRae, had once been a union man, but was now a turncoat, a drunkard in the pocket of the bosses. He was bustling about, shouting orders at the snipers, as well as his police on the ground, threatening the Wobblie organizers as they set up their platform where the Pentecostals had wound down. The newspapers said he was going to wire the Governor to bring in the National Guard.

The Wobblies didn't care. They weren't strong on paperwork but they made up for it in the ability to provoke. They had a proven flair for the dramatic. Just the year before, during a strike in Spokane, the IWW had called out all its members for a show of strength. Unemployed drifters flooded the city, coming in from hundreds of miles around, in boxcars, jalopies and by foot. That was what Everett was afraid of, a repeat of Spokane, so they passed an ordinance forbidding any Wobblies inside the county limits, hang the Constitution. And so, that day, the Wobblies were provoking Sheriff McRae just by being there, and to the city fathers they seemed the advance guard of a great flood.

The Wobblies had rented a storefront and planned to announce the opening of an organizing drive. That Sunday, at Hewitt and Wetmore, while the rank-and-file snored in their beds, a few pious ones nodding off in church pews beside their wives, the IWW was throwing down the gauntlet. All this was clear as we stood on the corner, scanning the positions of the snipers, listening to the Wobblie hammers and Sheriff McRae's futile threats. Horace seemed to be waiting, placid and confident. Suddenly, as if on cue, two rows of bedraggled men six abreast appeared from the direction of the train yards. You could tell they were Wobblies by the way they moved. "Soldiers of discontent" we used to call them, wobbly men culled from flophouses, a weaving defiant band. "We are Legion," so says the Bible. Well, what loomed up Hewitt Avenue was that , and it scared the bejesus out of Sheriff McRae. In Spokane, just processing all those hoboes, arresting and jailing them, feeding them, running kangaroo courts to ride them out of town, had nearly bankrupt the city. Sheriff McRae could see the same thing happening to Everett, the bill coming due on his watch. So he moved swiftly to arrest the dozen, personally whacked each head for good measure, then ordered his militiamen to herd them down to the county jail.

Horace watched all this, but once the performance was over he lost interest. "Let's go," he said, taking my arm and steering me down the hill to take one more look at the harbor. I had the impression he was expecting more Wobblies to show up in boats, but I was wrong. That plan was reserved for another day.

* * *

At the trial, the murder trial of the so-called *Verona* ringleaders, the prosecution claimed a pattern of IWW provocation tracing back to Spokane. They made the case that the test of Sheriff McRae's patience I witnessed that October day at Hewitt and Wetmore was linked inexorably to what happened on the docks on November 5. The prosecution saw a steady deliberate increase in lethal pressure applied by the IWW, something I saw as more like a game a dog plays with his master. Provoke and get slapped. Provoke and get slapped. Only by November 5, by the time the *Verona* docked, the master had taken up a crowbar instead of a slipper. All this had happened many times before. My pa slipping over the line, dynamiting a tool shed and igniting a fire that killed a night watchman. Did he do it? Well, somebody did. Who fired the first shot on November 5? Was the bullet from the *Verona* or at the *Verona*? Did Horace know it would come to gunfire or was he surprised, like my pa at the death of the night watchman, his bar stool buddy and treasurer of the local curling club? I don't know. I never knew. Still don't to this day. I lack the necessary confidence to assign blame. The world is complex. That's why I have always been attracted to as well as repelled by those who claim to know for sure. Sunday radio preachers. Cartoon heroes. President Roosevelt.

CHAPTER 5

That November 5th I was in a fraught state. Marcel had just told me he was leaving for a music conservatory in Chicago. This had long been arranged but his mother had contrived to move up the date. I was heartsick but did not dare broach the subject of my own plans—that I wanted to follow him, cook for him, clean for him, lay down my life. You know how it goes in the heart of a young woman. His impending loss made my whole body ache. That I would never again be able to reach down the length of his spine, hold in my hands his small hard buttocks. I was ill with the imminence of his departure, the prospect slick and stale on my tongue.

It was in this state that I went out that gray November afternoon to meet my brother. Since October the newspapers had been filled with plans for the so-called "free speech" rally in Everett. There were organizing drives to gain attendance among the students. Though never stated, it was assumed that this excursion was not suitable for women. So, in spite of claims that the event was only a festive picnic, there was an ugly undercurrent all along. I knew this without asking, knew that Horace would be among them. Perhaps I went out that afternoon to greet him as a way to reestablish my credentials as one of Fighting Joe Copper's clan, to spit in the eye of Marcel's mother and say, This is an older, deeper flame. If so, I set myself up for a double loss.

Waiting on the pier I distracted myself by watching a chipmunk. When I heard the newsboy's cry, "Extra, extra!

Massacre in Everett!" My stomach plunged. My eyes refocused and I saw, for the first time, the whole grimy concourse, the chipped iron railings, the small group of men breaking into a run. Numb, I walked over to hear the latest news—that the *Verona*, with nearly three hundred aboard, had taken gunfire from the wharf, that Sheriff McRae was shot, in the back apparently, by his own militia. The next wave of reports contradicted the first—that Sheriff McRae had been shot from the front, along with two of his men, proof, the mill owners said, that the first shots were fired from the ship. But later testimony at the trial showed that the bullets had indeed entered from behind. The prosecution had an answer to that detail, and enlisted witnesses to claim that the sheriff, at that exact instant, had turned to rally his men. Such a sad, sordid business. But at the time I knew none of this, only that a crippled *Verona* was coming back two hours behind schedule.

Twice more in that long afternoon news reports were relayed to a somber and increasingly angry crowd. They said that after Sheriff McRae went down, a huge volley of gunfire erupted. Panic led to a stampede on ship. As bullets raked the deck passengers rushed to the opposite rail, pitching the vessel so that scores were dumped into Port Gardiner Bay, a body of water ice cold in November, with strong undertows. Some reports said Sheriff McRae's men had run up the wharf to get better aim at the bobbing heads. At any rate, the final count was twenty-seven overboard, no survivors. The *Verona*'s captain, I can't remember his name, became a hero of sorts. In the midst of all this, he rallied his crew to cast off, letting the current take the boat a few yards offshore. Free from gunfire, he then persuaded frightened passengers to crawl back to the port side of the deck. The wounded were carried below, helping to further stabilize the vessel. On the long return home, fishing trawlers gathered reports from shouting passengers about the dead and wounded, so sketchy reports traveled from town to town along the way, and from there by teletype to the newspapers. That was how we came to discover what was going on: The *Verona*, crippled, making her way home. Conflicting numbers of casualties, both dead and wounded.

I can't say whether I thought then that my brother was dead or not. My mood was so bleak concerning Marcel that I may have been given to overdramatization. My sense of dread was, of course, as much for myself as for my brother. So when this fellow I mentioned, Gabe Rabinowitz, came over to me and said, "You're Horace Copper's sister," I was grateful to be recognized. Flattered, in a way. I fell in with him, not saying much, just the two of us together, shoulders hunched against the wind, walking back and forth as far as the police barricades would allow, for by that time the whole dock was filled with people who had heard the news. Even before the ballistics report at the trial, there was no question in Seattle, in the mind of anyone on the dock, who had fired the first shots.

And death shall have no dominion. That's what came to my mind when I first saw Horace's body carried down and laid on the bulkhead, one arm hanging limp, untended while the stewards scurried around to find a cloth to cover him. Someone offered a life jacket, but instead a steward produced a gunnysack stamped *Cargill Ltd., Alberta Depot, Dominion of Canada.* That may have been what put the word *dominion* in mind. Reverend Buck, at the First Everett Presbyterian, where my mother made sporadic efforts at our Christian education, was fond of that phrase. He had learned it, along with his deep sing song minister's voice, at some Bible school or other, and the way he sang out "do-min-i-on!" always stayed with me. At that moment, seeing the words on the gunnysack, I heard his voice with its particular intonation. *And death shall have no do-min-i-on!* I thought about Death and God, the Alberta grain depot and His Kingdom's temporal reach, probably not in such elevated phrases, but thought them none the less. I thought about waste, about my poor brother's dangling arm, the misaligned curve of Marcel's knobby back, the blank wall of my own life.

I remembered a piece of wood, split away from the pew where I sat each week in the First Everett Presbyterian. How often I longed to reach out and break off that long sliver, persuading myself that this small act of vandalism would be a good deed, the sharp edge a snare for unwary cloaks and trouser pockets. Many a Sunday when the sermon got too long, when the list of grievances in my own head made me tired in the reciting, I found my fingers itching to pull at that sliver. The last Sunday I attended I yielded to that impulse. The spectacular result kept me from going back— the yank took a much bigger piece of the pew than I had expected and the long section of exposed raw wood made me turn away from salvation. No one in my family took much notice, salvation being not high on the Copper family list of priorities.

And death shall have no dominion. Gabe took my hand and squeezed it. My soul was emitting a kind of curse on the whole earth, the whole of existence. Not a pious Christian thought at all. A bitter resolve overcame me, along with that first wave of grief, a sense that Horace's death had in some way released me, given me permission to be as hard and devious as Horace had been that day when I accompanied him to Everett. Ice was filling my veins and it frightened me. So I turned to the nearest distraction I could find, which was Gabe. He, alongside me, standing over the body of his dead cousin, the one he had come to meet on this ship. I watched with a sense of compassion for him I didn't feel for myself. Gabe seemed to sniff at the body as if confirming its relationship. Then he straightened, jerky separate movements that normally flowed together, as if the act of standing now required of him a dozen acts of volition. He looked gutted to me, lost, a look I never saw on him again. Then the expression was replaced by a ferocious anger. I envied that anger, having so little of it myself. It must have been then that I gave myself permission to turn away from the part of me that hurt so. The part that guided me in right and wrong, whether to trust or not. I was bruised, alone. I needed solace, and that moment Gabe seemed to offer it.

He caught my eye, as if to say, Watch me, then turned to address the crowd that had moved back into a ragged circle. "My cousin Abraham Rabinowitz has been murdered," Gabe announced in a harsh voice that somehow invited them into his sorrow. "And so has Horace Copper, the brother of this young woman." He motioned at me, catching me off guard. I remember my face struggling to find an appropriate expression, Gabe watching me like a patient acting coach. Finally he nodded. Hold that look. And I did. Then he pointed out, one by one, the bodies of the three others. "And these sons and brothers—Tom, Dick, Harry, no loved ones to claim them, they've been murdered as well. Dozens more wounded and killed by forces—" Here he seemed to lose his train of thought, and looked around at the shed rooftops as if seeing snipers, then rallied and took his oration in another direction. "We shall avenge them." This in a hard quiet voice. "Avenge their deaths. These—martyrs—shall not have died..." And here he stopped, aware, perhaps, that he was about to plagiarize Abraham Lincoln, and, seeking some more original ending, found none. So instead he simply dropped his hands, then his head, lifted one palm, an almost papal gesture. But the next moment, when he lifted his eyes, you saw the burning anger and the illusion of Christian acceptance in him died.

Judge not, lest you be judged. Do not give what is holy to dogs— they will turn and attack you. The Bible says that just before it tells us not to throw pearls before swine. Do you think the Bible, putting those thoughts so close together, was suggesting something? That maybe judging is part of what is holy and not to be cast away? In some hidden part of my brain, in the weeks and months that followed, as I tagged along with Gabe while he judged others up one side and down the other, I mulled that over. I was letting myself think his judging was holy when, in fact, the part of me that was holy was being thrown to the dogs. Marcel hadn't even left, I hadn't even faced up to telling him what was in my heart, when all of a sudden I allowed myself to be hijacked into the crusade of Gabe Rabinowitz—into avenging the death of his cousin, not to mention Horace, when I knew in my heart there was at least a small bit of complicity on my brother's side in the tragic confrontation in Everett.

As I said, I hid this knowledge from myself. The truthful reason was, I was afraid to be alone. Me, who had been alone all my life, was now spoiled by the balm of Marcel's lovemaking. I could no longer face the cold of my former solitary life. I wanted a place by the fire. Any fire.

The crowd on the dock started to disburse, the ambulances moving to take the wounded to hospitals. Another ambulance was being loaded to take the dead to the morgue. I became aware that Gabe was holding my arm and insisting on escorting me. I disliked this intrusion, I remember that, but lacked the strength or cleverness to find an excuse to go home alone. I was frightened, somehow, that he would find out about Marcel. That he was at least half the reason I was so bereft. I was afraid he would see into my grief that was bigger than the loss of Horace, and so I placated him, thinking he'd soon find something else to occupy himself, some bigger cause to latch on to. For even then, watching him manipulate the feelings of the crowd, I had formed an uncharitable view of him. I had seen his kind of lazy escalating rhetoric before. I knew what it led to. I had inherited my mother's scorn of big talkers. Horace, whatever he was doing, always had the sense to keep his mouth shut.

But not Gabe Rabinowitz. He was a talker and he talked my ear off the whole trolley ride home. I disliked the sensation of him being so near, the way he leaned into me, the smell of his wet coat, the way he kept trying to engage my eyes. His hair was matted, I remember that, dead looking in some places, oily in others. His lips were full, there was a raw cleft in the lower one, as if he had the habit of sucking on it before speaking. Which he did, repeatedly, to my growing discomfort. In short, I could not wait to be rid of him. But also, once gone, I found I could not get him out of my mind. Standing at my rooming house door, he asked to be invited in. No, I said, I think not. Why, I wondered, had I not thought of that reply before he boarded my trolley? Too late, he now knew where I lived, and looked me over in a claiming way that I knew meant he'd be back. I made some excuse, said that I was tired, and immediately regretted not having simply said good-bye. I had the foresight to stare him into walking away before turning to mount the inside steps but was left with the dispirited feeling that he had already captured the higher ground. I was ashamed, also, to have so quickly forgotten Marcel, his impending departure, my need for him, throughout the long interval of Gabe's speech over my brother's body. Ashamed that I had forgotten Horace, as well, during the trolley ride home in my distaste and fascination with this other man.

Later that night I found myself at Marcel's house, something he had specifically asked me never to do. Josephine, his mother, answered the door. She looked me up and down. I realized I must look wretched, feverish and groveling. She turned and left me on the unlighted porch, called back into the house to Marcel. After several minutes, in which I could hear him whispering with his mother, he appeared. He had on his nightshirt, with a plaid robe wrapped over and a pair of hastily put on trousers beneath. I guessed, in part, that's what the whispering had been about. There was sleep in his eyes and fear on his face, as if he thought I might be deranged and about to make a scene.

All of a sudden I saw him for what he was, a boy, too sheltered and half formed to be able to bear the weight of the burden I needed him to share. I whispered the bare facts, that my brother was dead, that I would have to go to the morgue the next day, that I would contact him when I could.

"Will you be working on Wednesday?" he asked. And then I realized that it would be three whole days before I saw him and that, by then, everything would have changed. I nodded yes, kissed him quickly before his mother saw and turned to go. I went down the long flight of stone steps and made it halfway to the corner before I turned for one last look and found he had gone.

CHAPTER 6

My brother lay on a slab in the morgue, face up, covered to the waist with gray canvas. Horace was again second in line, after Hugo Gerlot, before John Looney and Felix Baran. Gabe's cousin, Abe Rabinowitz, was last. Five bodies under harsh pools of overhead light, the rest of the room dark except for the three bright lamp-lit circles illuminating the midpoints of the first, third and fifth tables. Horace was in shadow, which suited me fine. All the bodies were partly in shade, so if the technician wanted to make an incision, in leg or neck, he would have to move the table to see. Three lights and five bodies—a lot of moving around required in a small room. The collecting gutters clamped along the sides of each gurney made me think this would be a cumbersome process. You can see the state of mind I was in, shell shocked, I suppose.

Family members had been assembled. My mother and I to identify Horace, Gabe and his uncle Sam representing the Rabinowitz family, a sister of John Looney. Felix Baran had family in Montana, but they weren't there. A grade school picture dug up from a helpful teacher in Billings was all the coroner had. The last body, of Hugo Gerlot, was identified by the night manager of his flophouse on Yesler Way. A couple of fellows sent by the Central Labor Council were also milling around. Thirteen people in all, if you count the lab technicians and the King County Medical Examiner plus the police cameraman. All of us crowded in with five formaldehyde-soaked bodies.

My mother was wearing a red dress. Not bright red, more of a chokecherry color, with gray leaves laid out in an alternating pattern that looked like feathers. I was bothered, somehow, by the choice of color, and wondered, for the first time, if my mother's behavior was not so much a product of distaste for me and most everyone she encountered but instead a kind of generalized poor judgment.

Gabe and his uncle were dressed in heavy woolen suits, old from the look of them, and Sam kept pulling at his cuffs to make the sleeves longer. Gabe, for his part, kept shifting from one foot to the other, in barely suppressed excitement, I suppose, or maybe it was grief, the circumstances were so odd, it was difficult to know.

My mother was composed, unnaturally so. She had come to Seattle as soon as the county medical office had wired her about the body. I had been torn between going up to Everett to tell her in person, or trying to get the university switchboard to let me use the telephone. In the end I did neither, or rather, took up the offer of the medical examiner to compose a wire, appended to the official one, free of charge. I had twelve words. I thought for a while, chewed on the pencil, scratched out a couple of attempts and came up with this: *Horace dead. Saw ship unload. Will meet train. Wire arrival time. Pennyjoe.* My name is really two words, but I collapsed it to keep to my limit. She didn't wire back, just arrived at the morgue Tuesday morning at the appointed time, in her chokecherry red dress, and nodded to me as if I were somebody else's relative.

The room was hot, the smell so strong I thought I was going to faint. The medical examiner, sweating in his wool suit, made a brief speech, read from dog-eared notes, expressing condolences and stating the forensic reasons for the autopsies. It came down to determining whether the corpses had been drowned, crushed or shot. As it turned out, none had drowned, and, while Looney and Baran showed signs of being crushed, all had been shot. Horace in the heart, Abe Rabinowitz in the back of the head, John Looney in the throat, Felix Baran in the stomach and Hugo Gerlot low in the ribs with the bullet coming up through the left lung. Pretty good marksmanship on a pitching ship from one hundred yards. I remember being thankful that Horace's face was not damaged. And that he had been facing his attackers when struck. My father's way of thinking, I realized, not being a coward more important than the trivial fact of dying. Then I realized that no one had wired Pa. I sidled over and murmured this to my mother. She didn't hear me at first, then looked up from where she had seated herself in the room's lone chair. "The union will tell him," she said.

As it turned out, the union did tell him, they sent a delegation later that same day with a full account of the events, plus the morgue pictures they'd secretly gotten from the police photographer, and took down Pa's florid account of Horace's idyllic boyhood. All that, plus a picture of Pa grinning in his cell, filled a two-page spread in the *Union Record*. And, of course, the line up of morgue pictures all edged in black. The whole story got picked up in the mainstream Seattle press and then by wire service and next day it was running throughout the nation. Even, I was told, in England and France.

In the next few months Horace became a martyr, and my father bobbed along in his slipstream. Pilgrimages to Eastern Washington State Penitentiary began in earnest. Ph.D. candidates rushed to claim Joe Copper and his martyred son as subjects for their dissertations. Famous journalists, including Lincoln Steffens and Max Eastman, weighed in. Emma Goldman made him the subject of one of her orations. Speeches denounced him on the Senate floor. The coffers of Fighting Joe's defense fund runneth over. Some of the money even found its way to support my mother. From jail, as a result of Horace's death, and, without lifting a finger, my father was finally able to provide for his wife.

I guess my mother took it as her due. I don't know. She left immediately after the medical examiner was finished, signing the forms authorizing the autopsy and release of medical records. When Gabe, later that week, went up to visit her with a request that Horace be buried in Seattle, in a martyr's grave paid for by the unions, she signed as meekly as she did for the medical examiner. This behavior displayed a submissiveness I did not know my mother harbored. Or perhaps it was merely disinterest in Horace's earthly remains. Perhaps she was persuaded that all this attention was evidence of her son's exceptional destiny and that he deserved a martyr's grave. Maybe she figured a free burial was the best bargain she could strike. As I said, I don't know. I never knew what led my family to do what they did.

As for myself, I emerged that day into a rare moment of November sunshine fighting down the urge to vomit. It was easy to accept Gabe's arm behind my back and his other hand supporting my elbow. With Sam Rabinowitz hovering in the background, we made a nice snapshot for the *Post-Intelligencer*. When the photographer was done Sam went over and murmured something to my mother. He took her hand and pressed it with his own, gave her a card and an encouraging smile. The photographer snapped away. A practiced performance, to my eye. I wondered that my mother was taken in. If she was. She came over while I was squinting in the sun and made a halfhearted attempt at patting my shoulder before announcing that she had to catch her train. I mentioned my rented room, that she could stay there—but something about the lovely memory of what Marcel and I had so recently done there, the sudden reticence I felt imaging all that in front of strangers, as well as the thought of staying in the same bed with my mother, we who had never caressed each other in living memory, stopped me. I let the half-voiced invitation run out. Silence gathered. Finally my mother said, "There's your room at home." Then she added, "Should you ever want to visit." She nodded, a dismissive gesture, smiled a fraction at Gabe and his uncle, pulled her gray shawl over her ramrod back and marched down the street in the direction of the train station. It was four months before I saw her again.

When I did go back to Everett it was to testify at the trial. My appearance was perfunctory. The prosecution called me as part of their effort to weave a conspiracy theory—that the three hundred men on the *Verona* came to Everett armed and intending to provoke mayhem. That they were anarchists, Bolsheviks, Jews. That my association with one Gabriel Rabinowitz, the spectacle we were then playing out in Seattle, proved this. On the stand my flat intonation and curt responses did not make for much drama. The prosecutor decided midway through that badgering the sister of a local hero shot through the heart was not helping his case. He cut short his questioning and the defense limited itself to establishing that I knew nothing about my brother's activities leading up to the massacre and that was that.

I had stayed at my mother's house the night before, timing my arrival late enough so that she was home from the canning factory but early enough so that we could make a pretense of catching up on local news before turning in for bed. I brought more Canadian toffee and a quarter round of Tillamook cheese as well as a jar of the kind of pickled mushrooms I knew she liked. She accepted all this with equanimity, as I later learned she'd accepted the bank drafts from the union defense fund. All the fire I'd known in her seemed burned out. We ate slivers of cheese and speared oily mushrooms from the jar with a long handled fork. It was as close to a party together as we'd ever had. She told me about goings on at the bean factory, which girl was fooling around with the foreman, who showed up Monday with a blackened eye and busted lip. I, in turn, told her about the laundry, the girl on the night shift who was pregnant by the deliveryman and left it at that. She must have known what was going on with Gabe, how I'd been roped into his circus, must have wondered if there was a seamy side to it, but she didn't ask. She didn't bring up the trial either, the fact that I'd be testifying the next day, didn't say anything about Horace, or my father and his new found celebrity in the penitentiary. About nine she said her back was bothering her and she boiled some water to fill her rubber bottle and said there were sheets and a blanket on my bed and that I could make it up myself. When I got up the next morning she was gone, but left a note, saying, "Thank you for the cheeze." It was the warmest communication from her I ever got.

CHAPTER 7

I never met Sam Rabinowitz until that morning at the morgue. But it was easy to see that Gabe and his uncle shared certain family features—a strong upper body not equaled by the lower. Long arms, hairy hands. Broad foreheads topped by masses of wiry hair. But there the resemblance ended. Sam had an altogether more likeable face, large tobacco stained teeth that served to soften his hawk-like eyes. Gabe's eyes were also sharp, but darker, almost black, and angry, but, since he rarely looked at people except when making a speech, his eyes were not the feature that stuck in one's mind. It was the rest of his face, and the coiled way he held his body that stuck with you. Sam groomed and oiled his hair to the point you could see comb marks, while Gabe left his long, so that its matted weight would lift with the wind.

The first time I really saw Sam was outside the morgue, when he went up to my mother and pressed her hands for the camera. Like any politician, I remember thinking, the kind of do-gooder "shop floor" Democrat that was then coming into vogue. He had something in mind for my mother, as he pressed her hands, something he wanted her to do, so it came as no surprise that he had something in mind for me as well. But, in my case, the details of that something were left up to Gabe. I do not know whether they decided this in advance, or whose idea it was, this division of labor. If it was Gabe's, as I am inclined to think, then there were probably dual motives at work. If Sam were calling the shots, the approach to me would have been more direct, an appeal to solidarity or family loyalty with my mother enlisted to press the case. As it was, Gabe relied entirely on his fine tuned understanding of my emotional state. Something only a practiced seducer could have read so clearly in those first few minutes we spent together on the dock.

But what was Gabe's plan? Again, I am assuming he had a plan, that he didn't just improvise as he saw the possibilities. There was that one great moment when he discovered my brother's body next to his cousin's, neither of us knowing until that moment that either one was dead. Whatever genuine rage Gabe brought to that moment, whatever sense of loss or retribution, instead of reacting with private grief, he chose a public response. *Don't mourn, organize.* Those were the famous words of Joe Hill. Well, that's what Gabe did. Seeing the bodies, sensing the mood on the docks, weighing his own stake in the tragedy, he gauged the possibility of creating a firestorm, and came up with two conclusions: one, that he was the man to run the show, and two, that he needed someone with better credentials than his. That was where I came in. Sister of a dead martyr, daughter of a jailed one. Vulnerable in a way he sensed but could not yet fathom. It takes a person of great cunning, or maybe the term is leadership, to see all that in one second and then act. That Gabe did, I give him his due. He shaped what came to pass. Except in the end. I shaped that.

On the sidewalk that day in front of the morgue, as I watched my mother walk toward the train station, part of me wanted to join her, so as to be a part of some plan, to be endowed with some purpose. I also wanted to get away from Gabe and Sam, from the rest of the motley group on the sidewalk. I realized just then, looking at my mother's retreating back, that no one had paid much attention to the bodies. It was the shock, I suppose, of seeing that line of naked chests, waxy, yellowish from the light or the fluid they were treated with, each with a tiny bullet hole, puckered and grayish at the edge, a plug of blackened blood announcing entry into the body itself. A canal, I remember thinking, an opening like an ear or a nostril. A punctuation mark. Had these deaths been ordained? When? At the moment of the bullet's entry? When the body turned to shield itself from gunfire? Or earlier, when some sheriff's deputy had pulled the trigger? Or earlier still, when the *Verona* first left port? Or even before that, when my brother rounded up these willing participants for his roustabouts' picnic? I asked myself these questions, remembering the bullet holes, feeling all energy drain from my body. Did it matter? Was it necessary to assign blame?

Gabe thought it was. He interrupted to ask if my mother had funeral plans. I was surprised he assumed I knew. She and I had not exchanged a private word the whole morning. As I struggled to formulate an answer, Gabe had a follow-up question. Did I mind him going up to visit my mother, in a day or two, to express his condolences, as well as lay out a proposition with respect to the burial? The phrasing of it, "lay out a proposition with respect to the burial" had an unfortunate effect. Perhaps Gabe was in the burial plot business, I thought. That's why he had been hovering around on the docks. I struggled to suppress explosive laughter, sure it would come out as a braying sound, as always happened when I was pushed beyond my limits. I closed my eyes and pinned my lips together, moving my head from side to side. No, I didn't mind. I struggled even harder as I imagined Gabe in my mother's parlor, hat in hand. If he owned a hat. But hat or no, he must have known what I did not, that she would welcome any young male that was a friend of Horace's in her parlor.

When I opened my eyes my vision blurred. I blinked and mumbled that I had to get back to work. Gabe asked which job I was going to. He had already wormed out of me that I had two. The laundry, I told him, wanting to keep him away from Marcel as long as I could.

"I'll go with you," he said.

* *.*

Later that day, as I struggled to feed my quota of wet sheets through the mangle, I thought about what to do next. I watched the wrinkled linens, still smelling from naphtha, disappear into the long padded arm, each sheet in its turn pulled deep into the maw. I thought about the word *mangle*, how such a term came to be used for a machine whose job it was to crush wet linens into freshly ironed sheets. A harsh restoration no doubt, to emerge newly bathed only to be steamed and flattened inside an unrelenting machine. Not something to be welcomed, but considered necessary by us humans, to restore sheets to useful life. A merciful God could have provided a more bucolic transformation, I thought, performed by Swiss maidens, using flat irons on a mountainside balcony. But this wasn't Switzerland, and I wasn't a Swiss maiden. I was in the basement of the Biology building, next to the heating plant, and my sheets were getting ironed according to the laws of the world they were consigned to. That grim thought gave me comfort, freed me from any sense I had control of my own destiny, so by the time my shift was over I had worked around my mind to the inevitability that Gabe was going to insert himself into my life whether I liked it or not, and that Marcel was going to leave me whether either of us did much to stop it.

Because there wasn't much I could do to derail Marcel's mother's plans. A shotgun marriage seemed out of the question. A baby wasn't something I'd done anything to prevent so there wasn't much I could do to start one. And then there was the painful realization that I didn't want Marcel to leave because I didn't want to be alone. That struck me as so pitiful I couldn't bear to admit it. Marcel had a future that I wanted him to relinquish. In my dark mood, that seemed like a lot to ask.

On that note, I climbed the stairs from my sweatshop and found Gabe. The girls alongside me were impressed by his wolfish energy. I didn't bother to introduce them. Gabe brushed past this. "I'm Gabe Rabinowitz," he said, shaking hands all around. Men did not normally do that in those days, shake hands with young women, so it had a seductive effect. He pulled out some cigarettes and offered those around as well. A couple of girls took him up. "You know Penny Joe's just lost her brother." The girls, who had been smiling, now pulled serious faces. "I lost my cousin in the same tragedy." All of a sudden their attention, their full sympathy, was with him. "I've been trying to think of a suitable memorial, a way to honor these men." Yes, they all nodded, a memorial. *Sheep.* That's what I was thinking. If he had said, "Run, run over a cliff," they would have happily trotted off.

He laid out his plan. A series of vigils starting that night. How easy, I remember thinking, how smooth a seducer he was. At first the girls looked tentative, then a little scared. "We might loose our jobs," one of them said. Gabe acted as if he hadn't heard.

Staring off into the distance he said, "In front of the university chapel."

A couple of girls agreed that the church was the spot, that piety would protect them. He told them how to fashion votive lights using brown penny bags, how two inch candles were best. Fold over the top of the bag, like this, he said, to strengthen the enclosure, make sure to hold them flat, supporting the bottom, watch so the paper doesn't catch fire. He asked them to check their purses, tallied how much money each had—then made assignments, who was to get candles, who paper bags. The girl assigned to beg the corner grocer for bags asked about signs. Gabe acted as if thunderstruck. Signs, yes, of course! And so she, blushing, got the job of lettering signs as well. With Gabe's coaching, they collectively picked a time, an hour to begin. One girl tried to quibble—wasn't it better to wait until tomorrow, to get better organized?

"No," Gabe replied, pulling rank, a harsh note coming into his voice. "It has to be tonight." How could she think of putting this off? The other girls were abashed. Of course, yes, it had to be tonight. The girl who had made the suggestion apologized, but to no avail. The others had shifted their bodies away. Already she had been cast out. Each young woman, just minutes before companionable coworkers, was now angling for Gabe's special favor. An exhibit of male power put on, I thought, for my benefit. As an offering and a warning.

Such is the devil's brew a virile actor in a potent cause can produce, intoxicating those willing to be led. If it is that easy, I asked myself that night, votive light in hand, why are we not every day cast down into damnation?

The vigil was a modest success, given its improvisational nature. Of course, had the girls not shown up, Gabe would have lost no face. Only I would have been the wiser. But the girls did show up. Seven strong, they were promptly dubbed the seven sisters. As soon as Gabe got them lined up on the chapel steps with their candles in paper bags, adorned by signs, he went off to get photographers. I was stationed at the collection basket with instructions to direct passersby to do one of three things: make a donation, buy a candle, or join the vigil. Most did all three. We did a land office business, considering it was mid-November. Fortunately, it wasn't raining. By the time the reporters got there sixty people were on the steps holding bags with lighted candles. Gabe filled in the reporters on my significance. One reporter, smelling of beer and cabbage, stuck his note pad in my face and asked about Horace, voicing his own conclusions first. "Yes," I agreed, "a life of promise cut short. A natural leader."

"Was Horace singled out?"

I blanked at this, not knowing where the question was headed. The reporter rephrased it. "Did they shoot him on purpose?"

I said I didn't know. Which was the wrong answer. The next day the headline said, "Horace Copper's Sister Suspects Deliberate Shooting." The story went on to repeat my coached phrases and those voiced by the seven sisters, each affirming her devotion to my dead brother, who, of course, she'd never met. Several of the male students who had joined the vigil spoke in terms of revenge. Presumably Gabe had coached them as well. A minister who'd joined suggested prayer. But Gabe had the final word. He was quoted as promising graveside demonstrations.

So you see, my mother's permission to let Gabe bury my brother was an essential element of the plan. The next day Gabe set out for Everett to secure it. And left me mercifully alone and free to figure out what to do about Marcel.

CHAPTER 8

These days I read the Bible a lot. That and seed catalogs. Do you know a mustard seed is so small, travels so easily on the wind, that once introduced to a habitat, it becomes nearly impossible to eradicate? Jesus said the word of God is like that, traveling on the wind, impossible to eradicate. I have seen fields taken over by mustard, heard farmers speak of it as a noxious plant, a species that, once established, chokes out all else. There are men like that, carrying a word they call good, who, once established, choke out the good of others.

My history with Gabe is instructive in that regard, though less for what good he smothered along the way than for the people he trampled. I was never blind to what he was. I was, rather, inert. Feeble as to the promptings of my heart, sickened soil, unable to fend off noxious growth.

The Wednesday following the docking of the *Verona* was my first day alone without Gabe to monopolize my senses. I returned to my shift at the diner. Mr. Panopolous was working, as usual, scrubbing the black stove with his wire brush. I, as usual, put on my apron and began to clean out crumbs from the pie rack. We said nothing. Students came in for their late lunch or afternoon coffee. Because of the vigil I was featured on the front page, so some spoke to me, awkward in their enthusiasm or subdued in their condolences. Others just shied away altogether. I was resentful of them all. I felt bruised, an imposition on myself and others. I realize now I was overreacting, but that day my black mood was sufficient to drive me to isolation behind the counter, leaving Mr. Panopolous to tend to the customers. He didn't seem to mind, perhaps he too felt I was a drag on his patrons' enjoyment.

Later, when the afternoon editions arrived, there was more unwelcome news. Spread across the front page were five morgue pictures, the ones that had been smuggled to the unions the day before. John Looney, pale high forehead over sunken eye sockets. Felix Baran, darker features set in a confused, furrowed brow. Hugo Gerlot had an altogether saintly expression, while Abe Rabinowitz had lips spread in a ghoulish smile. All unseeing, defenceless, as the photographer's flash exploded, a bullet hole showing on Looney's neck, another barely noticeable near Baran's armpit, a third beside Gerlot's small pinched nipple, another buried hidden in Rabinowitz's snarl of chest hair. Men I never knew, impossible to decipher in death. But my brother's face held an expression I faintly recognized but had long overlooked. In death his face revealed a pugnacious streak I did not recall in life. Examining his morgue picture while hiding behind the pie rack, I realized that in death there had emerged a whole side of him I never acknowledged, not because it was new, but because I could not see, would not see, what had been there all along.

I wondered then what unknown aspect of me would surface in my death. That day, I was sure, my death mask would have revealed forlornness. A loneliness so much like burning shame that it drove me behind the pie rack. I wanted to sink into the floor, or better yet, that piecrust—I wanted to burrow into the apple slices. But I did not die that day, did not hide my soul in any fruit pastries. And, though many times in later life that same impulse to die of shame came upon me, the basic question still remains unanswered. What will my death mask show? Perhaps I, too, shall reveal my brother's pugnacious cast, perhaps that is the trait that is taking a lifetime to ripen in me.

Lost in such morbid thoughts, I did not see Marcel come into the diner. A creature of habit, he moved to his usual seat, then thought better of it and came over to speak to me. I was emptying coffee grounds and kept my back turned. He retraced his steps to his table near the newspaper rack. Not wanting him to see the death pictures, I came over, wiping my hands on my apron, and sat down. "I only have a minute," I said.

He looked at me with his mild expression. "I'll wait," he said. Then, "Sunday night, on the porch—I'm sorry."

A lame excuse, I thought. I realized I was angry. "It's become quite a circus," I said, reaching over to one of the bamboo poles and tossing the afternoon paper in front of him. "My brother's last in line." Marcel took his time looking over the faces. I watched him, realizing the depth of my sense of desertion. "I'd hoped for more," was all I said.

Marcel looked up in a state I took, at the time, to be wonder. His face a mixture of confusion, shame and what I detected at the time to be pride. Male pride, the first woman to humble herself before him. "Do you want me to walk you home?" he asked. I wasn't sure exactly what he was offering, whether I'd managed to convey the sorry state I was in. Perhaps he'd taken my announcement as a request to make love, as if our usual Wednesday night engagement was the balm I was in need of. Maybe that's the only comfort he has to offer, I thought, and realized, now that he'd brought it up, that particular balm would be welcome, though what I was in need of was something altogether different. Solace was what he seemed to be offering, a certain comfort, but not protection.

The person against whom I needed protection next came to mind. "There is a friend of my brother's," I said, my voice flat, carrying a warning if only Marcel could hear it. "He has plans concerning my brother's burial. A commemoration of some sort, I don't know exactly what."

Again that bloom of wonder on Marcel's face, that gentle inability to comprehend. "Plans to—what? Take you somewhere?" Because Marcel was being taken away, his imagination traveled along that route.

"I don't think so," I said, realizing such a scenario was not out of the question. "He's using me to raise money. To cash in on this gruesomeness." I gestured at the death heads. Marcel finally caught the drift, that I did not see this fellow, his plans, as welcome. His face puckered.

"Can't you say no?"

I couldn't resist the jibe. "Like you do to Josephine?" Using his mother's name that way, saying it aloud, in that tone, that same tone he often used about her, was a provocation and Marcel took it as such. He colored, looked down, struggling to contain himself. Watching him gave me a kind of satisfaction. I waited to see if he might explode, defend her so I could attack her in his own words. But when he looked up his eyes were clear, his face still. He said, "You're not yourself. It's grief speaking."

That was the first time anyone had spoken that word. Grief. So, that's what I had become. A creature as fully taken over as my brother had been by Death. The idea came as welcome. To have a new name. To be anonymous. A universal self that had nothing to do with me.

I did let Marcel walk me home that night, did take him up on his offer. And his tender lovemaking and concern for me were a great balm.

But, as usual, he was not with me in the morning. Josephine saw to that. So I awoke, alone, the dull now familiar anger still there. I grasped to hold on to the night's memory, Marcel's always polite beginning, his hopeful expression, the boyish sudden move to take off his shirt, the shy offer to rub my back, his soft insistent fingers probing my spine, his violin player's hands moving down and across my body, and finally the slow progression into passion, the surprising suppleness of his unbalanced spine, my cries, his whispers, and then the graceful, besotted ending.

I wondered, as I brushed and pinned my hair, whether I

should simply kidnap him, take him like a Turkish bandit takes a bride, swoop down and catch him up on my steed. I teased myself with images of Marcel in a crimson burnoose, black eyes peeking out, myself in flowing robes, turbaned atop a frothing stallion. Why not kidnap him, I asked myself, why not take him by surprise and hide him out in some dusty border town? I studied myself in the mirror and considered my prospects. I could propose elopement, and, if that didn't work, demand it. But where would I take him, where could I find a music school to enroll him, where could I find work? Washing windows, scrubbing floors, it didn't matter. Had there been such a border town, had I known where to take him, I would have done so that day. Instead, I told myself that I needed more time, needed to think through this plan before I sprang it on him. If he would not rescue me, I decided, I would rescue him.

That afternoon, Gabe reappeared. I found him lounging in my room when I returned from the laundry. He had picked the lock. Such was my state that I was neither surprised nor angry. I had arrived full of plans to kidnap Marcel, but when I opened the door and saw Gabe, I became a different person. It was as if, sensing danger, all my energy suddenly withdrew. My life, my prospects for fullness, were banked instantly so deep inside as to be inaccessible. "Do you have a key?" I found myself asking.

"Yours," he said, showing me the extra one I kept hidden in my dresser drawer, dangling it in my face before putting it in his pocket. "For emergencies," he said. A relief, since I had expected him to say he intended to move in.

"I won't come here anymore," he announced, anticipating my unvoiced fear. "Until this is over. People must believe there is nothing untoward—" Here he smiled, a wolfish expression, his face turning his words into the exact opposite.

I bowed my head, accepting both the near term propriety of this arrangement and its longer term opposite, again with that odd sense of relief, and, to my dismay, a flicker of anticipation.

And Gabe was good to his word. In the next five months he never again came to my room, but left messages with Mr. Panopolous, instructing me on where to show up, when to beg off work. Because he relied on Mr. Panopolous, both to carry messages and to spy on me, he never asked that I abandon my shift at the diner. Rather, he instructed me to give up my class in biology, and, later, the laundry room. At least once a day for the next five months I was directed to appear at one or another rally or march or speaker's platform. I never knew whether Gabe organized it all or just claimed he did. Over the following weeks he set about to shape me, my personality, sculpt the expression on my face, the set to my shoulders, the way I rested my hands. I became companion to the death masks, Grief, the embodiment of all that was lost. I learned to sit silent, to let the rise and fall of Gabe's stage rhetoric transmit muted vibrations of his anger and pain to my face, let those emotions flare and then settle and pass over. Speech was a job for others. I was the movement's figurehead. An icon to be carted around but not consulted. And, mercifully, not understood.

There was one occasion, early on, where I was called upon to say a few words. A Sunday ecumenical service held at Queen Anne Presbyterian Church, which happened to be the church Josephine attended, having graduated from a lapsed Catholic to a Presbyterian, courtesy of her second husband. She was much enamored of the Reverend Sloan, pastor of Queen Anne, as were all the ladies of that church.

By that first Sunday in November Gabe had succeeded in rounding up permission to bury four of the five bodies. His plan had been for a grand five-martyr funeral. But his Aunt Esther outfoxed him and decided her son should be buried in Brooklyn. I heard Sam and Gabe arguing about it, whose fault it was that Esther had spirited Abe's body away. Gabe's position was that Esther was Sam's sister, that he should have anticipated her treachery, while Sam held that Gabe was guilty of not tending to first things first. A five-martyr funeral was to be their masterstroke. Thousands of mourners marching through emptied streets emanating from five different houses of worship. But to Gabe's great consternation, Esther outflanked him. Orthodox funerals dictate an immediate burial, but she managed some kind of dispensation, and got the body shipped back east while he was up in Everett sweet-talking my mother and Sam was in Billings doing the same for Felix Baran. Gerlot and Looney were local, drifters who would normally be buried in potter's field, so the union was easily able to secure permission to bury them.

But in the end Gabe was able to turn his cousin's departure into an occasion for press. Friday, somehow, he organized a ceremony at the train station, complete with Orthodox mourners, draped in prayer shawls and phylacteries, and a phalanx of black suited union leaders, sleek and pleased with themselves. Gabe and Sam arrived in a horse drawn carriage that carried a box, slightly shorter than a coffin, with a sign on the end that said, "Abraham Rabinowitz—Remaining Possessions," by which I suppose they meant his clean shirts and stamp collection. What I do know is that they called on the union leaders to assume the position of pallbearers and walked the box down to the loading platform, positioning it on the freight car so that the waiting photographers could shoot it from an angle that included the *davening* mourners and the honor guard of union officials. In the Saturday morning paper it looked as if they'd held the funeral right there on the train platform.

So, by Saturday, having said a public good-bye to Abe Rabinowitz's remaining possessions, Gabe had in hand four martyrs, and was making plans for simultaneous funerals the following weekend. The first Sunday was to be a grand ecumenical service at which he would unveil his next surprise, plaster of Paris death masks he had bribed a morgue guard to make. These he planned to fix on pikes to carry at the head of each converging funeral procession, but in the mean time they were displayed in red velvet cases at the church. My job, that first Sunday, was to stand beside the death masks and oversee a collection box.

I had not counted on the fact that Josephine was a parishioner, nor that the Reverend Sloan's sense of showmanship was as strong as Gabe's.

I was dressed in black, a dress Gabe had bought for me out of money he had already collected. As I stood in the waxy smelling hall listening to the organist grind out "Oh, Promise Me," attempting to hide the collection box behind a spray of bittersweet, Anna Mae Sloan, the Reverend Sloan's daughter, joined me. She took charge as if she knew all there was to know about getting parishioners to part with their money. As each filed past, she introduced the congregant to me, gave them a meaningful eye, and, when they blanched at the display of death heads, smiled at them to open their wallets. In snatches, she filled me in on her father's and her own political convictions. It seemed the Reverend Sloan was circumspect in his political views but decidedly progressive. Outwardly he hewed to the line of the Ministers' Alliance, but was always trying to move them to the left. She, on the other hand, simply plunged into whatever cause caught her fancy. Last year, for example, she had defended the rights of a woman tried for sedition, seeing it as her duty to show up at the trial each day and issue statements of support.

This did not sit well among the Progressive Ladies' Alliance, who had been major supporters in getting her elected as the first female member of the school board. Anna Mae dropped this last nugget with a modest blush. Not long after, unfortunately, she was the subject of a recall, the first female to have that honor as well. I assumed her eager involvement in my cause, or rather Gabe's cause, was part of the same pattern. But when Gabe emerged from the Reverend Sloan's office, a cubicle beside the washroom, I could see that Anna Mae had an eye for him that went beyond an enthusiasm for prospective causes and had no doubt influenced her attendance at the collection box beside me.

Anna Mae was well past thirty, buxom, almost blowsy. But that Gibson girl look was then still fashionable, and Gabe, looking more cleaned up than usual, gave her a gaze of frank appreciation. He had gotten a haircut, put pomade on his unruly locks, and the overall effect, in his newly pressed suit, was almost presentable. The "almost" was what attracted Anna Mae.

During the service, after the opening hymns but before the second collection, Reverend Sloan pronounced his eulogy to the "slain martyrs," exhorting the congregation to pay their respects the following week at the various concurrent funeral services and to join the cortege. I remember the use of the word *cortege*, it sounded so military and solemn, which was the effect he intended, though the event itself turned out hardly to be military and, at points, not even solemn. After that, without any warning, he called on me to say a few words. I could tell from Gabe's expression that this was not something Gabe had agreed to. Grief was to be seen but not heard. Nevertheless, I made my way to the pulpit amid scattered applause. I could feel Gabe's eyes on me, and, once at the pulpit, could see on his face both jealousy and possessiveness. On Marcel's face, which I encountered as I looked out and spotted near the back, I could detect only his usual befuddled wonder. His mother's face was set like a prune. Without knowing what I was going to say but, determined to make Josephine's expression even more sour, I plunged ahead.

"Horace," I remember starting out, "was my younger brother. Nearly six years younger." I realized that I'd given away my age to anyone who cared to count, and most particularly, to Josephine. "He was struck down at the age of—nineteen, he turned that in September." This drew a nervous laugh, settling the audience, who, I realized, were now hanging on every word. That made me bolder. I started mimicking the rhetoric I had learned at my father's knee. "Horace grew up in a family that lived the workingman's cause. His father—my father—was a shingle cutter like the men who went out on strike. My brother, in the normal course of events, would have been a shingle cutter, too, but my mother had other plans. Horace had plans too—not just my mother's plans, but his own plans. That is why he won every prize in school, got the scholarship that made a university education possible."

I looked out over the rows of faces. Where were these words coming from?

"But those plans changed. Horace joined an outing of men concerned about the fate of Everett's striking workers, men like my father, men who worked every day to put food on the table." A scattering of applause, stilled by the realization this was a funeral service. I started up again, aware that my pa had turned precious little of his pay into food on the table. "Horace boarded a boat, part of a just and legal gathering, in an expression of free speech sanctioned by the laws of the State of Washington and the U.S. Constitution. And then something went horribly wrong. My brother and four others are dead. Others lost at sea. Seventy-four of the so-called "ring leaders" in jail. My brother is dead, and I don't know why. I don't know what he thought he was headed into when he boarded the *Verona*, I don't know what he expected would happen when he arrived in Everett, I don't know what decisions he had made about the direction of his life or where it would find meaning."

My voice broke and I realized I had veered into territory far too personal. An image rose before me: that of my brother Horace when he was six, in the front parlor of my mother's house. It must have been his birthday, because he was dressed in his first long pants, his hair cut from baby curls, and he had a toy wagon, with red wheels, that my father had bought as a present. Horace was running the wheels up and down my leg. He was angry over something, some injustice inflicted on his newly proud six-year-old self. I, just by being there, was supposed to make it right. On his face the baby version of that stubborn face recorded on his death mask. "Rolling, rolling, rolling," I remember him saying as he ground the metal wheels deep into my skin.

"Cut that out," I said.

He looked up, startled at my betrayal, and burst into tears. But then he stopped. Tears are too babyish, his face said, and his expression returned to its original scowl. "Rolling, rolling, rolling," he dug the wheels in harder. The axle caught in my dress, he yanked it away, leaving grease tracks.

"Cut that out!" I said again, and this time, instead of tears, he pulled back the truck and jammed it into my side, hard, like a knife, then dropped it, grabbed me and buried his face in my neck. I remember holding him, rocking him, stroking his newly bristled hair, deciding not to notice that his hot little hand had cupped my just blossoming breast.

All this I remembered as I looked out at the audience, waiting for my thoughts to collect. The next moment I thought of Marcel, his hands, his urgent *rolling, rolling, rolling* as he visited himself on my body, and could feel the start of a deep cascading blush. I cleared my throat, pushing away both memories, Horace and Marcel, to examine later, although I never did.

"My brother's life was cut short," I found myself announcing, the tone changing to a plaintive note, sounding more like myself. "We can never know what he planned, we can never know what might have happened—" I could feel myself starting to break down, and, deciding this was a suitable moment, simply stepped from the pulpit. As I made my way back to my seat, dozens of hands reached out to touch me.

Afterwards, in the church basement, Gabe and Anna Mae relieved me from duty at the collection table so I could pass among the parishioners. I felt like a debutante, at what I imagined to be a cotillion. At this moment I first became aware of the narcotic effect of sympathy. Perhaps that explains, or at least excuses, my willingness to play the role of Grief. I do recall that the sympathy that day soon ended. Josephine, who had avoided me up until then, came across the room, pressed herself into my circle of sympathizers and positioned herself squarely in front of me. "Don't think I don't see," she hissed. "I know what you've got up your sleeve."

Such was my sense of entitlement, so borne aloft was I on a wave of sympathy, that I minimized her threat. "What?" I taunted her. "What do I have planned?"

Chapter 9

On the following Thursday Gabe took me on a pilgrimage to Eastern Washington State Penitentiary to get the blessing of my pa. Me in another dress, this time blue serge—not new, Gabe had borrowed it from god knows where. He found out my size and I guess he located some similar sized woman with a goodly stock of dresses. Or maybe he tapped into the wardrobe department of some theatre—I never knew. All during those months, dresses would appear, then disappear. Cloaks, hats, even jewelry. My hat on that trip to the penitentiary was very fetching, navy blue felt, with a jaunty brim and a cluster of red wooden cherries. At the last minute, getting off the train at Spokane, Gabe decided cherries were too festive, so he ripped them off, leaving a hole in the brim for the owner to notice. I gathered the cherries from under the wicker train seat and held them the whole time we were in the penitentiary. I kept those cherries for many years, but in one of my many moves, I lost them. Or threw them out. I don't remember.

Seeing my pa after almost a year was a letdown. Such diminished circumstances. It's odd I should say that, considering the heightened atmosphere of the occasion, but to me it all felt diminished. My pa felt diminished, the air thinned out between us. That day I saw him clearly, I guess that's what I'm trying to say. Saw him without embellishment. It was as if I had come to a blank wall and there, sitting against it, was my pa. Stuck, a sack figure.

Except he didn't know it, didn't know, or didn't recognize that Gabe was there to pump him up, inflate his ego, to use him as a prop in Gabe's crusade. Or, if my pa did know, maybe he was like my mother and figured this was the best deal he could get. I was ashamed to be a part of this sorry spectacle but didn't want my pa to see this, didn't want him to see me in the same cold light as I saw him. At any rate, it was an awkward hour or two, and I couldn't wait to get back to Seattle.

On the train back Gabe was pleased with himself and talkative. He had entertained a pack of newspapermen waiting outside the prison gate, letting them take flash pictures and scribbling accounts of our visit. I said little, which pleased him, even though what I did say made the next day's lead quote, which didn't please. But on the train back he was satisfied, and talked about his life, his plans, ambitions. To my mind it boiled down, more or less, to getting even. I've met a lot of young men like that, grown men as well. Encountered them as a child, ran into them all through the twenties and thirties and forties. In 1954, when my beloved second husband succumbed to a long illness in Detroit, I decided I wasn't going to allow any more ambitious men into my life. Not that Vernon was. He was an autoworker, ten years older than me, a soft-spoken man with creased hands and a rabble rousing past. Each morning of our married life he looked at me with eyes that held the same wonder as Marcel's, and, like Marcel, that was all I ever asked of him. He gave me more, of course, much more. His union pension, for one thing, which allowed me to move back to Snoqualmie and live with a widow's dignity. A snug life, if you want to call it that.

But back to Gabe, that day on the return train from seeing my father. He told me he had been born in New York City, that his parents had emigrated from Lodz, the garment center of Poland. He painted a picture of a hand-to-mouth existence, but I later found out his father owned a glove factory, not much of a factory, true, but an owner, so technically he was part of the oppressor class. Of course, like so much left-wing dogma, this distinction was idiotic. Being a Polish Jew was oppression enough in 1916. The fact Gabe's father hired a few relatives hardly made him J.P. Morgan.

But that was not how Gabe saw it. He was ashamed of his father's relative prosperity, and so hid this inconvenient fact in a flurry of rhetoric and crafted instead a public version of his origins that gave him the right to dismantle society however he saw fit. After telling me this concocted family history, he then proceeded to lecture me on scientific socialism, which I concluded was analogous to the theory of evolution I had been trying to master in biology class. Both favoring an iron law of ascent. A tolerance for aggression in the name of progress. These days in my garden I labor in the opposite direction. Trying to clear nature of all the progress that has been foisted upon it, letting wild seed reassert itself. It is solitary work. Tilling and waiting and watching. Best left to an old woman, one the neighbors think addled.

On the train Gabe told me one other thing. That he planned to go to Mexico when the draft was instated. Which everyone expected would be soon, unless the war ended quickly. He probed my political views, found them inadequate both as to content and vociferousness, tested my knowledge of international socialism. Lectured me on the Bolshevik and Menshevik positions on the war, revealed a desire, a burning desire, to be noticed, to be a *noticed* delegate at the next International. Of course, by the time such a conference was held, after the war, the socialists and the communists had split and Gabe had nothing to do with the socialists.

It is an interesting question, what attracted me to Gabe, compelled me, you might say, into his orbit. In my experience, such matters are always muddied when the sexes are involved. At a certain level maybe it was just hormones.

Or maybe I was just too timid to say no. In any event, I let him take over. But in spite of that, at another level, Gabe could never reach me. Never reach me in the way Marcel or Vernon could. Men like Gabe, who take what they want, can be exciting or demeaning or dangerous for a time, but in the end they are simply boring. They produce a toughening, not a tenderizing, of the spirit. An important part of you is blanketed, so that each encounter with a man like Gabe produces a new layer of skin. Dead skin, which can be sloughed off. Which is what happened with Gabe. That's what I think now, anyway.

When we got back to Seattle, I had to talk myself back into my job at the laundry. The foreman was not interested in my newspaper fame, the rightness of Gabe's political cause, the depths of my grief. I was allowed no more absences. Period. Gabe instructed me to give up my laundry work, said he would put me on the dole, a union allowance just like my mother's, at three dollars a week. Since Mr. Panopolous was sympathetic, I would be allowed to keep my job at the diner. But this did not sit well with me, not being able to earn my own way, so I defied Gabe in this one small instance, and talked my laundry boss into letting me take a half shift. Nor did I tell Marcel, or ask his advice in this matter. That was perhaps a sign that things were not well between us either, notwithstanding the continuance of our Wednesday night lovemaking. Since this was the sole interval during the week when we were able to talk, and there was precious little of that going on, key features of my increasingly complicated life were not well conveyed to him.

That day on the train, as Gabe ran on about the need for a Third International, I was thinking of the mechanics of elopement. There was the matter of Marcel's age, the requirement for birth certificates, blood tests, a marriage license. I recalled there was a place east of Vancouver, just north of Portland, where elopement was possible without the formalities of blood tests and waiting periods. Justices of the Peace there were entrusted to handle all those details in their parlors. But a birth certificate or some kind of notarized statement of age was necessary. And Marcel was still seventeen, a few months shy of legal age. So that seemed to leave me two choices: get forged papers or hide out somewhere until Marcel turned eighteen. I turned these options over in my mind as Gabe instructed me on the fine points of Italian, as opposed to German, socialism.

The next few weeks pulled me in two directions. The grand funeral came off almost as planned. It rained, so a somber mood blanketed whatever rabble rousing Gabe had hoped would adorn the climax. My mood was also sour. At the cemetery, Marcel showed up, stood off in the distance, speaking neither to me nor to other members of the entourage. That first time at Queen Anne church, over at the donations table after my speech, I had seen Marcel talking with Anna Mae and Gabe. I hadn't been able to tell what kind of conversation it was, except the fixed smile on Anna Mae's face made clear she thought Marcel just another member of her father's congregation. I knew Gabe was keeping track of me through Mr. Panopolous, so it was likely he knew about Marcel, his Wednesday night walks home with me. But I wasn't sure whether Marcel had put two and two together about Gabe. There seemed to be no tension between them, no male posturing. I suppose Gabe thought him no threat.

But I didn't understand what had prompted Marcel to approach Gabe. No subservient smile, that was not Marcel's expression when he walked up to Gabe in the church. Nor was there any such expression on his face at the cemetery. More a guarded stillness. As if he were puzzling something out. What did he say when he stood in front of Gabe at the church table? Did he introduce himself, ask about funeral arrangements, express condolences for Gabe's loss? Reverend Sloan had made mention of that fact in his sermon. That would have been like Marcel, to pick and choose among the various possible openings, to find the one true note he could safely express. The note that did not reveal.

I wish I had been blessed with Marcel's musical grace, his intuition. As it was, I was left only one choice in life, to hack out a rough path through sheer willpower. When I saw Marcel on that hill, separated from the multitude of mourners, I knew I had to run away with him. To save myself. The root of our problem turned out to be that he didn't need saving, however much I tried to persuade myself this was so.

* * *

The funeral over, I turned my attention to my situation: I no longer had any connection to the university, no brother to keep me in Seattle, no future beyond the phantom one manufactured by Gabe to be displayed on platforms in the weeks and months it would take to complete the trial. For I had no doubt that this particular cause would fall out of public favor as soon as a new cause rose to claim the attention of the populace. Sure enough, in April of 1917, the draft was declared, and the Everett Massacre slipped to the back page. It did not take a crystal ball to imagine this outcome. What, I asked myself, would I do then? Join the next cause like Anna Mae? Become the kind of needy female who hangs around at the edges? So running away with Marcel, subordinating my life to his, seemed a way out.

But first I needed a forger. Which is a bit like trying to find an abortionist—something you tried to do without calling attention. Oh, I knew what places to go to, which fellows to sidle up to, but I didn't know how to phrase my request. Why did I need a forger, I could hear them asking, why come to me? I thought about this for a while and decided I would represent myself as a do-gooder aiding a seaman who had jumped ship. I went down to Yesler Way one morning to a saloon I had heard about, the Brass Monkey, and sat at the bar running my finger through beer rings until the bartender noticed me. As there were only four other patrons, this should have happened quickly, but, as I expected, such was not the case. The bartender washed a whole rack of glasses and wiped down the entire length of the bar before he got to me. "This is not a place for you," he said. He meant to ply my trade.

"I'm not in trade," I said, matter-of-factly. "If I'd wanted to do that I'd have gone next door." He grunted in satisfaction, at least I knew this was a drinking man's bar, not a whorehouse.

"We don't serve women," he said.

"I know that too." I was beginning to enjoy this exchange.

"Well." He snapped his cloth as he finished wiping the space in front of me. I could tell he appreciated my sass. That I knew the rules. I phrased my next question as a statement.

"I came to find out if you know where I could find a forger. And how much a birth—" I stopped and drew in my breath. "Seamen's documents," I amended. "I need papers for a seaman."

I'd thoroughly muddled it. I could see amusement in his eyes. "Seamen's papers," he said, picking up the tone of my recital. "Now why might you need those?"

I lifted my chin. "You don't want to know." Then colored, thinking that might sound just like something he already suspected. "My boss," I said, thinking of Mr. Panopolous. "He has a nephew—"

"Then why isn't your boss here?"

"He doesn't go to such places." I got a bit angry on behalf of Mr. Panopolous, mustering an expression that conveyed what I hoped was obvious. "He's avoiding immigration."

That seemed to satisfy the bartender. At least enough for him to make a decision. "Well, you shouldn't be in such places either," he said. "But I'll ask around. Come back next week."

A week later I came back and he said he hadn't found

anyone with the requisite qualifications. The week after that he said he recalled a good fellow but that the man was laid up in a sanitarium. I was getting exasperated. "You know only *one* forger?" As if I were trying to employ a good carpenter.

That didn't sit well. "You can try other taverns." I relented and said I was running out of time. I could see he wanted to ask more, so to cut that off I said I'd stop by next week, and left it at that.

On the street I took a long breath. Here I 'd wasted three weeks to get the name of a forger only to find out he was confined to a sanitarium. And even if I got my forgery I hadn't broached the subject with Marcel. I resolved to do so that night. At the diner, I loaded fresh cream in my pitcher, poured it over the extra large square of cobbler.

Marcel looked up, interested in this beneficence.

"Will you go away with me?" I blurted out.

He thought about that, in that careful way he had, and then asked, "Where?"

"Portland," I said. "Or San Francisco, it doesn't matter." Another deep breath. "The two of us. Instead of Chicago."

"Instead," he said, tasting the cobbler as he thought through the meaning of this. The possible meanings. The only one it could be. Then that calm guardedness came into his eyes. "Are you asking—what are you asking?" So like him to turn the question.

"To run away. Maybe elope." I stopped, all of a sudden aware that people might hear. "You wouldn't have to give up your music. I'd find you a conservatory. I'd get a job— " Here I stopped, having no more cards to lay out. "That is, if you 'd like."

Another long pause, more chewing, an array of tamped-down emotions scudding across his face. Thoughts I could only guess at. It would have been better to have initiated this discussion in bed I decided.

At last he said, "It would take longer." He meant his

music education, the start of his career. That's what he had been thinking.

"We can do it," I said. "At least think about it." I was desperate not to be rejected outright. "Please."

My plans shifted after that. Became looser woven but more tightly focused. I went back to the tavern and told the barman that I wanted the name of the forger in the sanitarium. He whistled in mild disappointment and then went back into his rat's nest of an office, the place where the bookmaker held court. He came out with a torn slip of yellow paper: Otto Horvak—County Rest Home. The bartender gave a click of his tongue as he handed it over. "You'll find it at the end of the Madison Park line."

Chapter 10

The next morning I took the trolley to the rest home. I left early because I was supposed to be at the *Union Record* later that morning to finish giving an interview to Anna Mae. Her father's support was deemed critical to bringing the Ministers' Alliance, as Gabe so nicely put it, into a more confrontational phase. So I was to woo plump, breathless Anna Mae, so like a big baby, with a baby's prescient knowledge of where all this was headed. Harry Ault seemed to know about this next phase as well, and consent to it, although his motives in permitting Gabe to use the *Union Record* this way remained obscure to me as, I suppose, my motives with respect to Gabe remained obscure to him. At any rate, the *Union Record* was going to run a feature, spread over several weeks, about Everett's labor history, my father's and brother's role in it, so I was called upon, once again, to repeat the embroideries and fabrications Gabe had put in my mouth. The interview began the day before as I rushed in from the Brass Monkey with the yellow slip of paper tucked in my blouse.

Anna Mae was a haphazard interviewer. More interested in her own opinions than those of the person she was talking to. She was forever reformulating whatever I said, turning it around, embellishing it, then asking my opinion of her handiwork. After about an hour of this, the photographer showed up, and we all traipsed out to the Mount Pleasant cemetery for a picture of me draped against the headstone, Grief gazing in the distance.

The following day I was supposed to show up at ten. That meant I had to leave on the six o'clock trolley to get to the rest home by quarter to seven. I hadn't counted on the place not being open. I stood around on the sidewalk, walked back and forth, sat down on the wet granite steps until eight o'clock and then lost another twenty minutes trying to persuade the desk nurse that I had a legitimate reason to visit Otto Horvak. Apparently ladies in the trade were not unheard of visitors at the rest home. Just to be on the safe side, the nurse assigned an orderly to accompany me.

Otto Horvak was not in the best of health. Gray-faced, he was tucked in a gunmetal bed in a barracks of similarly pale and wheezing men. To even draw a breath he had to concentrate his whole body, the effort causing a line of spittle down the side of his jaw, but his eyes were alert, and he perked up at the sight of a female visitor. "Uncle Otto!" I cried, hoping this claim wouldn't be too confusing.

He processed this. Finally, a sly look emerged. "Aren't you going to give your old uncle a kiss?" So I had no choice and bent to give him a peck on the forehead, but, old sea rat that he was, he calibrated my trajectory, turned up his chin, clamped a paw behind my neck and landed my mouth smack against his. The orderly, a sallow fellow, took this display as proof of exactly the kind of relationship the desk nurse had enlisted him to guard against. Smirking, he moved a few feet off, to distance himself from whatever would happen next. Over the next few minutes, while Otto and I talked, he prowled the opposite side of the room pretending to study rain on the window while actually taking orders for tobacco.

I didn't have much time, and the kiss unsettled me. But Otto's talent for intrigue made me bold. I took a deep breath. "I'm planning to elope," I said, "with a young man who is under age, and the bartender at the Brass Monkey said you could fix me up with a birth certificate. For a price," I added.

A look of deep pleasure came over his face, whether at my mention of money or the thought of what would transpire after the elopement, I do not know, but that revery was soon replaced by regret. "I'm sorry," he said. "I could have. But not now." He motioned around, his confined state.

"Is there some one else?" I meant was there someone else he could refer me to.

"Chan," he said after a while. "But he's tricky. Chinese." All these words made Otto wheeze. He began to abbreviate even more. "White sla—" This came out with a bubble of spit and then a whoosh of air. I thought about supplying the full word "slavery" but decided against it. I kept to my polite, alert expression. His face conveyed concern about my future prospects. "Don't get...mixed..."

I pretended to reflect on this. "I can handle myself," I finally announced, wondering whether I could, indeed, get out of Chan what I needed without his getting from me what he wanted. On further reflection, Chan did not seem the ideal person to enlist. My plan started feeling hopelessly complicated, and dangerous as well.

"Not—Chan," Otto said, as if that settled it. I nodded in agreement.

Out of the corner of my eye I could see the orderly handing out wads of chewing tobacco in exchange for money. His transactions finished, he began to make his way back to us. "Can you think of someone else?"

Otto closed his eyes and thought. "Do you have a—certificate? To alter?" I shook my head no. He thought some more. "Where are you go—" He too could see the orderly getting close and his face became more guarded. How nice, I thought, to be in the hands of a professional.

"Portland," I said. "Actually, north of there, Vancouver County."

"Ah." He nodded at the wisdom of this. "A justice...of the peace." He concentrated, scanned his memory, but came up blank. Then his face brightened. "Or someone...in Portland?"

The orderly was back. If he overheard he probably thought I was in need of arsenic treatments or a coat hanger abortion. Otto's reputation as a fixer must have been well known. Otto thought some more behind his closed eyes. "Zellman," he finally announced, opening up to reveal bright blue pupils. "Rudolf Zellman. You can find him—" Deep breath. "Near the Burnside Bridge. Ask, someone will—" With that long speech he collapsed, shuddering. And gave himself over to ragged breathing, as if the memory of Zellman, the effort at calling him up, had exhausted the last of his reserves. He waved me away. "Good bye, miss." Then amended, "Mary's...daughter." With that bright thought he regained his old self. "Kiss your uncle," he commanded, settling in for my final kiss, then seemed to drop off as I gathered my coat. As I began to move away, he stopped me with an iron grip. "Give Victor a tip," he directed, still not opening his eyes. "For being so kind." I fished a dime from my purse, which, I could see from Victor's expression, was insufficient.

* * *

Later that morning, after I finished my interview with Anna Mae, I returned to my room and tried to figure out how to propose my elopement plan to Marcel. It was now mid-December, five weeks since the *Verona* had docked and the ringleaders had been arrested and transferred to Everett. The trial was to begin in January. Marcel was set to leave just after the New Year. I had two weeks, at most three, to make my getaway.

I considered all aspects of the plan. Money. A job. A conservatory for Marcel to study in. How to find Rudolf Zellman. What to do when Josephine found out. How to get Marcel to come with me on the train. These last two problems I put aside and concentrated on the ones I thought I could solve. Money was the first obstacle. How much would I need for two train tickets to Portland and a week's rent and food? Twenty dollars, I decided, twice what I had saved. I thought about asking Marcel to come up with ten, but decided to present him with as few complications as possible. I considered my mother, then decided that, even if successful, it would take five dollars in train trips and presents to get ten out of her. I thought about Mr. Panopolous, but decided against it on the grounds that he would tell Gabe.

Next I considered the laundry foreman but decided a loan from him would require payment in the currency that Otto had warned me against with Mr. Chan. I thought about Mr. Abbot, my biology professor, whom I had repaid by dropping out of his class, and felt too ashamed to ask. Surprisingly, after this discouraging inventory—there emerged not one friend, not one acquaintance I felt could turn to—out popped the name of Harry Ault. The editor of the *Union Record*, the gentle man who had hovered, hangdog expression on his face, listening to Anna Mae's interminable interview. What had he said, that first time I'd met him, that day I'd run into Horace on the street? He'd asked about my mother, said he'd recently visited my father, knew him from way back. Something about the concern in his voice had put me on guard, so that when he mentioned a possible job, to read proofs, the implication being that he was worried enough about me to want to take care of me—all that had seemed condescending at the time and I'd rebuffed him. But six months later, during the Anna Mae interview, with the image of the mysterious Rudolf Zellman hovering in my mind, I had been comforted by Harry Ault's concern, the sense of his knowing, better than I knew myself, that I was someone who needed looking after. I decided to go to Harry Ault.

But first I had to get Gabe off my trail and find a way to get Marcel to agree to join me on the train to Portland. Gabe had taken to appearing Wednesday nights at Mr. Panopolous's diner. To let Marcel and I know he knew, I suppose. He would never stay long, just drink a glass of seltzer in one long swallow, exchange pleasantries with Mr.

Panopolous. Then he'd walk over to where I was behind the counter and say a few words—tell me what I was supposed to do tomorrow, where to meet him the next day—and then, just as he was about to go out the door, he'd turn and nod at Marcel in his corner booth, who had been watching all this like a robin searching for worms.

That night, when Marcel walked me home, I had the sense we were being followed. I said as much to Marcel but he replied, "Why would anyone do that?" It seemed too complicated to explain. At any rate, by the time we closed and locked the door to my room, I was nervous, not only because of the notion of being followed, but also because of what I was planning to say. I felt the need of a good opening. I thought about going to my sewing box and showing him the ten dollars I kept there in the secret compartment. Then saying, We can use this to run away to Portland! or, There's more where this came from! or some such silly announcement. Then I had the idea of getting out my train timetable and studying departure times. Asking if he knew any good music conservatories in Portland. Or San Francisco or Sacramento. They, too, were on my timetable. I never thought in terms of going east, probably because I couldn't imagine getting enough money together for the tickets. Finally I said, "If I bought the train tickets, would you come with me to Portland?"

He looked at me for a minute and then asked, "Oregon?"

I nodded yes and showed him the timetable.

"You mean go down for a visit?" he asked, regarding me with his usual mild confusion.

I stood back, letting him read my face. Don't make me beg, I was saying. Finally I said I was thinking about going down there to get a job. And wanted him to come with me, that I would find him a music conservatory to study at.

There was another long pause while he took all this in. Then he made a counter offer. "For a day or two I could probably come, until you got settled." Then, "I don't know how I'd tell my mother."

"Don't," I said. "Don't tell her." I repeated all the arguments I had used to get him frog catching up at Snoqualmie Falls. Finally I got him to agree to ask his music teacher about good violinists who gave lessons in Portland. So there I left it, he was going to check out music tutors and I was going to book train tickets. I said no more, accepting his limited counter offer as well as his caresses, letting my mind drift while his long fingers worked the knots from my shoulders, knowing that I had every intention of keeping him in Portland, once I'd stolen him away. Knowing at the same time I'd never be able to hold him, would never be able to get him to sign his name on a marriage certificate even if Mr. Rudolf Zellman were able to fabricate proof of his age, but knowing I must try.

CHAPTER 11

I have forgotten to give you a full description of the funeral, the burial that was supposed to propel the Everett Massacre into the history books. The central idea, of course, was to have five coffins converging from five different churches into one massive funeral cortege. Then interminable hours of funeral orations to make the day indelible in the public mind, a springboard for future campaigns against whatever injustice Gabe next decided was the paramount issue of the day. Aunt Esther had robbed him of Abe's body, but he did have the other four. My brother's remains were assigned to Queen Anne Presbyterian. Felix Baran was placed in the care of All Saints Roman Catholic. John Looney was to meet his maker at St. Agatha's, also Roman Catholic. There was quite a quandary over Hugo Gerlot, most probably also a Catholic, but, being a drifter, and having no next of kin, Gabe decided to hand him over to the Wobblies who, in a shameless bid to gather the unaffiliated, staged a nondenominational pep rally at the Labor Temple.

The Labor Temple held over five hundred, counting the gallery, and on that day it was packed, though largely not with Christians. While the speakers exhorted, bottles were passed around so everyone left the Temple that morning pretty fired up. This ragtag army, marshaling in disorderly rows, was buttressed by red banners and Wobblie songbooks. Five mounted death masks weaved through the crowd. One fellow carrying a trumpet sounded the charge.

Off they marched toward the cemetery. The first group to intersect them was John Looney's two hundred mourners from St. Agatha's. That cortege drew its inspiration from a life size effigy of St. Agatha, dimpled and demure on her satin-draped platform held aloft by four standard bearers. Twenty well scrubbed alter boys followed in lace surplices over watered green silk. St. Agatha's was an Italian parish, and when it met up with the Wobblies, the priest made it clear he was not against rabble rousing so long as St. Agatha led the way. The Wobblies, however, would give no quarter to a plaster saint. So both sides started shouting and soon enough the alter boys started to shed their surplices and the Wobblies began to roll up their sleeves. Sam Rabinowitz, who had been assigned to manage the Labor Temple mourners, pulled Father Rocco aside, and, after a suitable interval of dickering, diplomatically gave way. He announced that St. Agatha would lead the combined march. The Wobblies booed this proposal but finally acquiesced when Father Rocco agreed the St. Agatha contingent would join the Wobblies in group song.

Off they went, a fragile coalition belting out "Hold the fort for we are coming" planning to meet up with Queen Anne Presbyterian at Denny Way. Ours was the middle class contingent, three hundred teachers, shopkeepers, housewives, and a sprinkling of Norwegian fishermen from the Ballard District, Lutherans, Baptists and Methodists reluctant to join the Wobblies and unwilling to enter a Catholic Church. The parade stopped again, Gabe and the Reverend Sloan trying to negotiate the terms under which Queen Anne would join the procession. The Wobblies, having given pride of place to St. Agatha, were not about to yield to a bunch of Presbyterians. The well-oiled trumpeter shouted out, "One pack of God scrapers, that's enough!" Reverend Sloan polled his delegation, noting that since Queen Anne didn't have an icon, maybe it should just intermingle with the two other groups. Nix to that, the Wobblies said, they needed to maintain unsullied cohesion. St. Agatha's alter boys looked like a nasty lot as well, so, after much hand wringing, the Reverend Sloan proposed that his band of three hundred take their place to the rear. This burst open the Protestant front faster than you could spit sunflower seeds. Gabe saw his ideal of a fused mass of mourners melt before his eyes.

A few Wobblies were now plotting a coup against Sam and threatening to go off on their own. Father Rocco was also threatening to secede, taking his St. Agatha contingent down Dexter Street to meet up with All Saints and form an all-Catholic group. The sky, which up to now had offered only intermittent rain, opened to a downpour. Our red banners, already drooping, started to bleed. St. Agatha, on her platform, began swaying in preparation to move out. Gabe and Sam had commenced bickering. Then, in one of his lightning decisions, Gabe decided to join Father Rocco. Sam, left to handle the Reverend Sloan, told the Right Reverend in no uncertain terms to gather his mourners and fall in behind the Labor Temple. Thus two corteges moved separately to the cemetery.

The graveside orations, which were to have been the culminating political moment, became a barely papered-over disaster. Gabe blamed the weather as well as the presence of paid agitators, both a perennial Seattle curse and thus a handy excuse whenever an occasion fell flat. But the newspapers covered it, I was featured in my Grief pose, Gabe's best lines made the front page. So the day met his expectations and donations had been ample.

From there on Gabe concentrated his energies on planning a May Day commemoration, raising money to erect a granite memorial. Joe Hill, the famous Wobblie organizer, had been killed recently by Pinkertons at a copper mine in Idaho, and Gabe became hell-bent on getting Joe Hill's ashes to spread over his graves.

So, in early December, Gabe announced another reception at Queen Anne Presbyterian. Anna Mae and I were put in charge of collecting for the granite memorial. I remember I had on a coffee-colored shirtwaist that did nothing for my complexion. I was irritated by Gabe's insistence on dressing me for these events, forever having to change clothes in closets or washrooms, then having to change back after the event. "Why don't you just give me the dresses and let me pick out what I'm going to wear?" I complained as he handed me the outfit.

"No," he said. "Do what I say. Hurry up." He had a bad smile, small teeth that were discolored and crooked. When he smiled, he became a nasty little boy. As time went on, I used to provoke comments like that, to see him smile, to remind myself of what he was.

But that day, the smile just made me mad. "You don't own me," I said, a statement sounding false even to my own ears.

He gave me a fish eye. "Oh?" And left it at that.

The Reverend Sloan came down to the basement with Sam to talk with Gabe about the sermon. Sam had a preexisting connection to the good Reverend. Sam was a union official at City Light, the municipal utility that supplied power to the schools, hospitals, and most of downtown. The fight to establish City Light a few years before had been a great civic cause, and the Reverend Sloan and Sam shared many platforms. So Sam considered the Reverend Sloan a key partner in this cause.

I could see from their doting expressions that Sam had persuaded the Reverend that Sam's nephew was a real comer. I knew Gabe's expressions well enough to know he considered Reverend Sloan a fool. But a useful, well-connected fool. What was passing between Gabe and the Reverend Sloan's daughter, the pink plump Anna Mae, was an assessment of a different sort. Was her interest in him political, physical or on a higher spiritual plane? Gabe, from what I could tell, had no higher spiritual plane, except what his Marxist politics provided him.

As yet there was no Communist Party in the United States. Socialism, anarchism, but no Soviet-style Communist party. The first Russian Revolution did not occur until March of the following year. Lenin had not been spirited back in a closed railway car to the Finland Station. The Bolshevik revolution did not happen until the following November. Only after that, in a summer cottage, hidden in the dunes near Benton Harbor, Michigan, did the official Communist Party of the United States get born. It was, I was told, about as sorry a mess as Horace's funeral, but I was not there and that is another story.

But to get back to the church basement. I was standing outside the closet sweating to get the buttons done up the back of my dress. Gabe, lounging against the green wainscoting was eyeing Anna Mae. She, hand to her throat, was in high color. The Reverend Sloan was counting brochures I had laid out on the table and messing up the alignment. I wanted to slap his hand but restrained myself and continued to work the row of buttons down my back.

"When's this show go on the road?" I asked. I could see Reverend Sloan did not appreciate my informality. Upstairs, the church organist was warming up. We could hear the parishioners filing in.

"Shhh!" Gabe commanded me. He put on his ferret smile and ushered the Reverend Sloan up the stairs. Anna Mae tucked in her organdy blouse and heaved her bosom to set out after him. I was glad, for once, of my bony frame. My blouse, at least, stayed tucked in. Anna Mae must have read my thoughts because she came back with a poisonous smile to attend to two pearl buttons I had missed on my spine.

Josephine arrived a few minutes later with Marcel in tow, swishing right past me as I came up the stairs. I was just as glad. Our secret life, our secret plan, felt almost ready to burst out from me as Marcel and I stole glances. Gabe somehow caught whiff of this deepening complicity, and later, after the church coffee hour, after the last of the parishioners had left and I was heading into the closet to take off the brown dress, Gabe reached out and grabbed my arm, pulled me close so I could feel his intention. "Keep away from the prodigy." I yanked my arm away and went in the closet, heart hammering, wondering how much he knew.

Later, on the way back to the Labor Temple, where we stored our cash in their safe, Gabe told me I was going with him on a trip to Boise, to talk to the keepers of Joe Hill's ashes. He figured if he could get Hill's ashes, he could then go down to San Francisco and talk to the big labor organizations about bankrolling his May Day celebration. He complained that all the local money was being funneled into the Everett defense rather than to his graveside memorial. Such was the depth of his political commitment. At any rate, I kept my mouth shut and made a vague remark about never having seen Nob Hill and left it at that.

My next stop, Monday, 8 a.m. sharp, was to visit Harry Ault at the *Union Record.* Harry was surprised but pleased to see me. He had an editorial conference going on, and asked me to wait, showed me to a chair near the window, but I didn't want to be near the window, so I said I had an errand to do and promised to come back at quarter to nine. I used the time to go over to the train station and check out schedules. There was a Northwest Empire Limited that left each day at 7:40 a.m., with stops in Tacoma and Olympia and Vancouver, that got into Portland at 2:17 p.m. That ought to do fine, I thought, leaving us almost three hours of daylight to find a room. I asked about the fare. The ticket seller said three dollars and thirty cents per person. He asked if I wanted reserved seats, which would require a deposit as well as passenger names. I thought about whether I wanted to give my name and covered my hesitation by pretending to check my purse. "No," I said, "I'll come back," and hurried off to my meeting with Harry.

Harry showed me into his glassed-in office and asked me if I wanted a cup of coffee. I said no, and could hear the quaver in my voice. He said okay, the coffee was lousy anyway. After that, we both relaxed and he asked me what was on my mind. I said I'd appreciate it if he didn't say anything to anybody but that I was wondering if there was something I could do on his newspaper. He whistled a little between his teeth, as if he were assessing if I had any genuine aspirations in the newspaper business, whether he could afford any more help. During this interval I got nervous, and broke from my plan, which was to get a job first and then ask for a loan. Instead I went straight to the loan. I don't know what made me trust him, made me sure he would go into his own pocket if need be, but it was almost as if I knew he was in my corner. I abandoned any pretense of seeking employment and said, "Mr. Ault, to be honest, even if you offered me a job I couldn't take it. I'm going to be leaving town for a while—" I realized I was blushing, but struggled to carry on. "On personal business—that's why I need you not to say anything."

He gave me an encouraging smile. I realized he thought it had to do with Gabe, that I was trying to get away from this unpleasant fellow. Well, in a way he was right. I concluded on a lame note. "Of course, I really do want to work for you. I think I'd like the newspaper business. Anything you want, I'd get coffee, sweep the floor—" Here he stopped me.

"Hold on. Joe Copper's daughter is not going to sweep floors. Have you ever written anything? Can I see something that shows you've mastered the King's English? Of course we can't start you on reporting, but maybe proofreading, or writing ads, or bookkeeping if you're good at numbers."

"But I can't work for you," I reminded him. "I'm here to ask for a loan."

"A loan?" As if he'd forgotten. My heart sank. "How long are you leaving town for? A month? Two?" He pulled out his wallet.

I held my breath. I'd never be able to pay him back in two months.

"How much?" he prompted me.

I hesitated. "Twenty dollars."

He checked inside, then shut his wallet. "Tell you what," he said. "Write something. Doesn't have to be long, a paragraph or two. It can be on anything—"My Favorite Christmas." I just want to see how you write. Then bring it in, I'll set you down at a typewriter and see how you do at typing. If you pass muster, I'll make you an advance of, say, ten dollars, and put you on the payroll as an occasional correspondent at six dollars a month. Will that do?"

It was a gift. As long as I could write a legible sentence, I would pass muster. I wanted to throw my arms around him but didn't dare because of the staff on the other side of the glass. For the first time in weeks I had some real hope. I could do this, I could get out of this tunnel. I would go down to Portland and keep Marcel with me as long as I could, get some day work and at night learn to write well enough to be a reporter. I was sure that Harry Ault would keep whatever confidence I needed him to and was also sure that I would eventually pay him back—either by becoming an adequate employee or robbing a bank, if necessary.

CHAPTER 12

The next day, Tuesday, I tried to think through what I was doing. I was running away, yes, but from what? Away from Horace's death, the hopes I had had when I first came to Seattle, surely. Away from Gabe, the circus he had roped me into, that I had let myself be roped into. Away from the moment when Marcel would leave, when I would be alone in all my neediness, for Gabe to make use of for whatever purpose he had in mind. Of course, in my own mind, I was running to something, marriage, a new start, all the usual illusions we poor humans concoct to shield our gaze from our own sorry condition.

Years later, in the 1930s, when I actually did embark on marriage with my first husband, Ashton, a professor at the University of Illinois, I can't say I had made much progress in the matter of my shameful malleability. I was living in Chicago at the time, having arrived there as the events I am telling you about more or less reached their conclusion. I was going to night school and making a living writing for the union press, as part of a drive to unionize the meat cutters. Meat packing is a trade that leaves nothing to the imagination. If I had a choice between dying from cedar asthma or having my gorge filled daily by the smell of the slaughterhouse, I'd pick sawmills. I was writing for poor Slavs who earned their daily bread by killing animals pulled out of reeking railroad cars, butchering and boiling them into Vienna sausages. I was living on the north side, in a single room near Lincoln Park. I had come to Chicago to find Marcel, but it came up a dry hole. So I fell back with a union crowd and met Ashton.

He came from Cumberland, Maryland, his father an executive with a utility company while his mother, he said, mainly put on airs. That was the way Aston described them. I never met his family so I can't verify his version of the truth. Like Gabe, he felt it necessary to dissemble about his origins. "*Petit bourgeois,*" he said. "Very *petit,*" thereby excusing his social class and a lot more. Ashton, though I did not know it at the time, was a quiet but purposeful drinker. And an all around weak-willed person, who disguised those facts with a lot of flowery rhetoric that led him eventually to join the Lincoln Brigade and go to Spain and get killed. For the five years I was married to Ashton, I often asked myself what weakness on my part had led me into that fix, and all I could come up with, then or now, was that I had run out of better ideas. Ashton, like Gabe, offered a script, a trajectory that I could coast along on without believing in.

That was the glimmer of insight I was struggling to avoid that December in 1916 as I set about deciding what to do with my clothes and the few furnishings I had accumulated. I was stricken with a bout of conscience about not paying my landlord. The rent was due on Friday, but if I went off to Portland on Thursday, I would be giving him no notice. On the other hand, if I paid my rent early, I might signal something was amiss, such were my fears of being watched and spied on. In the end I decided to do nothing, to take my clothes but leave behind the curtains and bedspread and the knickknacks I had been so proud of purchasing and hope the landlord did not check on me until well after the rent was due.

What to do with my clothes was the next question. I was afraid to involve Harry Ault any more than I already had, and afraid to be seen lugging a big valise down the street when I left for the station. So I split my belongings into three piles, one for packing in a small satchel to take on the train. The second pile went in a cardboard box that I planned to take to the laundry and hide. The third pile went in a suitcase to take to the train station the day before our departure to store in the overnight luggage section. At the last minute I took a few knickknacks off the dresser, an oval hand mirror, a picture of a girl with a donkey cart, my sewing box with the secret compartment, and packed them in the suitcase and felt satisfied.

Now all I had to do was wait eight days and write a sample news story that would satisfy Harry enough to collect my ten-dollar advance. I spent all day Tuesday mulling over topics. The more I considered it, the more it seemed that my choice of topic would augur my future. I made lists of titles: "Frog Reproduction," "Shipping on Lake Washington," "Recreation in Seattle's North Side." None seemed of interest to a labor newspaper. I thought of describing my first visit to the university library, but that felt too personal, too girlish. Finally I decided on "A Visit to a Lung Ward," and wrote a few pages describing an interview with a shingle cutter named Ole Nilsson. I gave Ole Otto Horvak's personality, and made the purpose of my visit gathering evidence on conditions in the county rest home. I took a muckraker's point of view, used the nurse's suspicions of my visit as a lighthearted opening, then went on to describe the orderly to a tee, and how Ole immediately picked up on the idea that I was his niece. Then the slow turn of the orderly around the ward, selling tobacco to men too sick to breathe much less smoke. I put words into Ole's mouth that were unintentionally comical—I was better describing scene than I was at making up dialog. I had him say valiant things about living with lung disease, how the city fathers should be proud of their investment in the county home, a rant about mill owners who failed to provide ventilation. I ended with the bit about my under-tipping the orderly, and that was that. Four handwritten pages. More than Harry had asked for. But I knew I wasn't much of a typist and Harry Ault would soon see that as well.

That composition took much of Tuesday and Wednesday. Gabe, of course, had me running around to various union halls to watch while he whipped up the troops. And I still had my half-shift at the laundry and three nights a week with Mr. Panopolous. On Wednesday Marcel was later than usual and Gabe, for some reason, didn't make his customary appearance. That bothered me, both things bothered me, but I shook off the unease.

Marcel, when he did arrive, was quiet, and I didn't bother him, just took his usual order and left him alone. He studied sheet music until I was ready to go. Later, in my room, the packed luggage made it clear that the trip to Portland was going forward. He didn't say anything, just that he was tired. His usual offer to rub my neck seemed half hearted. Or maybe I was just nervous. Anyway, the knots in my neck stayed. I told him about Harry Ault, the offer to hire me dependent on my writing sample. I read him the article about Ole Nilsson, then flushed in the middle, it suddenly sounded girlish to my ears. I could tell he wasn't paying attention. To startle him I told him that there really was an Ole Nilsson, except that his name was Otto Horvak, and that I had gone to visit him because he was a forger. I showed him the piece of paper with the name of Rudolph Zellman written on it, and asked if he knew what the area was like near the Burnside Bridge. I could tell he didn't, and that was good, because the Burnside Bridge was a pretty rough place, fellows in my pa's saloon used to talk about it. I didn't tell him why we were going looking for Rudolf Zellman, how I needed Zellman to forge Marcel's birth certificate and then steer us to a shady justice of the peace, and Marcel didn't ask. It was as if Marcel were already defeated by the monumental task of holding all these plans of mine in his head. He had on his usual puzzled look, but this time it was also wary, and I could see I was the cause of his unhappiness. But the unease hadn't broken through to downright rebellion, so I was content to let things be.

I told him that when he came to the train he should just bring a change of clothes. I let him think it was still a two or three day trip, until we found Rudolf Zellman, until I found a job and a place to live. I look back and wonder what kind of Mata Hari I thought I was. But all this intrigue kept my mind off other things, and later that night, when we snuggled down in my single bed for a few minutes before Marcel had to get home, I was content to have him hold me, before his usual excuse that he had to leave. But there must have been some deeper knowledge in him, that this trip was a momentous step, because when I put my hand out to stroke his belly, he turned to me with such ferociousness that the next twenty minutes made my head spin. Well, not just my head but other parts as well.

I waited until Monday to go back to Harry Ault. I rewrote the composition a couple of times, nearly weeping in frustration when the whole thing started to sound flat. I was reaching for a crisp breezy style that I admired in certain magazines, but that was clearly not my own. When Monday came I arrived clutching all three handwritten versions, and then in a show of—what? savage humility?—shoved them all at Harry. He smoothed down the corners, damp with sweat, and put them face down on his desk. "Good," he said. "Now I want you to take a typing test." I was nervous and made a botch of it. "Common Four Letter Words," that's what I remember as the heading of the exercise. Different four letter words kept coming to my mind.

After about twenty minutes Harry took pity on me and put a stop to it. He showed me the typesetting operation, the rows and rows of type in tiny cubbyholes, letters and punctuation marks and slugs—blank spaces you put in so that words and letters didn't run together. And that was just lower case. There were also capitals in four or five sizes of bold and headline type. In all, a bewildering forest of tiny boxes filled with grimy ink-stained type. I loved it from the minute I saw it. It was the source, the wellhead of the printed word. Harry saw my face, and murmured, "Well, I think we've found your spot." He gave me a sheet of rough-set type and asked me to proofread it, looking out not only for spelling and punctuation errors, but also flies—small bits of metal that butted poorly against the neighboring type and left tracings of ink. I got a big red grease pencil to mark errors and happily made a mess of that job as well. Of course, as I went on in the field, I got to know all the editing shorthand and could mark up rough print with the best of them, but that day I was just happy to be scrawling away with my red grease pencil, circling and bracketing and question marking like my old school teachers used to do.

When I left Harry's office to head over to the laundry, planning an excuse about a sore tooth, I had my ten dollars. And was so excited about the prospect of typesetting and proofing that I almost didn't want to leave town. Then I thought about Gabe, how he would never allow me to take Harry's job, for the independence it would give me, and I concluded that staying in Seattle would never work. What's more, I feared for Harry Ault if Gabe should ever find out about the offer. That sober note strengthened my resolve, but I decided that when I got to Portland I would look for a job on a newspaper or even a print shop if it came to it.

I was tired after my laundry shift, a case of nerves building, I expect. I had spent all day Sunday with Gabe going from one meeting to the next. Negotiations with the Wobblies over Joe Hill's ashes were commencing in earnest. Gabe had me typing letters to various union leaders seeking money to make a trip to Boise to secure the ashes and requesting further money if he should prove successful in landing the prize. Monday held the prospect of yet another night meeting.

On Tuesday, when I went to the laundry, I brought with

me the cardboard box of clothes. Some of the girls saw me lugging it in, and asked what it was. I said it was a parcel for my mother that I had to take to the post office. When no one was looking I took it to the boiler room and tucked it away in a corner and covered it over with old shingles and surveyed my handiwork. It would be ten years before anyone thought to clean out that mess. One of the girls noticed me coming out, and gave me a funny look, but I put it from my mind.

The next day, Wednesday, I took the suitcase to the train station and went up to the storage desk and gave them a dime and wrote down my name on the luggage tag and got a receipt. I had to claim it by 7:15 the next day or forfeit another dime. My heart was singing as I went to my last day at the laundry, thinking about the week's pay I was going to forego. The sun was shining—a rare event in Seattle in December. There was spring in the air and for the first time in months, or maybe years, I had a sensation of unadulterated happiness. So this is what happy people feel like, I remember thinking. I wanted more of that.

We had agreed between us that Marcel was not going to come home with me that Wednesday night. I was distracted at the diner, dropping a sugar bowl, mixing up orders. Mr. Panopolous regarded me with a studied expression. "Where's your friend?" he asked as we were closing up.

"Pleurisy," I said, then realized my gleeful expression didn't match the news. "I might be getting a new job," I added, to account for my smile, then realized that also begged clarification. "Instead of the laundry."

Mr. Panopolous shrugged. As long I showed up for his shift. I was sad to be a disappointment, leaving him in the lurch, but told myself that there were other girls who could take my place.

The next morning, Thursday, I awoke at four. In the dark—for some reason I did not want to turn on the lamp—I washed my face and put on my traveling clothes and pinned up my hair and counted my money and checked the contents of my small valise. I said good-bye to my bedspread and curtains and felt an actual stab of pain at leaving them behind. They had been the first things I had bought to make a home for myself. All through my life, as I moved from place to place, there was always something—a peony bush, stenciled flowers on my bathroom wall—something I couldn't take with me that broke my heart. That day it was my curtains and bedspread.

I arrived early at the train station. Too early. I reclaimed my suitcase and sat down and drank a cup of coffee and pretended to read the paper. After I finished the *Post-Intelligencer* I started on a discarded copy of the university paper. On page three was a notice of all the rallies and meetings planned for the coming week. That night the Young Socialists and the next day a trip to Everett to protest conditions in the county jail. I was supposed to be at both.

By quarter to seven I was getting nervous. What if Marcel didn't come? I forced myself to relax, to stay seated with my valise and my suitcase, reminded myself I'd said seven, that as of that moment Marcel wasn't even late. I had put off buying tickets and now there was a line of about two dozen people at the sole open ticket booth. I got up and waited in the slow moving line until Marcel arrived at 7:15.

He was lugging a much bigger suitcase than I had instructed and was also carrying his violin case. That made me hopeful, maybe he had decided to stay in Portland. I was suddenly shy, and blushed and didn't know how to greet him. "Hold my place in line," I told him, and went up to the front to see if I could speed up the process. "We need tickets for the 7:40 to Portland," I said in a loud voice, too loud because several people turned to look.

The ticket seller motioned me back into the line.

"It's important," I whined, calling even more attention to myself. A man at the front stepped aside for me to take his place but the ticket agent would have none of that.

"Get back in line," he told me. "Train's late. Won't be here till 8:23."

I got back in line, and finally bought our tickets at 8:15 and together we rushed down the dark corridor with three bags and one violin case in tow. With three minutes to spare we arrived at the track as the Northwest Empire Limited chugged to a stop.

We found seats in the last car, bumping down the aisles and through the folding doors on the swaying metal platforms. I was exultant but Marcel seemed exhausted. As I settled into my seat he kept staring out the window and chewing his lip.

"You'll get a sore," I told him, sounding to my own ears just like my mother. He stopped chewing, but wouldn't look at me for the next several miles. By the time we pulled out of Tacoma his color was better, and he actually turned to see me when I spoke to him a second time. I had no idea what he thought this trip was for—to elope or keep me company for a few days while I looked for a job. I should have tried to clarify that, but I lost my nerve and instead suggested a game of *Paper, Stone, Scissors* to pass the time. Paper covers stone, scissors cut paper, stone breaks scissors. I liked the quickness of it, the randomness, the sense of destiny cast by almost involuntary choices of the hand. I noticed Marcel favored scissors, so I switched from paper to stone, then he caught on and chose stone as well, so I moved to cover him with paper. We continued this game until we were nearing Olympia, then Marcel shook his head and pushed away my hand and said, "I don't think I can do this."

I was about to ask what it was he couldn't do, when the conductor came through announcing that only forward cars would unload passengers. I said, "When we get to Portland we can decide." But we never got to Portland because the ten-minute scheduled stop stretched to twenty and then thirty minutes. Finally the conductor came through saying there was an unforeseen delay. Then two police officers boarded our car and told us to take our luggage down from the overhead rack and come off the train with them.

I knew the jig was up, but not what was going to happen next. The policemen were polite enough, and took us to a small room in the station, a detention room, I suppose, because there was only one small window with bars on it. I asked if I could go to the washroom and was told no, not until a police matron arrived. I wondered why this was happening, if this had anything to do with the Everett trial. If the landlord was after me for his rent. But deep down I knew it was simpler than that, that it had to do with Marcel, and my trying to take him away.

We sat there for three hours, until the next train arrived from Seattle. On it was Josephine, my mother and Gabe, as well as a deputy from the Sheriff's office who told me I was being held in violation of the Mann Act, which made it a crime to transport minors across state lines for immoral purposes. With Josephine looking on, and my mother acting as if she wasn't even there, and Gabe smirking through the whole proceeding, the officers confiscated our luggage as proof of intent. Not once in the entire time did Marcel and I have a chance to talk, and when the deputy questioned him, about why he was on the train with me, what we were planning to do in Portland, he kept saying, "I don't know," which sounded fine the first time but lost authority after the fourth or fifth repetition.

Josephine kept breaking in, trying to make sure the deputy knew of our previous amorous behavior, claiming I'd already broken the law, corrupted her son, despite the fact we hadn't yet gotten as far as the state line. I realized then that Gabe was running the show, that the point, his point, wasn't to get me locked up, I would have had to cross the state line for that, which would have been easy enough to let me do. Gabe's point was to keep me from leaving Seattle and his clutches, to humiliate me and end things forever with Marcel. Once I realized this I refused to say anything and, after a while, even Marcel stopped saying "I don't know." We all sat in silence for several minutes and then the sheriff's deputy snapped his notebook shut and said we should all get started back. The next train was in twenty minutes. At that point I succeeded in getting permission to go to the ladies' room and managed to rid myself of the yellow slip of paper bearing the name of Rudolph Zellman before coming out to board the train.

* * *

I wish I could describe how heartbreaking this all was. How crushing my sense of shame and failure. My own mother listening to me being accused of corrupting the morals of a youth. Saying nothing, looking as if it had nothing to do with her. Gabe, Josephine, my mother—how had they all managed to get together? Who had found out, who had organized this posse? Maybe Marcel had signaled something. Maybe Harry Ault, for all I knew, had told Gabe. Maybe the ticket salesman or someone else in the train station had recognized me, put two and two together. Maybe Gabe was having me followed. I didn't know. I would never know. But I would never doubt that Gabe had organized the trip down to Olympia. Had managed somehow to coach the sheriff's deputy in his part. If the fellow was indeed a sheriff's deputy. I never knew that either. But I knew Gabe had won. Had succeeded in crushing my revolt, had stopped my bid for freedom. He was the one who held the cards, could either move the Mann Act charges forward and ruin my reputation or not.

As for Marcel, he was hustled off by his mother to another train car. Without so much as a backward glance. My beloved. What had made me think I could lean on that slender reed? When the train arrived back in Seattle, the deputy had a brief conference with Josephine and then told me I was free to go. Josephine marched her charge off in one direction and I was marched off by Gabe in another. My mother stayed in the train station to catch the Interurban back to Everett. Never, for the rest of her long life, did I ever discuss that day with her. I never found out who had summoned her or why she had come, although I suspect it was Gabe. She and Josephine had never met before to my knowledge and never exchanged so much as a passing remark in all the time we sat in that room in Olympia. On the other hand, she never spoke to anyone that day. I watched her ramrod back as she stood at the newsstand to buy a magazine as Gabe steered me outside to take me back to my rented room, the room the landlord never even knew I'd left. Once there, I put my luggage on the bed and stood looking at the floor until Gabe ran a hand down my back and then turned to leave. I listened to him lock the door from outside and whistle as he went down the hall. I sat down on my bed to examine a life that seemed, that moment, in ruins.

I never saw Marcel again before he left for Chicago. I went back the next day to the laundry, although I did not retrieve my cardboard box from the furnace room. For many years I lived in fear that a police charge of violating the Mann Act would surface and find its way into the press. I could not face Harry Ault and found excuses not to go to the *Union Record*. Most of all I felt I had dishonored my father, Fighting Joe Copper, the only man, it seemed, who ever loved me, who was moldering away in Eastern Washington Penitentiary. Why I should have felt I dishonored him I don't know. Except that no man had ever owned him, and I now felt that I was owned. Gabe Rabinowitz had broken my spirit as surely as any mustang put to halter.

I had ceased to be Joe Copper's daughter, that's how I felt. It was as if I had become some pale imitation of him, a namesake who dishonored him even as I trotted around Seattle posing on speakers' platforms to glorify the martyrdom of his son.

Part Two

CHAPTER 13

Gabe wasted no time. Or rather he took his time, in a manner designed to make it clear, to me at least, who was in charge and whose timetable was being followed. He left me alone. For several weeks. All through Christmas and New Years and on to the last week of January. By then I was in a pretty sorry state. Self-pitying, grieving the loss of Marcel, what seemed like my life. Years later I read somewhere, "I never knew that grief could feel so much like fear." That was me. Not fear, but what felt like fear. At the time I thought I was a coward when what I really was, was bereft.

Come the end of January, Gabe decided it was time to reclaim me. He walked into Mr. Panopolous's diner and the disgraceful thing was that my poor impoverished heart leapt. Hope flowed into my face. Someone had finally come, and knowledge of this weakness made me fearful. Gabe surveyed me, examined the menu, then ordered his usual. "I told Spiro you need a couple of days off," he told me. "I'm taking you to Boise."

He said to give up my job at the laundry. I gave notice the next day. But left my clothes in the boiler room—because I was too ashamed to retrieve them or as some kind of remnant of freedom? Maybe both, that's how mixed up my feelings were. At any rate, the next day Gabe and I were on the train to Boise. He had rented a room near the train station, in the kind of hotel where you hoped the sheets were washed and the food wouldn't kill you. The kind that didn't notice when two unmarried people signed "Mr. and Mrs." to the guest register. Gabe didn't even bother with that. He signed his name and then shoved the register over to me and left me crimson as I tried to fathom what I should put down. Finally I signed P. J. Copper, then hesitated and added (Secretary). Gabe took the registry back and looked at it and then me in amusement. I studied the tips of my shoes and then with a huge force of will raised my eyes and dared the desk clerk, who by now was also enjoying this signature, to do anything about it. He finally dropped his eyes and put away the book and handed us the key. I counted that as one win and didn't press my luck any farther.

We went up to the room, fifth floor, a long climb up rickety stairs. When Gabe opened the door I was relieved to see twin beds. And twin nightstands and a bureau big enough to put all my things in one drawer. I realized then I had never been inside a hotel. I'd been in lobbies and read about what went on in hotel rooms besides sleeping, but had never been inside an actual room, unpacking my clothes and watching myself in the bureau mirror as I put away things in a drawer. It was not so different from my own room, all in all, and that made me feel better, the only difference I could see being that I had a roommate. Or so I told myself.

Later, after I'd gone down the hall to inspect the toilet facilities, we went to the dining hall to eat dinner. I ordered pork loin, it was the special, and though I did not care for cauliflower, it was the cheapest thing on the menu. When Gabe ordered brisket of beef I remembered he was Jewish, and that he wouldn't, or couldn't, eat pork, and that small difference gave me an illusion of freedom as well. I ate a lot of pork in the months ahead.

After dinner, which Gabe paid for with a roll of bills he took from his pocket, he went out for a walk and I went back to the room. Then went down the hall to vomit up dinner, whether from nerves or the cauliflower I don't know. I spent the night huddled in my bed, unsure whether to stay on the far side, crouched into a ball, or splayed across the whole mattress in hopes my bed would look too crowded for Gabe to bother with. Sometime late in the night Gabe came in and undressed and pulled down the covers on his own bed and never so much as appeared to notice me. The next morning we both got up, I got dressed while Gabe used the facilities, then I went down the hall and slipped out of my shirtwaist and washed my underarms as best I could, then the other parts. I was glad I had brought my own washcloth.

We set out for the union hall after a breakfast of coffee and dinner rolls saved from the night before. There was some jam on the table, I remember that, apricot, with pits, one of which I bit down on, and while it didn't break my tooth, it did cause me to bite my tongue, which I took as a sign, and said as little as possible in the negotiations that followed.

Gabe, as I mentioned, wanted Joe Hill's ashes to scatter on the graves of his martyrs. When we got to the local office of the Western Federation of Miners, he laid out his plan. He was a good salesman, I give him that. I found myself beaming in the way candidates' wives do, and when I caught myself, felt so foolish it cheered me up a bit. Looking foolish, I discovered, was far preferable to feeling cowardly. They dickered back and forth, the Boise men pointing out that Joe Hill's ashes were a limited and revered commodity, Gabe pointing out that ashes sitting on a shelf in a union office in Boise did the movement not one whit of good. The union officials quoted Prodhoun and made vague threats against stoolies and scabs, while Gabe railed against the Pinkertons and state militias. In the end Gabe got half the ashes. For a promise to split the May Day take.

I knew the union guys in Boise would never see a dime but that didn't bother me, the whole transaction being so tawdry it hardly warranted jumping in to protect their interests. Gabe and I then spent the afternoon shopping for an urn to take our share of the ashes in. In those days it was common to store a loved one's remains in a certain kind of ceramic vase, flowered, with a stopper that screwed down tight. The enameled flowers were of a suitably funereal tone, mauve or green, with blackish leaves that spread out in a kind of indeterminate swirl. To signify eternity, I suppose. Anyway, we bought one of those, child sized. And got a nameplate affixed to the wooden stand it sat on engraved with letters from a wheel that cost five cents a letter, punctuation extra. There wasn't a lot of space, and since this was temporary transportation, Gabe settled on just "Joe Hill, RIP" which cost fifty-five cents on top of the two dollars for the urn.

We went back to fill up our small urn from their bigger one. There was more back and forth, about what was the best implement to use to transfer the ashes, who was to do the honor, and finally Gabe had enough sense to let Hennessy, the big fellow in charge of the negotiations, "the keeper of the flame" as Gabe liked to call him, do it his way. Hennessy went out to the kitchen—they had a little closet in back used to brew coffee and the like—and came out with a soup spoon and a battered tin funnel. He'd put on a leather apron, I remember that. A blacksmith's apron. All very ceremonial, as if he transferred ashes every day. It was then I realized that some people had a gift for improvising the kind of dignified ritual that we seem to require when we honor loss, and some don't. Hennessy was, at best, an amateur in this business of ceremonial dignifying and so the whole thing had a slightly comical air—a big hulking fellow in a leather apron spooning ashes down a battered tin funnel. I had to cast my eyes away and pull in my lips to keep from laughing.

On the way back to the hotel Gabe was in a triumphant mood. With the urn in a box under his arm he had an air of giddy pleasure, such unalloyed self-regard, such boyishness, that I forgave him for making me come in the first place. A mistake. I put myself off guard by being eager to join in the fun he was having. The upshot was, he had me that night. Before dinner, when the last light of day was extinguished. Afterwards, in the dining room, I ordered pork, even though that night it cost an extra quarter. It still came with cauliflower, creamed this time, with sprinkles of caraway seeds that reminded me of mouse turds in cotton batting. I threw up again that night, though whether the cause was the cauliflower or my more general predicament, I couldn't say.

My deflowering by Gabe was not, of course, a technical one. I remember him taking off his pants in front of the bureau, the one that had my clothes in the top drawer and his in the second and third. I remember thinking that that was the same order my mother and father used in their shared bureau, and it was that, more than anything, that made what was going to happen next seem inevitable. Gabe took me the same way I suppose my pa took my mother, with exuberant, clumsy self-regard. Thoughtlessly, as if it were his due and no one else was a party to it. When Gabe was done he wrinkled his nose and said I stank and to go wash up. I have always wondered who men think they are smelling, after they spill their seed into a woman.

The next morning we went home. It was many years before I saw Boise again, and I can't say I held it in fond regard. I had an abortion later, in Kansas City, and I felt the same way about that town. At any rate, we got back to Seattle about four p.m. It was nearly dark, raining, and Gabe took my elbow and steered me to the trolley, then came up to my room and spent the night. That, more than anything, spelled the end of my dreams about Marcel. To have Gabe in that bed, that place of such joy and hope. I put away my dreams that night, so they couldn't be touched, so I couldn't feel them or grieve for their loss.

Things got better after that. At least I wasn't confused about where I was or what I was doing. I went back to the same routine. Working for Mr. Panopolous. Letting Gabe dress me up in other women's clothes, to sit on platforms, to look ethereal and gaunt. That last wasn't hard, I was loosing weight, and Gabe used to complain about that as well. We went up to see my mother once, before the trial, and she looked me over with some satisfaction, although what the source of that satisfaction was I couldn't say. And back once to see my father. He was getting soft about the middle, from the prison food and lack of activity, and he didn't look well, but got on famously with Gabe. He had written a poem about Joe Hill in the pantheon of angels to read at the May Day ceremony. I wrote it down as he dictated and flailed his arms. And then, of course, there was the trial, in March of 1917, at which I testified, unblinking, without tears, as if all this had happened to someone else, and not me.

The jury acquitted. "Everett Martyrs Redeemed" the *Union Record* headline proclaimed. "Justice Hijacked," mourned the yellow press. Meanwhile, the nation was mobilizing. On April 6, 1917, President Wilson asked Congress to declare war. The next week he instituted the draft. By June 6, all men aged eighteen to twenty-four had to register. Union issues got pushed to the side as young men wondered whether to comply. More troubling, for those who cared about such things, was that the socialists and the progressives had split on the question of war. I, on the other hand, found all this a relief because it took attention away from me, and focused Gabe's mind less on the Everett Massacre and more on saving his own hide. I suppose I thought one day he'd get tired of me and abandon me in some roadside ditch, but no such luck. After the May Day ceremony at the graves, which was something of a dud, although the weather was nice, Gabe announced we were going to Mexico. "Oh," I said, and wondered whether he was going to supply me with clothes for that. He didn't. He just informed me one day that he'd told Mr. Panopolous I was leaving and not to bother with the rent. I packed my clothes again, the ones I'd unpacked from my trip to Portland,

and put in the sewing box and ivory backed mirror and the picture of the girl with the donkey and left everything else in the room just as I'd done the first time. That marked the beginning of a new chapter between Gabe and myself. He had lost interest in me, as I had hoped, but he wasn't yet willing to let me go.

The night before we left we had dinner with Sam and his wife Etta. They lived in a little house south of downtown, on a street near where the new port was being built. That's an area of town that is now miles of paved industrial land and loading docks. In those days it was a dumping ground for fill taken from the leveling of the downtown. The city fathers were terracing hillsides, filling in tide flats, carving out new land for commerce. In those days Seattle was at war with its landscape as much as it was with the Huns and the anarchists. Anyway, Sam had this musty little house on a street that led nowhere. A failed subdivision I later found out had been some kind of utopian cooperative that was caught up in the city fathers' plans for leveling the earth.

Sam spent a good part of dinner fulminating about how he used to see red-winged blackbirds from his kitchen window. He blamed President Wilson for that and a lot else. We talked about Mexico, the potential for shaping the situation there to Russia's liking. During the hectic four months between when I got back from Boise and when we left for Mexico not only had our country gone to war but the Russians had had their first revolution. To Sam and Gabe, at dinner that night, the possibilities seemed endless. Lenin, emerging as an international figure, the head of a tiny Bolshevik faction, was putting pressure on the Kerensky government to quit the war and move the revolution to its next phase. No one believed Lenin was going to be able to manage anything of the sort. But Sam and Gabe did. What's more, they decided Mexico was going to be an ally in that process. The *Verona*, union issues, no longer existed. Move the troops, shift the battlefield, concentrate all energies down in Mexico.

By this time my head was spinning. Or maybe it was more accurate to say I was in a state of wonder. I was back at my father's side in a saloon where he was spinning his vast plans. Except here everyone was sober. And I had a ticket the next day on a train for New Orleans, en route to Mexico. As we left that night I watched Sam give Gabe an envelope and realized that's what the evening had been for.

* * *

I often wondered where that money came from, who it was intended for down in Mexico. Wondered whether I had been involved in raising that money, its diversion from one cause to another, or whether I was giving myself, the *Verona*, the whole Everett Massacre, too much weight. But the money had come from somewhere, as had the clothes I had worn on those many speakers' platforms. And Gabe, for all his air of improvisation, was taking orders from somewhere. As was Sam, I suspected. I could tell that less from Sam's demeanor than from the way his wife Etta opened her eyes and looked pleased when certain subjects were introduced, then would relax and let her face settle into its habitual scowl at others. I became a detective that night, on the trail of something to explain all this. Why I had been chosen by Gabe. For what purpose.

Chapter 14

The train to New Orleans took four days. I sat mostly in the club car, watching the mountains and desert and scrub prairie go by, cushioned in the sound of the rattling tracks, savoring the shudder as the long line of cars edged through slow curves. Gabe left me mostly alone, I was grateful for that, and we even got two separate pull-down pallets in our sleeping compartment, so I was able to spend each night without his hands grazing over me, checking me, making sure I was still his. We stopped in Kansas City, switched trains, to get rid of the business I mentioned. Gabe had contacts everywhere, I had to give him that. And it wasn't too painful, not too much of a fuss. I bled for the rest of the trip, and on into the first week in Mexico, which was an inconvenience, keeping clean, keeping my things clean. As soon as I got a chance I burned all my clothes.

In New Orleans we got off and stayed in a run-down hotel, in the old quarter, a place where moss grew in the corroded iron balconies and crippled vendors sold strange foods in the streets below. The smell of coffee was everywhere and made me homesick for Mr. Panopolous's diner, which was the closest thing to home I had. For two days Gabe left me alone in the Bon Chance Hotel. I had no money, it having been spent on our side trip in Kansas City. I prowled the room, making tight circles like I was in a cell. Gabe had left a valise, containing his clothes and some toiletries — not used often enough, I might add — some kind of hair oil I have never been able to abide the smell of since. And a ragged note pad, with a long cardboard cover, a receipt book I guess you could call it. It had yellow paper, the bottom half lined, with a box on the upper left, where I guess you were supposed to write orders, or the name of the person buying your goods. Each yellow page was numbered, with a numbered onionskin copy page beneath that. A long purple carbon paper was originally attached to slip in between the yellow page and the onionskin, but it was ripped out. Anyway, in the front were a whole host of blank onionskins, missing their yellow order form, and then a few complete sets in the back. And tucked in the very back was a business card, in Spanish, with the name of a person or company in Vera Cruz.

I have a very good memory, a visual memory, I can store pictures in my mind, remember a pattern of markings without understanding, without recognizing what it means until some later incident puts the pattern in some useful order. I discovered this talent years ago when I was working on seeds, a government job that was part of the New Deal, after my first husband perished in the Spanish Civil War. I could look at plants, and at the seeds they produced, and after I looked at them long enough, turned them over and studied them, I could sort them, match the good seeds with the good plants, a useful trick in classifying strains of hybridized corn, which is what I was working on, all without knowing how I knew. I could just tell which seeds produced which useful properties based on having seen seeds like them before. God grants us strange gifts, which we can make use of or ignore. Once I recognized my strange gift, accepted it as a talent stamped on me like a birthmark, I came to rely on it as my secret strength. Only then was I able to accept myself and that acceptance gave me peace.

As I said, my first inkling of this uncanny talent came in the Bon Chance Hotel, holding those flaps of onion skin to the light, trying to see imprints of handwriting, feeling the pages with my fingertips, trying to sense, like a phrenologist, what was on each page, what had been going on inside Gabe's head when he had used this order pad or, if he'd taken it from someone else who had used it, what had made him bring it on the train to New Orleans. I thought I might gain power over him by studying those pages, letting that hidden part of him seep into me, letting the dumb, passive part of my nature open like a flower, storing things, collecting impressions like those blank onion skins, a whole library of hidden impressions, stored without knowing. Waiting for the moment when it would all take on meaning.

The onionskins seemed to include a record of money. Given or accepted. And notes in a language I didn't recognize, which I later came to think might have been Polish. The handwriting was not Gabe's, except at the very end, and I don't think it was Sam's either, although it might have been Etta's.

I should tell you what I knew of Etta and Sam. Sam and Gabe, as I mentioned, had a family relationship that masked something more complicated. I was never able to discern whether Sam was the leader or Gabe. Or Etta, for that matter, it is possible she could have been calling the shots for them both. But I don't think so. Sam was big, rough hewn, with wiry gray hair he brushed back from his brow. He always wore woolen shirts, and hobnailed boots, and looked like a lumberjack, although he had an indoor job as a union steward at City Light. He was a self-taught mechanic, an intelligent man, with a much warmer personality than Gabe's, and it was hard not to like him. Gabe played off him, acted the bad boy, showed off, asked advice, then rejected it with a mock rebellious air. There was a tension between them, but it was a tension of shared affection. I always relaxed around Sam, because I sensed a kind of paternal oversight that I hoped would extend to me and serve to keep Gabe's demands on me within bounds.

Etta was another matter. She didn't like me. Whether it was because I was a *shiksa*, or for some other reason, I never knew. She was a sullen person, at least around me, heavy and given to shuddering sighs, and I can forever see her standing in her little kitchen, over a smoking stove, burning those crumb-filled meat rolls in a frying pan full of chicken fat. She was old world, miserably unhappy in a way neither Sam nor Gabe could be. She was short, the flesh around her ankles encased in heavy gray stockings, the black-laced shoes making me think she suffered from bad circulation. Her sighs reminded me of my mother. The same coiled anger, the same suffocating sense of grievance.

The handwriting in all but the last few transactions on the onionskins was small but wasn't, I decided, necessarily a woman's. It could have been an accountant's, a shipping clerk's. On the edge of a couple of the pages I saw blue ink, which made me think the person filling out the order might have also used a stamp. The more I examined the ghost traces of those past orders, the more I came to think of it as a shipping book. A record of things paid for and then sent from one place to another. Gabe and Sam were running some kind of business, I decided. But what kind?

After several hours, I set these musings aside, buried the invoice book back in the underwear section of Gabe's valise and went down the hall to wash out my bleeding pads. In those days girls didn't have disposable sanitary napkins, the pads we used were washed and reused. You can imagine what a pleasant job that was and how the custom grew up for men to leave us alone at those times. I was still bleeding pretty heavily, and was rotating the use of four or five pads, and I set out the freshly washed ones on the sun-filled window sill to dry, to aggravate Gabe if he should come back, and then went out on the street to find some food or a way to get money to buy some. I had with me a brooch that my father's mother brought over from Scotland, and, tucked in my deep pocket, the ivory backed mirror. My intention was to find a pawnshop. I found instead a whorehouse, and, since it was early afternoon, the ladies were just getting up. I spent several comfortable hours with them eating cornbread with treacle, drinking strong black coffee and picking seeds out of pomegranates, crushing an occasional one to let the juice run down my fingers. I had never seen a pomegranate before, and was entranced with the story one of the girls told of Proserpine and Minerva and the six months in Hades. I returned to the Bon Chance with crimson fingers and my brooch and ivory-backed mirror in tow, calmly lying to Gabe, detailed in my description of the torn fruit I'd found in the gutter. "Here, smell my fingers," I said to him, pushing my red cuticles at him, watching him turn away and taking pleasure in that. Good, I repelled him. That was a start.

The steamer we took to Vera Cruz was what was known in those days as a tramp steamer, because it had no set schedule of ports, simply plied the Caribbean picking up bananas or junk cars, or illegal passengers according to what would pay. It seemed an appropriate mode of transportation for two Americans with no papers, running from the draft, up to business they didn't care to discuss. We were hidden away in the hold, in a small room next to the engine, near some crates of chickens, whose presence attracted rats. I kept the door shut as much as possible, and ventured out onto the deck only after midnight, to breath in the sea air, to wonder what I was doing there, to wonder why I had so little wonder.

It was during one of those brief spells on deck that I decided the invoice pad must contain records of explosives, bought and transported, or stolen and transported to various sites of civil unrest. The book probably went back a dozen or so years, and must have been maintained by some quiet wild-eyed clerk in some mining camp who had sworn to some violent cause in compensation for his miserable existence. There had been several spectacular cases, involving the Western Federation of Miners, the union we had visited in Boise, and all of them involved dynamite, a commodity found in abundance in mining camps and easily converted into bombs. The trip to Boise and Sam's odd farewell dinner made me think that Gabe must have inherited this portfolio of responsibilities and that we were now heading toward some similar site of civil unrest, and that the money Gabe carried was to purchase something to further that cause.

Mexico was in a state of civil war. There were Zapatistas and followers of Pancho Villa in the countryside, an assortment of middle-class people who called themselves republicans in the provincial capitals, and radical anti-clerics who were running the show in Mexico City. Other parts of the country were strongholds of the old ruling elite and the embattled Catholic Church. What government you had depended on what part of the country you were in. Wealthy ranchers raised their own armies and used them in running battles with what they called outlaws but were considered by others to be liberators. Someone looking to aid the revolutionary cause would find plenty of opportunity to supply goods to blow up bridges and poison cattle and run guns in the mountains. That's what I thought might be ahead of us. Gabe spent lots of time up in the captain's grimy cabin, and down in the hold checking various crates stored some distance from the chickens and this made me think a shipment of guns was being transported. I had picked up a Spanish grammar, a children's book, had actually stolen it from a library near the Bon Chance Hotel. Years later I sent the New Orleans Public Library one dollar, in a blank envelope, and called it even.

I spent my five days in the cabin pouring over that Spanish grammar, determined to get a hold on the language, certain that it would be essential in some way I had not yet determined. Gabe, of course, made no effort to learn Spanish in the entire seventeen months we were in Mexico. Once we docked in Vera Cruz I moved up to studying Bible tales, picture books that the local cathedral used in Sunday schools. It may be then that I developed my taste for the Bible, for the comfort of it. The sanctuary that those embattled Mexican cathedrals provided to the weary populace.

It is, of course, an irony that the Catholic Church is both a sanctuary and despot. A lesson the Marxists and the radical unionists were slow to learn about their own faiths. I was learning to tread lightly in all those camps, to keep my peace, my own counsel. Seeing everything, keeping judgments to myself. Soon enough in Vera Cruz I graduated to paperback Mexican westerns, which told of rustled cattle, endless feuds and lovesick women shipped off to convents. After about a month I told Gabe I was ready to look for a job. Surprisingly, he agreed, whether because his money was running low or he was sick of having me always in his room, which required that his various secret meetings be held elsewhere. When we were together, sitting in a cafe nursing coffee, and some fellow would show up, he would have to revert to a clumsy code.

Most of the fellows he met with were Europeans or Americans. I never saw him talk to a Mexican. One time we met an Indian, a Brahmin named M.N. Roy with a blonde girlfriend he introduced as his wife. It turned out they were both from New York, so Gabe and this fellow talked about the people they knew, mutual friends. They only used first names, and clarified with additions like, "Ike, who lived on Avenue A," or "Herman, whose wife was a seamstress" or "Ilse, off in Amsterdam last year." They both seemed to know what all this meant. There was a lot of looking around, checking to see where the waiters were. It seemed very un-spy like to me, for I had decided by then that they were both spies.

Roy's girlfriend, Evelyn, was of more interest. She was about thirty, with a narrow face, high cheekbones, and she wore her hair in a Gibson girl flounce held by tortoiseshell pins clamped to keep the wavy mass in place. A few years later all this hair on girls would be cut to the nape, but then I was jealous. I had always wanted hair that stayed thick and wavy on the top of my head. I asked about her embroidered dress, where she had gotten it, because I was, by that time, reduced to wearing one oversized blouse, belted over a limp dun-colored skirt. A priest had let me take it from a jumble pile intended for the destitute and victims of fire. This, after I had burned all my clothes and showed up at the cathedral clad only in my poplin raincoat. I figured I, too, had been the victim of fire and said, "*Si*" when he asked if I was destitute.

Evelyn said all her clothes were made by the woman who kept house for her in Mexico City. She said if we came to visit she would give me some fabric, that Rosa was a wiz with embroidery as well as sewing. Then, on second thought, she asked why we didn't consider moving to Mexico City, they had plenty of room in their villa, and urged on us at least an extended visit. She seemed pleased to make this offer, and looked at Gabe with a sly expression of the sort I had seen before. Gabe looked at Roy, who made a dismissive gesture with his cigarette, of course there was room, and then blinked at me. I weighed the look, Roy's shrug, thought about the line of ants I was forever sweeping out of our tiny kitchen, the scorpions that were our constant company in the toilet, and said I would need a job. That if I was going to have Rosa make clothes for me I would need to pay for them.

That set off a four handed discussion about jobs, what an American with no papers could land in the way of employment in Mexico City. I had had only modest success in Vera Cruz. A Lebanese who ran a tortilla factory let me sweep up at night and gave me a few pesos and a large pinch on the buttocks when no one was looking. An offer by his nephew to sell flowers at a restaurant near the bull ring that seemed to entail more than selling flowers. Evelyn laughed with the rest of them at this story and then said she had an idea. Why not introduce me to Senior Cisneros, the owner of the English language newspaper, at which their two American houseguests were employed as reporters. I could be their dogsbody, getting coffee, keeping accounts, placating the owner with my broken Spanish. This last task turned out to be the most important one since the two reporters claimed to speak no Spanish and Senior Cisneros spoke no English. I wondered aloud how the pair found anything to write about, but learned soon enough, once we moved to Mexico City and took up residence in Evelyn and Roy's crumbling villa. I took my dogsbody job at the newspaper. Fifteen pesos a week, and I did all the work, while the twin reporters held revolutionary meetings, smoked revolutionary cigarettes while dictating denunciations of America's entrance into the war and the glorious prospects for continuing revolution in Russia. This instead of which ladies played bridge at what garden club.

The situation wasn't likely to last, and it didn't, since the owner thought his American reporters were writing social news for American ex-patriots. Women whose husbands worked for mining companies or managed the local offices of American corporations trying to do business with the assorted regimes competing for power. One of my jobs was to make up bogus translations of the irate letters that poured into our office, to explain away in my pidgin Spanish the fury of the occasional reader who showed up in person and made her way through the louvered mahogany doors to the inner office where Senior Cisneros napped.

But in the mean time Gabe and I were given a decent, if somewhat musty, room in Evelyn's mansion, and I was allowed to escape for hours each day to a newspaper office, with enough money to pay Rosa to make me an embroidered dress, with a yoke of crimson camellias set against inky blue leaves and a circling of blue cornflowers with tiny yellow centers at the hem. It's funny, that's what I remember most about Mexico, the pleasure I took in that dress, standing for the fittings of it, running my fingers over the embroidery, circling the flowers below my collarbones. I never had anything quite like it, the weight and drape of that heavy white cotton. I felt like a bride, but a bride to whom I did not know. To myself, maybe.

CHAPTER 15

I should tell you something about this Mexico City household I moved into. It was at once more and less familial than the one I had been born into. This one, of unrelated adults living together, each for his own reasons, had patterns of habitation different from the Copper household. Except for Evelyn, who, like my mother, wanted everyone to sit together and eat, no one in this little band ever concerned himself whether he arrived for dinner on time or not. Rosa shopped and cooked and cleaned and we all acted as if it were a free cafe. People who happened to be at dinner either talked to each other or didn't. Smoked and stubbed out the ashes in their leftover food or not. Those who didn't like each other juggled their meals so they didn't have to talk with whatever person got on their nerves. Folks came and went—the villa was a way station for young Americans avoiding the draft—and Rosa just cooked and served and cleaned up after. Now that I think about it, that must have been my mother's grudge as well.

However, sheer habit and hunger drove most of us to the table most of the time. And we did talk. And argue, and in this regard it was similar to dinnertime in Everett. Little attention was paid to the Mexican revolution. Trotsky and Lenin were our nourishing staples. The Wobblies, Everett, the Triangle Shirtwaist fire, all ceased to be important. Even the war was a subtext to our new big picture: what would happen in Russia. Was worldwide communism at hand?

It was about that time, in the summer of 1917, that radicals consciously shifted their rhetoric from the old tenet of the slow, inevitable maturing of social relationships, to the militant imperative of Lenin's Bolshevik doctrine: seizure of the state by force. People nowadays think that the November Bolshevik revolution came out of nowhere, but it didn't. Among the *cognoscenti*, of which we, in Mexico, were a minor outpost, violent overthrow of the newly installed Menshevik government was a given. The April revolution was both a step in an inevitable process and an obstacle to its completion. If Kerensky, God forbid, were successful, where would that leave wild-maned Trotsky? Smooth stubborn Lenin?

Such were our arguments, loud, exuberant harangues, about which of the two was the better man to lead. Trotsky has visited New York earlier that year, before the Russian army revolted and Kerensky was handed power. Of course Trotsky knew nothing of what was to come, Lenin's returning to Russia and seizing the reins of state, but he managed nonetheless to dazzle all the left-leaning young men caught in his wake. Trotsky fed on disciples, anyone who ever met Trotsky became a disciple. Lenin, by contrast, fed on splits. He didn't so much build a cadre of followers as distill an elite through factional opposition. Those not on the scene became his armchair followers via the printed word. Book readers, we called them, Lenin's disciples who poured over English language translations put out by his publishing house in Switzerland that arrived each month at a post office box in New York. These intense young men favored the self-proclaimed father of Bolshevism and considered Trotsky a blowhard. Conversely, Trotsky's followers considered Lenin an academic, dry, brittle, out of touch. This battle was to go on for some time, until Lenin died in 1923 and the blowhard proved he could lead men in battle but not administer his way out of a paper bag. Stalin finally deposed Trotsky in 1927, and it is an interesting footnote that Trotsky established his regency-in-exile in Mexico City. In this same crumbling villa, I used to imagine, although this was not the case.

The permanent members of our household were seven: M.N. Roy, and his so-called wife, Evelyn, Gabe and myself, and the two New Yorkers, a playwright named Mike Gold and a wild-haired Columbia University student who went by the name of Manny Gomez. These were the pair of reporters hired and fired by *Senor* Cisneros. The seventh was a Russian, who arrived in early 1918, who said his name was Mikhail Borodin. Of all the men, only Gabe did not use a *nom de guerre*, and that soon changed. The women used their own names, of course, including Rosa, who was invisible, and not considered part of the household by anyone, it seems, but me.

You have heard enough about Gabe and myself, that happy couple. Let me describe instead the other two couples in that household—M.N. Roy and Evelyn, and the two guys from New York. Then how the arrival of the Russian changed things.

M.N. Roy was, I would guess, about forty, a well-preserved aristocratic specimen. Copper skin, black hair shot through with one arresting gray streak (a Hollywood touch, I always thought) and a commanding set to his narrow shoulders. He dressed in a Mexican version of Hindu garb—Rosa, I suppose, tailored these pegged trousers and side-slit tunics to his specifications. He had an engulfing smile, not engaging, engulfing, unpleasant to my taste, and I always thought of the wolf in the fairy tale, dressed up and pretending to be Grandma. With regard to Evelyn, Roy was both solicitous and dismissive. She, of course, was bankrolling this sojourn, and required at least a modicum of deference.

Evelyn, for her part, wore a hectic air. Hectic in the sense of hectic fever, an aura of false brightness, a display of energy that presaged a relapse into some vague chronic illness. We tried to avoid her without seeming to do so. She made a great display out of being the mistress of the manse, calling out orders to Rosa in fractured Spanish, trying fruitlessly to get us all to sit down to dinner. She took a special interest in me, once Gabe had filled her in on my status as minor heroine in the Everett tragedy. She seemed bent on perfecting me to the role of good wife to the man of destiny, a junior version of her own starring role, cast opposite her more handsome and talented leading man. She was right about Roy—he was a leading man, and became, after many twists and turns, the head of the Indian Communist Party, subverting both Gandhi and Nehru, but Evelyn, of course, was pitched long before that happened. She was, I heard, jettisoned as soon as the household broke up. Such are the spoils of war. I knew this, in that peculiar way I had of sensing the future, but she didn't.

Manny and Mike were a similarly mismatched pair. They had known each other casually in New York. Mike, part of the Greenwich Village set, an impoverished playwright/cab driver, of Polish stock, while Manny, though trying to look Mexican with oiled hair and droopy moustache, was in fact the privileged son of a German Jewish banker. Manny was ferocious in his Marxism, analytic and slashing in his argumentation, untempered by romanticism, and ravishing, he liked to think, to women. He religiously read the brown-wrapped packages that arrived from New York and was betting all his marbles on the theoretician from Switzerland. Mike, on the other hand, had been courted by Trotsky, and was prone to thinking of revolution in terms of charismatic leaders. The two were thrown together in Mexico. Manny, the more energetic and manipulative, had gotten them jobs at the English language newspaper, then left Mike to do all the work. It was an arrangement that suited them both, Mike able to use the typewriter to bang out plays and Manny free to roam around the city making contacts in furtherance of the revolution.

It was Manny, of course, who had stumbled onto M.N. Roy, newly arrived with Evelyn in tow, without papers, one step ahead of U.S. Immigration officers that were deporting Indian radicals suspected of having ties with Germany. It is another interesting historical footnote that, like the Irish, Indian nationalists supported Germany in the First World War. Roy, before Evelyn's monetary support, or maybe in addition to it, was rumored to be on the payroll of the German government. To Marxists of a certain stripe that made no difference. Maybe added flavor to the stew. Gabe and Manny used to argue about this with Mike, when Evelyn and her swain were otherwise occupied. Whether Roy had, in fact, taken money from the Germans, and, if so, what import it had. Then the corollary, whether Roy should be considered a *bone fide* Marxist, or just an Indian nationalist, useful, but not central to the cause.

Rosa and I stayed out of this, Rosa because she understood so little English and had no interest in the subject at hand, and I because I was working on becoming like Rosa, invisible. Opinions were a danger, prone to exposing the contours of the soul, that much I had figured out. These arguments between Manny and Gabe and Mike would generally take place during siesta, when Roy and Evelyn had retreated to their private quarters, and were conducted in hushed tones, in case the host and hostess might hear, as presumably Roy and Evelyn conducted their business in similarly hushed tones, so we would not hear. I once went up to their private sanctum during an argument, stood close to the door to see if sound passed either way, and it did not. But I never told Gabe and the others of this, just let them continue to stage whisper, and then, in the heat of argument, their voices having risen to a shout, hush themselves and look up at the ceiling.

Through all this Rosa would clean and sweep and polish the tile floors. I would watch for minute shifts in her expression as the subject of Evelyn would come to the fore, if what they were discussing about Roy was personal. Roy's using Evelyn, her using him. Then the political questions:

Roy's German connection, his tenuous relationship to Lenin's Bolshevism and Trotsky's call for world revolution. All of this, I thought, was revelatory of Roy's character.

And Evelyn, the bargain she'd struck, was surely revelatory as well.

So I'd watch Rosa, trying to discern what she was thinking, how she felt about her employers, the permanent guests who had taken up habitation in the villa that she was assigned to clean and cook for, how she felt about her own country's revolution, her place in it, if any. I knew only that, of all the people in this house, she was most partial to Mike Gold. I also was partial to Mike, his gentleness of spirit. We became a sisterhood of sorts, girls with a crush, allies straining to protect Mike in his innocence against the self-aggrandizing young bucks.

It was into this layered web of alliances that the Russian arrived in the late spring of 1918, an emissary of the new government of Vladimir Illych Lenin. Mikhail Markovich Borodin—he later became famous, briefly, during the first, failed, Chinese revolution, and then disappeared into Stalinist imposed obscurity, or worse, I never found out— Borodin was a Russian by birth, but also an American with a family still living in Chicago. He had been part of the 1905 uprising against the Czar, and had been deported, or escaped, I'm not sure which, and wound up in Chicago running some kind of language school connected with Jane Addams's Hull House.

I found this out over time, not all at once. When Borodin arrived in Mexico he closeted himself with Roy for a couple of days, and then some kind of decision was made, and he moved into a spare room, one over the garage, the former stable, which Evelyn protested was not good enough, that it was for servants, but Borodin made a good show of being egalitarian, and even helped Rosa sweep it out, which was a smart move, as it solidified Rosa's loyalty, and impressed me. This was a man who knew what he was doing.

Evelyn, of course, was in a swoon. All of her best furniture was dispatched after being dusted and oiled. Lamps were lit, fragrant boughs brought in. You would have thought the Pope himself had arrived. Which, of course, he had. Or the next best thing, Lenin's man. That was the impression. Hush hush, of course, not to be bruited about outside the little household group. With just a few suggestions, a couple of anecdotes about the old days—Borodin seconding Illych's motion at a fateful conference, how he ran guns and smuggled spies in the forests of Estonia—with such nuggets our new guest placed the entire household in thrall. We were at his unquestioning service. For what exactly was not immediately clear, but we extended our patience, sure our mission would become evident in the fullness of time.

While we were waiting, a strange alchemy began to play itself out. For one thing, arguments about Lenin and Trotsky and Roy's credentials as a *bone fide* Communist ceased. Now that the commander had arrived, Roy and Manny and Gabe began to jockey for position. Who would become the lieutenant, the favored one, the one trusted with the as-yet-unannounced mission? Among the women the same sort of question hung in the air, although the favor we were seeking was of a different sort. But the game among the women lacked interest to the men. It was their contest that had world import.

What was the mission, why was the Russian here? Borodin spent most of each day in the hot courtyard, paring his nails or cleaning his boots. This drove Evelyn to distraction as she felt that the paring of nails should be done in private, if not in a barber shop, and boots were to be left to the servants. Rosa did offer to do both, but Borodin, after letting her inspect his hands, cluck over them, rub salve into a persistent hangnail, withdrew his rights to a manicure and gave her instead a shirt with a collar in need of turning. She retreated to her room behind the kitchen bearing the prize.

Evelyn he seduced by ignoring her. Complimenting her, of course, in a formal way as befits the wife of the man of the house, but ignoring her. To Roy, on the other hand, he gave his undivided attention. The two sat for hours playing chess under the papery bougainvillea—no amount of water seemed to revive that plant in the dry spring of 1918—a chess game that seemed to have less to do with bishops and knights than it had to do with ritual expressions of fealty. Borodin gave Roy the compliment of assuming at the outset that he was loyal to Lenin. Even though he knew this to be questionable. Flatterers pick their marks carefully. Narcissists are especially vulnerable. I used to sit in the shade of that crimson bougainvillea, studying my Spanish, writing out verb tenses, looking up phrases in my battered dictionary, listening to the ebb and flow of their play, the deferential questioning. Borodin, in his low voice, asking some seemingly spontaneous question, as if he had been troubled by a thought, an unfortunate gap in the logic of Marxist canon—what did Roy think of the colonial question, how was India to deal with evicting the British, where did caste fit in, culture? What should Illych do about the nationalities question? The Tatars, the Pamirs, the many tribes of the Caucasus? And what about borders, that vestige of outmoded empire—how would a revolutionary India deal with its neighbors, the religious, the nationality implications?

I could see what he was doing. Treating Roy as the future Lenin of India. Which is exactly how Roy thought of himself. I wondered what Borodin was going to do when he got around to harnessing Manny and Mike. And Gabe.

I didn't have to wait long. After several days of cleaning boots and playing chess, Borodin and Roy went off for several days without explanation. I never did find out what they were doing, but I assume it had to do with meeting some revolutionary contacts.

When Borodin got back, alone, he turned his attention to Mike and Manny and Gabe with that same polite but absolute focus. So famished were they for his attention that I'm not sure they noticed they had waited in line. He began to stay up late at night with them, after Evelyn had retired to her room, began to smoke Cuban cigars and talk of his trials as a young man before the Revolution, drawing parallels between the arc of his life and what they saw to be theirs—early idealism, foot soldiering, exile, finally a return with great glory. I wondered at his tactic, treating these *tres gatos* as they called themselves—three cats, not in the hip sense, or only slightly in the hip sense, but more in the sense of strays—of treating these three strays as a set. For all their good natured camaraderie, both Manny and Gabe treated Mike as a hopeless sophomore, an apple polisher, a Trotskyite before that was even an epithet, while they regarded each other with thinly concealed contempt, contenders for the same prize. Borodin must have seen all this, and kept Mike in the middle to lend an air of civility to what was, in essence, a group audition.

In the fullness of time it became clear that there was a task to be carried out, one that involved certain things Borodin had brought from Russia, things that needed to be taken by boat, to Tampa, by way of Cuba, a suitcase with a false bottom, a fountain pen with a special ink cartridge. It was not clear what was to be smuggled or the plan of conveyance. That would be revealed later. Instead Borodin conducted a tutorial on smuggling. Case examples taken from his past. Interrogation techniques. The all-important role of distraction. The little scene it was necessary to play out at the critical moment when customs officials examined papers and decided whether to search luggage. Listening to all this, I wondered why Borodin didn't simply contact the captain of the tramp steamer we had used to sail from New Orleans. He seemed to have sufficient bribes in place to dispense with all this tradecraft, but I kept my peace. By that time I was learning to embroider crimson flowers on a smocked bodice that Rosa had helped me sew. I kept my head bent under the thin yellow light of the oil lamp and listened to all this boyish bravado in mild wonder, each

131

hopeful trying to outdistance the others with his own hypothetical example of what the Tampa port authorities were likely to do while trying to intercept the lucky carrier of the false-bottomed briefcase.

CHAPTER 16

In order to explain how the smuggling expedition wound up, I need first to go back and tell more about who was sleeping with whom. Before Borodin's arrival, assorted wayfarers sleeping under our roof had participated in their fair share of short-term liaisons. Any new face at the dining table produced a frank appraisal of the night's prospects. Sometimes this resulted in a late night pairing and sometimes not. Manny, of course, pounced on anything female, as did Gabe when he didn't think I was noticing.

Not that I cared, I would have been grateful if he'd shucked me and waltzed off with some more avidly revolutionary *senorita*. It is not as if our occasional physical relations produced any joy. So when Gabe cast his eye on some firebrand from Rochester or Mexican schoolgirl in the marketplace, it was fine with me. But dinner table revolutionaries of the female persuasion were few and far between, so Gabe and Manny mostly had to make do with what they picked up in town.

The dinner table offerings, being mostly male, fell to Evelyn, although she was often constrained by the presence of Roy, who, of course, knew what was going on, and knew it was his right, nay duty, to be shocked by it. After all he was Brahmin, she was a woman, she was his. On the other hand, she was an American, she had the money, he was a brown-skinned foreigner, a step outside the law. So it was an even match, and they played it with cat-like intensity, involving all of us as their audience, an audience that was supposed to notice, but not notice, know and not know.

It was a wonder we had the energy for it, what with the heat, Evelyn shouting at Rosa all day, herding guests into meals, entertaining them, entertaining Roy in sweaty couplings each afternoon. Then to feel bound to seduce any attractive male guest in a manner not ruffling the surface propriety of the household.

It took me a while to figure out what Roy was doing all those nights when Evelyn was accommodating some wayfarer in the guestroom. As it turned out, availing himself of *seigneurial* rights in the servants' quarters. There being only one servant, Rosa had the honor. Such was our egalitarian household.

All these sexual proclivities took a while to become manifest, so enmeshed were we in the fabric of our daily living that they were either not noticed or not remarked upon. Our conscious attention was focused on Lenin, Trotsky, the nationalities question. Then along came Mikhail Markovich Borodin, who put an end to the debate on the relative merits of Lenin and Trotsky. An end to the dinner guests as well. We became a closed household, bent on some secret mission, each household member being groomed for his or her part.

Given the strength and free ranging nature of the various libidos, something was bound to explode. At first I thought Borodin himself might become an object of play, as was clearly Evelyn's intent. But he treated her with a grave courtesy, which drove her mad, which he chose not to notice, which pleased Roy hugely, which was the point. For Borodin's first task was to bring M.N. Roy to heel. This he did with several weeks of *mano a mano* conversation and inept chess moves under the fluttering papery petals of the bougainvillea. That done, he sent Roy off on a second mission, again to the mountains, to a clandestine meeting with high level rebels who were open to political conversion in exchange for cold cash. That is my speculation, of course I never knew the exact nature of what the trip entailed. Only that the lack of amenities caused poor Roy to return with his elegant demeanor considerably diminished.

Borodin had a stash of convertible paper with him, in the form of Cuban bank notes, tobacco futures as I recall, something that required a lot of notarizing to convert to local currency. This is where Evelyn was pressed into service. She was well known in town as a rich American, who employed the services of a left-leaning Mexican attorney, who in turn maintained some kind of affiliate relationship with a Philadelphia law firm in charge of dispensing her monthly dollops of family fortune. Manny, whose father was a banker, claimed to possess a passing talent for financial manipulations, and was thus assigned to accompany Evelyn on her trips to the *abogado* to sort out a marginally legal way to turn those bearer notes into Mexican currency. Over the course of the several weeks that Roy was gone, Evelyn and Manny's trips to town got longer and longer, and it was the remaining household's opinion that the high enthusiasm in which they returned each day was disproportionate to the zeal which they brought to the processing of tobacco futures. I waited to see what would happen when Roy returned.

Also during this interval Borodin got Manny and Mike and Gabe thinking about how they should arrange to smuggle his precious cargo into Tampa. He had some Cuban connection, the man who had produced the tobacco futures, presumably in exchange for some part of what Borodin had carried with him into Havana, the balance being still hidden in Cuba. So my idea, of simply taking the goods and going to Vera Cruz and bribing our way back to New Orleans would not do. Not that I said anything. After all, no one was asking me. Listening to the four men go round and round and never come up with a decent plan, I began to wonder why not, but cautioned myself that I hadn't yet broken any laws, at least any major laws. I wasn't dodging the draft, engaged in sedition, I was merely trying to learn how to embroider red camellias on stiff cotton. So I kept my head down, driving the dull needle through tough fabric and only occasionally stabbing my finger and having to stop to suck the blood dry.

When, late in the summer, Roy returned, his elegant clothes badly in need of repair, his slim frame twenty pounds lighter, Evelyn decided an elegant victory meal was in order. Much to my surprise, Borodin seconded the idea, and added the notion of a *mariachi* band to commemorate the occasion. Considering the cloistered nature of our household, this was a departure. Borodin seemed never to leave the house; he had arrived incommunicado and presumably would leave that way. Of course, some people must have known, hiring a *mariachi* band wasn't the act of a person who was *persona non grata.* The government certainly kept their eye on Evelyn and Roy, indeed it was the government Borodin and Roy were trying to woo, so somebody in a position of authority must have known that Borodin was there. But whether Borodin feared assassination, or was simply a man of deep caution or whether he felt this cloistering was a necessary part of bending us to perform his tasks, I do not know. At any rate, Mike Gold and I were given the mission of finding a *mariachi* band, and a *pinata,* which was out of season, and this entailed spending a full day visiting the back rooms of dry goods stores all around the square.

Mike and I were friends, in the sense that we had an affinity for each other, but we rarely had the opportunity to talk about personal things. Partly it was Mike's silent nature, his reluctance to engage in chatter, not because it was idle but because of what it might reveal. He was the most dedicated communist I ever knew, dedicated in the sense of possessing a deep interior life in which the tenets of communism, as he understood them, possessed a profound spiritual value. It was he who taught me the concept of *Tikkun,* the Hassidic belief of a shattered godhead, man's unending obligation to gather all the lost shards of light in the darkness, ultimately to restore our lost paradise. I longed to become one with that grace-filled, passionate existence, but, alas, unlike Mike, I was never able to believe that Lenin and Trotsky were adequate to the task. In the end, I suppose, belief of that kind requires a temperament that can look wholly within, see past the harsh reality of everyday existence. I have never been able to sustain the effort of such introspection nor persuade myself that looking past reality is not morally reprehensible.

But to get back, Roy's arrival required Evelyn's return to toeing the line. The trips to the *abogado* ceased. Manny, on starvation rations, became quite surly, salving his pride through jibes at Gabe, whom he feared might be selected as Borodin's favored boy. Gabe naturally gave back as good as he got. This rivalry broke into the open at the dinner table with the welcome-home *pinata* and *mariachi* band, a disagreement about what exactly was being stashed in Havana for smuggling to Tampa. Jewels, Borodin clarified. Loose gems to be secreted in the fountain pen, and other jewelry still in its casings, to go in the false-bottomed briefcase. That information did nothing to stop the bickering. Borodin watched this red-faced scrap escalate without comment, until Evelyn finally put a stop to it on the grounds that no one could hear the band. She spoke to Rosa, who took the musicians off to the kitchen to feed them, and the mood of festivity was patched up.

After dinner, we adjourned to the living room, where Evelyn had hung the *pinata* in the door jamb. Roy was loosing enthusiasm for all this attention, but Borodin, again to my amazement, insisted that the party continue. He called back the band, three small men in big hats, one with a battered horn, another a guitar and the third with a outsized drum on his belt. They sang a mournful Mexican tune not fully in keeping with the mood Borodin hoped to reestablish. He motioned them to step up the beat, so they segued into a meringue, to which Borodin proceeded to demonstrate some Cossack dance steps. He had been drinking brandy that night, something I rarely saw him do, and I couldn't tell whether his edge of manic festivity was calculated or inadvertent. Evelyn began to dance with him, mirroring his steps, then, abruptly, he cut off the demonstration. He turned back to the band, humming and showing them he wanted a waltz tempo, which they managed more or less. Then he assembled the group into three dance couples, Mike and me, Evelyn and Gabe, and Manny with Rosa. I wondered if we were being paired off for a reason, wondered how much Rosa knew or could understand, what she thought of all this. Roy, left out of the pairing, put an end to the evening by taking a broomstick and smashing the *pinata.*

Over the next few days the situation deteriorated further. Gabe, feeling pressure, confided in me more about what this Tampa excursion entailed. I've noticed this about revolutionaries, their recourse to self-bolstering through the attention of women, though maybe this is just a weakness of men in general.

At any rate, Gabe confided in me that the jewels Borodin had stashed in Havana were taken during the sacking of St. Petersburg. Silverware and candelabras melted down went directly into the Soviet treasury, but the jewels were siphoned off to finance the international payroll. These particular jewels Borodin carried to Havana were destined for New York, to pay for expenses associated with establishing a Communist Party in the United States, either by taking over the Socialist Party or by splitting off and forming a new organization. You must remember that Lenin, at that time, had been in power only a few months, Russia had pulled out of the war, but the war was still grinding on. Lenin's new state was momentarily free of enemies only because no other armies had yet had time to crush him. But as soon as Germany was licked, the White Russians, who were gathering forces in the Ukraine, were expected to call upon the capitalist nations to evict the Marxist roundheads. So Lenin was looting the throne room to buy support overseas from nations like Mexico, which had just had its own revolution, and nationalist groups like the one Roy belonged to in India, groups that had no love for capitalists either.

I had to admire, as we lay in bed at night, how Gabe laid all this out, no doubt quoting direct from the mouth of Borodin. You had to admire Lenin's response as well, sympathize with the guy in such a box, the boldness of his moves. Jewels, hidden in velvet sacks or in a golden strongbox, buried under some Cuban moss-draped tree. The idea of it took on a swell of romance, intrigue disconnected from any sense of right or wrong, any sudden change in ownership or ultimate disposition. Like Gabe, like every one else in that household, I was seduced. I wanted to see the jewels. I wanted to join in their safe passage.

All this worked on me, as it was undoubtedly intended to. I have described how Borodin sized up and then played upon the aspirations and vanities of each member of our household. I was not exempt, nor was I unaware that eventually I would become the object of the Russian's attentions. When it came, Borodin's attention, it arrived from an unexpected quarter. Borodin asked my advice. Just like that, as if he wanted help in picking a suitable hat. He asked whom, did I think, he could trust. After some hesitation, I started to answer. But then he opened a little side conversation about grammar, *who* or *whom*, and I gave my best opinion on that. As to the bigger question, it was clear he meant those in our household, who among us was trustworthy, who cared enough about his cause, who admired him enough to willingly put Borodin's interests, and by implication, Lenin's interests, above self-interest. Borodin did not voice these nuances. But the questions were in his eyes, the timbre of his voice. The implication, of course, was that he had already put me in the category of the trusted. That was the hook. He was asking me which of his male apprentices should be entrusted with this delicate smuggling operation.

It was like one of those moments in a movie, a few words and a smoldering look. Well, Borodin's look wasn't smoldering, he knew I wouldn't be taken in by that. It was more the kind of look a hero gives, a fugitive on the run from dangerous enemies, when he asks the young girl to shelter him, to lie for him, to switch sides. No one ever needs know, his eyes tell her, only him, only her. *Do this out of the goodness of your heart, because I am so vulnerable, so right in my cause. Nothing more will be asked.* And so she switches sides. Rises to full womanhood. The music swells; she does what he asks; he escapes, the movie ends. And, though she has only a bit part, the audience remembers her. That was the hook Borodin was offering me, the hidden moment of immortality.

Borodin took my hand, cleared his throat, then repeated his question. In giving my answer I gave him my loyalty. After all, he had given me his. Or so it seemed. After a moment of reflection, I said, "I'd trust Mike." He waited to see who else I would recommend.

"Is that all?" he finally asked, a touch of surprise, or maybe disappointment, in his voice.

There's me, I wanted to add, but didn't, fearing that would spoil the moment. "Rosa," I said, needing to say something.

He looked confused. I could see him turning this over in his mind, the possibilities of this recommendation. "Yes," he finally agreed. He dropped my hand. "Thank you." It took me a while to figure out the confusion was because I hadn't included Gabe on my list.

CHAPTER 17

Of all the members of the household, Manny was most proficient in Spanish. I have mentioned that he was from New York, with a given name Frederick Goetz, but he fancied himself a Mexican, and had adopted the name of Manny Gomez, and spent a lot of time perfecting the accent and mannerisms of a *louche* son of the *bourgeoisie,* the kind who populates certain cafes and bordellos the world over. It was this impersonation that finally decided Borodin. Whoever it was supplying tobacco futures had connections to the cigar factories in Tampa. The plan was to go to Havana, get the jewels and working papers for the two-person team (Borodin had decided it must be a team) and, upon arrival, go to work in Ybor City rolling cigars. Then, after a suitable interval, the pair would travel to New York, turn over the jewels to the Left Wing Socialist League, which would hock them and use the funds to bankroll operations around the country.

Mike Gold was to travel separately to New York, to establish things at that end, while Gabe would go to Chicago to work with a new organization called the Communist Propaganda League. Borodin's wife still lived in Chicago and she was to be Gabe's contact. I was surprised, after all the hush hush when the plans were hatching, how out in the open everything became as we got close to the departure date. Borodin planned to travel with Manny to Havana, where he would be teamed up with a Cuban for the trip over to Tampa, but then, just a couple of weeks before departure—this would have been in September of 1918— word got back that the Cuban businessman's activities had been discovered, and so the plan got very risky. There was much discussion about whether to go ahead, how to devise a backup plan that would be secure. This is where the idea of taking Rosa along came about. To be on the safe side Borodin felt identities and travel documents would have to be put together in Mexico, the stop in Havana only to pick up the jewels, with minimal contact with the Cubans.

Borodin approached me one afternoon in the kitchen, where I was helping Rosa prepare *flautas*—I was learning to cook by now, as well as to grind corn and spices. "May I see you in private," Borodin murmured, placing a hand on my shoulder and letting it run down my arm. Interesting, I thought, and wiped my hands on a dishtowel then followed him to the far corner of the courtyard where the wood was stored. I had taken up smoking and used the excuse of a cigarette to hear him out.

"I wonder if Rosa might be willing to marry Manny," he speculated, looking up at the sky.

I thought about that, thought about Rosa's circumstances, her prospects, how drastically they might change under Borodin's plan. "How about Manny?" I asked, meaning what did he think of this plan.

A small detail, Borodin's face seemed to imply.

How about Roy? I wanted to ask. How would he take to this change of bedding? Then I remembered Manny's fling with Evelyn, and decided that Roy would probably enjoy Evelyn's chagrin more than enough to compensate for his loss of Rosa's company. Borodin broke in on my reverie. "Will you arrange an interview?"

"You mean with Rosa?"

"Yes," he said. "We will have to start her political education."

Do they have a rulebook? I wondered. Or was this just

Borodin's slightly pompous way of setting up an arranged marriage? "My Spanish's not good enough for that," I finally offered. Both of us thought about asking Manny to translate and decided that was out. "Mike might be able to help," I suggested. "Between the two of— "

"Yes," said Borodin, breaking into a brief smile. "Set it up, this afternoon. During siesta." I thought of Evelyn and Roy and what went on at their siesta.

So that afternoon, in the hottest part of the day, the four of us assembled in Borodin's room above the garage, splendidly decorated by Evelyn but airless and musty just the same. After some nervous minutes of standing around Borodin urged Rosa to the room's only chair. "Rosa," he began, then cleared his throat. "If we could take a moment of your time." I translated as best I could. She looked up at him, at Mike and me. What else did she have but time? Then, her dimples came out and she bobbed her head. Borodin let out a breath he had been holding. "Rosa," he said, "I need to ask you some questions, to get your views on certain political matters that are commonly discussed in this company." I simplified that, asking Rosa if she had listened at all to the arguments at the dinner table.

"*Si*," she said, and then giggled. "*Loco*," then giggled again. Mike flushed, remembering, no doubt, his spirited defense of Trotsky. I decided not to translate. Borodin was having enough doubts. I was glad he hadn't managed to pick up a word of Spanish. Mike, as we exchanged glances, offered to take over.

"Let me see if I can explain." He spoke gently, asking if she knew anything about the revolution that had been going on in Mexico.

Of course, she said, how could she not?

Did she have any brothers, cousins, who might have taken sides?

Of course, how could they not?

Borodin cleared his throat, irritated at being left out.

"You keep talking to her," I told Mike, "I'll translate." And so we went through it, Mike phrasing the political interview in the basic terms of the Mexican struggle, my translating back into the tortured jargon favored by the international left. Between us we managed to establish that Rosa was not in the clutches of the landowners or the church. That she was able to distinguish *banditos* from insurgents—at least in theory. In practice in Mexico, at the time, it was hard for anyone to discriminate. But in theory she was willing to accept the premise that Russia—a country she had never heard of until she started working for *Senor Roy*—that a country called Russia had clear lines, clear sides, with the monarchy and the landowners and capitalists on one side, and the revolutionary army of workers and peasants on the other. And that the leader of the workers and peasants in Russia was now in power—

Un Rey, she asked? No, not a king we assured her. *Un General?* No. Here Mike took the opportunity to backtrack to the dinner table arguments, and establish that *Senor* Trotsky, whom they had often discussed, was an heroic general—*Ah, si, del mismo Zapata*, she chimed in. Like Zapata, Mike agreed, nailing down at least that flank.

It remained how best to characterize Lenin. This seemed a good time to turn things back to Borodin. He surprised me by taking exactly the right tack.

"Do you have in your family a very revered man—not necessarily a relative, but someone in your village, someone everyone looks up to, goes to for protection? A man with a superior intellect, someone who has had an education, perhaps. But not someone taken in by the lies that come with an education, not someone who has lost sight of where he came from, not someone who betrays the people he loves. Someone who is the salt of the earth—" Here he stopped, while I, rushing to translate, got hung up on the metaphor. After a moment I translated 'salt of the earth' just as is, hoping it didn't mean alkali or have the connotation of death.

Rosa bobbed her head up and down, trying to take this all in, and seemed to accept my metaphor, however odd it sounded to her ear.

Now Borodin moved in close the deal. "That man is our leader, Vladimir Illych Lenin." Opening his hands, he announced this simple truth. "I have known him since I was a boy. He has taken me to his breast." He made a slow sweeping movement, a gesture of the godlike Illych reaching down and gathering up the young Borodin. Something about that movement of his hands, its religiosity, grabbed Rosa, I could see. Borodin could too. He locked his eyes to hers and asked softly, "Are you ready to help this great leader, this friend of mine, who needs you?"

Rosa looked to me, to Mike. "*Si,*" she finally agreed.

As she had pledged her loyalty, Borodin called the session to a close, in part because Evelyn would be soon looking for Rosa, wondering about dinner. Also the room was sweltering. This was a high-wire act, and we were all exhausted and elated we had come through it together. Such, I noted, is how real alliances are struck. The hard part, the sausage making, comes later.

The next day we reassembled in Borodin's room without Mike. That in deference to Rosa, because Mike was Manny's friend. As Manny's role in the scheme became clear, the conversation became quite candid about Manny's faults, as a prospective husband and otherwise. So it was just as well Mike wasn't there to hear it.

Borodin's opening was brisk. "I am here as a courier," he said. That last word set me to leafing through my Spanish dictionary. He waved his hand. "To transport some funds." I took a stab at that. Rosa nodded. With all our conversations in the library she had figured that out. "The funds will go to New York. I must find people to take them there. Then, I will go back to my own country." At the mention of New York I could see her eyes light up. Something Borodin also noted. "Would you like to go to New York?"

"*Si.*" A pause, a shy smile then the lowering of her eyes. It was like watching someone being asked on a date.

"It would be dangerous." Now Borodin pulled back a bit. "You might get caught."

This Rosa dismissed. She had been in danger all her life.

"You would not go alone. You would have a traveling companion."

This should have been reassuring, but it wasn't. Something in Borodin's voice. Rosa's hands went to her lap. She waited, head down.

"You would have to cross the border. You would need papers. A legal reason to enter."

Yes, her body said, tell me the rest of it.

"We—that is our group, Penny Joe, Mike, your employers, *Senor* Roy and *Senora* Evelyn—all of us have decided it would be best, when you make this trip, if you were married."

Brief hope flashed through Rosa's eyes, then she remembered Borodin said he was going back to Russia. And so confusion replaced hope, then came disquiet. "*Que?*" she asked in a small voice.

"Manny," he said. "*Senor* Gomez."

Rosa let out a breath of disgust. "*Puerco,*" she said. Then looked at me not to translate.

"*Si,*" I said. "*Un puerco.*" A disgusting male pig. "*Tambien Senor Gabe.*" We both exhaled, a kind of gallows laughter.

That strengthened her a bit. "*Porque?*"

"She wants to know why," I said. "She understands about the papers, but what comes next? What is she expected—" I was making this up, it was I who wanted to know what would happen to poor Rosa in New York.

"You mean when she gets there, when the—ah, funds— are delivered."

"Yes," I said. "Will she have a job, will she be expected—" I waited. Rosa, who seemed to know I was negotiating on her behalf, also waited.

Borodin considered what he had asked of this young woman, what Manny's assumptions about this arrangement might be, what he could be relied on to do and not do. "I will tell *Senor* Gomez that this arrangement is exclusively a matter of business. That you are not to be—engaged— against your will. That when you get to New York he will find you suitable employment, that you can make whatever—"

"I will give her an address to get in touch with me," I said. This just popped out, I was so sure Manny would do none of what was asked. "I have a friend who runs a paper—" It seemed I had suddenly made plans for the next part of my life. I would go back to Seattle, take up Harry Ault on his offer. I would work for the *Union Record* and use the labor network to keep in touch with Rosa and make sure she was all right. I had found a friend, I realized. My heart filled with the prospect of protecting Rosa. I smiled, and that made Rosa smile, and her smile infected Borodin.

"It is settled then," he said, and rose to go.

"*Puerco,*" Rosa said behind his back but in reference to Manny.

"They're both *puercos,*" I said, including Gabe in the compliment.

* * *

It was not so easy of course. Getting papers arranged. The big question was whether to marry Manny to Rosa under his own name, Frederick Goetz, and risk the prospect that he would be picked up at immigration as a draft dodger, or forge papers to make him a different American citizen, or leave him as Manny Gomez, Mexican national and then have the problem trying to get them both through as immigrants. This last made no sense, marrying Rosa to a Mexican. And as for using other American papers, all the Americans we knew were draft dodgers. Time was running out. Borodin had to get back to Russia, and he was afraid that the longer he left the jewels in Cuba the greater the chance that they would get discovered, and so, for lack of a better plan, the decision was made to marry Manny and Rosa under the name of Mr. and Mrs. Goetz. Borodin figured that even at worst, if Manny were jailed, his father could bail him out. Rosa, unless the jewels were found on her, could claim ignorance.

This was probably the source of the change in plans that led Gabe and me to wind up with some of the jewels. In the end, four people went on the trip to Cuba: Borodin, Manny, Rosa and Roy. Manny and Rosa took off for Tampa with their portion of the jewels and Borodin and Roy returned to Mexico. Manny did get in trouble at immigration, but he had already handed off the case with the false bottom to a traveling salesman who agreed to meet him three days later. When Manny did clear immigration, the salesman had gone.

This story got changed over the years, got told and retold until it was Borodin who handed off the suitcase. I heard through the grapevine that Borodin did get in trouble, at one point, with the Soviet version of the star chamber, over the suggestion that instead of just bungling the jewel caper he had made off with the goods. That was unfair, and goes to show you what jealousy can do. But there is more to this story because when Borodin and Roy returned, still believing that Manny and Rosa had gotten safely through, Borodin took Gabe and me aside and showed me what he had brought back. Three Faberge eggs.

CHAPTER 18

In the 1870s, Peter Carl Faberge, Russia's jeweler extraordinaire, made an Easter egg for Czar Alexander to give to his wife. The egg—a white enameled shell opening to a golden yolk that opened in turn to reveal a golden hen—was a success, so much so that the Czar's present became an annual one. When that Czar was assassinated, his son, Nicholas II, continued the custom, giving a Faberge egg each year not only to his wife, but to his mother. Over the years the eggs got more and more elaborate, ovals of gold encrusted with crystal and jewels. Each egg had some trick, a hidden clasp, a secret spot when pressed that popped open to reveal a portrait: a miniscule carriage, a warbling songbird. Jeweled eggs became the rage among the aristocracy, so others besides Romanovs soon possessed Faberge eggs. But none were so elaborate, so jewel laden, as the ones given to the Czarinas. Who, of course, were shot along with all the other Romanovs in 1917. So Lenin wound up with the Czarinas' eggs. But Faberge eggs were not so easy to hock as jewels pried from tiaras, so Lenin or his henchmen included a few of those eggs along with tiara-lifted rubies and pearls in the cache sent to Cuba, and left it up to Borodin whether to take out his pen knife and prize apart those beautiful objects.

Fortunately Borodin could not. And, so as not to make things harder on Manny and Rosa in Tampa, or maybe because once having seen them he could not bear to part with them, he brought the three eggs back to Mexico. They were extraordinary to behold, each nestled in a cream colored case, a velvet box, itself egg shaped, with satin lining, the interior molded to an exact impression so that the egg, placed inside, fit exactly like a child inside its mother.

I was entranced, sitting in the dining room, Borodin having brought them out and placed them on display like a traveling salesman. One, fairly plain, about the size of a goose egg, was enameled a deep reddish brown, laced over with gold scallops like a pinecone. The scallops, in turn, were dusted with small stones—I seem to remember seed pearls but they could have been diamonds—and then inside, the surprise: an elephant, jeweled, topped by a Sepoy rider, complete with gold hunting horn and tiny black lacquered whip. How perfect, I remember thinking, touching the flexible crop. And the ivory tusks, the elephant's jeweled headdress, the little embroidered seat, all rendered in the most infinite detail. Only a barbarian could have melted this down.

The second egg I found easier to imagine dismantling. A turquoise bauble with gobs of gold rope and, when the hidden spot was pressed, four framed miniatures that sprang out to reveal seasonal scenes of blossoming cherries, autumn birch, stag reindeer.

I turned to the third. This one, not entirely egg shaped, was tapered at the bottom, then attached to a pedestal not more than a penny's width in circumference. A letter seal, the egg its handle. Made for cupping, it worked with rolling ease, like the gear shift in an expensive automobile. The deep green object kissed your palm as it rolled it back and forth. Even the rounds of platinum swag engaged the senses, touching bone as the egg rolled side-to-side, back-to-front, pressing down wax that would seal the letter.

A pleasure to remember even now. During those last days in Mexico I would sit for hours, rolling the green oval back and forth, back and forth. The design cut into the stamp was mysterious, a few feathery lines that seemed almost Japanese. I asked Borodin what it meant, and he speculated that it might be the Romanov herald from some far-flung hunting estate. We got out candle wax and mixed it with stove black and stamped the imprint many times on butcher paper as if we were issuing Imperial edicts. M.N. Roy, for his part, became entranced with the elephant and its Sepoy rider, telling us fantastic stories of his own royal lineage among the Maharajahs, but I loved the wax seal. It felt exciting, danger filled, summoning some power in me I did not know I possessed

After those first few nights the Faberge eggs were put away and plans were made for Gabe to smuggle them back to Chicago, to turn them over to Borodin's wife who would, in turn, deliver them over to their intended recipient in New York. It was by now late October and everyone knew the end of the war was near. Revolutions were springing up in Austria and Hungary and Bulgaria as the Axis armies collapsed. When the time for departure came, in late October, Gabe and I took a surprisingly casual leave taking of those left in the villa. Borodin, and Mike Gold I would miss, as I already did Rosa. Our host and hostess I felt grateful to, for their hospitality, but Gabe was nonchalant. I think he expected to meet up with them all again one way or the other. For my part, I was sad to leave. I had grown to love the house, the climate, at least some of the people. Even Evelyn in her way. Roy, I never took seriously, but didn't really dislike. And Rosa I had come to feel deeply grateful to, for teaching me something ineffable about life.

At any rate, Gabe and I traveled to Vera Cruz by bus, the Mexican kind bearing chickens on the roof, and it took two days, what with a broken axle and overheated radiator. When we arrived we took up residence in the same seedy hotel. I took to visiting the cathedral once again, lighting candles and thinking of the wax seal and its faintly Japanese impression. Gabe had the eggs hidden somewhere in his luggage, packaged as gifts, but wouldn't let me see them. It was as if, freed from Borodin's presence, he reverted to his normal distrust, his instinct that I was not an ally to his cause. He was right, as I had concluded that his primary cause was himself.

Borodin and I never discussed Gabe's trustworthiness outright, we never discussed anything outright. There was simply a gentle irony between us, a kind of truce, not an alliance exactly, it was more personal than that, a loyalty that sometimes comes between a man and a woman based on their mutual sense that they can see inside the other. It was the lack between Gabe and me of any mutual empathy that prompted him to hide the eggs even though our possessions amounted to one suitcase apiece. I bided my time.

After five days Gabe came back to our room and said we were sailing in the morning. I asked if it was on the same ship, and he said yes, but with a different captain, and that made him nervous, but he was taking the chance because he wanted to time his return to the expected Armistice, because port supervision would be light. The next morning we were installed in the small cabin in the hold next to the rats and the chickens. Gabe spent his days sleeping and nights drinking with the captain. I lay on my bunk smelling diesel fumes and not thinking. I had become an expert at not thinking. I had been not thinking for an entire year. Late at night I sometimes prowled the deck and looked at the inky sky. Swirls of light emanating from somewhere, perhaps inside my brain, cast the same impression as made by the wax seal. I felt explosive, restless, deadly calm.

After four days we stopped to off-load bananas and rum at an oil refinery outside Corpus Christi. The captain said that we should get off because Texas was less heavily patrolled than New Orleans. So, before dawn on the morning of November 11, we found ourselves put ashore on Padre Island, and hitched a ride on a cattle truck into Corpus. No one noticed our disheveled appearance as we checked into the first hotel we found because by mid-morning the town was bursting with parades. Armistice day in Corpus Christi was an explosion of tin whistles and cowbells and truck horns. Prayer meetings and parades. As day passed into night the celebrations became torch lit and drunken. I spent the day wandering around, fending off the occasional sloppy kiss and over enthusiastic hug, glad to be back, glad to have no identity other than a happy American, and later, when Gabe was taking his bearings in the downstairs saloon, glad to be enjoying cool sheets, diesel free ocean breeze. The next morning, as Gabe snored, I went through his luggage to find the Faberge eggs.

He, or Borodin, had, quite cleverly, separated the eggs from their holders, nesting one holder inside the other and hiding the whole bunch inside a pair of rolled up socks. The pinecone egg had been hidden inside a Mexican pot, kitchenware used to hold honey or *salsa*, sealed so that on casual inspection it looked like a rooster instead of something that came apart. The turquoise egg was concealed inside the matching hen. These two chickens were boxed as a set, tied with ribbon, a lovely gift for a mother or sister. I untied the box, opened the figurines by twisting the seal, examined the eggs, resealed the birds, placed them back in the box, redid the wrapping paper and retied the ribbon. Two eggs accounted for. It took me longer to locate the green wax seal. Finally I found it, disguised as—what?—a wax seal, but now encased in a leather pouch, with a flap that came over the top and snapped, the whole thing fitted inside a tooled leather writing case that held a supply of expensive paper and envelopes. This writing case I found inside the battered briefcase Gabe used for his odds and ends—shaving soap, a Spanish dictionary, a sketchpad with halfhearted renderings of bullfights. This, too, I could see as Borodin's handiwork. Only a real spy would know to hide something in plain sight. A letter seal disguised as a letter seal, what could be better?

I wondered where the yellow receipt book was, the one I had found in New Orleans, whether it had stayed behind in Mexico or been destroyed.

Gabe seemed to be carrying enough money for us to travel well, and the next day we took a train that changed engines in Houston and then went east to New Orleans. We stayed this time at a good hotel on Bourbon Street, ate oysters in the bar and washed them down with Jax beer, and Gabe spent the next day at a men's beauty emporium, coming out with hair straightened, pomaded and cut like a gentleman's. His eyebrows were tweezed, and he had picked up a pair of gold rimmed glasses, and, what with the seersucker suit, the new shoes and necktie, and the ten pounds he had gained in Mexico, he looked like an altogether different man.

His last acquisition before heading to Chicago was a new identity. He had business cards printed up, advertising himself as Howard Green, civil engineer, with an address and phone number in Chicago. Again, I could see evidence of Borodin's handiwork. Borodin had carried with him a few identifying items from Chicago—a library card, membership in an automobile association, a driver's license. In the back room of a watch repair shop near the railway station, while I perused the jewelry cases up front, Gabe took these bits of Borodin's identity and had them transformed into a passport and set of cards that certified to the existence of one Howard Green. That done, we went shopping one more time, bought and filled two new suitcases with winter clothes suitable for Chicago and then took the train north. It had been two years since I had hatched my plans to take Marcel on a train down to Portland. Now, as I sat at the window watching red clay levees fly by, I took out old thoughts of Marcel, examined them, and tried to imagine what two years of his life in Chicago had wrought.

CHAPTER 19

I had never been to Chicago. As a matter of fact, when I counted it up, my two years with Gabe had delivered me to six cities, three times the number of places I'd been to up until then. After Gabe I was to live in another dozen places before I came back and settled in Snoqualmie, and in some sense those dozen were also the result of Gabe, defensive moves to get myself out of the box he had put me in, or I had put myself in. That is the question. Whether others do to us or we do to ourselves. When I finish my story you can judge for yourself.

We arrived in Chicago at 4 a.m. on the morning of December 1, 1918. I still hadn't answered the question of whether I was going to look up Marcel. What had happened to him in the two years since he'd left Seattle was anybody's guess. Was he still studying in a music conservatory, was he enrolled in a university or playing in an orchestra? Maybe he had moved somewhere else, or gone home. I didn't know, and however well I imagined I understood Marcel, I didn't know him well enough to answer that. A boy of seventeen living with his mother is a different person from a young man of nearly twenty who has spent two years on his own. I was a different person, too, older certainly, three months shy of twenty-seven, but that seemed the only shy still left in me. In its place was a kind of hardness, a core of fused judgment and experience. I was different in other ways as well. For the first time in my life my skin was brown (it would never be that brown again).

Mexico had made inward changes as well. As always, I kept my counsel, but now it was a surer counsel, more tempered, less fearful. Never again would I be that young woman on the dock. Fate had dished out its worst and I had absorbed its blows. I was no longer unmoored by others' neglect or scorn. I had learned that even in inhospitable environments one could draw sustenance from simple courtesies. People like Rosa were everywhere, gentle, overlooked, waiting to be recognized.

Armed with this newly crystallized insight, I watched the intermittent lights of southern Illinois flash past and pondered where my first love fit into the picture. Certainly Marcel was gentle enough. Overlooked, waiting to be recognized. I was more or less sure that his intentions toward me had been infused with good will. The adoration he accorded me in his lovemaking had been genuine. So I didn't doubt his essential goodness or good will. The problem was knottier than that. It was whether my intentions toward him could be so characterized. Had my motives been honest and honorable? I searched my past conduct. Had I been too forceful, too clutching? Had I used him to rescue me from Gabe or from myself? Yes. But was he not in the same need of rescue from his mother? Or was that just a convenient excuse for my own actions? More importantly, could we start over again two years older and wiser? I laughed when I posed that question, rousing Gabe from his sleep. He looked up with a frown. I pulled in my smile and wondered who was the wiser, the girl on the train two years ago or this one, still on a train, this time with the wrong guy. First things first, I decided as the train pulled into Chicago's Union Station. Deal with obstacles one at a time. First Gabe, then Marcel.

* * *

In spite of my newfound resolve I muddled the two problems together almost from the start. Gabe moved us into a rooming house near the University of Chicago, on the near south side. Under his new name of Howard Green, Gabe started frequenting the library and book shops, noting the locations of various student meetings, getting a sense of where student opinion was heading a bare three weeks after the end of the war.

I was sent out to earn a living, a welcome relief from ships and trains and smuggling jewels. I found a coffee shop on Blackstone Boulevard that was advertising for help and told the owner I had worked a similar job in Seattle. I gave him Mr. Panopolous's name, knowing he'd never bother to check, and was in my apron cleaning crumbs from under the pie rack that same afternoon. I immediately started pocketing my tips, keeping them from Gabe, because I was already planning to run away, that's how I thought of it, running away, because I doubted my departure would be a civil one. Maybe that is an example of doing to myself what I saw then as having been done to me. Should I instead have had it out with Gabe the moment the train pulled in?

At any rate, within two days of our arrival, I was working six days a week, 6 a.m. to 4 p.m., while Gabe went out every afternoon and night, assessing the student mood, lining up his next moves. After about week of this I asked him what he was going to do about the eggs, whether he had yet contacted Fanya Borodin and the Communist Propaganda League. That was the first time he hit me. Not a heavy blow, just a slap, which he converted into a hard pinch and a jibe that I was too nosey and that Mikhail Borodin was no longer around, that now he was in charge. That's what I mean about having things done to you versus doing them to yourself. I took three lessons out of that incident: one, that my tone in addressing him had changed, and that at some level he recognized this and that this new use of physical force was recognition on his part that stronger measures to contain me were going to be necessary. That both pleased and concerned me. The second insight was that he was jealous, that he had noticed some regard for me from Borodin. That of course pleased me as well. The third lesson had to do with my mention of Fanya Borodin. I had a distinct sense that he was afraid of me. Of what I could tell Fanya Borodin. And that also made him do what he did. Were those three lessons worth the slap? At the time I thought so.

The next day, Sunday, in a show of submission, Gabe took me on the trolley to the west side, to an address on a scrap of paper that Borodin had given him. We rang one of the doorbells fixed on an unpainted board beside the door of a dilapidated tenement, then climbed to the third floor and knocked on the entrance to Number 8. A square of card paper stuck in the nameplate said "Borodin" in both English and Russian. Fanya Borodin opened the door with a cautious expression. She was a large dark woman, squat but muscular. The air from the apartment smelled musty, but she covered it with her strong lilac perfume. She looked from one of us to the other as we stood trying to look both businesslike and pleasant, at least that is what I was trying to do. Only with great effort could I imagine Mikhail Borodin in this place, with this wife, this identity. Then Mrs. Borodin wiped her hands on her apron. "Who are you?" she asked in a surprisingly high voice, and then "*Kto eto?*" in case she had misjudged and we were Russians. Gabe announced that he had come from Mexico, which sounded kind of abrupt to me, and indeed, that announcement set her to looking down the hall and ushering us in before Gabe decided to say more.

Inside, the apartment was clean, though over furnished, and was more welcoming than the outside stairwell or the first waft of odors would have suggested. I made myself at home on the horsehair sofa and accepted a glass of tea. I was from Everett and had visited worse. Gabe seemed unable to sit down and stood near the lace-curtained window and put down her offered tea untasted. A boy of about ten peeked out from the hallway that went back to the kitchen. None of us were sure how to begin. "Mrs. Borodin, I brought you something," I said, reaching into my satchel for a package of day-old cookies. "I work in a coffee shop," I explained as Fanya unpacked them from their makeshift wrapping in a fit of nervous exuberance and rushed off to the kitchen to find a plate.

"Shut the f— up," Gabe instructed. Maybe that is too modern an expression, but I remember the 'F-word' was in there somewhere. And that it was directed toward me. So I shut up, and contented myself only with a smile when Fanya came back and passed around the cookies. She motioned to the boy to come and eat, which drew another glare from Gabe that pleased me enormously. I smiled and gave Gabe my stage look of adoration in return.

He cleared his throat, oddly nervous at being the center of attention.

"Yes?" Fanya prompted, as she shifted her lilac scented bulk from one buttock to the other. The boy watched us as we each spoke in turn, alert to the unfolding possibilities. How much he reminded me of his father.

"I have a gift for you, from your husband," Gabe announced, motioning for me to bring out the other package, the wrapped one with clay chickens. I handed it to Mrs. Borodin, watching her closely, wondering why Gabe had not brought the writing case that contained the third egg. Slowly she unwrapped her gift, smoothing down the paper, looping the red ribbon as it was untied into a little nested circle. Finally she opened the box, drew forth first the tissue wrapped hen and then the rooster. She set both figurines on the side table where she had placed the box, stood and examined them, breathing heavily. She did not touch them, or comment, and when the boy moved to examine them she spoke sharply to him in Russian, warning him away. Then she carefully wrapped each one up again in its tissue paper and put each back in the box and closed the lid. "Is there anything else?" she asked in a voice that attempted calm but belied her agitated state.

I could see Gabe's mind working, and knew that if she had not asked this he would have neglected to mention the other present of the writing case. *Thief!* I was pleased to have finally plumbed his essence. Then I smiled, because I knew what I was going to do. "Next time," I said, breaking my silence, and letting my words cover the real meaning of my smile.

To change the subject, to cover what he must have thought was a slip on my part, Gabe asked about what contacts he was to make. He phrased it differently of course, as if he were simply a newcomer to the city, looking for someone that might help him find work. He gave her his phony business card, explained that he was trying to discover what people he should talk to, how to establish the right contacts. They chatted a bit about work he had done in the past, mining and road building. I doubted there was much call for that in the west side of Chicago but kept my peace. He asked about ward politicians, whether those were the right people to ask for help. Fanya demurred, said those were important people, surely, but there were others. She pretended to think about who was the best person to refer him to. Finally she wrote down a name. And said this person could be found most evenings at the Workman's Circle, or at the lectures at Hull House, or failing that, Friday afternoons at the Turkish bath. Gabe pocketed the scrap of paper, thanked her, and said he'd be back in a few weeks time, to visit again and tell her of his progress. Fanya rose quickly, now that business was done, and escorted us to the doorway. "I, too, will look after your progress," she said, in a voice both motherly and, to my ears, holding a bit of warning. The last thing I did was catch the eye of the boy, Norman, exchanging with him a bucket full of knowing, as I had done so often with his father.

I figured that when Gabe said "a few weeks," he meant at least two before he would go back to Fanya Borodin. That meant if I were going to find Marcel I needed to do so soon.

I wasn't yet sure that I wanted to find Marcel, not sure I wanted to face the distance between where things had been and where they might be now. But if I were going to make a clean break with Gabe, I told myself, I might as well also face the music with Marcel. In truth I was hoping for some kind of miracle. When I spoke of Marcel going to a conservatory in Chicago it was somewhat misleading. In those days, a music conservatory was more of an informal system of tutoring, usually connected with an orchestra such as the Chicago Symphony. At least that was my first guess about where to start looking. I found an excuse to go downtown one afternoon after work and went to the symphony box office. It was closed, as was the administrative office located behind a mahogany door with a posted notice. I went back home with a phone number, and tried, unsuccessfully, for a day or two to call. When I finally got through, a cultured and very disinterested receptionist told me that such information was confidential. I tried the telephone book for a listing, but, as expected, found nothing. I thought about other Chicago orchestras and going through a similar search with them, but then it occurred to me that Marcel might have taken a musicology class at the University of Chicago, much as he had in Seattle, so I went to the university administrative offices and got a course listing and picked what seemed to me the most likely classes he might have taken, and wrote down the names of the professors and their office locations. All this took me the better part of a week.

At the same time I was sorting through the other part of my plan. I needed money, that was for sure, for a train ticket back to Seattle if nothing else. I decided to take another job, four to nine, at a bookstore, and made arrangements for them to hold my first pay. That pay packet fixed the timetable for my departure. Christmas day, or Christmas Eve if there was a late train somewhere, anywhere that got me out of Chicago. I figured if I didn't pay that week's rent, could hold the landlord off until I left town, I could get away with enough money to buy a ticket and eat reasonably well until I got to Seattle.

I briefly considered taking some money from Gabe's ample supply, but didn't, in part because he always kept it with him, and counted it religiously every night before getting in bed, in part because I didn't want any connection that might give him a pretext to follow me. There was another reason. I had decided to steal the Faberge letter seal.

You might ask why, besides the fact that I coveted it, and the answer is I don't know. Partly because Gabe wanted it, and I didn't want him to have it. Partly because it had already been stolen, by Lenin, from some poor Romanov (I guess you could call the Romanovs poor at this point), although whatever family member it was that owned it, he or she was most likely dead. But mostly I don't know why it was I wanted to steal it. Because I wanted it. As a souvenir. But more than that, the egg and my act of taking it felt symbolic of everything that had happened to me up to that point, everything that was going to happen. It was my turning point. My moving from having things done to me to doing them to myself, for myself. By doing this, I told myself, I was declaring myself to be something of value. An outlaw. I was stealing fire.

CHAPTER 20

As I got close to the time of my departure I was again feeling bereft. My brave bargain with myself, of being no longer afraid, was just a front. The thought of seeing Marcel, then heading back to Seattle, made my stomach ache. But I had money, at least, and a plan, and that was better than nothing. I comforted myself by making a list. First, the Faberge egg (how to steal it). Second, Marcel (how to find him). Third, (when I found him), what to say. After that I stopped, that was more than enough to chew on. My thoughts then went to Rosa, the promise I'd made to go back to the *Union Record* so she could find me if she ever needed to, and then to my mother, and so I put down a Number Four: everything else. I decided not to worry about Number Four, or Number Three, for that matter, and just concentrate instead on One and Two. I returned to the university library and looked at the bulletin board and studied train schedules. There was an 11 p.m. departure for Denver on Christmas Eve. That sounded fine. I had never been to Denver. Going straight to Seattle was probably not a good idea in case Gabe found out too quickly about my departure. I realized that whatever plan I came up with for stealing the egg would have to be executed at the last minute, so I put that problem aside and concentrated instead on how to find Marcel.

There was a course offered in the fine arts department called "Musicality of the Baroque." Something about that appealed to my ear, and I thought it might appeal to Marcel's as well. So I begged off from work one afternoon and made my way to the music department, room 207, arriving just as class was ending. It was a large rehearsal hall, three rows of chairs bolted on tiers in a semicircle. In the pit, along with a grand piano and a disorderly collection of music stands, stood a long-haired maestro, waving his slender hands and chopping the air and talking about tonal variations. I waited in the back, studying him with Marcel's eyes. When class was finished, I followed him down the hall and caught him wrapping his muffler around his long neck. "Professor Danzig," I ventured.

"Yes?" He flashed a smile somehow both wolfish and courtly. I had an odd sensation, the first time in my life it occurred to me I might be attractive. Maybe my Mexico sojourn had altered my exterior. I was browner, certainly, but maybe something else as well. I told myself not to stammer and asked about Marcel, whether he had ever been the professor's student, whether he knew where I might find him.

"You are, also, a musician?" He looked as if this were an unlikely prospect.

"No," I said. "A friend from Seattle. In town for a few days."

That seemed innocuous enough, but Professor Danzig seemed to think there was more. After examining me enough to make me blush, he at last recalled that he had met a young man named Marcel—Freed, or was it Freedman?—at a party. A party given by the first violinist at the Chicago Ballet. Maybe this Freedman fellow was in the orchestra there, or taking private lessons with his friend. At any rate Professor Danzig gave me the name of his friend, and a telephone number, and said to mention that we had spoken. But in the mean time, he suggested that I go to the free Sunday concert given by the orchestra. It was nothing much, he said, Christmas music, the dance of the sugar plum fairies, but I might find my young man there, playing in the Palm Court at the Art Institute. He smiled his benign and knowing smile. I could have hugged him, but thought better of it.

Sunday was my day off, and, as Gabe usually slept in until noon, I planned to start off as soon as I could thereafter. This particular Sunday began as usual, me waking up about seven, then sitting in our narrow bed for three or four hours with Gabe's arm wrapped around my middle and his head in my lap while I listened to him snore. I was permitted to get up and relieve myself once during these Sunday mornings. Otherwise Gabe liked to have me handy while he slept. It seemed too much to argue the point that I was awake and he was asleep when all there was to do in the room if I did get up was to sit in the one straight-backed chair. Besides, when Gabe finally did awake, I had other responsibilities that required my presence back in bed.

Gabe was a once-a-week man. Since that first time in Boise, neither Sunday nor morning, our coupling had settled into an unvarying routine, the only change being how long it took. The first few times, because I was scared, or ashamed, it seemed to excite him, and he took his time, to make sure I was properly humbled. But then his attentions drifted to other excitements, and he lost interest in his weekly servicing of me. I became part of a larger routine, an end-of-the-week equivalent of a beer and a chaser. I accepted this, indeed considered it part of the blessing of becoming invisible. But, as I had learned when I provoked him regarding the visit to Mrs. Borodin, I stepped out of invisibility at my peril. So I was compliant that Sunday morning to get my duties over as quickly and uneventfully as possible.

Sometime around noon Gabe woke up, scratched his belly, then reached over and began scratching mine. After this was done I was expected to get up, cook breakfast on our hot plate, while he went off to the bathroom to relieve himself. Then he came back to put on his weekly change of underwear (that I had dutifully put out), then eat while reading the newspaper I had fetched, finish dressing and go out to visit one or another of his new friends. Sometimes he took me with him and sometimes not. This Sunday I was hoping not. I had prepared an excuse, Christmas shopping for my mother, overtime at the bookstore, but it wasn't necessary. This day, after his bath in the tub of water I had heated and poured, after he tore open his neatly wrapped packet of laundry I had collected and paid for, after he slapped me on the rump and said he was going out and not to wait up, I nodded and kept my face neutral, reminding myself that this was the last Sunday he got to maul my body and that I would never have to do it again. That made me quite cheerful, and I must have smiled, because he took my expression as some kind of affection, or satisfaction, and made a comment that flattered himself in the sexual performance department. I had to laugh — Rosa was right — he was a pig! But Gabe took the laugh as mockery and so I had to work my way out of that, which I did by more or less telling the truth, that Rosa and Manny had popped into my mind, that I was wondering how they were making out in New York as man and wife.

That got Gabe to laughing too, and he told me various unflattering stories about Manny, various things that had gone on down in Mexico that I wasn't supposed to have known about, and I asked him whether he thought Roy and Evelyn were still in Mexico or whether they had moved on, and if so, where. At this, he shut down, and said I shouldn't ask about such things, that I ought to know better. So I apologized, said I was curious, and left it at that. After he was gone, in the few minutes before I had to take the train downtown, I thought about the matter of the Faberge egg and how I was going to steal it.

I was pretty sure the Mexican writing case was somewhere in his suitcase, or dresser drawer, somewhere in the room. But the chances of the egg being in it, instead of hidden separately, were slim. If it wasn't in the room, the only other possibilities were with a friend, and I guessed he didn't yet know anyone he trusted enough in Chicago, or in a locker somewhere to which only he had the key or combination. The combination lock possibility bothered me, because he would have no particular reason to go there in the next few days, and even if I followed him night and day, unless he took the egg out of the locker while I was watching through a telescope, there was no way I could discover the combination. Of course, I didn't even know if there was a combination, or if he had a locker.

I found the writing case in his drawer. Inside were the original paper, envelopes, as well as the yellow invoice pad I had first discovered in New Orleans, some receipts and a train schedule. But no Faberge egg. So I spent an hour going through everything in the room, all his belongings, every nook and cranny in all the furniture as well as looking in the bathroom down the hall. Where was it hidden? How was I going to find it? As I took the train to downtown Chicago I kept thinking about where Gabe could have hidden the egg, trying to fathom his mind, instead of thinking about what I was going to say to Marcel at our hoped-for meeting

It was just as well. I got there late, and the palm court was filled to capacity, and I wasn't able to get anywhere near the orchestra, to see if Marcel was down there in the violin section. I spent the next half hour standing behind a marble pillar, among the potted plants, thinking about how beautifully sound carried in all this marble, thinking of palaces, and how someday I would like to see a palace, go to Europe or Byzantium. With murmurs from the audience, a dozen little girls, skinny and tall, short and plump, decked out in lavender tutus, rose to pass around baskets of sweets, and I thought how, when I was that age, I would have liked a dress like that, to be among the sugar plum fairies. But I took hold of myself, told myself such day dreams were not productive, that I was twenty-six, no longer a child, as close to an orphan as a person could be with a mother still alive, and I'd better get to wishing for things that were possible. I promised myself I'd someday visit a palace, but gave up on the notion of a lavender ballet dress.

With the final applause, the orchestra stood and bowed. People got up from their seats and moved past me toward the exit. I tried to make my way forward around the palms and pillars to get to where the orchestra was packing up. It took me a few minutes moving against the crowd to get to where I could scan the musicians as they folded their music stands and talked with relatives and admirers. I admit nerves made me take longer to get there than was absolutely necessary. When I did get to the front, I could see a few of the musicians had already left. Reluctantly I moved my eyes away from the door where the musicians were leaving to the place where the remaining violinists still congregated. There was Marcel, head down, putting his chin pad into his violin case. He continued to look down, finding specks of dust to brush off the velvet lining. All of a sudden I knew he had seen me, in the back, behind the potted palms. And, instead of making a hasty exit, he had waited.

This gave me the courage to speak. "Marcel."

He looked up, flushed, a fearful look in his eyes.

"I found out about you from Professor Danzig. I'm staying on the south side. For a few days." I added this last to give us both some protection.

I waited to see what he'd make of this. Eventually he smiled a painful half smile, whether because I was here, or only for a few days, I wasn't sure.

"I'm glad you're doing well," I added, to imply I accepted that he'd moved on with his life.

He didn't say anything, just continued to look at me with a combination of awe and uncertainty, as if I were about to ask something of him he couldn't possibly fulfill.

He needs time, I decided. "I'm going back to Seattle," I said. "I've been away the last few months." Still no response. "I suppose you get back there, from time to time."

He nodded, still not sure where I was going.

"Next time you get back, I'll probably be there. Working at the *Union Record.*"

I waited. Wanting to add, Call me. Or, better yet, Let me come with you, for coffee, a slice of raspberry pie.

Still that same pleasant, wary look.

"I enjoyed the concert. I miss hearing you play." That's not all I miss, I could feel myself trying to tell him. His look of frozen fear grew. Time to end this, I decided. I stuck out my hand to prevent myself from throwing my arms around him. When he didn't reciprocate even that small gesture, I took his hand, the left one that held the bow, that same one that had ranged so beautifully over my naked skin. I held his palm and thumb and lovely fingers in my hands, stroked them, remembering, and then, unable to stop, bent down and kissed the open center.

"I miss you," I told him, and then fled.

On the train back to the south side, I thought about what had happened, or not happened, and how I felt. Mostly, I felt elated. That he had waited for me after the concert, that, at some confused level, he still wanted my company. He hadn't turned our abortive trip to Portland into some kind of awful memory that withered all feeling. In some way he still loved me, and that seemed enough for the time being. I decided that even if I couldn't steal the egg, I would take the mysterious yellow invoice pad. I didn't know what it was or what it meant, but I wanted some leverage, some way to hurt Gabe if need be, and figured that might be the best I could do.

CHAPTER 21

I had four days until Christmas Eve. That was when I got my pay packet from the bookstore, the first day I could leave. How to find the egg, get Gabe to produce it, how to steal it without his knowing it was me. I thought about hiring a thief, a real one to come in and ransack the room, but without being sure if the egg was there it seemed hardly worth the risk—much less the cost. Much less trying to find a reliable thief four days before Christmas. I hadn't given up on that idea, I knew a couple of disreputables, who hung around trash bins in back of the coffee shop, but the more I turned over that idea the more I could see its faults.

For one thing, for theft to work to maximum effect, I should be with Gabe at the time, then come back to the ransacked room, share his dismay, fury, urge him call the police, etc. Of course, Gabe would not want to call the police, would not want to attract the attention, so I would be spared that interrogation, but not the one that would come instead from Gabe, who would, of course, suspect me of complicity, even if I had been with him the whole time.

That got me to thinking about Gabe's suspicious nature, how, whatever I did, if I took one thing, his tooth powder, he would think I stole it. Imagine when I left town. The only way to throw him off track, I decided, was to plant his suspicion on an alternate thief, and that set me to thinking about Fanya. Not Mrs. Borodin herself, but the whole Bolshevik apparatus she was the broad face of. Gabe knew he was supposed to hand over three eggs. She had clearly expected something more, whether she knew about the third egg, or was awaiting further instructions or just voicing pleasantries, I didn't know. And Gabe didn't either. But, as part of my return pleasantries, I had promised "something" the next time we visited. So Gabe was in a pickle and he knew it.

What if I invented a scenario in which I went back to visit Mrs. Borodin? Then it came to me that it would be better if Fanya Borodin came to me. Or Gabe thought she did. Came to our door, unexpectedly, when I was alone, and so I became flustered, wasn't sure what to do, and told her Gabe wasn't home but that I would relay a message. What if she, indeed, had left a message—a note saying "Come see me"—or some such? Gabe wouldn't know her handwriting—but I remembered the handwriting on the card on the door saying "Borodin"— could I approximate that script? I had studied Mikhail Borodin's handwriting, had noticed the peculiar formations of the letters "m" and "n" and "p," a style that seemed to flow from the habit of writing Cyrillic. I sat down and practiced some words, writing first "Borodin," which was all I had to go on from the tiny card, then, when I was more or less satisfied, worked on "Mrs." and then, at the last minute, decided to change it to "Mme." which seemed more mysterious.

I worked on different versions of my short request and finally settled on "Visit soon." I thought about how to form the letters "c" and "s," tried to remember what I had seen of Mikhail Borodin's hand writing. Then it occurred to me there might be a note in a Russian hand posted on the bulletin board at the Slavic languages department. So I decided to do my best copy and then compare it with what I could find posted there. I was counting on my note from Fanya Borodin to scare Gabe and force him to retrieve the egg so I would know where it was and also that the note would create a plausible explanation when his room was ransacked.

Of course, there remained a problem of Gabe's interrogation of me when I gave him the news about Fanya's visit. Also the question of whether he would retrieve the egg soon enough for me to steal it and escape before Christmas. But for the moment, that was the best I could do. On my way to the coffee shop I took my practice pad and went by the Slavic languages department and stole a posted note about the test scores on a Pushkin exam, and spent the afternoon between customers tracing letters and rearranging them into Fanya's hand for her summons to Gabe.

That night, after my shift at the bookstore, I changed into my nightgown and lay down on the bed and thought through my plan. I went over it several times, trying to find holes, trying to imagine how I would deliver the note from Fanya, how I could manage to prey on Gabe's fear of being found out by the Bolsheviks—as a thief, an unreliable comrade—all the while protecting myself from his suspicions and wrath. I was not expecting Gabe until eleven that night, the earliest he typically came back to the room, and so, still immersed in my feverish preparations, I got up and went down the hall to get water to make tea. On my way back, carrying the kettle, I remembered the mattress. I had forgotten to check the mattress. Of course! How could I be so stupid? If I were going to hide an object the weight and size of an egg, I would put it in the mattress.

I got back to the room and put on the kettle and then sat down and tried to think. How would I go about hiding something in a mattress? In a way it wouldn't be found? It would have to go in a place where the lump couldn't be felt, and also where an incision in the mattress ticking could easily be covered. It was now ten-thirty, and I thought about getting out my nail scissors and starting in, but decided the risk of Gabe's coming back and finding me was too great. How could I explain the mattress on the floor with me slicing holes in it?

So I forced myself to wait, and drank my tea, and thought about all the mattresses I'd ever known. The manufactured ones, sold in stores, all had a label. If I were going to make an incision in a mattress, to insert a small object, I'd pull the stitching out of the label and then make a cut in the fabric beneath it, put in my egg, burying it as deep as I could, then stitch the mattress together and finally sew the label back in place. I doubted Gabe, if he did this, would be a good enough seamstress to make the repair invisible. Indeed, I counted on the fact that he was too fatheaded to realize that his improvised skullduggery wasn't perfect.

In the few minutes left before Gabe's arrival, could I at least find the label and see if it had been tampered with? Or locate it and feel if the egg might be nearby? I couldn't resist. The label could only be sewn in one of four places, top center upside, top center downside, or bottom center up, bottom underneath. I ruled out top upside and top down as too likely to be discovered. So the egg would be found, if at all, underneath. I went to the bed and pressed both hands, top and bottom, along the lower several inches of the mattress. About four inches in I could feel the sewn edge of the label. Moving my hands in unison, I pressed down and up, one small section at a time, as if I were a doctor examining a stomach. Found! A small hard lump just to the right of center and about eight inches from the bottom edge. I got up, and tucked the sheets and blanket back in, then sat on the bed and tried to feel the lump just by pushing down with my hand. The outline was faint, a lump of batting, nothing more. Satisfied, and with pounding heart, I lay down again in the bed, pulled up the covers, and tried to slow my breath so that when Gabe came home he would think I was asleep.

I don't think I slept a moment that night, or if I did, had

feverish dreams of marble halls and potted palms and escape.

The rest was relatively easy. The next day, after the lunch crowd left the coffee shop, I begged off work for an errand, went back to my room, pulled the mattress down on the floor, turned it over, undid the clumsy white stitching Gabe had used to sew up the label, then picked apart the even rougher stitching that held together his three-inch incision in the mattress. Out came my precious egg. I put it quickly in my pocket and then, sweating and heart racing, I sewed up the cut, trying to mimic Gabe's poor handwork, and replicated his clumsy stitching of the label. The whole thing, including making the bed, had taken less than thirty minutes. I thought about where to keep the egg, and decided back in the coffee shop, behind the scouring powder and rat poison, in a part of the kitchen no one went but me.

I was nearly home free. There remained the part about Fanya and the visit, Gabe's interrogation about the note and then the getaway itself. It was now December 22, two days from my planned escape. As I lay in bed that night, waiting for Gabe, I went over and over the scene between us that I was sure the note would produce. Should I deliver it the following night? Or wait until the last possible moment? Maybe I shouldn't do it at all. Maybe just leaving the note at the scene after the ransacking would be sufficiently ominous, maybe Gabe would just hightail, confused as to who suspected him of what. I decided, in the end, that that was the better plan, the least likely to expose me, less clear-cut. Gabe would suspect me anyway, but what I didn't want was for him to know for sure.

That left me all of the next day to compose the note. I drifted off to sleep in a kind of exhausted bliss and didn't even wake when Gabe came in that night.

* * *

Of course, the next morning I wasn't so sure my plan was

perfect. How could I disappear on the same night the room was ransacked and not have him think I was involved? Why wouldn't he presume the truth, that I was heading back to Seattle, and follow me? What if he went to Fanya Borodin and she told him she had never been to visit or left a note? Finally, I decided it was too late to come up with a better plan, except to leave earlier in the evening and take whatever train was leaving the station. I had agreed to work at the bookstore on Christmas Eve but my two weeks pay packet was due me that afternoon. When I collected my money at the beginning of my shift, I asked if I might leave at eight that night instead of nine, and was given a lecture about responsibility. So I apologized. And decided to leave at seven.

I didn't dare pack or do any ransacking until just before I was ready to leave. So that night, at seven, I excused myself and went to the ladies room, then gathered my coat from the storeroom and let myself out the back. I was feeling very anxious. Six whole blocks to the rooming house. It was starting to snow. I was feeling feverish, but I was sure it was just nerves. I had borrowed a boning knife from the coffee shop — well, taken it, stolen it, I suppose, this wasn't the time for scruples. I had it wrapped in a dishrag in my purse. I'd taken the egg from behind the borax and wrapped it in a clean cloth as well. Both lay in the bottom of my now very heavy purse. Along with thirty-seven dollars that I hoped would get me to Seattle through points in between.

When I opened the door to the room my hands were shaking. I half expected to see Gabe sitting on the bed. But no Gabe, just the same dreary room, with my clothes in the top drawer and my suitcase on top of his in the wardrobe. I took it down and threw in everything I owned. Then I took the writing case from underneath the underwear in Gabe's drawer, and started to replace the egg in its brown leather compartment. Then I changed my mind, taking only the yellow invoice pad and adding that to my purse, then pulling out the boning knife and slashing up the leather-tooled writing case, the mattress, the bedclothes, pulling out drawers and throwing Gabe's clothes around the room. I cut up some of his shirts and pried off the soles in his extra pair of shoes. I was enjoying this, but it was taking up too much time and so I left off that and took out the note from Fanya Borodin and placed it on top the dresser—only after I had swiped off the hair oil and the rest of Gabe's toiletries that had accumulated on the grimy doily since we moved in.

I was almost ready to go. I straightened up, took a deep breath, put on my coat and took hold of my suitcase. I started to leave. Then turned around and decided my clothes and suitcase had to stay. I took everything out, retrieved a pillowcase, which only had a slight cut in it, and selected only a skirt, two blouses, my Mexican dress and two changes of underwear from the pile I'd just dropped on the floor. The rest I cut up with the boning knife and left intermixed with Gabe's. Then I took the bottle of Gabe's hair oil and hit the edge of the door. The bottle broke and I gauged a few scratches in the wood near the lock. I wondered if it looked like someone had broken in and I'd been kidnapped. I hoped so, and considered if I should use the broken glass to cut my finger and smear blood around, but decided not to, because I doubted Gabe would notice a little blood and I didn't feel I had a lot left to contribute at that point. So I looked around one last time, checked to make sure no neighbors down the hall had peeked out at the noise, and put my pillowcase over my shoulder, kept my purse close to my side and marched down the hall, down the stairs and out the door. The streetcar stop was two blocks away and I made it without once succumbing to the urge to look back.

CHAPTER 22

All my life I seemed to make my getaways on trains. This departure was no exception. I arrived at Chicago's Union Station with all my worldly possessions in a used pillowcase and a big heavy purse. After what had happened in my escape to Portland I was taking no chances, and went straight to the counter and bought a ticket for the next train. That was how I found myself heading to Milwaukee, a scant ten minutes later, trying to decide whether to connect on an overnight to Minneapolis or stay where I landed. I settled in for the three-hour milk run that stopped in Evanston, Wilmette, Highland Park, North Chicago, Kenosha and Racine. That suited me fine, I was going nowhere, just leaving somewhere and someone.

I decided to set myself a late night topic for reflection and ruminated on several before settling on two: 1) "How I let myself in for the likes of Gabe Rabinowitz (now known as "Howard Green")" and, 2) "What to do when I got back to Seattle." A secondary question was why I was going to Seattle in the first place, considering that Gabe, when he took a mind to, could find me there in ten seconds flat. Particularly if I went back to the *Union Record* and asked for a job.

As I turned all that over in my mind it became clear that I was not inclined to be run off, that the time felt right for me to hold my ground. There were few people in this world who cared for me and that I could rely on, and Harry Ault was one. (I put Marcel and my pa in the category of people who cared for me but couldn't be relied on, while my mother could be relied on, but only to be herself.) I was no longer feeling bereft, merely determined, and that meant going back to Seattle and taking up my life where I had left off.

The train was pulling into North Chicago, would soon to be crossing into Wisconsin, so I turned my attention back to Gabe, why I had let myself be led into his lair in the first place. The more I pondered that time on the docks, the more it seemed that I had been like someone buried alive, and when someone feels that way they just claw to daylight anyway they can. That's what I had been doing. Gabe and his aura appeared as a kind of daylight, an opening to a world. Mostly what he gave me was an excuse to shut down. My heart lay frozen for the entire two years I was with him, and maybe distance was what was allowing me, on the train, to breathe again.

I touched my slim wad of cash pinned inside my camisole. Should I spend the night in a hotel and then move on to Minneapolis? I decided to wait and see what kind of reception I got in Milwaukee and move on only if it felt right. When we pulled into the station at 2:25 a.m. I stood on the snowy loading dock and looked around. Then walked across the street to a hotel that seemed respectable and asked for a single room. As I signed the guest register I realized I was beginning to enjoy the sense of being a woman on her own, the slightly racy air of it, relishing my anonymity. When the train pulled into the station I had been remembering that fateful trip to Portland, my interrogation in Olympia. Mostly I remembered Marcel's face, the guarded, frightened eyes. The relief when he saw his mother accompanied by the sheriff's deputy and Gabe.

I'm saved, that was the expression on his face, and that, more than anything, was the bitter pill. That and the painful realization that I still loved him, still needed something only he could provide, while it was unlikely to be forthcoming.

But, as I toted my pillowcase and heavy purse up the stairs of the Terminus Hotel, I reflected that at least I felt no remorse that day, no shame in kidnapping him. In making the decision to take him away to Portland I had felt strong, stronger than ever before in my life. It had been a flight blessed with purpose. I had sworn to protect him, to sustain and honor him. In my heart I had married him. The thwarting of that, the discrediting and discarding of it, that is what shamed me. That is what led me to Gabe and to Mexico. That's what got stirred up when I saw Marcel in the Palm Court.

Gabe's was the other face I spent my sleepless night studying. The Terminus Hotel was located hard on the freight yards, which came alive well before dawn. As I tossed and turned, I saw Gabe's eyes as I had first encountered them on the docks. At the coroner's office when we identified my brother's body. In the hotel room in Boise. Mirrors in which to see myself. Eyes taking me for a weakling, someone to be used. A pitiful creature who had bet her life on the big casino, trying to hook on to her brother's winning streak. Well, now, in Milwaukee, cradling my Faberge egg, I decided Gabe was the one who had made the bad bet. And I was the one who had an ace up my sleeve. I didn't know who held the power in the new faction he was angling for position in, but I knew its rules would be ruthless. Loyalty above all, reliability in toeing the line. Not Gabe's strong suit. He coveted power, but didn't have the temperament to play on a team. That was my reading. Poor Gabe. How was he going to explain I had stolen the booty he was instructed to guard?

I settled into my bed as the sky grew lighter. Christmas morning. How did I feel this moment, how had I changed? Some things were clear. I knew how to check into a hotel and stare down the night clerk. Thanks to Harry Ault, I knew the basics of typesetting. Thanks to Mexico, I knew a fair amount of Spanish. I had learned how to judge people. How to live in a household and yet keep my peace. I'd learned the pleasure of coded communication between friends who trusted each other but not the rest of the world. As sleep began to catch up with me that daybreak I remembered my first train trip, the one on my leap year birthday almost three years before. I'd been setting out to attend my brother's university. Well, I hadn't done that, but I had gotten an education.

* * *

Later that morning I awoke a second time and remembered it was Christmas. Christmas Day, it had been a long time since I'd felt anything hopeful about that. I tried to remember a time when I had looked forward to waking up on Christmas morning, and finally recalled a year when I was about seven, when my pa had promised me a pony and I'd known I wasn't going to get one. He had watched me with a sly satisfied grin while I dutifully went through the lumpy stocking full of nuts, an apple in the toe and an orange in the heel, and then after breakfast he'd started whistling and then Zeke, his drinking buddy, called from the yard, and sure enough, the two of them had rented an old dray horse for the day, and we spent the remainder of that Christmas, the part that didn't rain too hard, visiting his pals, me set atop this old sway-backed mare, perched like the queen I was.

That cheering thought in mind, I dressed and went downstairs and found the restaurant and just about everything else in Milwaukee closed. There was a sideboard set out with coffee and rolls, so I breakfasted on that, and then went out to find something to occupy myself. Churchgoing was the order of the day, so I went to the early Catholic mass, down on Greenfield Avenue, and then, when that broke up, found a Lutheran service just starting. The Lutherans had cookies and cider afterwards for which I was grateful. Next, I listened to what the Congregationalists had to say about Christmas, then the Episcopalians, and finally, about two in the afternoon, showed up at the Pentecostal mission and had a full turkey dinner with the rest of the lost souls washed up in Milwaukee that day. All in all, the best Christmas I'd had since the horse showed up, and, as the sun set in my hotel room overlooking the freight yard, I topped off the day with a little display of lit candles I'd collected on my visits, all arranged on my battered hotel bureau with its scant burden of my clothes spread out between all five drawers. For the first time that day I thought of Gabe and what he would have made of the cut-up clothes he'd found on our floor, then corrected that thought—his floor, his alone. And with that, I fished out one of my good lisle stockings, a run in it but no matter, and put my velvet encased egg in it, then threw on top the small bag of sweets I'd taken away from the Pentecostal dinner, and hung the whole thing up with the stocking top wedged in the upper drawer of my bureau. I turned off the overhead light and sat back on my bed and squinted my eyes so I could see the dance of the five candle flames and sang "Good King Wenceslas" twice through, remembering all four verses. And found myself happier than I could ever remember. I unwrapped my present, kissed my egg and used the top of the stocking to wipe away my tears.

The next morning I asked the desk clerk to hold my pillowcase luggage, checked to make sure the Faberge egg was tucked in my purse, and took the streetcar out to Marquette University. I went to the library first, to breathe in the smell of the place, to remind myself again how much my life was the same and how much it was different from three years ago. I asked at the circulation desk if there was a coffee shop nearby, and got directed to the commercial strip that lines every urban university, walked past the bookstores and cheap restaurants and Chinese laundries, found a restaurant that was looking for a waitress, promised to start the next day and asked the manager where I might rent a room.

So, twenty-four hours after making my escape from Chicago, I was settling my clothes in a new bureau, this one all my own, my few sets of underwear in the top, what little else in the middle and bottom. I hung up my coat, my one skirt, two blouses and my Mexican dress in the wardrobe, and laid my toiletries out on the dresser. I remember humming my pa's favorite tune as I did this: "Hold the fort for we are coming..." I wondered how long I would be there, when I would make my promised return to Seattle. Wondered whether I should get in touch with my mother, how my pa was doing. I thought about my brother's grave, Joe Hill's scant portion of ashes dusted on top. Wondered if my brother was happy in the company of Gabe's assembled martyrs. Was my brother a martyr, I asked myself, or a simple fool? Was he, perhaps, not the boy I had thought he was. I had taken a train to meet him, like a lover almost, but he had not turned out to be the gallant swain I had wanted him to be. Perhaps he was simply another version of Gabe, charming, ambitious, good at pleasing his elders, at manipulating events, at gambling with history and other people's lives.

I remembered again my Christmas with the horse. How my mother's face had lit up, then settled into a kind of quiet happiness. For me? Because my pa had finally done something right? But Horace, he'd been jealous, first whiney and then throwing a tantrum. I recalled that it had been me— out of pity almost—that had let him climb up behind me on the mare, to be consort in my court. Maybe, I told myself, it was time for me to stop wondering about things I had no answers for and start making a life.

Part Three

CHAPTER 23

I had no particular plan for how long I was going to stay in Milwaukee, until leaving felt right, I suppose, by which I meant when it felt safe. But it turns out I left before that, and that decision, if you can call it a decision, always bothered me. Two parts of me were warring, one part wanting to keep safe, against the other part calling itself a coward for choosing safety over—what? courage? conviction? That other side propelled me to take precipitous action one afternoon in February of 1919, no more than six weeks after I had arrived.

I had rented a room, as usual, and gotten a job at one of the shops that lined Wisconsin Avenue near Marquette. In my spare time I haunted the Marquette library, reading magazines and newspapers, trying to piece together the events of the world I had missed during my year and a half in Mexico. The Spanish Flu had killed over a half million people in America. Popular belief was that troop ships had imported this infestation. But that was not the only infestation brought on by the war in the public mind. Germans had been supplanted as the alien enemy. The Justice Department, through its aptly named Alien Enemy Bureau, was officially switching the nation's vigilance from Germans to Communists, especially alien ones. Milwaukee, with its German population and socialist politics, was a fishbowl in which to see our government lash out in both directions at once.

Eugene Debs, the head of the Socialist Party, and Victor Berger, a Milwaukee congressman, were on trial for espionage under a sweeping new law. The U.S. Attorney General, A. Mitchell Palmer, had lobbied hard for the bill, which, he believed, would aid his presidential ambitions. Woodrow Wilson was ill, hidden from view, his wife rumored to be leading the country. Strikes in all sectors were sweeping the nation.

All this I read in the Marquette library, shifting from daily newspapers to right-wing magazines to the labor and socialist press. Filtering events from one side, then another, I was trying to orient myself, to find some ground on which I could stand. Coming home to the United States, I felt no identity, no right to an identity at all, as if that had been scrubbed clean by events since my brother's death. Any effort on my part to put on a fresh face, any fresh trappings of political views, would be immediately attacked—as inauthentic, manufactured with the intent to deceive, as deeply, dangerously suspect. Or so I thought. I had done nothing wrong, except cross a border without going through customs, live in a Mexican commune more or less against my will. But that, of course, would be enough for the Justice Department. Eugene Debs and Victor Berger were on trial for much less. Under the Espionage Act, my actions were criminal. That much was clear. My father and brother's colorful history only sealed the case.

So what to do. I was neither enemy nor alien, but had spent time with those who were. I was an "associate." A trophy to be mounted and put on display. A. Mitchell Palmer would make good use of me. So my impulse to hide, to piece together a safe life was understandable. But a part of me—a growing part—was tired of being pushed around.

So when I read toward the end of January that the Seattle Metal Trades Council, the union that represented the shipbuilders, was calling for a general strike, I felt an old familiar pang. This was a reprise of the same unruly politics that had led to the Everett Massacre. The union was in a bind. The nation no longer needed warships, thousands of returning troops had been promised jobs. But during the war, the Seattle Metal Trades Council had succeeded in forcing up wages far above the standard paid at other shipyards around the country. So the Emergency Fleet Corporation, the quasi-government entity that contracted for ships, was adamant that Seattle's shipbuilding wages had to come down. The union was equally adamant they would not. When unions all around the country were striking to raise wages, a government order to cut wages seemed a provocation. Or so the radicals declared. So what if calling a general strike got them labeled "alien communists."

On January 22, a rump group of unions allied with Seattle's Central Labor Council voted in favor of a general strike. The regular leadership, including Harry Ault, was in Chicago at the time. When I read this I had an urge to rush back to Chicago, I wasn't sure whether to protect Harry or *visa versa*. What protection I could provide seemed obscure, but that was the seed of my subsequent action. I started to check train schedules, went down to the local labor press to get the breaking news as it came over the wire.

On January 27, the newly returned leadership met with the General Strike Committee, as the self-appointed strike organizers now called themselves. Reading between the lines, it seemed to me that Harry and the rest of the union leadership had already lost control, following, not leading, events set in motion while they were absent. The critical question, at that point, was whether the strike could be averted through some kind of diplomatic intervention, or, if not, contained in such a way as to not fatally damage public support for the labor movement. I listened to this argument, back and forth, in the Milwaukee pressroom, sure the same argument was going back and forth at the *Union Record* in Seattle.

Still I wavered whether to go back. What for? To be a witness, a participant in what some were saying would be the first American Soviet while others were saying was the biggest mistake ever made by America's organized labor? To throw my body in front of the mob? To stop them? Stop who?

The rabble-rousers. The purveyors of zealotry who had coaxed my brother up to Everett. Enraptured romantics whose call to revolution always included a good punch in the mouth. Or even better, guns. Dynamite. Turpentine soaked rags. The underside of the American labor movement, the rough pranks so loved by my father.

At any rate, I bought a ticket, but was still hesitating whether to pack my bags, when I saw yet another Seattle news story. My old nemesis Anna Mae Sloan had written an inflammatory editorial in the *Union Record*. "Who Knows Where?" ran the huge black headline, and what followed was a drumbeat of rhetoric making the point that Seattle's general strike was a giant step into the unknown. With girlish enthusiasm Anna Mae declared, "We are starting on a road that leads—no one knows where!" Well, the right wing press knew where. Proof positive that this was no mere wage dispute, no colossal error in judgment by the labor movement. No, this was ironclad evidence that alien communists were about to launch their first salvo in an American Bolshevik revolution.

A second story, farther down the page, mirrored the first. It recounted the threat made by an unnamed figure, someone representing the Electrical Workers on the General Strike Committee. This fiery spokesman was quoted as saying that City Light, the public utility that provided power to the city's streetlights, hospitals, government buildings and all of downtown, was joining the strike. "Fear Strikes Heart Of Seattle's Citizens!" the headline read. There was a quote by the utility's director, downplaying the threat, then reference to Sam Rabinowitz, the union's business agent, who was unavailable for comment. Sam Rabinowitz. Uncle Sam. Who, then, might this mysterious firebrand be? I read the article again, but found no name. Frantic, I went to the union hall, trying to find out the name of this firebrand who threatened to shut down Seattle's power. Finally, a fellow at the news ticker pulled up a story. I scanned the herky-jerky type trying to find a name, a description. Woolly hair. Dark complexion. Scanty beard. And a name—Leon Green. Green! The name Gabe had picked in New Orleans. Now not Howard Greene but Leon. After what famous leader, I wondered. I thought of our dinner arguments in Mexico. Was Vladimir Illych too much of a give away?

* * *

So I got on the train. Mad that Gabe was, so soon, up to his old tricks. The more I thought about it, the more convinced I became that he had written Anna Mae's editorial. Oh, he wouldn't have been able to imitate her gushy style— that was hers and hers alone. But the ideas behind it, the push to inflame an already incendiary situation. And smug Sam, not being available for comment, inserting his beloved nephew into the Electrical Workers union at just the right moment, under a false name, with false papers and a newly grown beard. They must know, I thought, people must know. Harry Ault must know what's going on. How could he have let that editorial run? And then I became worried again, about Harry Ault, a man who had faith in me, the man I had run out on, taken his money. So anger got me on the train. But anger petered out around Eau Claire, and, by the time the train pulled in to St. Paul, I was stuck between panic and gloom. At the layover I got off the train, scanned the return schedule, then bought some crackers and a creme soda. While I hesitated, trying to decide whether to go back on the train to retrieve my bag, a paperboy came along with fresh news of what was going on in Seattle.

I snatched it up and devoured the latest—a last minute effort by the Ministers' Alliance to head off the strike, Reverend Sloan's defense of his daughter's editorial, casting

"Who Knows Where?" in biblical terms—and I got mad all over again. The only villain not accounted for so far was Marcel's mother, who was such a good friend of the Reverend Sloan. What, I wondered, was Josephine's position on the general strike?

While I was stewing this over, a hand brushed my arm. "Pardon me, miss." A short oily-haired man stood close by. I touched my purse, to feel my Faberge egg was safe. The man doffed his hat, a felt bowler, dove gray. He wore a black overcoat with padding in the shoulders that made his square frame even more so. His face was square, too, topped by wavy hair brushed back from the forehead, his dark eyes with shadows under them and a bulldog expression that reminded me of Mr. Panopolous. "Pardon me, Miss," he repeated. I looked him over, closed my paper and rearranged my expression. "I noticed you sitting across the aisle," he began again, then motioned to the newspaper. "You seem interested in events taking place in Seattle."

Immediately I thought of Pinkertons, the hired detectives found at every union conflict. Was he on his way to Seattle to join the fray? Was he following me? Or was he just another oily-haired man on a pickup?

"I live in Seattle," I said. Then regretted that. "My mother does. Near Seattle."

"Oh, yes," he said, motioning me toward the train. The conductor was boarding new passengers, and we would have to hurry to claim our seats. He didn't touch my arm again, but corralled me toward the train by the power of his presence. I forgot I was planning to take the train back to Milwaukee. "Seattle is a dangerous place these days," he added.

Once on board he settled me in my window seat, and then took the seat next to mine instead of his old one across the aisle. I'd never noticed him there, and wondered if he had been there at all. But it was too late, they were letting on new passengers and the train would be crowded, so I didn't see how I could move without making a fuss I wasn't prepared to make. I told myself I'd been in worse fixes and this was probably just a lonely bore and wished I had some reading material—a Cosmopolitan or a Harper's Bazaar or some Bible tracts. Come to think of it, Bible tracts were probably just what he was looking to discuss. I didn't like this man, there was something unsettling about him, but he wasn't burly, didn't look like the type to press his luck with the ladies, and he was too well dressed to be a drifter. I thought about turning brightly to him and asking, "What brings *you* to Seattle? Are you an undertaker? A munitions salesman?" But I didn't. I waited for him to ask what I knew would be another set of questions.

He surprised me. Settling back in his seat, soaking hair oil, no doubt, into his headrest, he took a snooze. I was greatly relieved, and watched the night sky as it whirled past the Minnesota plains. We flashed through half a dozen towns, Brandon and Evansville and Melby, and I was starting to get hungry, but didn't want to wake him by stepping over his feet. Then the conductor came by and announced that the dining car was open. I was thinking about how much money I still had and whether to splurge on a sit-down dinner, with napkins and silver utensils, when the man opened his eyes and apologized for falling asleep on me. He said to make up for his rudeness he felt compelled to buy me dinner, that crackers and creme soda was no meal for a growing young lady. He spoke as if I were fifteen, fresh off the farm, and in need of some guidance, which didn't seem to me to be the mark of a crusher, and, as I thought about it, I found there was something genial about him that I hadn't noticed before. I wondered if maybe he had sensed my indecision, if that's why he had come up to me, and that maybe my initial sense about him had been wrong.

Anyway, I let him buy me dinner. Roast chicken, with mushroom gravy, with a dab of sherry in it, he said that's what made it so delicious. I was starving, and embarrassed myself by eating everything in sight, four Parker House rolls and most of the butter pats, and a second helping of string beans with pearl onions that the waiter was passing around. After the dishes were taken away he ordered me apple pie, with a slab of cheddar on top, and asked if I wanted tea. Coffee, I said, as he waved away the inquiry about dessert for himself, indicating his strained vest buttons, and gave me a sad smile that said that weight had always been his problem. He ordered a brandy instead, a brand I didn't recognize, and asked if he might smoke. He took out a cigar, a large one, with a thick gold band, which he removed slowly, and placed in front of him, like a little crown. He patted his vest pockets, and took out a silver scissors, shaped like a pelican, and snipped off the tip of his cigar. He handed the pelican over to me for inspection. "I like nice things," he said by way of explanation. "My house, my mother's house really, I live with her, is full of souvenirs I bring back."

I thought about a response. *Back from where? Why do you still live with your mother?* But settled for, "Where does she live?"

"Washington D.C." he said. "The District of Columbia. That's what the natives call it, D.C. So as not be confused with your State of Washington." I could tell he thought this clever. "This is my first time traveling there."

Now was my turn. To ask him what he did. Why he was interested in me. But I let it pass. I smiled and forked in yet another big bite of pie to demonstrate how good it was.

"I notice you read a lot," he said. "Newspapers, magazines. You don't see many young women doing that." I hadn't been reading any magazines.

"My father always read the paper," I said, and then immediately wished I hadn't.

"Your father," he said, blowing out smoke and then smiling at me. "Now, what does he do?"

He's in prison, I wanted to say, for lighting a night watchman on fire. Instead I said he no longer lived at home.

"I'm sorry," he said, as if he'd expected as much. "And what does your mother do? To support herself," he added.

I said that she worked in factories, mostly canning factories. Then said that Washington produced a lot of fruit. He said that was very interesting and then spent a lot of time talking about his fondness for cherries. Finally he got around to what I supposed was the point.

"And you," he said, "what have you been doing to support yourself in—" He acted as if he didn't know where I'd gotten on the train.

"Milwaukee," I said. "I worked in a shop near the university."

We talked for a while about universities, public *vs.* private, the advantages of secular *vs.* religious education. He asked if I were a Catholic. I said no, I just liked universities, especially the libraries. He asked which university libraries I had been in and I told him about the University of Chicago and the one at the University of Washington, and he nodded and exclaimed at each detail I gave him, about the high vaulted ceilings, the waxy smell, the way the little drawers stuck when you pulled out the card catalogs. I told him about going into the library in Seattle and not knowing what the little drawers were for, thinking they held screws like the ones I'd seen in machine shops. He burst into a hearty laugh, a little forced I thought, and then wiped away a tear. He was on his third brandy by then. I was wondering if it would be polite to ask for another piece of pie. Then he started telling me about what he said was the greatest library of all time— a temple, a repository of learning equal only to the departed libraries of Alexandria. He asked if I knew about the libraries of Alexandria and when I said no, he gave me a little lecture on that.

The Library of Congress, he finally announced, was the greatest library of modern time. Then gave me a lecture about its founding, by Thomas Jefferson, the various locations where the books were housed during the early years of the

Republic, the disastrous fire that had destroyed the first collection, how it was replenished by the purchase of Jefferson's personal library, how the collection grew and grew until finally, in 1897, came the dedication of a wondrous new edifice, a mere three blocks from where he still lived with his mother on Seward Square. Then he launched into a detailed description of the galleries, their ceiling frescos, the mosaic arches that lined the marble halls. And, most spectacular of all, the great reading room. The waiter interrupted to say the dining car was closed and berths were being made up.

My dinner companion turned serious, rose, smoothed down his vest and said he had worked as a clerk at the Library of Congress while he was going to night school—the George Washington University Law School—and that after he passed the bar, unfortunately, he found it necessary to transfer to another agency where his law degree could be put to better use. But, sadly, he missed the hallowed halls of the Library of Congress.

For a moment we were flung together, negotiating the swaying platform between cars. Again I touched my purse to make sure the egg was safe. Then I thanked him for his company, the lovely dinner, thinking myself lucky to have escaped telling him about myself. He said I was a lovely young woman, bright too, and a good listener, that I would go far. But that I needed an education, that, regardless of my origins, with hard work and pluck, I could rise above. That working as a typesetter was a good occupation, although unusual for a woman, but it showed respect for the written word, and that was good. He said my mind was a sound one, our conversation had proved that, and that I should consider moving to D.C., where there were lots of opportunities for smart young people, and that the U.S. Department of Agriculture ran a night school, with a vast array of course offerings that were free to government employees, and that while government pay was modest, opportunities for advancement were many. Why his own agency—he didn't say what it was—had openings for smart young women. With that he stopped outside his sleeping berth, where the porter had delivered his carrying case, and pumped my hand, once, twice, then bade me good night.

I went back to my coach seat, over-full and slightly dazed by the descriptions of mosaics and ceiling frescos in the Library of Congress. It wasn't until dawn, as the train pulled into Fargo, that I realized I never told him I aspired to be a typesetter.

CHAPTER 24

About 6 a.m. the next morning the train pulled into Spokane. I had slept poorly, forgetting how big the lumps in a train seat can become by the second day. I was starting, too, to have second thoughts about the whole enterprise of returning to Seattle to face Gabe. From that I began thinking about my egg, what I was going to do with it, whether to hide it, and, if so, where. I didn't suppose I could go back to the laundry and leave it behind the boiler with the rest my clothes. I snuck a look, touched it's creamy velvet wrapper nestled in the bottom of my purse. It reminded me of an Easter egg, of a picture I'd seen of well-mannered children hunting for eggs on the White House lawn. That set me to thinking about the man on the train, why I had let him buy me dinner, what he had wanted from me. He was a Pinkerton agent, I was pretty sure of that, heading to Seattle to knock heads. Although he didn't look as if he knocked heads for a living.

I thought about his fascination with libraries, his vision of the Library of Congress as a palace, and decided I wanted to see that palace. I'd promised myself one in my lifetime, and that was probably the only one I'd ever get. I thought about the idea of taking free classes at the U.S. Department of Agriculture, and from there my mind wandered to the frog capturing trips I'd taken with Marcel, how standing beside him ankle deep in slime had made all the senses in my body come alive. I decided someday I'd go to Washington and see that Library of Congress and take a class or two at the U.S. Department of Agriculture.

Maybe it was that thought, of classes at an unseen government office, of myself as a citizen who owned part of a library that looked like an Italian *palazzo*, that made me do the things I did in later life. I remember turning over those grand thoughts as I tried one way then another way to prop up my legs, to get comfortable as I tried to blot from my mind the image of a man whose name was now Leon Green.

Spokane is on flat ground, at the edge of the Eastern Washington desert, and was not then nor is it now a very prepossessing place. When the train chugged to a stop I counted my money and wondered whether I should get off and buy a real breakfast. That got me to thinking about the bulldog-faced Pinkerton and why I hadn't seen him in the last twenty-four hours. Was I expecting him to buy me another meal?

I opened the window a crack, because even though it was dead winter, the train had gotten stuffy during the night. That's when I heard the newsboy cry, "Red Copper killed in prison scuffle!" I immediately got off the train, leaving my suitcase and almost forgetting my coat. The story wasn't top right, that column was reserved for the general strike, but it was above the fold, a picture of my pa twenty years ago, also a recent one of him being led away in chains, on his way to the Eastern Washington Penitentiary. This story was not news in Chicago, I remember thinking, or even Milwaukee, except in the labor press, but in Spokane, home of all those guards and their families, prison riots and Red Copper were news. Far-away labor unrest was fine, but even better was a good murder, especially a local murder, a murderer's murder, though, in Pa's case—since he had plea bargained—it was technically a manslaughterer's murder.

Thank goodness I had the wit to go back and retrieve my bag, to stow it in a locker in the station. I was feeling both revved up and adrift, like I had felt the last time I had stored a bag in a train station. I was on automatic, going through the motions of protecting my scant possessions from some as yet unknown onslaught. I tried to think what to do next.

Once again the bulldog-faced stranger appeared at my elbow. "You should contact your mother," he murmured. "Go to the police station and ask for Leif Johnson. He's the detective who handles prison matters." He thought for a moment and added, "My condolences," then tipped his hat and gave me his card, which I shoved in my coat pocket and forgot. The conductor was calling for passengers to reboard. My bulldog-faced friend had to leave. He looked at me carefully, to see how I was taking this, then hesitated. The picture of his face is clear in my mind, I can see the hypnotic intensity of his eyes, as if he were trying to infuse me with something, his certainty, his sense of decorum. *There is a right sequence to all this*. That's what his eyes seemed to say. *First deal with the necessities of the deceased, then your mother's needs, then the mechanics of paying honor. Seattle can wait*. That's what I got out of it anyhow. I have no idea what he really meant.

The train whistle blew and he turned to go, squeezing my elbow one last time, then told me to get something to eat. That was the last I saw of him, the back of his black coat. The train pulled out. I was alone on a loading ramp in February, two days short of sleep, trying to figure out what to do about the news my father had been killed in a prison scuffle.

I decided the first thing to do was eat breakfast, which I did, three eggs, bacon and a stack of pancakes. The next thing I did was count my money to decide whether to get a hotel room or wait and see what the day brought. I went to the ladies' room and washed as best I could, combed out the snarls in my hair, and wondered whether it was better, when I arrived at the police station, to ask for detective Leif Johnson and be forced to explain about the stranger on the train or just go in and say I was Red Copper's daughter and let detective Leif Johnson find me.

A trolley left every twenty minutes for downtown and I waited with the other passengers and townspeople who were claiming their parcel post. The trolley was late, snow on the tracks someone said, but I was content to stand there, having no appetite for what lay ahead. At least I wasn't going to see Gabe anytime soon. That thought cheered me and got me downtown and into the police station where I waited in another line for twenty minutes until I was able to speak to the sergeant at the desk.

Finally he looked up. "I just got off the train," I said. "I read in the headlines my pa was killed." He sighed and hauled back the notebook he'd just put away. I watched him lick his pencil.

"What'd you say your name was?"

"Copper," I said. "Penny Joe Copper."

He looked at me for a long minute, as if I were some kind of apparition. "I just got off the train," I repeated. "I heard the newsboy say my pa was dead."

That got him going. He stood up and proceeded to shoo the others waiting in line, decent folks reporting stolen bicycles or cats trapped in trees, ordered them all to the straight-backed chairs near the radiator, and announced in an important voice that he had to take this young lady in for questioning, by which he meant me.

The interrogation room reminded me of the paneled office in the Olympia train depot where Gabe's detective and Marcel's mother had given me the third degree. I settled in on the straight-backed chair I was directed to, wondering if I should have gone back on the train and let my mother handle it. Presently a middle-aged fellow with lank blond hair appeared. I surmised he was detective Leif Johnson but said nothing. I was starting to enjoy this, the thought that I was the aggrieved party, that they were the ones in the hot seat, but then my enthusiasm failed. In spite of the fact that the incident had no apparent connection with any wrongdoing on my part, I was not sure they would see it that way. My last visit to my father, to enlist his support for Gabe's May Day scheme, could hardly be called a family reunion. My overwhelming sense of being guilty by association smothered any grief or outrage. When I left the prison that last time I had already said good-bye to my father, had let go of my last hopes for comfort or illumination, so his death, now, seemed a mere confirmation of something that had already happened. I wasn't sure whether my mother even knew this news, or what she would make of it, and so when the detective got done studying his file notes, and cleared his throat, it was me that asked the first question. "Does my mother know?"

He said she did. That he had wired the Everett police and they had stopped by her last known address, and, finding her no longer living there, had asked neighbors where she might be, and had finally tracked her down and given her the news.

"Where is she?" I asked, not really caring, just trying to make conversation while my mind spun in several directions. His answer surprised me.

"At Archer's store." He studied his notes. "Mr. Archer is a dry grocer. On—"

"Oh, yes, I know it. Archer's," I repeated, thinking of the round man who owned it, a bald fellow with a ready smile and a spotless white apron folded twice over his ample waist, a proprietor who had a firm policy about offering no credit. Needless to say the Coppers did not patronize that establishment. What was my mother doing at Archer's store?

Detective Johnson interrupted my reverie. "When was the last time you saw your father?"

I knew he knew. It was in those records of his, so I told the truth. "February of 1918. I was up here with a fellow who was trying to get my father's endorsement for a rally at my brother's grave."

He knew all about that, too, but didn't follow up with any questions about my brother or the May Day rally. "Where did you go after that?"

199

Not caring to let him probe too far in that direction, I unloosed several questions of my own. "How did this happen? Is my mother coming? When can I see my pa?" Tears were coming, tears that felt more like fear than grief, but I decided to let them flow.

He got up and fetched me some water and then waited while I pawed through my purse for a handkerchief. During this whole interlude my mind was running a mile a minute. "I want to see him," I announced and stood up. I felt stronger that way, more in control. He nodded to the sergeant, who was still by the door.

"They need to alert the coroner. It will take a few minutes. In the mean time, I need your help to fill out this report." With a smile, an apologetic one that might have been put on, he led me through a series of questions that started with my arrival at the Spokane train station and led backwards. I told him truthfully about Milwaukee, my job in the coffee shop, reading in the papers of the Seattle general strike and being concerned about where it was headed. "What made you want to come back?" he said, implying there was some ulterior purpose, and I pasted together a partial truth. I said I had been away almost two years, I mentioned New Orleans, hoping if it came to that I could use the address of the whorehouse and leave the impression I had spent my time there. I said I had been in Chicago since early December, then in Milwaukee, that I was thinking about getting a job of a more skilled nature, or maybe going to school to learn a trade. I said I had a standing offer with a friend of my father's, to work on a newspaper, to learn typesetting, and that I was going back to see if that offer was still good. He asked the name of the friend. "Harry Ault," I finally said. "Of the *Union Record*." As he wrote down that name his face changed, as if a ball had finally rolled into a slot.

"Your friend Ault has his hands full," he said quietly as the sergeant came back and we rose to go out to the squad car.

* * *

My pa's body, when I saw it, had the same look as my brother's. Gray and waxy and dead. It is amazing how life goes out of a body. How little feeling you have for the remains. Dutifully I touched him, ran my finger over his brows and eyelids. Touched his lips and felt the stubble of a two-day beard that had stopped growing. His hair, red when last I saw him, had lost its color. It had become mousy, dry, poorly cut, even by my father's slapdash standards. "What happened?" I asked, repeating my first question, asking in a huge sense, not really interested in the answer. I could see no evidence he had been beaten. Many times I had seen his face bloody after a good fight, but this wasn't one of them. They said a scuffle. I could see no scuffle. My pa had survived many a scuffle.

"He was pushed," Detective Leif Johnson said. "He was part of a protest. Something about food. There was a scuffle—" Again that word, so innocent sounding, so deceiving. Even Detective Johnson must have thought so, for he amended his words. "There was a fight. Someone had a lead pipe. A guard got struck. Then retaliation." My mind followed his words. The mechanical order of them. I knew about such things, had seen it, some version of it, all my life.

"There was a scuffle, and men got hurt," I summarized for his benefit. "My pa got killed." Suddenly I was tired. I didn't want to hear the rest. Finally I said, "How?" Meaning what injury did he die of.

"Blow to the back of the head." He touched the base of his own skull. "Snapped spinal column. It shut off breathing. I don't think he felt much."

"A lead pipe." I filled in the blanks for him. "Someone hit him in the back of the head with a lead pipe," knowing now for sure which side had wielded the pipe.

"Most probably," he agreed. He looked uncomfortable, and sure now that he also had questions he didn't want asked, I took up my purse, took out my handkerchief, wiped my eyes, stuffed the cloth back in and snapped the clasp shut. The noise was like a gunshot. "Is there anything else?" I asked, knowing there wouldn't be.

As we headed back to the police station I asked if he knew of my mother's plans. They had wired her again, telling her I was there and asking what she wanted done with the body. Detective Johnson suggested I stay overnight until they got word back, and offered to pay for my room at a hotel at the taxpayers' expense. I allowed as how I would accept the taxpayers' offer and told him my bag was still at the train station so he commandeered another squad car to take me back to retrieve it. This time when I checked into a hotel, with a policeman at my side and signing for the bill, I got no fish-eye from the clerk but instead a nervous stammer. Once in my room, I changed into my nightdress for the first time in three days and then broke down and cried. For all that had happened. To me. To my pa.

The next day, when I walked across the street to check on word from my mother, I was given a telegram, with twenty-five dollars and instructions to bury him in Spokane. The return address was Archer's General Store.

CHAPTER 25

It took me three days to bury my pa. First an inquest, by the state, to establish that they had done nothing wrong. Then the paperwork, back and forth with my mother over power of attorney, so I could file his probate, have the state declare him legally dead, take possession of his effects, a cardboard box with his shaving mug, a few dog-eared books, a picture of me, my mother, and Horace down at the sawmill squinting in the sun, and another of Pa and his mates, hoisting beers, with a banner behind declaring an end to wage slavery. I did not claim the muslin bag containing his "worn personal effects." The state was still paying for my hotel room but not my meals. I had mother's twenty-five dollars, and a chit that said the prison owed one Joseph Augustus Copper $4.35 cents in back wages, payable quarterly by check from the general treasury of the State of Washington. I did not count on those funds arriving any time soon. My own small stash was now reduced to eighteen dollars and change. The question was whether to take a pauper's funeral or pay for something more.

This was not an easy question to answer. I could have gone to the Spokane Central Labor Council and enlisted their aid for a dignified funeral. But the memory of my brother's funeral, our trip to Boise to dicker over one half of Joe Hill's ashes, stuck in my craw. I doubted that whatever ensued from my requesting union help would result in anything that could be called dignified. I tried to figure out what my father would want, what I wanted him to want, what my mother expected, what I could afford.

All the while, events in the general strike were moving apace. I had stepped off the last train destined to arrive in Seattle. While I was evading Detective Johnson's questions, all forms of public transportation in Seattle shut down. At 10 a.m. on Wednesday, February 6, whistles sounded and the dockyard workers walked off their jobs. Then other factory workers joined suit. Teachers closed their books and ushered what few children there were out of the classrooms. Municipal employees, known conflict-avoiders, simply took the day off. Hospitals could only admit urgent cases. With no fresh produce, grocery stores closed. Dry goods establishments shut down for fear of vandalism. From Wednesday until Friday, Seattle's wheels of commerce locked. Then, on Friday afternoon, things started to turn.

The left-wing papers, including the *Union Record,* had shut their doors in solidarity with the workers. But the mainstream press, those opposing the strike, managed to get out broadsides offering rudimentary news coverage and much alarmist editorializing. The mayor called on the governor to activate the National Guard and by Friday morning the Guard was marching in to restore order. This much I read in the Spokane papers. What was going on under the surface I had no idea.

This backdrop as much as anything made me avoid walking into the office of the Spokane Central Labor Council. My pa had died from a lead pipe applied to the base of his skull. I did not want his demise to be wrapped in with the chaos of the general strike. In the end, I chose what I wanted, cremation, one mourner, and instructions to send the ashes, parcel post, to my mother c/o Archer's General Store. The total bill came to thirty-one dollars. I did not begrudge my mother the extra six.

So, Monday morning I set off again for Seattle, with barely seven dollars in my purse and little idea what I was heading into. I would have liked to leave on Sunday, but the station master said that trains were still not running to Seattle, that I could only go by a circuitous route, taking eighteen hours, and winding up in Tacoma. That or wait a day and hope regular service would be restored as promised by the National Guard. I had no desire to spend the night shuttling between trains only to wind up in Tacoma and, as the state was still paying for me to sleep in a clean bed, I booked my ticket for Monday and hoped for the best.

I arrived at 2 p.m. to a station not swept for days and filled with exhausted passengers camping out while trying to book passage to safer climes. They looked at me with tired amazement, one of only a few passengers to get off the train, their eyes asking why I would want to come into this, but since I had no sense of what "this" was, I couldn't answer. Fittingly, my arrival was accompanied by freezing rain. I stood under the canopy on Alaskan Way, looking up and down the mostly deserted street, and tried to figure out what to do. My first thought was to hike up to the university district and throw myself on the mercy of Mr. Panopolous, but that was several miles away and the chance of his shop being open, given his student clientele, was slim. My next thought was to spend my last couple of dollars on a hotel room across the street, but that impulse, I knew, was born of a fatal urge to burrow myself away. So, deciding there had to be someone working at the *Union Record*, I resolved to present myself regardless of the complexities.

When I arrived a half hour later, wet and shivering, the sidewalk in front was awash in competing protests. One group of diehard strikers was protesting Harry Ault's decision to begin printing again that morning, while another group of Central Labor Council loyalists was trying to persuade the hotheads that if the unions didn't publish there would be no strikers' voice. The old-line unionists shoved leaflets at passersby, a copy of a telegram from Samuel Gompers authorizing the *Union Record* to continue to print, as if this exonerated their actions. Inside, through the window plastered with fresh broadsides, I could see a few employees trying to get out a second edition, but most reporters were sitting with feet up and folded arms. They wore paper hats that said, "General Strike Means General Strike." I waded through the sidewalk arguments, fought against the wind to open the heavy door, then made my way through the newsroom, glad everyone was too busy with their own political posturing to notice. I knocked on Harry Ault's door, aware I was making a puddle on the linoleum. The curtains on the glass were drawn, but I could hear him arguing with someone inside. Anna Mae, I guessed.

"Come in," he barked. Whoever he expected, it wasn't me. At the sight of me, his argument with Anna Mae broke off. My arrival must have come as both a welcome surprise and a distraction. "Penny!" he said, coming over to give me a hug. It had been a long time since I'd been hugged and I let him take his time. I stood with my eyes closed and told myself to remember this moment. Anna Mae must have been jealous because she came over and kind of wedged herself in the middle. She pretended she was trying to rub my head, and mussed up my hair while trying to separate the two of us. She told me I looked awful. Then got to the point. "You're too late," she said, meaning there was no room for me in this high political drama.

I savored that news and then stepped away from Harry's protective arms to give her a look up and down. She had put on weight, the Gibson Girl freshness now a thing of the past. "I'm sorry." I said, meaning sorry I was late for her party. "I was delayed. By the death of my pa." She had no answer to that and Harry decided to reclaim control by putting a protective arm around my shoulder.

"I'm glad you came," he said and I nodded in agreement. To keep me away from any further Anna Mae pronouncements, he guided me out the door to his assistant, Mr. Bowles, who pointed out the washroom and offered to run across the street for coffee and crullers. A few minutes later, after I had managed to dry my hair and Anna Mae had gone on her way, I went back into Harry's office and closed the door. He sat with his feet up on his desk and motioned me into his big visitors' chair and looked me over like I was his favorite hunting dog just come out from the woods.

I was eventually to tell Harry Ault a fair piece of what had happened to me over the months I had been missing, but not that day. That day we mostly concentrated on how I had happened upon the news of my pa's death in Spokane. He laughed at my description of mailing Red Copper parcel post and said my mother was a hard one. He asked if I were going to visit her, and I said soon. Then he asked if I had a place to stay, and I said no, and he thought for a second and then asked if I would like to stay with his family. He began apologizing about their cramped quarters, said because of the strike everyone had kind of let things go to the dogs. Then he apologized for making it sound like his wife was a bad housekeeper. I laughed and said I wouldn't tell, thanked him and said I was most grateful for his offer. And realized that two years ago there would have been something in me that prevented him from making that invitation and something in me that would have prevented my acceptance.

Then Harry became all business, and asked if it would be all right to get someone in to interview me about my father's death, and I said yes, Pa would have wanted a fitting account. Harry said he had a few things to attend to but he'd be back in an hour and then I might want to go with him on his round of meetings so I could get "up to speed," as he put it, on Seattle's moment in history.

I spent a few minutes with Mr. Bowles, who took some notes on my pa's death and the arrangements I'd made for his funeral. He asked who had attended the cremation, and I said, "Just me," and he thought about that and wrote down *private service*. I had the feeling he wanted me to make some accusations against the prison, the speedy and slipshod inquest, but I didn't offer any details, and when he asked if I had consulted legal counsel I shook my head no. I suppose he thought my lack of outrage was caused by sadness, or its stronger cousin, grief, and in a way it was. But not in the way he assumed. So, rather than try to explain the tremendous sadness I felt about the entire world and my precarious place in it, I just left it at that.

Harry returned about five and gathered me up for a trip to city hall to hear the mayor, Ole Hansen, explain his views on the various skirmishes of the day.

Hansen was a large man, built like a block, with blunt-cut hair that he brushed over his crown, so it often fell forward when he was making some energetic point. He made a lot of energetic points during that hour-long news conference, beginning with a generalized tirade against the striking workers and their leaders, and then moving into a gleeful listing of all the factories and retail establishments that had reopened that day. The fact was that, for most workers, three days without pay was about the sum total of what they could sign on for. Their wives were getting tired of having no fresh produce, with children underfoot because there was no school. The strike leaders, Harry told me in whispered asides, had neglected to figure out a precise set of demands, so negotiations soon became a shambles. Whoever showed up for either side at a bargaining session, whether organized by the Ministers' Alliance or some other self-appointed intermediary, immediately laid down a new list of demands. Added to that problem was that there was no announced date or procedure for ending the strike. A general strike with no announced goals and no set ending could hardly be expected to conclude successfully, Harry whispered bitterly as Ole Hansen read through a seemingly endless list of establishments now open for business. The mayor had worked his way through bakeries and booksellers and was now on coal companies. Reporters were starting to drift away. Ole Hansen sped up the pace. "The local unions are voting today on whether to go back," Harry told me. "We tried a vote on Saturday but it was no go."

"Maybe the strike leaders had other objectives," I murmured, thinking of how the Bolsheviks I had lived with in Mexico had so valued destabilization as a political tactic. A neat arithmetic, mayhem as an absolute good, undertaken for its own sake. No need to think through strategies. Or tally costs. Just sow the seeds of discord and something would happen. I kept these thoughts to myself, however, because I could see Harry was struggling to persuade himself there was some purpose in it all. Even though he had opposed the strike, once it was called, he felt loyalty to support it. "Solidarity," I murmured, sad at the irony.

"Yes, that's it," he agreed, looking hopeful, as the few reporters who remained peppered Hansen with questions. Was he going to round up the ringleaders? Would they be tried? What about reports of vigilante justice? How about deportation?

The mayor spread out his hands. That was not his bailiwick, he said. People from Washington were here, people from the Justice Department. Time would tell. Then his natural enthusiasm broke forth. "If you ask me, gunny sacks and nooses would be too good for them." Then immediately added, "Seattle is a God-fearing community. We don't condone violence." Unlike Everett, I thought.

Next we went to the Labor Temple for the tally of strike votes. Not like the gathering for the burial of my brother, this time access was controlled. Then the object had been to rally support, so the building had been thrown open to the crowd. Now the object was to put the best face on failure, so entrance to the meeting hall was strictly limited. Each local that had voted to join the strike less than a week before had polled its members anew. Delegations carrying vote tabulations from around the city arrived and made their way past a gauntlet of reporters and milling Wobblies into the hall where the leadership of the strike committee was assembling on stage.

The Strike Committee had seated itself on one side of the podium with empty chairs left for the leadership of the Central Labor Council on the other. Harry, when he saw this arrangement, went up on stage and had a short but intense discussion with the head of the Strike Committee. I thought I recognized Sam as the man he was talking to, but as I was in the back of a crowded room, I didn't make a lot of effort to identify faces. There was a fresh stir behind me and someone called out to make way for Jimmy Duncan. The head of the Central Labor Council was pushed forward by his retinue of burly coat-carriers. When Duncan saw the arrangement of chairs, he stopped in mid-stride. Harry nodded to him from the stage, and motioned as if to bring the chairs all together. Duncan nodded and held his position. Harry went over to Sam on his side of the platform and the two huddled. Sam then conversed with some of his colleagues, and it was decided. Chairs were rearranged, made into one long line, and, once that was completed, Jimmy Duncan resumed his entrance, making his way forward to take his position in dead center of the line of chairs, next to Sam, who, as leader of the Strike Committee, sat on his immediate stage left. Harry took his own place four chairs down, to the right of center, as strike symbolism required.

What ensued in the next three hours was speech making, interlaced with vote tallies, as one by one the various local unions proclaimed their undying loyalty to the strike and then voted to go back to work. Each delegation head, and sometimes all the members of a delegation, felt compelled to give a rousing personal account of the splendid solidarity witnessed by all in the struggle. Acts of heroism were cited. Nefarious deeds by Mayor Hansen testified to. Calumnies were heaped on Governor Lister, President Wilson, the War Labor Board, the Department of Justice. In the end, all but two locals voted to return to work. The two holdouts were saved for last. First the dockworkers, the initial grieving party, announced its intention to continue the strike. The assembled cheered and stamped their feet as if they were all about to go out on strike once more. Then came the electrical workers, the spokesman for City Light. I was still in the back, hidden behind a row of men a head taller than me, but I immediately recognized the voice. Gabe, introducing himself, amid wild cheers, as Leon Green.

CHAPTER 26

Hearing Gabe's voice made my skin grow cold. My insides became clammy. I felt as if I were going to vomit. My one clear thought was to flee and so I pushed through the men behind me toward the double doors. A guard, seeing me, asked if I was ill. To get away from him, I ran down the steps and onto the street, clumsy and shivering, trying to get my coat on, pushing my arms at the sleeves. I had no sense of where to go. Finally it occurred to me to go back to the *Union Record* and wait there for Harry. My stomach settled during the five-block walk, but I was good and wet when I got to the front door and found it was locked. Eventually he would come, I thought, and settled down on the wet stoop just outside the stream of water gushing from the gutter, trying to blot any further thoughts from my mind.

An hour later Harry did find me. By that time my nose was running like the gutter. He looked at me with his usual mixture of sternness and amusement. "You look like a drowned rat," he said. "Showing up wet is getting to be a habit."

"Yes," I said, "I'm stubborn. My mother always said that." He helped me up and used his ring of keys to open the front door and then his office. My luggage was still there, so he stepped outside and ordered me to put on dry clothes. Then he opened the door a crack and tossed in a white tea towel with an apology it was the only one he could find. I thanked him and stripped out of my soaking dress and opened my battered suitcase and tried to figure out what combination of unlaundered clothing would provide the least objectionable outfit with which to make an entrance into Harry Ault's household.

I had never met Harry's wife, knew nothing about the family except that they had four children. Harry told me once that his wife's name was Minerva. Goddess of the harvest, that seemed a good omen as I rubbed my neck and hair with the tea towel.

Strike leaders all had extra gasoline rations, so Harry, unlike the rest of Seattle, still had gas to get around town. He informed me of this while inserting the key to start the motor, having deposited my wet clothes and suitcase in the trunk. I'm not much good at cars but I recall this one was a Reo—an early version of the Oldsmobile, named after its founder, Ransom E. Olds. I have a picture of myself with Harry standing in front of his car that my second husband once saw in a scrapbook and identified as to the make and year. He said it was a great automobile, but the ignition was tricky in damp weather, which was what was happening then, but I only half noticed. I was thinking about Minerva, and the prospect of being laid down to sleep in some all encompassing bed.

Which is what happened. Minerva couldn't have been nicer. She moved one of the twins, apologizing for the fact that the sheets were a couple of days old, but that made it even more inviting, sinking down into the hollow of warmth left by the missing twin. I slept like a rock and awoke long after dawn. Harry had already left for the newspaper and Minerva was puttering in her kitchen. She poured me tea with a spoonful of honey, fed me corn cake, felt my forehead and ordered me back to bed. I spent the next two days there, sleeping on and off, then woke Thursday morning feeling brand new.

"I guess you needed the sleep," Harry said as he tasted his coffee and buttered all four sides of his corn cake.

"I guess so," I said, embarrassed for treating his house like a hospital ward, displacing his eight-year-old daughter from her bed. "I should have been helping out."

"Nonsense," he said, waving away this thought. "There's always time to repay hospitality." Something I've since remembered.

"How are things going?" I asked, meaning at the newspaper. I wasn't sure I wanted to know, but felt pressed to change the subject.

"It's over," he said, meaning the strike. "Only thing now is the mop up."

"Meaning what?" I asked.

"Rounding up the ringleaders," Minerva put in. She was coming out of the kitchen. "You know, the ritual game."

I liked her toughness but not the prospect it suggested. "Are you one of the ringleaders?" I asked Harry.

"Gracious," he said. "Not according to the strikers. They call me a traitor to my class." He said this with a half smile, as if such a grand indictment were above him.

I smiled back, glad to hear he didn't feel in any danger of arrest.

"I saw Gabe," I told him, I'm not sure why. "Heard him, actually, on the stage." I left the rest unsaid, not knowing how much Harry was aware of my past association, if he knew where I'd gone, and why.

"Oh, yes," he said, suddenly taking an interest in the bottom of his cup. "The mysterious Leon Green. Did you know he was back?"

"I thought he might be. I saw his picture in the Milwaukee paper."

There was a long silence while Harry put down his coffee and rearranged the silverware.

Minerva was midway on one of her trips to the kitchen. She touched my shoulder. "Did that upset you?"

"No," I said, blood rushing to my face, all of a sudden feeling exposed. I looked down. What was I doing, I asked myself. Why was I blushing, was I denying some truth, was that what I looked like, some smitten fool? Humiliated, I pushed away from the table and stumbled into the kitchen.

They let me clatter away with the dishes for a few minutes, then Minerva came in with more cups to wash. We stood side-by-side, cleaning dishes in the soapy water. She said, "It was rude of me to press."

I was astonished someone could be so polite. I had never known families where feelings were something others did not intrude upon.

"I'm sorry I brought it up," I said.

Later, Harry asked me if I wanted to go to the office, or did I want to stay in the house for another day. I was torn between a growing fear of meeting Gabe at the *Union Record* and shame at staying for another day in Minerva's care. So I said, "Take me to the university library, there's something I want to do there." So he dropped me off and then went off to his day at the newspaper. I stood outside, looking up at the massive doors, remembering the first time I had entered, that day in February, when I had come down from Everett. Three years ago, in some respects, a lifetime. I went in, smelling again the waxy lemon of the floor polish, the musty scent given off by the old books, the sulfur aroma thrown off by the freshly printed newspapers. I breathed in all this and felt peace come over me. The librarian looked up. Did I need help?

"The archives," I said, not sure what I was asking for.

"Manuscript Division?" she asked.

"I want information on the Library of Congress, when it was built."

"What year was that?"

"I'm not sure." I thought about the man on the train. What date had he mentioned? "1897 I think." Why was I asking for this? I needed an excuse, that's why, to spend the day doing something.

For three hours I read everything the librarian could get

her hands on about the Library of Congress. Two gray manuscript boxes full of clippings, plus some dusty volumes she called up from the stacks. I learned that the Italian Renaissance building was designed by two architects named Smithmeyer and Peltz. That some forty-two sculptors and painters, all American, had been hired to adorn it. Their designs were heavily allegorical, a bronze door peopled with figures representing Tradition, Writing and Painting, mosaic floors and frescoed ceilings filled with Greek and Roman deities carrying sheaves of wheat and tablets of law. The grand hall was in a style copied from the Paris Opera while the grand staircase was inspired by a Vienna museum. In all, a veritable Temple of the Arts. The main reading room stood three stories tall under an ornate dome topped by a lantern cupola which, in turn, was circled by a fresco depicting the great periods of civilization. On the roof, a Torch of Learning pointed to the sky. So said the dedication pamphlets and news descriptions of the day.

Poring through these accounts, I was taken with a longing to walk those frescoed halls, to sit in the hushed silence under that golden dome. I had asked Harry to drop me at the library because I needed to find a place to hide my Faberge egg. And gotten waylaid in the manuscript archives dreaming about visiting the Library of Congress. I could expect to encounter Gabe soon enough, and could predict he would find a way to ransack my belongings. So the question was not whether but where to hide my egg. I thought once again of the boiler room at the laundry. But going back there would surely be noticed by the girls. There was the biology room directly above, all those glass jars with floating frog parts and pickled brains. Could I hide my egg in there? But who knows what formaldehyde would do to enamel. So where to put my egg, a secure place, where no one would think to look, but where I could easily return to retrieve it?

I studied the gray cardboard box in front of me, its catalog number and content description, "Library of Congress—Dedication" and decided—why not? I slipped the egg, still wrapped in its beige cover, into the bottom of the box. Then picked the box up and moved it from side to side, feeling the egg shift and thud. I put the box back down, looked around to make sure no one had noticed, then thought about how to muffle the sound. More stuffing, I decided, but where to find it? A few chairs down a man had left his muffler on the chair. I went over and felt it, but found it too wet. Should I go downstairs and take some paper from the ladies room? I had another thought, and stepped behind a high row of reference books, out of view of the two researchers still in the room. I unbuttoned my blouse, pulled off my wool camisole. I was going to be chilled the rest of the day, that's for sure. Buttoning up, clutching my camisole in my fist, I made my way back to my chair.

At the far end, a lady raised her head, sniffing the air. I took up the second gray box and began lifting out clippings. I spread them around, took one after another to study further. After I was satisfied that the lady had returned to her research, I gathered up the clippings and replaced them in the second box, then took back the first one, opened it and lifted out the egg. Wrapping it in my woolen camisole, I carefully stuffed it back into the bottom of the box, then lifted and shook it. The weight was off, it was too heavy for a clipping file, but it didn't thump. I hoped the student assigned to replace this box in the stacks would be attentive enough to file it correctly but negligent enough not to wonder about the odd weight. I wrote down the catalog number on a scrap of paper and buried it in my purse, then retrieved the cart on which manuscript boxes had been delivered and placed the entire collection, two boxes and three books, in the location designated for reshelving. I left the archival reading room, thanked the research librarian and promised to be back within a week or two.

That done, I walked out feeling stronger than I had in

days. I took the trolley downtown to the *Union Record*. Harry was out, so I spent the remainder of the afternoon talking to reporters about the general strike. Most of them knew me, by reputation at least, as Red Copper's daughter. A few remembered me as someone who had worked briefly at the paper two years before. Others recalled my involvement in the burial of the Everett martyrs. But if they knew I had disappeared with Gabe Rabinowitz they didn't say. What I gathered from their talk was that they were worried about retaliation. Worried for their jobs because the *Union Record* was now branded as part of the right wing, a mouthpiece for Samuel Gompers. Broken strike or no, the radicals were in charge in Seattle, and that didn't bode well for the *Union Record*. I longed to ask them about Leon Green, but instead inquired about Anna Mae Sloan, her infamous "Who Knows Where?" editorial that made the *Union Record* national news.

"The truth is," one old hand put it, "she just marched in, with Sam Rabinowitz and the other guy—that bearded fellow—" They all laughed, the old reporter struggling to keep from smiling. "You know, Leon What's-his-name? Anyway the two of them had little Miss Sloan in tow and this typed-up editorial, you know how she gets all pink and puffy when she has something important she's written. Well she was pink and puffy that day, I can tell you."

"But why did you print it?" I asked.

The old guy shrugged. "There was no one to say no," he finally offered. "Harry and Jimmy Duncan were in Chicago. Eli Marsh was the nominal editor-in-charge." He looked around to make sure Eli wasn't in earshot. "But he didn't want to make the call, what with all the goings-on, so he assembled us all together and we played soviet and made a collective decision."

"To fold," I said, then thought maybe I was stating it too baldly.

"Correct," he said, not offended at all. "You see how it is

in the new soviet state of Seattle."

Then Harry came in, and the news guys around me broke off and went back to their desks. It was as if they didn't want to burden Harry with their bleak view of the circumstances. I wondered, when the time came, whether they would stand by him.

Somehow, after hearing that story about the editorial, I lost my enthusiasm for working at the *Union Record*. I didn't tell Harry though, and let him spend the rest of the afternoon talking with various staff about where I could best fit in. I thought of Rosa, in New York, how my original resolve to come back had been so that she would know how to find me, and realized that leaving a forwarding address with Harry would serve that purpose just as well. It was becoming clear there was no pressing need in the newsroom for my services.

"I probably should spend a few days with my mother," I ventured. The relief on Harry's face was quickly smothered. I would be sorry to leave Minerva's nest but if I did not go soon, I would never pull myself away. "I can't thank you both enough," I said the next morning. "When I get back maybe it will be clearer how I can help." Help Harry, I meant. But of course he thought I was speaking of the newsroom.

CHAPTER 27

The next day I packed my luggage once more and set off on the Interurban. Harry insisted I take a few dollars "advance" against an, as yet, unspecified story I would write. I felt badly taking the money, because I knew union coffers were depleted by the strike, that support of the newspaper would be adjusted accordingly. "Nonsense," Harry assured me. "It will come out fine." I doubted that. Neither of us mentioned the obvious—that Harry was hanging on by his fingernails.

I asked myself was I running away from my meeting with Gabe. The answer was yes, I wasn't ready for it. At least that is what I told myself as I folded my newly washed clothes into my newly borrowed Gladstone bag. I still had Gabe's yellow invoice pad tucked in the bottom of my purse. I didn't know what importance it had, but it felt like a bargaining chit.

I told Harry and Minerva that I would come to visit when I returned, that I had taken up their daughter's bed for too long. It was a small house, and though Harry was generous with their hospitality, I could see that Minerva was aware of its limits. When I got to the train station there was quite a crowd of policemen, one half of the waiting room cordoned off. Behind the lines of police and a cluster of reporters I caught a glimpse of the day's story. Thirty-six Wobblies—so called "enemy aliens"—were being loaded into a railway car for transport across the country to Ellis Island and deportation. A. Mitchell Palmer, the man later famous for the Palmer Raids that scooped up "enemy aliens" around the country, was testing his methods in Seattle. I thought I caught a glimpse of the man I had met on the train, who seemed to be directing the effort. I had forgotten the calling card he gave me, it still waited undiscovered in my coat pocket. I was anxious to get away from the complexities of the general strike and the *Union Record*, and so I detoured willingly enough to the other side of the train station and caught my Interurban and spent the next hour thinking not about the man I'd met on the train but about what kind of reception I would get from my mother.

Everett was awash in a rare interval of winter sunshine. I had not wired ahead, partly to save money and partly because I was already exhausted by the prospect of renewed communication with my mother. I didn't want to presume more welcome than I would get. I rehearsed over and over in my mind the pretext for my visit—to make sure Pa's ashes had arrived, to carry out any further instructions regarding their disposal. This latter was a fine point since my mother's instructions had been to bury him in Spokane. I debated various excuses for my failure to do so. The cost, the potential for unseemly behavior by old (and well lubricated) labor comrades. The implication at the inquest, that Red Copper had been the victim of murder, or at least manslaughter, at the hands of a prison guard. Should I bring that up, ask her advice about whether to pursue it or not? Should I redeem my ten-dollar advance from Harry Ault by writing an account of the inquest and raising those very questions? With all these matters tumbling about my mind I paid little attention to the deportation of thirty-six enemy aliens at the train station in Seattle.

Since the weather was good, and I was in no hurry, I walked to our old house, a good mile uphill, to find out, to my less than complete surprise, that my mother no longer lived there. The woman who answered the door, a thin woman with two feverish children, one on her hip and one at her skirt, gave me no information. So I was forced to assume that she was now in residence at Archer's dry goods store. I walked another mile there, but by that time the weather had turned and I was tired from hauling my Gladstone bag. Mr. Archer was ensconced behind the counter. He looked up and smiled when I came in, whether because he recognized me or because of the bell announcing a customer I wasn't sure. "Penny," he said, walking out from behind the counter, wiping his hands on his apron in advance of shaking mine. The welcome seemed genuine. At least he had recognized me.

"I stole candy from you once," I blurted out, to set the record straight. "Olga Froll did too." I just remembered that part and hoped her complicity would help clear the decks between us.

Rudy Archer brushed aside this admission, along with its addendum. "Your mother has been waiting." He colored deeply. "She and I—" He took a deep breath and struggled to go on, then lost his courage and side stepped the announcement.

Instead, he turned and led me through a storeroom filled with crates of sewing goods, work gloves and coveralls. "This is the back way," he informed me, hastening to add, "There's also a front entrance, from the street, a proper entrance." I was charmed, he was so concerned about my mother's propriety, that she have a proper entrance, and found I was not at all distressed that the two of them had found comfort from the world's gaze by using the back stairway. I gave Rudy's rear end a big smile as we mounted the stairs. This new alliance, the prospect of one, buoyed me, gave me a new angle from which to approach my formidable and distant mother.

Rudy knocked on the door, then announced he had to tend to his customers and fled. I was left alone with a closed door and the frail hope that it would soon open. A half-minute passed and I knocked again. Finally I heard sounds, and presently the door opened and my mother stood before me. "Forgive me," she said, "my ears aren't what they used to be."

"Did you get pa's ashes?" I asked, getting right to what I imagined to be a bone of contention. "I didn't know what else to do. It didn't seem right to leave him in Spokane."

Mother never took second place in blurting out hard truths. "Rudy and I are fixing to be married," she said. "These ashes are causing some consternation between us. Whether to invite them to the wedding or not."

I could see what she meant. Me sending Pa back had muddied the protocol. She looked hopefully at me, thinking I might be able to sort out this mess. "I think Pa'd like to attend," I said. "I'll keep him with me. No one else need know. Afterwards, I'll—" In my mind's eye I could see the wharf where the *Verona* had docked, the place where my brother had been shot. "I'll take care of it," I said. She nodded. That settled, she invited me in for a cup of tea.

The apartment above Archer's store was surprisingly comfortable, a kitchen off the back landing, a parlor to the front, two small side rooms, one fixed as a bedroom, the other as a sewing place. Apparently my mother had gotten work running up aprons and other stitched goods for Rudy to sell in his store and he had offered the rooms above at a reduced rate. He was a widower, with two small boys, and, since my mother was always hopeful with boys, the match seemed a good one. Pa's unexpected death had just hastened things along, allowed them to bring to light what the town already knew but had not acknowledged. "Rudy is a God-fearing man," my mother explained. She seemed to treat that as a minor flaw, as if he approved of cockfighting. "He has his reputation to protect."

"So you're being made an honest woman." She looked uncomfortable at this teasing, but pleased as well. "Well, I think it's time you took up with a God-fearing man," I said, and meant it, and with that a lot of the tension I had brought with me dissolved.

But even so, my mother was not an easy woman to be with. She was still cold, and remarkably uninterested in the events, much less the emotional parts, of my life. But if we stuck to outer appearances, if I put aside any need of comfort or protection, things worked out well enough between us. I stayed for six weeks, working at Rudy Archer's store, sleeping on a cot in the sewing room, earning some money to take back with me to Seattle. I witnessed my mother's wedding, a stiff affair at the Methodist church, attended by Rudy's two sons, his former in-laws and the minister's wife. Mother had made herself a new black dress for the occasion, with a shorter, almost fashionable skirt. Rudy wore his Masonic pins and a purple sash that must have meant something. Mother insisted I wear a hat, and when I protested that I didn't have one, lent me one of hers, a brown one, that didn't go well with my one decent blue shirtwaist. We had considerable discussion about how to bring my father's ashes to the occasion. I pointed out that if Rudy's ex-in-laws were coming I thought that gave enough latitude for a deceased husband. "But Pearl can't come," my mother pointed out. "She's in the ground." The implication was clear. If I'd left well enough alone and put Pa in the ground too, we wouldn't have this problem.

I sighed. "All right, Mother. I'll sneak him in some way."

"And out," she pointed out.

"Yes."

What I wound up having to do was take the urn to the church the night before, while Mother and Rudy were off moving her wardrobe over to Rudy's house. I hid it in the grass behind a fir tree, and then, the next day, after the meager assortment of guests assembled, made the excuse of having forgotten my hat.

"Don't worry, dear," my mother patted my hand. I couldn't decide whether to be astonished to be called 'dear' or irritated she was missing the point. I left anyway, holding up the ceremony while I pretended to walk two blocks back to the store. Rudy was a punctual man, and by the time I returned with the urn, and the hat that I'd stowed out of sight in the entrance alcove, I could see that everyone thought I had marred the occasion. I am my father's daughter, I thought, a bull in a china shop. I put on my ugly brown hat and took off the blue tartan shawl my mother had also lent me and wrapped the shawl around the urn and carried it in like Jesus in swaddling cloth. No one noticed, or if they did, they thought it just one more thoughtless gesture by the bride's daughter.

I left the urn in the pew while we went downstairs to eat cake and drink fruit punch. This was my first chance to visit with Rudy's boys, aged seven and nine. I had agreed to stay at their house for two days while Rudy and my mother took a honeymoon near Port Townsend. They were nice boys, well mannered. The younger one, round-faced, reminded me of Horace. The older one had a chip on his shoulder I didn't care for, but I suppose it was because he reminded me of me.

The next day I retrieved the urn from behind the fir tree and took it to Port Gardiner Bay. "Well, Pa," I said as I stood on the dock where the *Verona* had crashed up against the pilings, where the sheriff's men had opened fire. My thoughts went to those innocent college boys and grizzled drifters Horace and the other ringleaders had persuaded into boarding. How easy it is to fire up a crowd, to create a crisis. But I knew Pa wouldn't see it that way. He would see it the way Horace had, the way lots of men do, as some kind of test of manhood, putting your life on the line, standing up to oppressors. "Well, Pa," I said as I reached in and took out a handful of ash. "I guess you're better off here rather than in prison. Or Spokane," I added. "You died how you wanted to, in a fight." I thought a bit more. "Horace would have been proud." The next part was harder. "I'm proud too. In spite of the stupid things you did. The many stupid things you did." I released the handful of ash, the wind caught it and blew it out into the bay. I took up another handful. "Now that Mother's married, maybe she can forgive you as well." I released my second handful. "The thing is, Pa, we were mightily vexed with you, most of the time. Except Horace, he never seemed bothered one way or the other." I released a third handful, then checked to see how much was left. I had run out of words and could feel tears coming. "But, vexed as we were, Pa, we all loved you." There, I'd said what I'd come for. I dumped the remaining ash over the rail and called it a day. Called it, also, the end of my childhood.

When mother and Rudy returned, I wished them well and returned to Seattle. The camellias and rhododendrons were beginning to bloom, I had enough money to rent a decent room and was carrying with me a eulogy I had written for my father that was honest enough and loving enough to give me peace. I gave the eulogy to Harry in payment for my ten dollar advance, and the paper ran it a few days later, but there was such turmoil going on at the newspaper that once again my father was upstaged.

In March, communist delegates from around the world had assembled in Moscow to establish the Third International, better known as the Comintern, an organization charged with spreading the Bolshevik version of socialism around the globe. In practice this meant delegates going home, country by country, and attacking the socialists, just as Lenin had done to the Menshevik wing of his party in Russia. Years later I learned that both Mike Gold and Manny Gomez had been there, along with John Reed, who was famous for his book, *Ten Days that Shook the World*, an eyewitness account of the October, 1917 revolution. John was a Portland boy, a northwest native son, and got lots of press in the State of Washington. He wrote a column from Moscow that was picked up in all the various labor newspapers, so I was following these events in Everett as I helped Rudy sell overalls and pipe tobacco.

Just before I returned to Seattle, John Reed and a band fresh from Moscow had succeeded in taking over the executive committee of the American Socialist Party. Harry Ault had been among the committee members deposed. By the time I got back to Seattle, the left-wing socialists, from their new perch on the executive committee, were attempting to clean house to rid themselves of the vestiges of old-line socialism. In Seattle, Harry Ault and the *Union Record* stood in the way.

There were a few minor problems with this plan for deposing Harry from his editorship. For one thing, the *Union Record* reported to the Central Labor Council not the Socialist Party. For another, the old socialist leadership was not taking its ouster lying down. Before their terms expired, they planned to call a full membership convention with the intention of booting out the new executive committee, and, to make doubly sure they would carry the vote, they set in motion a plan to expel all rank-and-file members of any affiliate organization that happened to espouse the violent overthrow of any government.

This was the fray I walked back into at the *Union Record*. Harry looked both exhausted and enraged. I could tell he was running out of energy, defending his shrinking promontory. I tried to stay out of the way, doing bits of layout and typesetting, running errands, cleaning up after late night meetings. Anna Mae Sloan, who had guest credentials with the paper, was playing worm in the apple. While the fellows who put out the paper were not fond of her, she had longevity and a national writer's reputation that made them give her a grudging deference. To outsiders she seemed harmless in her bosomy breathless way, a cheerleader for the revolution. *Why can't everybody just go along?* This was the kind of useless advice she was good for. *Russia is our leader. Be boosters and get on board.* It was an easy logic to fall in with, for those tired after the war and all the labor strife. First one, then another, then a third reporter sidled up to her way of thinking. I kept my head down and out of the way. Sniffing the air. Where was Gabe in all this? I knew he was in there somewhere. Why was Anna Mae avoiding me?

I found out soon enough. One evening, Harry asked me if I wanted to attend one of the public communist rallies, to see what the opposition was up to. I still had not told him of my time in Mexico, my familiarity with all that rigmarole, but I said yes, why not, and so we slipped unnoticed into the back of a room full of students at a rented hall near the university. The target of this particular rally was University President Suzullo, the nemesis my brother Horace had used to whip students into political action three years before. Up on stage, his arm draped behind Anna Mae's puffy neck, sat Gabe Rabinowitz. A new female conquest to enhance his podium presence.

Gabe was being introduced by the moderator as Leon Green, City Light activist, hero of the strike committee. Wild applause. On cue, Anna Mae turned to him, blushing and smiling just like a candidate's wife. Gabe unglued his hand from her shoulder, then stood to acknowledge the adoring audience. The applause built into whistles and hoots and thunderous stomping. A sharp snake of pain wrapped through my gut but I didn't know if it was disgust or fear. Finally, Gabe signaled for quiet and started to speak on the subject at hand, the sundry evils of the university administration. Then he must have caught sight of Harry in the back, because he shifted his rhetoric to enemies within the labor movement, the toadies who gave only lip-service to the strike, those whose continued positions in seats of power held back the full flowering of the common man. He called them enemies of the vanguard, Judases to the One who would lead Seattle's workers out of the wilderness.

Garbled metaphor, I thought. Old and new testaments, casting himself as both Jesus and Moses. *Don't they see?* Alas, being students, they didn't. Or did and didn't care. Didn't care who he was attacking or why. Just there for the spectacle.

Ready to follow Gabe because he fed their sense of grievance and flattered their self-importance. It begins again, I thought. And then, He's not going to get Harry.

What I meant by that I didn't know. I just knew, when the time came, I was going to stop Gabe from hurting Harry.

CHAPTER 28

Every day at the *Union Record* I watched Harry Ault lose ground. Leaders of the Central Labor Council were targets for a union membership bruised and sore from the shellacking they'd taken in the general strike. Not only had the bosses done them in, but also their own officials, men like Harry, whom they had not heeded in the first place. Of course, there was the larger arena, the struggle between the socialists and the communists, that also inflamed the local situation. Harry was a target on that score as well. Then there was the personal angle. I felt, in some way, that the animus directed at Harry was really aimed at me, that his kindness to me, my very presence at the *Union Record*, made him Gabe's special target.

But I could do nothing about Gabe. He had started coming into the office, strutting around like he owned it, leading a delegation of former strikers, along with Anna Mae and Sam. They would all crowd into Harry's office, and after a while voices would rise. Then there would be silence and Harry would open his door and, grim-faced, usher them out. The second or third time this happened, Gabe stopped and made a point of coming over to me and making a slight bow. He had a mouth that lent itself to a sardonic smile. That smile had many meanings but this particular one I took as a warning. I did not smile back.

The next time Gabe came with only Anna Mae and Sam. He left Anna Mae outside Harry's office and, when the door closed, she marched over to me and announced in a breathy voice that I needed to be "set straight." I told her I had been set straight enough and didn't need any further help. Anna Mae was burdened by a literal mind and, as usual, failed to grasp what I was talking about. She started explaining details of Trotsky's defense of the Ukraine, how White Russian Armies were, at that very moment, demolishing whole villages. She said she was thinking of going there to help. She meant help Trotsky, of course, not demolish villages. I agreed it was something to consider. She asked what my position was. I said I was helping out in the newsroom. No, she said, my larger position. I said I had not formulated one. She said the world was polarizing and that one was either with the forces of progress or against them. I said I was still trying to identify what those forces of progress might be. She said any fool could see. Indeed, I said.

At that point the door opened and Gabe came out, leaving Sam inside. He came over and placed a possessive hand on Anna Mae's backside, then gave me one of his bow-shaped smiles.

"Congratulations," I said. "You've taken hold of the minister's daughter." He laughed. Anna Mae did not look pleased.

"No hard feelings," he said.

"None yet," I said, thinking of Harry, but I could see that he misunderstood or was at least confused as to my meaning.

When they all left I marched into Harry's office and said I needed to know what was going on. "I'm being offered a graceful exit or an inglorious one," he said. "So far I've opted for inglorious."

"Can they make you go?" I asked.

"Eventually," he said. "If they can keep up the pressure." Just that week Eugene Debs had announced, from prison, his intention to take back the leadership of the Socialist Party. Morris Hillquit, his deputy, was taking the necessary steps to convene the national convention. "If I can hold out till

August," Harry said, "maybe the tide will turn. Don't you bother—"

"My pretty little head." I could play this game, but I took the occasion to say something serious. "I have evidence on Gabe," I told him. "Things I could use to stop him." I thought about the paltry evidence I did have. "At least I could try."

Harry looked interested but doubtful. "What evidence?"

I didn't want to go into that. "Papers that could implicate him in sedition."

"I'm not going to help convict anyone of sedition," Harry said.

I tried again. "How about avoiding the draft?"

"Not that either."

"You have too many scruples," I said.

He smiled. "We socialists are often so accused."

"Well, I'm not a socialist," I told him. "And not burdened by your scruples." He ruffled my hair to put an end to that discussion and asked how I was getting settled in my new place.

My new place was a room and a half. The first time I had ever had a washing alcove, a real sink and a flush toilet, curtained off from my bedroom. I was living in an attic in a fisherman's house in the Ballard district, with a family named Ahlberg, old friends of Harry's. I helped Mrs. Ahlberg with the laundry and baby tending, so the rent was low. There was a vacant lot next door, and a rickety back stairs that took me up to my apartment. I felt safe enough going around the back, because it was April, and light when I usually got home, but one evening, a day or two after that last meeting with Gabe, I got home after dark, and there was Gabe waiting for me in the vacant lot. He stepped out as I rounded the back edge of the house.

"Penny Joe," he said, his thin smile loading that simple announcement with menace.

"You don't belong here," I said, trying to think whether it was better to run, yell or stand my ground. What happens in these situations is that women lose sensation in their limbs, so that flight or even protest seems impossible. We must be made more like possums than hares. This weakness I struggled to overcome. "What have you come for," I asked, my voice flat, trying to sound calm, trying to deflect the menace to somewhere outside myself. I focused on a nearby tree, the wooden fence in the distance.

He whistled between his teeth, sizing up my question. "What have you got?"

"Nothing," I said. "Get out of here." I turned and started back toward the street. There was no way I was going up those rickety steps. I thought if I could get around the corner of the house and into the glare of the streetlight, I might get him to leave. He grabbed my arm but I kept going. Fortunately, I was moving fast enough so that he didn't have good purchase and I dragged him a step or two before he got a second hand on my shoulder, uncomfortably close to my neck. I had the urge to turn my head and gnaw at his fingers, but I decided that would slow me down. I got another step or two, just shy of where the streetlight cast its beam, but under a lighted window. If I raised my voice would someone hear?

"Get away from me!" I shouted. "Get your hands off!"

His response was to pull me close, my back to his front, his arm around my waist, and clamp a hand over my mouth. I bit the inside of his finger while trying to drum his shin with my heel.

"Stop!" he hissed. "I just want to talk." He loosened his hand, which was now bleeding, and stepped back. "Jesus Christ!" he said, examining his finger.

"That's not nice," I said peevishly.

"Are you my mother?" he said, sucking his wound. That seemed to break the tension. Jokes like that don't usually go along with rapes.

"How's your new boyfriend?" he asked, meaning Harry.

"I wish," I said, although I didn't mean it. I snuck a look at the lighted window.

He noticed the look, and the implied fear. His tone changed, became satisfied. "I think you took something of mine."

I could deny it or not. "If I did, I don't have it now."

"No?" he said, smiling as if I had confirmed possession of the egg.

I smiled back. A sweet smile, full of poison. I had just remembered the card in my coat. I took it out of my pocket, looked at it, saw the name and job title for the first time. "It says here that this gentleman is an assistant to the U.S. Attorney General, Department of Justice, Washington D.C." I waited a minute, watching Gabe try to control his breath. "D.C. stands for District of Columbia," I added, waving the card a little. "I met him on the train, then here again, after the strike. He was at the train station, loading soon-to-be-deported aliens." I could see Gabe only half-believed this. But half-believing was enough to give me the advantage. He tried to take the card but I snatched it out of his reach. His injured finger was still leaking blood.

I looked up at the window, this time with more assurance, as if I assumed a listener was just out of sight. "He knew about the jewels. And the eggs," I told him, thinking about Manny and Rosa and Mme. Borodin. "Not just the one you kept." There, I'd said it. Implied I'd told the man not only about Manny and Rosa but also about Fanya Borodin and the whole apparatus of Mexican Bolsheviks. Gabe's smile changed. My enjoyment of this moment made me reckless. Had I been thinking better I would have known that provoking fear in such situations is unwise.

"You gave it to him," he whispered, implying I'd told everything. I could see his body coil and knew I'd gone too far.

"He knew about the eggs. Knew about you. I didn't tell him anything." I wasn't sure he believed that, but at least I'd avoided confirming I had the egg.

"I want the egg," he said. "And the other thing."

Ah! Now, that bit of information was worth the whole caboodle. He'd as much as confirmed the invoice pad was gold. I pasted a puzzled look on my face. Out of the corner of my eye I could see a shadow passing behind the window shade. I raised my voice. "I don't know what you're talking about. The man was following me. He asked me questions. Could be after me! I'm at risk, too!"

"I want my egg!" he said, raising his voice and reaching for me again.

"I don't have your egg!" I shouted. "I never—" At this point the window sash came up, and Mrs. Ahlberg stuck out her head. "Penny Joe?"

"Here," I said, waving to make sure she saw me. "Just coming."

She smiled a nervous smile, looking directly at Gabe, then turned back to someone in the room.

"Get out of here," I hissed at Gabe, part warning, part command. "I didn't take your egg," I told him one more time. Then I was gone, to the front of the house, scooting up the stairs, into the just opening front door. I was never so glad of a welcome.

The Ahlbergs calmed me down with a mug of hot milk. At first I was evasive about who the man was, but finally told them it was Leon Green—everybody in Seattle knew about Leon Green. I told them Leon was pressing for Harry to resign, that I had had some words with him in the newspaper office earlier that day. Mr. Ahlberg, a big man, was used to settling things with his hands, and he was all set to hightail out to find Leon Green right then and there, but I stopped him, saying that Harry was in a precarious position, that going after Leon Green for what was essentially a personal quarrel was bad business. So he calmed down and asked if I felt safe alone upstairs, and I said yes, though I wasn't sure I meant it, and finally it was decided that from then on, if I came home after dark, I would knock at the Ahlberg's front door and one of them would go with me up the back stairs to my room. Then Mrs. Ahlberg took me to her second floor, past the kids' room, to a big linen closet and showed me a ladder and trap door that she said came out at the far end of my attic room. "I'm going to keep this unlocked, and this ladder in place, so if you ever need to get downstairs quick, you'll be able to." I thanked her and said I hoped such an escape would not be necessary.

The next morning, after thinking about it, I dug out the yellow invoice pad from where I'd hidden it and took it downstairs. Mr. Ahlberg was just finishing his coffee and I took him outside on the porch and showed him the pad. "This is what Leon Green was after last night. I don't know why it's so important, but it is. If something happens—" Here I hesitated, I wasn't sure what I had in mind. "If something happens, and I don't come back for it, you can give it to the police if you want. If you think it would be right." I hesitated again. I still wasn't sure what I was getting at. "Sam Rabinowitz gave this to Leon," I said. "I think it has something to do with explosives. The handwriting is foreign. Polish, maybe, I don't know." Mr. Ahlberg raised a hand to stop me. Explosives and mysterious bombings were common enough among union circles in those days so as not to warrant surprise. But neither did most people want to know too much about it.

"I'm sorry to do this," I added. "I'll move out if you want. It would be safer, in case—" Again he raised his hand. Then he put the battered invoice pad in the pocket of his oil slicker. "Don't tell the Missus," he said.

I walked down the hill and took the trolley to the newspaper office as if nothing had happened. Indeed, nothing had. I had called attention to myself, made Gabe more wary, but had done nothing to save Harry Ault's job. It was now mid-April. The next ten days brought a steadily increasing drumbeat of pressure on Harry to resign. Petitions signed at all the union halls and forwarded to the Central Labor Council and Samuel Gompers in Washington D.C. The

Reverend Sloan, in a letter to the *Post-Intelligencer*, suggesting in the "interests of harmony" Harry Ault step down. University students staging demonstrations and boycotting classes to make Harry throw in the towel. It was as if everyone in Seattle simultaneously decided that all the wrongs of the world could be righted if Harry Ault just quit. Astonishing, how a scapegoat is selected and then sold to the masses. Impressive, Gabe's orchestrating all this.

I had stopped eating, unable to keep down food. I lost weight and Harry noticed. He asked if I was feeling the strain and I allowed as how I might be. "How do you think I'm feeling," he joked, then said nerves only made him pack in more potatoes. All this harassment ended abruptly when a dramatic new event filled Seattle's morning papers. On the afternoon of April 28, 1919, a bomb exploded at the office of Ole Hansen, Seattle's mayor. In the next three days some thirty-four more bombs were sent to various political personages around the country. Some went off and some didn't. No one claimed responsibility. In Seattle a mysterious flier appeared claiming the bombings were the work of right-wing provocateurs. Of course, the mainstream papers and local politicians claimed it was the communists. On May Day, all around the country, parades were disrupted. Seemingly spontaneous riots broke out, well-organized mobs stormed socialist and union headquarters. The *Union Record* was not spared. In the fray Seattle forgot about Leon Green and the campaign to oust Harry Ault. At the *Union Record* we kept our heads down and spent the time repairing machinery and sorting through ransacked files. Then someone came into the newsroom and announced that Anna Mae Sloan had been found, snowbound in the high Cascades. And that Leon Green, to all appearances, had disappeared.

CHAPTER 29

While I didn't much care for Anna Mae, I did feel duty bound to visit her in the hospital. Her father was keeping the news quiet, but one of her pals at the paper knew and somehow it got around. Anna Mae was an outdoors enthusiast, so the fact that she was in the mountains, in a cabin, when a late storm hit was of no particular surprise. That she was alone struck folks as odd, but I didn't think she had been alone.

What was odd is that people who knew her, who were part of the movement, did not allow themselves to draw conclusions regarding certain changes in her personal life. Anyone who had eyes could tell that Gabe, or Leon Green as he was then known, was keeping her company. But radicals are a surprisingly prudish lot. Not that they don't have sexual proclivities, but they don't like to call attention to it, the act, the lack of discipline it implies. For women, this is especially true. Serious women are somehow supposed to be exemplars of free love while remaining chaste, participants without entanglement. Men are allowed their male compulsions but not so as it interferes with their work or the stature they bring to that work. To get involved with a colleague is asking for trouble—one or the other suffers disrespect within the inner circle. Anna Mae would have understood that she would be the one to suffer. Gabe, I imagine, made it known he was jollying her up, recruiting her deeper into the cause, whereas Anna Mae would have handled this entanglement by treating it as if it didn't exist. So, of course she was alone in the cabin. The fact that Gabe disappeared simultaneously wasn't a connection people would have speculated upon.

The whole matter of Gabe Rabinowitz pretending to be Leon Green was another example of the double thinking that was, and still is, necessary to survive in the world of radical politics. Dozens, perhaps hundreds, of people in Seattle knew Gabe well enough to deduce he was Leon Green. After all, Gabe spent the better part of a year on platforms all around town purveying death masks and other mementoes of the Everett martyrs. Then, suddenly, along with scores of other draft-avoiders, he disappeared. The politic thing was to blot them from one's mind. After all, good socialists should support pacifists. So draft-avoiders first became heroes and then became nonexistent — they simply dropped from public and private notice. That was the safest way. After the war, when Seattle radicals were bursting with bravado, plunging into their pointless and ill-conceived general strike, an unknown leader appeared, a protege of Sam Rabinowitz, who immediately catapulted this mysterious fellow into a key position at City Light. Bingo, the emergence of Leon Green, Gabe-like, bearded, incarnate, ready to push the strike rhetoric to the limit. But this wasn't Gabe, the draft-avoider, a hero who didn't exist. This was a new unknown, heaven sent, a stranger with no past or future to take center stage.

And even then, after Leon Green became the spokesman for the strike, when his picture was on every front page and his words teletyped around the nation, no one seemed to notice that he possessed an uncanny resemblance to the missing nephew of Sam Rabinowitz. Except the man on the train. Somehow I think he knew, and was biding his time for his own reasons.

At any rate, I went to see Anna Mae. A day or two after I heard, three or four since she had been found. The hospital was only admitting guests Anna Mae wished to see, so I was mildly surprised when I was allowed to enter her room. She was sitting up, pillows tucked behind her, and looked bruised on the left side of her face. She noticed my gaze and put a hand up to her cheek. "I fell," she announced. "There was ice everywhere." I murmured something about late storms and left it at that. I had brought a gift, an Indian souvenir, a birch bark canoe glued on a pond of glass, a small velvet fish underneath coming up to feed. The warrior was missing, maybe fashioning one was beyond the talents of the souvenir maker, or perhaps the brave had fallen out of his canoe and been lost in shipment. Something about the scene's loneliness, the missing canoeist, appealed to me, and I bought it on impulse and now felt foolish offering it to Anna Mae.

"What are you going to do when you get better?" I asked, as much to distract her from this gift as anything. I expected some noncommittal reply. Instead I saw her face crumple as she turned away into the bank of pillows. Her body heaved as she struggled to regain composure. She's in love with him, I realized. And then, this is a woman gravely injured. I adjusted my voice. "Is there anything I can do?" Then added, "He's not worth it." There was a moment of silence while we both absorbed what I had said. Then she turned back to face me, her mouth working like that trapped fish.

She said, "He—he's—" Then she stopped and pulled back her hospital gown to show me a dark bruise running from her neck all the way down to the top of her breast. Her modesty prevented me from seeing the rest. Part of me wanted to see it all and part of me didn't. "You should go to the police," I said. That turned her ashen.

"No," she said, mouth working to make sound come out. "No one can know."

"I know," I pointed out, partly to argue, partly as a kind of solidarity. At least one other person knows about Gabe Rabinowitz, I was saying. The kind of things he is capable of. "I know," I repeated.

She absorbed this without apparent reaction.

"You'll heal," I tried again, to infuse her with some hope. "Think about what you'll do next."

She looked at me with deep sadness, as if a part of her was cut out, incapable of any assemblage of will.

"You have to try," I insisted. I heard my voice carry a mean, mocking tone. All of a sudden I understood the voice with which my mother had greeted my tears. She had been trying to strengthen me, to toughen me. She had been trying to help. But it hadn't helped, it had only been an added weight to my desolation. I tried a different tack. "What would you do If you weren't such a squashed frog?" My brother speaking, this was how he used to cheer me up.

As I hoped, it startled a laugh. "Oh," she said, "I can't even think."

"Why not?" I challenged. "Don't think about tomorrow, think about a year from now." Then, to set an example, I announced, "I'm going to Washington D.C. to see the Library of Congress. And get a job so I can go to night school at the Department of Agriculture." That was news to me, but it seemed like a good enough idea now that I'd said it. "What's your plan?" I asked again. Go along, just pretend, I was trying to tell her. This was the game Horace would play to help me out of my doldrums.

She started slowly. Opened her mouth, motioned for water. She put the glass down, then announced she wanted to go to the Ukraine. The Quakers were organizing a relief brigade out of Warsaw, she said, and while it wasn't possible to go directly into Soviet territories, she was sure once she got there she could find a way to slip across. I sat like a stone, contemplating the mountain of deceit she was about to climb. But I kept my silence. It was her life. Just as Rosa had agreed to go to New York as Manny's wife, weighed that against the prospect of staying in Mexico, now Anna Mae, out of the wreckage of a love affair, was flinging herself into a new maelstrom. I could not reckon the wisdom.

"Hold on to that," I said, and reached out to squeeze her knee, then stood up to go.

"Good-bye," she said, knowing it was a final parting, her voice signaling that any lingering bad feeling between us was cancelled, now that we were going our separate ways.

I smiled. She turned to look out the window.

Going downstairs I ran into Reverend Sloan. He was accompanied by Marcel's mother, which maybe accounted for my outburst. I had always wondered if there were something between them, suspected that Reverend Sloan was a ladies' man, his piousness a calculated mask. Coming on them now, in the stairwell, unaware of any eyes to see them, I could spot the signs. The way she held his arm, his head inclined toward hers. He was starting to say something, and then, on seeing me, they sprung apart. My mood was such that my normal reaction, to crow at this sign of moral turpitude, was smothered by my concern for Anna Mae. I stopped a stair above them, blocking his way. When he tried to smile and move past me I reached out and grabbed his arm. "Gabe Rabinowitz did this to her," I said. "Your friend, Leon Green."

The Reverend gasped, flustered at this linking of Gabe to Leon Green. Also relieved, I suppose, that I had not commented on his companion. Offended as well, I am sure, that I had presumed to visit his daughter, learn about her condition and then feel free to speculate as to who might be the cause of it.

"There was an ice storm," he said.

"I know," I said, skipping over that. "And Leon Green disappeared."

"Well, yes," he said, trying to deflect this new topic.

"And Leon Green is Gabe Rabinowitz," I said, forcing him like a dull child.

"I thought perhaps—" Then he conceded the point, looking uncomfortable, so strong was the taboo against speaking of draft-avoiders.

"That's neither here nor there," I said, impatient with all this. He really is a silly man, I decided. And warranted one chance only. "Gabe and Sam Rabinowitz are involved in these bombings. I can't tell you how I know, but I do. Stay away from them. They're rough customers. You see what happened to your daughter."

Then I brushed past them and left.

* * *

The *Union Record* had shut down for a couple of days following its sacking after the May Day parade. Since reopening, it had been running editorials protesting the claim that organized labor had been behind the bombings. The kernel of truth behind the notion of labor involvement was, of course, that the bombings were somehow connected to a Bolshevik uprising, a vast, worldwide conspiracy, furthered by a disciplined cadre stationed right here in Seattle. The nation-wide pattern of the bombings gave further fuel to this fear. The left's attempt to discredit this notion by publicizing its own version of a vast right-wing conspiracy was not effective. More aliens and radicals were rounded up. Seattle's general strike was cited in editorial after editorial as the turning point in America's fight against Godless Communism. The *Union Record's* editorials were mere spit in the sea.

Harry Ault, while still its nominal editor, was spending less and less time in the office. In mid-May he left for Chicago, to attend a rump session called by the old leadership of the Socialist Party. They were meeting one last time before handing over the reins to John Reed, and, as their last act, voted to expel two-thirds of the voting membership, some 40,000 people, for the crime of belonging to affiliate organizations that espoused the violent overthrow of governments. The fact that the governments these immigrants advocated overthrowing were in Eastern Europe did not matter. They were John Reed votes, not Morris

Hillquit votes. This plan for wholesale expulsion seemed to me a sign of panic. And it served to increase the white-hot anger with which Harry Ault was greeted in Seattle labor circles.

When Harry returned he looked haggard. From sun up to sundown pickets blocked the entrance to the building, shouting insults to all who entered. From her hospital bed, Anna Mae sent in her resignation. Several union locals began withholding dues from the Central Labor Council until the "Ault issue" was resolved. Rumors began to circulate about Harry's past—a drowned pregnant girl, misappropriation of money, connections with Seattle's opium trade—all standard slanders, impossible to refute. And not only had Gabe disappeared, Sam Rabinowitz, after being so prominent in opposition to Harry, now faded into the background as well. Evidence by his absence, I supposed, that he was pulling the strings, but, like Harry's opium connections, impossible to prove or refute.

I began having trouble sleeping. Not knowing where Gabe was, what Sam was doing, made me jumpy. I was beset by shadows, torn between the impulse to hide, run away, or stand and take revenge. For that is what that last impulse was. Not a matter of a good citizen bringing forward evidence. No, this was personal. My blurting out Sam's name to Reverend Sloan now seemed, in retrospect, no more honorable than the ugly rumormongering about Harry. If I had evidence, then announce it. If not, tuck it in the corner of my mind where suppositions are kept. That is what I told myself, but the lack of fighting back wore on me. To see Harry not fight back wore on me as well.

June passed into July. It was hot that July, with little rain. I remember reading in the *Post-Intelligencer* that frogs that summer were dying in the dried-out ponds. I thought about our frog collecting trips, Marcel's and mine, the evenings that came after, and these thoughts kept me awake those hot nights as well, if you could call such pain and longing thoughts.

On June 2, 1919, another bomb, the last of the series, ripped open the front door of the Attorney General's house in Washington D.C. It is a little known fact that the then-Secretary of the Navy, Franklin Delano Roosevelt, lived across the street. I don't think today people can understand how frightening to the average American it was, all those bombs going off. In July there was an article in the paper with a picture of the newly appointed head of the Alien Radical Division in the U.S. Department of Justice. The new appointee was quoted as saying that ninety percent of the communist and anarchist agitation in the country was attributable to aliens. I thought of Gabe and Sam, both American born, and decided he was wrong. On the other hand, I remembered the Eastern European writing on the yellow invoice pad, my stay in Mexico in the villa of an Indian Brahmin, the mysterious Borodin who had been a Latvian spy, and decided maybe I was wrong. Where were Manny Gomez and Rosa now? Had they gone with Mike Gold and John Reed to Moscow? Was it a coincidence that John Reed came back from Moscow and promptly took over the executive committee of the Socialist Party? Were the old-line socialists right, along with the new head of the Alien Radical Division, in attributing all the violence and menace to the foreign born? My head ached from the weight of it. I knew I was heading toward a decisive moment, a question of loyalties, of taking, or switching sides. What was I going to do with the yellow invoice pad, with my Faberge egg? How was I going to end this association with Gabe Rabinowitz? Of course I recognized the picture in the newspaper, the man who had been named head of the Alien Radical Division. The man on the train. J. Edgar Hoover.

CHAPTER 30

The conviction settled upon me that, since Gabe already thought I had given the egg to J. Edgar Hoover, I might as well do so. But the question was how. I was, to the thinking of the Justice Department, technically complicit in what Gabe had done, so I was under no illusion that a chicken dinner would convert Mr. Hoover into an ally. I had broken one law, leaving and reentering the country without going through customs, and had taken a valuable object that didn't belong to me. Depending on who you thought it did belong to, that also might be considered a crime. More worrisome, I feared I could be made to testify, paraded around as part of someone else's political drama. This I did not plan to do. So the problem remained, how to get the egg to him, for whatever use he would make of it, without entangling myself?

One Sunday morning I went with Mr. Ahlberg down to the fish pier and retrieved the yellow invoice pad from where he had buried it under some old ship's manifests. A few days later I went back to the university and requested the Library of Congress papers and retrieved my egg. Now that both were safely back with me, I thought about contacting the local police, or the Justice Department, to find out who from the Alien Radical Division might still be snooping around Seattle looking for alien radicals. But these approaches seemed unsatisfactory. More and more I settled on the notion that I would go to Washington D.C. myself, and find the house where Mr. Hoover lived with his mother on Seward Square. I would go inside and meet his mother and then hand him the invoice pad and the egg. That was the picture I spun out for myself, a fantasy just ludicrous enough to assuage my fear.

Each morning I still had to fight my way through ugly picket lines to report for work at the *Union Record*, though fewer and fewer others seemed willing to brave the threats and insults. Harry emerged less and less from his glassed-in office, but one day he came out and asked if I wanted to go to Chicago, to the Socialist Party convention at the end of August, to the purging of its leftist membership and subsequent reinstatement of the old-guard leadership. This was to be the final break. The communists had already rented separate space and planned an inaugural meeting of their own organization immediately after being thrown out. I thought about whether I wanted to attend. The place would undoubtedly be crawling with spies of Mr. Hoover, as well as the likes of Manny Gomez and Mike Gold. And probably Gabe and Sam Rabinowitz.

Yes, I said, I'd go. I presumed Harry wanted my clerical help. Also my company, I suspected. He said we would be leaving in ten days time. I hesitated, then told him that after the meeting I probably wouldn't be coming back. He nodded and said that he probably wouldn't be holding this job much longer himself.

So it was with some sadness that we embarked on the train in mid-August, both of us feeling we had a task to do that was not a pleasant one, with the prospect of an uncertain future. We settled in a small hotel near the Palmer House and plunged into a round of pre-convention caucuses. I was not in any of the important ones, Harry mostly had me running errands and mimeographing announcements. The convention itself was predictably tumultuous. Outside, pickets, policemen and newspaper reporters all jostling for space and attention, while inside the proceedings were unexpectedly listless. A three-day recitation of old grievances and well-practiced defenses of loyalty, punctuated by bursts of anger at those demonstrating outside. But truth was, none of the old socialists took any pleasure in expelling 40,000 immigrants just because their nationality-based affiliates advocated the violent overthrow of unjust governments. It was the death of the American Socialist Party. It wasn't labeled as such, but that's what it felt like.

When I wasn't attending plenary sessions or taking minutes at rump meetings, I made a halfhearted effort to find Marcel. He was no longer at the Ballet Orchestra, it had taken me only one phone call to find that out, but I was not able to get any further information on where he had gone. One morning I took the train down to the university, to see if Professor Danzig could tell me anything. He was out when I got there, so I left a note under his door, asking if he knew where Marcel was and leaving my hotel phone number.

As the meeting wound down and my time in Chicago grew short, I was close to giving up hope that I'd be able to pick up Marcel's trail. I'd kept the egg and the invoice pad with me, in the trusty bottom of my purse, because I was positive that Gabe and his uncle were somewhere in the city. I used the back door to the convention hall, to avoid pickets, to avoid running into them. I worried that the Reverend Sloan had repeated my remarks to Sam. I wondered where Anna Mae had gone, whether she might show up on the arm of Gabe. As it became less and less likely that Professor Danzig would phone, I grew more and more jumpy. I kept dreaming Gabe would come up and snatch me from behind. Or that Anna Mae would denounce me from the floor of the convention. I just wanted to disappear, to give Mr. Hoover my egg and be gone.

But the next day, after I came back from one final and fruitless trip to the music department, I discovered my room had been searched. Not trashed, like I had done to Gabe's room, but mussed up enough so that I would know someone had been there. Gabe or Mr. Hoover's men? I didn't know. I thought about going to the hotel across town where the supposedly secret meetings of the new communist organization were to be held. Finding and confronting Gabe a second time. But after seeing Anna Mae in the hospital, the whole idea of going head-to-head with Gabe scared me. The better, ignominious plan was to steal away, to let both Marcel and Gabe slip into my past. And so, without thinking too hard about it, I packed my suitcase and checked out, left a good-bye note for Harry at the hotel desk, took a taxi to the train station and bought a ticket for Washington D.C.

* * *

I seem to have been a creature of half-baked plans. Certainly the idea of going to the house on Seward Street to have tea with Mrs. Hoover was one. As I sat on yet another train watching the smoky hills of Western Pennsylvania sweep past, I thought that my first attention should be given to planning what I would do after I gave the egg to Mr. Hoover. I would have to disappear, start a new life without anybody knowing or caring who or where I was. I reviewed what Mr. Hoover knew about me, my habits, predilections, and decided that this time I would not get a job at a coffee shop near a university or typesetting at a labor newspaper. Once I had done my deed, I would change my name and my appearance. I thought about whether to dye my hair or merely cut it. Get it marcelled, in honor of my lost Marcel. Then, like a schoolgirl, I started doodling names. Mrs. Joseph Capstan. Miss Gertrude Dogsbody. Nothing seemed to fit. In this way I put off thinking about what I was actually going to call myself and what I was actually going to do about giving the egg to Mr. Hoover. All that could wait, I told myself, until I found a place to stay and had a full night's sleep.

Union Station in Washington is an imposing place. I could see the lighted dome of the Capitol as I stepped through the heavy bronze doors into the hot night. I looked at the cluster of hotels off to the right and decided to take my chances with the Negro bellman who was carting bags for well-dressed passengers standing in the taxi line. "Can you tell me of an inexpensive hotel? Or better yet, a room to rent?" He studied me, then flashed me a smile and motioned me over to the marble archway to wait. After he had loaded all his passengers into taxis, he came back with a small pad and pencil and wrote down an address.

"My cousin," he said. "She takes only colored boarders but for me she sometimes makes an exception." I thanked him and asked how far away it was. "Six blocks," he said, motioning off to the left.

"Is it near the Library of Congress?" I asked.

"Close enough," he said, looking at me in an odd way. "Are you some kind of researcher?"

"Close enough," I said, then asked more detailed directions on how to walk to his cousin's place.

Henrietta Boland's rooming house was a three-story brick row house on D Street N.E. I rang the bell and waited on the marble stoop and looked at the day lilies and clipped boxwood hedge that edged the tiny front lawn. Just the kind of place I was looking for.

The door opened to a large middle-aged Negro woman with her hands on her hips waiting for me to explain what I wanted. I showed her the slip of paper. She studied it, then noted that this must have come from Lysander. I nodded and said I had asked him for help at Union Station. "You asked help from a colored man?" she said in mock surprise. At least I took her tone to be a joke. I said Lysander looked more honest than what I saw of the taxi drivers, and his advice was cheaper. She smiled and said maybe this once she'd make an exception as long as I didn't go around announcing where I was staying. She asked if I wanted to rent by the week or the month and I said by the week, then thought maybe that was the wrong answer and added that I didn't know how long I'd stay. She asked what I was doing in town and I said research, at the Library of Congress, and she seemed to buy that and told me what the room would cost, and said, "Cash now please." I gave her the cash, most of what I had, and asked where I might get a part-time job while I was doing my research, and she said she'd have to think on that and that breakfast came with the room, served six to seven a.m., no exceptions.

She led me up two flights of stairs covered by a threadbare but clean runner, to a narrow room, third floor rear, with a bath down the hall shared by two other ladies, both colored. I said that was fine. She gave me one towel and one washcloth and said the sheets and blankets were in the dresser. The room was big enough only for a single bed, the dresser and one straight-backed chair. There was one window, which I promptly opened to let in some air. But the room was quiet and I was in a place where no one would think to look. That seemed heaven. I sat on the bed and realized how tired I was. It must have showed because my new landlady said I could sign the guest register in the morning. That gave me all night to think up a new name.

The next morning I awoke sticky from the humid air and confused as to my whereabouts. Oh, yes, Washington D.C., in another strange room, starting up another vagabond existence. I remembered the egg, my half-baked plan, and felt if I could just deliver it, get rid of it, get past those last three years, my unwanted association with Gabe and Sam Rabinowitz, I would be home free. Free to invent myself, to become whatever was waiting inside. With those uplifting thoughts I took my towel down the hall to the pink bathroom and washed up and brushed my teeth and got ready to face the day. When I arrived downstairs for breakfast, 6:45 a.m., my landlady was waiting. I called her Mrs. Boland, which she said she appreciated, but to call her Henrietta. She waited expectantly for my name. "Jo," I said, then amplified,

"Josephine." Well, I had a new first name. I looked down at her polished mahogany table in the gold brocade dining room and took up a white linen napkin in a silver ring. "My," I said, looking for a fresh topic of conversation. "How lovely." I meant the hominess of the welcome, the elegance of the table setting. But I could see she misunderstood. "I come from a factory town," I added. "My ma never had silver napkin rings, much less napkins."

Henrietta's face forgave me. "I could tell you're not from around here." Meaning, I later figured out, I was not sensitive to the language and customs of race. I also later found out I was putting her in some danger by simply being there. But at that time, in Washington D.C., I was not breaking the law. Had we been over the river in Virginia it would have been another matter. At any rate I recognized all this only dimly, and was so bent on not revealing anything about myself that all this went over my head and I just smiled and dug into my porridge, which I later found out was called grits.

She asked where I was from, and I said out west, and she took this to be cowboy country, that where I came from they had ranches, and I let her think that. She told me that the house was her mother's, that two sisters, both teachers, had bought this house in 1887 and she, Henrietta, had lived in it for over thirty years. And that she and Lysander, her mother's sister's child, had been brought up almost as siblings. I had never heard someone use that word before, *siblings*, and it put me in mind of Horace, and something urgent and pain-filled came into me on hearing that term *sibling*, how she used it so proudly to describe what was between them. Horace and I were linked that same way, that was it, two kits from the same litter.

"Lysander stopped down on his way to work," Henrietta said. "He wanted to see if you'd made it."

I smiled again. Two sibling guardians and I'd only been in town twelve hours. "Tell him thank you," I said, tasting the coffee in the thin porcelain cup.

Dimples showed on her cheeks. "Lysander doesn't usually pay much mind to white women," she said. "Thank goodness." There was a pause before she started up again. "But he seems to have taken a liking to you."

We both laughed, to cover the awkwardness, for me to absorb the warning. "A good Samaritan," I offered, thinking this a neutral characterization of Lysander's motives.

"Um," she said, considering that. "Lysander always did like doctoring to lost puppies."

I came to learn a lot about this family. Henrietta began that morning by filling me with tales about growing up in a house run by two schoolteachers. I learned about the world-within-a-world of D.C.'s educated Negroes, the "Dunbar set," products of the city's elite school for the light-skinned Negro middle class. Lysander and Henrietta had grown up in this small world, then faced the realities of a city in the process of returning to southern-style segregation. Twenty years before, when Henrietta was attending Dunbar, the streetcars had been open to all. Now they were segregated, colored to the back, and, if the car was crowded, the Negroes stood or were put off to make room for the whites.

"Thank goodness my mother and aunt bought this house back then," she said. "Don't think they'd get to buy something like this now."

She managed the boarding house, and Lysander, who lived on the second floor with the male roomers, brought in extra pay with his job as a bellhop. Neither had married, though she said she kept company with an older man at church, an undertaker who was now a widower. Lysander she wasn't sure about, he had sown his wild oats, and was now steadying down, but hadn't fixed on any particular woman as yet, although there was a lovely lady at church Henrietta especially liked who wore wonderful hats. I asked about his age, and she said he was six years younger, which made him thirty-five.

Again I thought about Horace, the almost six year age difference that separated us, how he and I might have lived as a similar companionable pair, except that Horace was dead, and hadn't wanted my companionship anyway. Lysander's name, she said, was Shakespearian, a character from *A Midsummer Night's Dream*. Lysander's mother was an English teacher, don't you know, and had spoiled her son from birth. I wanted to tell Henrietta about how my mother chose the name Horace, for an Egyptian god, how I'd always wanted to be Isis, but instead had been named for my father. "Joe," I said, more to myself than to her, "Josephine." Then added, much to my surprise, "I was named after an Empress." I straightened up at that thought. Well, this business of naming yourself could have some benefits.

Just then, another of the lodgers came down, a Mr. Grimes. Henrietta busied herself with his breakfast, and when the time came to sign the guest register and get a rent receipt, I completed my new identity by choosing the last name of Nichols. In just one day, I'd gone from penny to nickels. A fivefold increase.

CHAPTER 31

Rent receipt in hand, I spent the rest of my morning walking up and down the streets of my new neighborhood. Washington is laid out on a grid, with letter names running north/south and numbered streets running east/west. There are four quadrants of letters and numbers, with the U.S. Capitol at the center. Henrietta's house was in the northeast quadrant, at 607 D Street, N.E., which meant that I was six blocks east of the Capitol and four blocks north. This tidy system pleased me, anchored me in a way that felt calming. I went up and down the grid, back and forth from 6th and D to 12th and H, then cut across Independence and Constitution into the southeast quadrant. At Sixth Street S.E., I found Seward Square, named for William Seward, Lincoln's Secretary of State. Nearby was a public library, so I went in, showed my rent receipt and got a library card in my new name.

Now I had two pieces of identification, so I set about looking for a job. The Eastern Market, just around the corner, seemed like a good prospect. It was a large public building that rented stalls to local farmers who brought in produce for sale to housewives and restaurants. Around this market had sprung up bakeries and meat markets and stores selling house wares. I walked up and down Ninth Street trying to decide whether I wanted to sell sausage or baked goods or lampshades. In the end I decided it didn't matter, I would work for the first store owner that would have me. I got my first lesson in race relations when I tried to apply for jobs in a couple of Negro-owned businesses only to be politely turned away. Finally I had to settle for a pharmacy on the corner with a hand-lettered sign in the window saying "position open, whites only." The owner explained that colored people were served at the back and were not allowed to purchase on credit. I thought about what Henrietta and Lysander would say about my new employment, but decided to put it from my mind.

I returned to my room with a library card, a job and a fierce set of foot blisters. A good beginning, it seemed to me, a new life both safely hidden and yet out in the open. As the days went by I became less anxious about the egg, whether it might be discovered or stolen. Since I had decided to get rid of it by giving it to Mr. Hoover, I figured if some thief snatched my purse, my only real loss would be the evidence of my new identity, and even that loss could be turned to advantage, since I could tell the police even more identification had been stolen as well. To my new employer I was, of course, guarded about exactly where I lived, careful to keep my "whites only" world separate from Henrietta's home. My friendship with Lysander began to blossom as well. There was about him a shy courtliness that seemed evidence of some attraction, but it was a hopeless, dangerous path, as I had been warned by Henrietta. So there were boundaries not to be stepped over and that seemed to free both of us to be just what we were. And in the pleasant confines of the parlor that autumn, the three of us, along with old Mrs. Hattry, another Dunbar teacher, played whist and read Alexander Dumas and talked about castles in France.

I would have liked my time there to go on forever. But one day, in mid-November, when the days were already woefully short, when the newspapers were filled with the deportation of the anarchist, Emma Goldman, I decided it was time to get back to my purpose in Washington, which was to track down J. Edgar Hoover and give him my egg.

Up until then, I had avoided going to the Library of Congress, out of a kind of superstition, not wanting Penny Joe to be discovered. But by that time I had cut my hair, bobbed it in the new flapper fashion, and didn't need a finger wave since my hair fell into a frizz that Henrietta said made me look high yellow. That pleased me, to be taken for one of the Dunbar set, even though my Scots-Irish skin and sharp features were hardly the mark of a light skinned Negro. I thought about rinsing my hair, and even experimented, but the lavender rinse came out muddy and henna made me look like a showgirl—a skinny small-breasted showgirl, but blowsy in a way that called attention. So I stuck with the carrot-red God had given me and finally one night, my head bent in the circle of light thrown by the fringed parlor lamp, trying to read aloud from *The Count of Monte Christo*, Henrietta said that I ought to get glasses. So I went down to the local eye glass store, to a man from Henrietta's church, who knew everything a real eye doctor did, and he sized me up, made me read charts, diluted my pupils with belladonna, then pawed through a dusty bin of lenses to select two he polished up, then set them in tortoiseshell frames that seemed too big for my face. But they served to hide my eyes, which were, according to my mother, my only good feature.

So now I had a complete new look: new haircut, glasses, a new style of dressing. Lysander had an artistic streak, and was fond of eyeing the racks of ready-made clothes that lined the sidewalks along Pennsylvania Avenue. He bought me a shawl from Trinidad, thin wool woven in zigzags of cherry and green. One Sunday night we defied convention and walked together to see an outfit in a store window—a tobacco-brown twill jacket worn above a bias-cut maroon skirt, silk and cut to the knee. "My, that's elegant," I said.

He said he would buy it for me. I protested. He insisted, and so, the next day, I walked back and parted with twenty dollars of Lysander's hard earned cash. He was so sure I'd agree that he'd already asked Mrs. Hattry to make me an ivory silk blouse to go with it. That night we celebrated in the parlor, Mrs. Hattry with pins in her mouth, fitting the sleeves, and Lysander smoking a cigar and drinking brandy as if he were the father of the bride. I told them about the last time I'd been fitted by a seamstress, wanted to tell them all about Mexico, wanted to show them the beautiful white dress with the red embroidered camellias I still had upstairs in the bottom of my suitcase, but dared not. I wanted them to know nothing that would implicate them if Mr. Hoover came to visit. So I kept that memory to myself and drank a sip of Lysander's brandy and counted my blessings.

The Library of Congress, when I finally stepped through its heavy bronze doors, was everything Mr. Hoover had promised. Endless gilded ceilings, frescoed walls and mosaic floors that seemed more like a museum than a book repository. I signed my new name and asked the guard directions to the reading room, then settled in at one of the mahogany desks ringed around the great circulation desk under the oracle skylight. I needed something to do—a topic of research to warrant my time looking around. I spotted magazines along one wall, and went over, looking through the technical journals and popular magazines, trying to settle somewhere between anthropology and arctic whaling, needlepoint and nephrology. Finally I picked up *Symphony Digest*, a magazine that looked to be a cross between classified ads and a newsletter. Most of its dozen or so pages were given over to advertisements, boxed announcements by agents who were accepting new clients, posted schedules of symphonies, help-wanted columns, a notice of a violin audition at the Minneapolis Philharmonic, a percussionist's position available with the Toledo Brass Ensemble. I skimmed all this without thinking, reading as if it were a phone book, taking in random bits of information to be filed away or dismissed.

Only after I had read through the entire copy, replaced it and taken out the previous number, did I realize I was looking for a name, reference to the whereabouts of one Marcel Freid. With whoosh of breath it dawned on me that this was the way I could find him. Somewhere in this great library, this giant maw that sucked up a copy of everything printed in this United States, there was a list, a reference to the members of some unknown orchestra that included the name of Marcel Freid. He was there waiting to be found. But not now, I told myself. First, I had other things to do. Nevertheless, I spent the next hour reading back issues of *Symphony Digest*, not expecting to find anything, just getting a sense of all the orchestras in the United States, their names, how they communicated with one another, how the many parts of this fluid society fitted together. Then I put Marcel out of mind. Just as Mr. Hoover was doing his detective work on me, I needed to concentrate my detective work on him.

The next free afternoon I went back to the Library of Congress and asked the librarian to find me a street directory of Washington. Seward Square was bound by six short streets, Seventh and Fifth, D to E. A District of Columbia telephone book listed no Hoover on any of those streets, but I had expected that. Next I asked for a telephone directory of the Justice Department, and found that the Bureau of Investigation did not list the home addresses of its employees. I sat for a while, looking at office phone numbers in the Alien Radical Division, thinking about how to proceed, whether to follow the postman up and down Seward Square, looking in mailboxes as he marched ahead, or pretend to be a delivery person with a mislabeled package and ask the neighbors for the correct address of Mrs. Hoover. I was clear that I did not want to walk into Mr. Hoover's office, did not want to go through a phalanx of questioners, did not want my gifts extracted from the bottom of my purse and then myself become an object of their interrogation.

I thought of the letter I had forged in Mme. Borodin's hand, the one I had so labored over to confuse Gabe in my escape, and it seemed to me some similar effort might work in this instance. I needed a letter, I decided, so that when I handed over the egg and the yellow invoice pad, Mr. Hoover and his aides would have enough information to point them in the right direction, but not enough to conclude I knew any more than I had put in my letter. So that when they tried and failed to find me, it wouldn't seem like I was avoiding them, it was more that I was just an anonymous and unimportant bearer of information. I needed to get the weight and tone of it right, the letter had to say just enough and not too much.

I went over the facts I would present. Gabe had received the yellow invoice pad from his uncle, and thought it valuable enough to take with him to Mexico and back. He also thought it important enough to try to get it back from me. But I did not know why it was important or what wider enterprise it connected to. That was for Mr. Hoover to figure out. Then there was the question of what had made me take it from Gabe in the first place.

The Faberge egg was another matter. About this I knew a lot, that it was part of a shipment sent from Lenin's inner circle, that it was smuggled to Mexico and then smuggled again into the U.S. That it was supposed to be sold to finance various activities of the Russian government. I wondered about the other jewels, the ones routed by way of Tampa. How much money they had fetched in New York, whether Manny and Rosa had gotten through. Whether money from the sale of those jewels or the eggs given to Mme. Borodin had supported the cost of the recent organizational meeting in Chicago. I wondered whether Mme. Borodin had sent her eggs to New York, or whether she had kept them in Chicago and used them to finance the Chicago wing of the party. I didn't know, these were issues Mr. Hoover would care about, but I didn't.

My real question about the egg I was proposing to give him was what did I want him to know. About me, about Mexico, about Borodin. Did I want him to know it came from me? Well, the fact that I had imagined giving it to him at a tea party arranged by his mother more or less answered that question. I wanted him to know I had it and that I had stolen it from Gabe. But did I want him to know about Mme. Borodin, the stuffed ceramic chickens, the existence of the other eggs? Or did I want to narrow the story down to just Gabe—that he had gone to Mexico, gotten a Faberge egg destined for sale to finance American Communist Party business, then kept it, failed to turn it over as instructed for sale, and that because of that, I had, in turn, stolen it from him. For what reason? What was I going to say? Because I liked it? Or that I intended all along to turn it in for evidence—that that was why I had taken the mysterious yellow invoice pad as well, because I thought it, too, was evidence, because I was a patriot, just like Mr. Hoover.

Alas, that trail ended by making me feel ill. The idea of any interview with Mr. Hoover made me want to dispose of both items in the ladies' room trash receptacle and be done with it. But then I remembered the bruise along Anna Mae's shoulder, the sad folly of my father's life, and I told myself it had to end. The little war against shadows that I had been conducting all my life had to end. I had to face J. Edgar Hoover and try to parse my way through the morally ambiguous thicket I had created for myself. And come out the other end whole. Free, with it all behind me. I didn't know how I was going to do it, whether I could do it, but I had to try.

In the end I constructed a letter to go along with a neatly wrapped package:

> *Dear Mr. Hoover,*
>
> *I am providing you with two items I obtained (without permission) from Mr. Gabriel Rabinowitz, who is (or was) also known as Leon Green, a spokesman of the Seattle General Strike Committee. The yellow invoice pad was given to*

Mr. Rabinowitz by his uncle, Sam Rabinowitz, prior to Gabe's disappearance in June, 1917. Gabe Rabinowitz was then preparing to leave the country to avoid the draft. The second item, a Faberge egg fashioned into a letter seal, is a genuine article from the Romanov family estate, expropriated by the Soviet government, and then transported to the United States with the intention of selling it to finance activities beneficial to the Soviet Government. Gabe Rabinowitz, upon his return to the United States in late 1918, was entrusted with the egg and chose not to deliver it to the designated intermediary, but to keep it himself. Upon my departure from Mr. Rabinowitz' company, in December, 1918, I took both items with the intention of keeping them safe until I could determine a proper place for them. Since I do not know the origins of the yellow invoice pad, nor what transactions it details, I cannot say what its proper return would entail. However, Gabe Rabinowitz was very anxious for its return. As for the egg, I do not believe the Romanov family can any longer claim possession, and, since the Soviet government has elected to sell this item, I presume the item legally belongs to them. Perhaps the egg can be placed in trust until the question of its appropriate ownership is resolved.

Sincerely,
   Penny Joe Copper

P.S. Thank you once again for the delicious dinner on the train.

I had my letter. Now I needed the courage to deliver it.

CHAPTER 32

In addition to having my letter, I needed a plan to deliver it. I thought about various ways I might ingratiate myself with Mrs. Hoover, but in the end decided it would take too long. Something had made me aware that time at my present living establishment was running out. A rock crashing through the bay window in Henrietta's front parlor. It was tied with twine, and carried a note accusing Henrietta of harboring a "white girl nigger lover." The implication was clear. Why else, but for immoral purposes, would a white girl be living in a colored boarding house?

Whatever the merits of the charge, however dangerous my presence was to Henrietta and Lysander, it was, in fact, also dangerous to me. The sheer fact of being noticed. Just as in Mexico, as was our little household, in spite of our efforts to persuade servants and the authorities that we were idle Americans (plus one Indian Brahmin and one Russian spy.) Presumably, with rocks coming through the window, Mr. Hoover would catch the drift of my presence in the nation's capital soon enough as well. So I didn't have much time, not enough time, certainly, to court Mrs. Hoover and persuade her to invite me to her home.

As I saw it, that left me three alternatives: one, to deliver my letter and the egg anonymously, say, in a package of household laundry. The shop next to mine did laundry so I could filch some of their unclaimed goods and wrap up my egg and note inside. The second possibility was to study

Mr. Hoover's comings and goings, trail him when he left his office, intercept him on the street near his home. Third, I could walk right into his inner sanctum and declare myself, tell my tale, leave my goods and hope to escape without arrest. Of the three choices, I decided intercepting him on the street, outside his home, with or without the laundry, was the safest bet. But to do this, I had to find out where on Seward Square he lived.

After thinking about that some, I took the trolley to George Washington University Law School, Mr. Hoover's *alma mater*, and, under the guise of inquiring about becoming a legal secretary, found out how land records are kept. I was astonished to discover that they are all public, that any citizen can walk into any city hall and ask to see the evidence on which a town decides how much tax property owners pay. Apparently this is how other owners keep track of what their neighbors are charged, as well as where lawyers search deeds to determine if properties have what are called "clouds" on their title. So, armed with that scant knowledge, I marched the next day into the land records office of the District of Columbia, signed in using my new name of Josephine Nichols, and said I was a clerk at a law firm I saw advertised in a second floor window down the street. When the pale man who stood behind the counter asked if I wanted land records or tax records I said, "Tax."

He asked, "By name or street address?"

"Both, " I said. Then, thinking Hoover was a pretty famous name and that I didn't even know Mrs. Hoover's first name, I changed my mind. "Street."

He sighed. "What street?"

I was getting nervous. "Seward," I said. "Seward Square." He began to look this up in an index of street maps. "South East," I added, to help him along, and wished I hadn't.

"What block?" he finally said. There was scorn on his face, as if he were beating me in some game with unknown rules. "There are several on Seward Square."

I hesitated. "All of them," I said, narrowing my eyes as if daring him to cross me.

He pulled out a heavy book, opened it to a section near the middle, scanned the contents, then dropped the volume on the counter. It landed with a thud, then, with one finger, he pushed it in my direction. "This covers the two northerly blocks," he said. "If you want the rest, you'll have to go to Volume 38 or 42." He turned away, that unpleasant task done.

I cleared my throat. When he turned to see what I wanted, I gave him a big smile. "Thank you so very much," I said, laying on the charm. "Is there somewhere I can take this?" He motioned to a chair at a table pushed up against the wall.

"You can't take it out of the room."

"I wouldn't dream of it." I widened my smile and took the cracked leather book over to the long table to begin my study of Volume 29 of the District of Columbia tax records. I spent the next half hour taking notes, although it was clear there was no Hoover property in that volume. When I got the second volume, after going through the same "please" and "thank you" rigmarole, I found it. Estelle Hoover, owner of 228 Sixth Street S.E., a property valued at $4,358 and taxed at a rate of $79.38 a year. I wrote all that down, added it to the list of information on all the properties on the north side of Seward Square I had written down. To be on the safe side, I went back and got Volume 42 and took notes on those properties as well. It was closing time when I finished. I returned the last volume, thanked the clerk, put away my papers, got on my winter coat and went out into the evening darkness. It was late November, Thanksgiving two days away. The following week, I told myself, I would move. And make my move on Mr. Hoover as well.

It was with deep grief that I told Henrietta that night that I was leaving. I did not know where, but it seemed best to say I had completed my work and was leaving the region entirely, to avoid any suggestion I was departing because of the rock. Henrietta did not ask more, but I could see Lysander was troubled. "You all right, girl?"

I nodded, although I wasn't all right, just hanging on, not knowing where I was going next. That Thanksgiving I felt more alone than I had in my whole life. To give up the only protection I had, to go out in the world once again, was almost too much to bear. I was reaching some kind of crisis, for the first time wanting something for myself, something that wasn't provisional, that wasn't just a shadow of real life. I had started on a train journey on leap year's day almost three years before, hoping for a new life that my brother would bring. Well, my brother was dead. My pa dead, too, and my mother with a new family to raise. Marcel, the love of my life, had disappeared. Harry Ault, the one employer who had seen something of value in me, was now probably out of a job. That moment, all I wanted was to stay with Henrietta and Lysander forever, but I couldn't. So that drizzling holiday weekend we went through the motions of normal holiday festivities in the front parlor, but in more ways than one, the heavy curtains were now permanently drawn.

Maybe it was cowardice, but that weekend, I changed my plans again. I decided I would leave Henrietta's house, but not Washington. I would find some other rooming house, in Glover Park or Silver Spring, then confront Mr. Hoover and repair to my new hideout. The second thing I decided was that, before dealing with Mr. Hover, I would find Marcel. I had to know if that door was still open, even just a crack, before I set about fashioning yet another new life. So I stopped thinking about 228 Seward Street, and started thinking about how to find Marcel.

It was clear from my brief study of *Symphony Digest* that there were people whose business it was to keep track of where musicians came and went. Booking agents of one sort or another. All I had to do was find one of those people to find Marcel. Having put off my confrontation with Mr.

Hoover, I took myself back to the Library of Congress and spent the last days in November poring over newspapers and periodicals, looking for announcements about new members of violin sections, scanning photos in season programs, writing down information about the dozen or so agents who specialized in placing performers. One of those agents had an office in Baltimore, so on the last day in November I found myself boarding the train to Baltimore to meet a Mr. Isaac Sigismund.

His office was on the third floor of a run down commercial building on Lombard Street. Symphony Hall was just a few blocks away. Mr. Sigismund was a small man with tufts of hair growing out of his ears and tiny blue eyes that gleamed when he spoke. He smiled often, reflexively, his face then gathering into a web of wrinkles. When he was not smiling he looked wan, so I was glad when he smiled, because then he didn't reminded me of me. Mr. Sigismund told me he was happy to be of whatever help he could.

Looking around, I got the impression that business was slow. Before I could explain the purpose of my visit, he suggested that he first show me Symphony Hall, which turned out to be locked, the orchestra on tour. Next he said he was hungry, and so walked me to his favorite raw bar, and made me sit beside him while he ate a dozen oysters. I declined the offer of oysters but took one of the deep fried fritters that came with his order. Most of the other men at the high mahogany bar were fishermen drinking midday beer and stronger stuff. I was surprised to see Mr. Sigismund in his worn three-piece suit settled so happily in their midst.

He sensed my thought and told me, "I used to be one," then smiled as he did a bottoms-up with his oyster. "A harbor rat, in Vilnius." His eyes closed, head tipped back, the moment seemed to me a private one. The oyster safely down his throat, he opened his blue eyes and winked. "Years ago, in the time of the Czars."

There it was again, the Czars. I touched my purse,

checking my Faberge egg. A sense of unease washed over me. Was Isaac Sigismund the next step in the journey of this Romanov jewel? "I haven't told you what I've come for," I announced, to put an end to this unsettling sensation.

Mr. Sigismund waved away this detail. "Wait," he said, standing while he slipped the last oyster down his gullet. Finished, he patted his lips with his napkin.

I announced, "I have a friend. Someone I've lost track of. A lover." Then blushed. I had meant to say violinist.

"Ah," he murmured. "A lover." He nodded as he absorbed this information.

"A violinist," I amended, staring at the bowl of corn fritters. I picked one up, pretended to study it while he waited. Finally I gave up and returned the fried mound to its oily paper nest. We said nothing more about my problem until we were back in his rabbit warren of an office and he had taken out a bottle of Cherry Heering.

"For the digestion," he said, holding it to the light and then pouring three fingers of thick red liquid into short cordial glasses. It was now mid-afternoon, and I had had nothing to eat except two corn fritters.

An hour passed, two large refills. From his desk drawer he took out some hard cheese, wrapped in a checkered bandana, which he opened to make a tiny tablecloth and then cut off thin slices of cheese with a letter opener. He offered this on a tray he'd made out of old newspaper. I accepted with great pleasure. While we continued our little party he filled me in on the vagaries of his business. He said he was a matchmaker, a go-between among orchestras that needed cheap labor and musicians who were willing to accept starvation wages.

"But how do you get paid?' I asked.

"Ah! Smart girl," he exclaimed, then gave me one of his beaming smiles. "That, indeed, is the question. Not much room for the middleman!" This he offered up as proof of the dignity of his calling. He and my pa would have got along famously. He poured another round to celebrate the mystery of life. We still hadn't gotten to the whereabouts of Marcel. The afternoon was heading somewhere but I didn't know where. I was mulling over how I was going to deflect what I assumed was coming—a pass, a clumsy attempt to take advantage. But he surprised me. The pass, when it came, was clumsy, but not unwelcome, and not to take advantage. The bottle emptied, he tucked away his disastrously astray collar, stammered a bit and finally came out with it. He asked if I would work for him, clean up the mess of his office—he lifted an arm in a gracious arc as if he were showing off Buckingham Palace. And answer the phone, he added. He pointed to a stack of uncollected invoices, said he couldn't afford to give me a salary, but that I could have half of what I collected and also a share of any new business I brought in.

"How would I bring business in?" I asked, already taken by the prospect of unlimited afternoons filled with Cherry Heering and hard cheese.

"You're young, pretty. Musicians like pretty girls," he said, as if that answered it.

I frowned, trying to be businesslike, and asked where I'd stay. I pointed out I couldn't afford a place to live if I were making no wages. He said he had a friend who had a room over his tobacco store. If I put in a few hours a week at the cash register, he was sure I could have the room for nothing. "What about food," I said, thinking hard, trying to find a flaw in all this. He shrugged, a detail.

"I will feed you," he announced. Then he confessed that he missed his dead wife and that I reminded him of a daughter he had lost to typhoid back in Vilnius.

I took the late train back to Washington, my head swimming from the Cherry Heering and the unexpected turn my life had once again taken. Lysander was working late storing bags and when he saw me his face broke into a huge smile. He wanted to hug me, I could see that, and I wanted to hug him. But that was impossible, we were in a public place. He told me to wait, said he was off in a half hour, that then he would walk me home. Although it had been a long day, I was content to sit on a carved marble bench in the great domed waiting room. American palaces, I thought, libraries and train stations. I dozed off and then woke to find Lysander shaking my shoulder. I liked the touch of his hand on my houndstooth coat, and rubbed my cheek against it, rough tweed and leather skin. On the walk home I told him that I had taken a job in Baltimore, that I would miss him and Henrietta, that I hoped they could visit me, or I visit them, when things calmed down. Lysander didn't ask what I meant by things calming down, but I think he knew. One of the things I meant was when it became clear what my feelings were for him and what, if anything, I would do about it.

CHAPTER 33

I stayed with Siggy seven years. Seven years over the tobacco shop, seven years of Siggy cooking me meals on a hot plate in his cramped office, or bringing in stuffed cabbage he had cooked at home and then kept warm on the top of the radiator. Occasionally he invited me to his home, an equally cramped apartment near Johns Hopkins that smelled of Baltic cooking and oriental rugs badly in need of cleaning. In the last months of his life, in 1927, I moved in to care for him when he was too weak to take the streetcar down to his office or climb the stairs, still keeping up the pretense to the end that we were running a business. In those seven years he told me a lot about his life, his dreams and illusions, the things that had sustained him. Music, his wife, the memory of his daughter. The simple freedoms of an independent existence. "Never," he used to say, "never did I work in a factory." That was a point of pride with him, avoiding the regimentation. But he seemed to have no political views, no ax to grind one way or the other. In this he reminded me of Marcel, who existed on another plane that he was led to through music. While Siggy was not particularly musical himself, he kept a *balalaika* and a battered tambourine, but on the rare occasions he took them down from their places in the dark mahogany bookshelves that lined his parlor, he played folk music, which he sang in a high nasal voice quite unlike his speaking one.

His speech was raspy, and varied from a bark to a coo, depending on what worked best with a client. Most of the musicians he placed were with orchestras on the Eastern seaboard. In former days he would personally visit all the conservatories in the train corridor from Boston to Richmond, but, as he got older, he ventured no farther than Philadelphia, preferring to send me to New York, and not bothering with Boston at all. As for the orchestras, they generally communicated through the mail, or occasionally by telegram. Sometimes we approached them, using Siggy's encyclopedic knowledge of the strengths and weaknesses of each orchestra in order to entice a director into taking an interest in one or another musician Siggy was trying to place.

I liked auditions best, the informal ones Siggy arranged in his office, and more formal ones, when occasionally a visiting orchestra director would ask us to rent a rehearsal hall and line up a dozen or so prospective bassoon players or violinists. I never succeeded in understanding much about what I was listening to, and my trips out of town were, to my mind, a waste of money, but Siggy was right, musicians did like pretty girls, and I guess I was pretty enough to sign them up, and then Siggy would work on finding them somewhere to play.

It was a world separate enough and calm enough that I spent seven years there, as if the world I left behind evaporated, as if Penny Joe Copper didn't exist. I didn't miss my old self when I settled into a life as Siggy's long departed daughter and all around Girl Friday. There were, of course, the outstanding matters of Mr. Hoover, my search to find Marcel, my feelings about Lysander. But after I had been in Baltimore a few weeks I took the train back and found Lysander as I had first found him, helping people into cabs. We beamed at each other, then he told me to wait, and found another red cap to cover for him. We retreated into the porters' rest area, deserted in the middle of the afternoon.

Once the door closed we gave each other a big hug, then he stroked my face and said, "My, my," and commented that I had put on some weight and said that was good. I told him

I missed him, and Henrietta, too, and that was the truth. I asked if they had had any more trouble with the neighbors and he said no, but we both understood that it was not wise for me to go back, so I scribbled an address on a piece of paper and said that I'd like them both to come visit me, that Siggy would cook us all dinner, and play the balalaika, and afterwards we could play cribbage or read Alexander Dumas. He looked at the paper carefully, folded it and placed it in his breast pocket and said he'd do that. Then gave me another quick hug and said he had to go back to work. I waited a few moments after Lysander left before slipping out and going on my way.

A month or two later Henrietta and Lysander did come, one Sunday afternoon, and we had a fine dinner laid out on the work table in Siggy's office and after went to a jazz club near the Gaiety Burlesque that had paid off the police and was thus exempt from the local segregation laws. Two or three times a year we would get together, twice including old Mrs. Hattry, whom we tried to match up with Siggy to no avail. In later years the dinners moved to Siggy's house, and Henrietta would do the cooking, bringing a chicken with greens and her famous pineapple pie. This blending of the two most comfortable families I had ever belonged to seemed almost a miracle to me, and it must have seemed so to Lysander as well, because neither of us further tested Henrietta's injunction to keep our friendship just that.

The matter of J. Edgar Hoover kind of petered out as well. On December 29, 1920, less than a month after I'd arrived in Baltimore, the famous Palmer Raids began. Within the next ten days some hundreds of people were rounded up in cities across the nation. Lists had been prepared—names from the Finnish Workers' Alliance, the Bulgarian Self-Help Committee, Wobblies anywhere and everywhere—members of any organization thought to be radical or composed of foreign born. Like the May Day ransackings of the previous year, offices were stormed and files taken or destroyed.

Assembly line processing of the subsequent arrests resulted in imprisonments and mass deportations. A. Mitchell Palmer, the Attorney General whose house had been bombed seven months before, gave his name to the campaign, but J. Edgar Hoover was the mastermind. Several of Siggy's friends were arrested for no other reason than their membership in Baltic fraternal organizations. At least that is what Siggy told me and it seemed reasonable to believe.

Now that I was away from Seattle, my anger wasn't so white hot, and was more evenly distributed between Gabe and Mr. Hoover. I wondered whether Harry Ault was still running the *Union Record* and hoped he had had the sense to withdraw quietly. Somehow I doubted it. But it was no longer my war, if it had ever been. And I was loath to open myself to its all-consuming anger by communicating with the Justice Department. Another thing that bothered me was a widely published photo of Mr. Hoover, grinning from ear to ear, showing off trophies he had taken from the raids just conducted. Flags and other memorabilia hung on his office wall, the smaller stuff displayed in a glass-front cabinet behind his desk. I didn't want my egg there, a trinket in his trophy case. But I had no such concerns about the yellow invoice pad. So, after considerable thought, I rewrote my letter, now a year old, typed it out on Siggy's battered Remington, took out all references to the egg and my enjoying his dinner on the train. I took off my name as well, folded the brief note implicating Sam and Gabe by way of the yellow invoice pad, put the letter and incriminating evidence in a manila envelope addressed to Mr. Hoover c/o the Justice Department. I took the train to Washington and the trolley to where the Justice Department stood and put my envelope in a mailbox just across the street.

I thought no more about it, but years later, in the mid 1930s, when I ran into Anna Mae on one of her visits to the United States, she told me that Sam Rabinowitz had, seemingly out of the blue, accused her father of turning states' evidence during Sam's 1921 conspiracy trial. I thought of Reverend Sloan in the hospital stairwell, taking his hand off Josephine's rump, and decided that one way or the other my message had gotten through. "How about the other Rabinowitz?" I asked in an ironic voice, as if we were discussing the weather.

"Disappeared," she said. "Rumor has it he turned margin trader on Wall Street and lost it all in the crash."

A nice picture, but somehow I thought his talent for mayhem would have found more conducive channels. I knew by then Anna Mae was deep in the Moscow bureaucracy, so it could just as well have been that Gabe was an undercover operative for the Soviets and Anna Mae was hiding that fact. But I doubted that as well, because I had stolen Gabe's egg, and I doubted the powers in Moscow would take kindly to Gabe's pilfering of Romanov souvenirs.

* * *

One winter afternoon in 1922, after a half-dozen schnapps, while Siggy was telling me tales of Latvia, he once again mentioned the Czars. I took a deep breath and told him I had something to show him. He made no comment, but eyed my nervous preparations as I proceeded to bundle him up and lead him through the snow back to my room over the tobacco shop. Once there I pulled out the sewing box in which I stored my few personal keepsakes. Inside was the egg. He whistled as he turned it over, rubbing the deep green enamel and blowing at the gold filigree.

"It's a letter seal," I told him.

"I can see that," he said. "Where did you get it?"

"I can't tell you."

He asked if I had any ink and I got some out of a drawer and watched as he poured a little into a saucer, then rolled the seal into it and stamped five or six times on a piece of paper.

"Do you know where it's from?" I asked, remembering how Borodin and I had gone through the same ritual process.

He looked at me carefully. "No," he finally said. "It's Russian, of course, possibly Faberge. But it could be a forgery."

"It could be," I said, suddenly happy at that thought which had never occurred to me. By unspoken mutual consent we said no more about my possession of a potentially fake Faberge egg until three years later when Siggy's business had dwindled to a trickle and his lung condition made climbing stairs to his office an ordeal. "Let's sell the egg," I proposed. "How much can we get?"

He thought for a bit and then said, "Too dangerous. First we would need a provenance." I asked what that meant and he explained that every valuable art object needs a documented history before it can be sold on the open market.

So began my second encounter with a forger, this one an art expert. Siggy knew a lot of people on the margins in Baltimore, a business netherworld that populated the storefronts in the few blocks around Siggy's office. The Estonian art expert had a shop even shabbier than Siggy's, from which he sold cufflinks and watches from dusty velvet trays while running an appraisal business in the back. After a few mumbled greetings, we were escorted through a black velvet curtain to a windowless room. When Siggy took the egg from its wrapper the Estonian grunted. He reached out, removed the egg from its cover, looked the egg over, hefted it, examined the markings on the seal, then examined the beige velvet cover with even closer attention. "Where did you get this?" he asked in a sharp voice.

"That is for you to tell us," Siggy replied.

"Do you want to sell?"

"Not yet," Siggy replied, giving me a measured look. "I'd like your advice about how to position it for later sale. Say, in ten or fifteen years."

"Oh, that's easy," the Estonian replied, handing the egg back with a wistful expression then watching Siggy polish off any fingerprints and replace it in its velvet casing. "I take it this piece belongs to the lady?" He gave me an appraisal equal to the one he had just given the egg.

"Maybe," Siggy replied. "She has a friend who has been most generous."

I took this as my cue to blush.

"Then she is free to give it to someone else? Someone who might have had occasion to come into legitimate possession? Who might, after a suitable time, be open to giving it back?"

"I don't see why not." Siggy looked thoughtful as he mulled this suggestion.

And so that afternoon the egg was recorded first as pawned at the Estonian's shop in 1916, brought in by a questionable person known to the police as a jewel thief, then recorded as sold to Siggy on November 4, 1918, along with a pair of silver earrings. The second transaction was dated a few months before Siggy's wife's death, and the sales receipt was placed in the appropriate drawer in the Estonian's haphazard records. Siggy tore up his carbon copy. The Estonian nodded in approval. But the notations of provenance were kept by Siggy, handwritten on the Estonian's stationary, ascribing the egg to the late 19th century, "A curio letter seal, possibly Faberge but more likely a copy done in the Faberge style." The earrings were described as mid-ninteenth century English, machine-stamped silver.

"Keep it for a few years," the Estonian instructed. "Then give both items to the lady—" He motioned at me as if I were part of the woodwork. "Better yet, will them to her. She can keep the earrings and take the egg to someone who will undoubtedly discover it is genuine."

"How much is it worth?" I asked.

He shrugged. "Hard to say. The longer you hold on to it, the more it will bring."

So the egg became our nest egg. Every time things got really tight, we'd joke about selling the egg, but never did. Sure enough, in Siggy's will, I got not only his balalaika, and his wife's jewelry, but a return of the Faberge egg. To pay for his funeral, and in accordance with his instructions, I sold his heavy well-loved furniture, and then buried him much more reverently than I had buried my pa. It was an Orthodox funeral, attended by a dozen or so of his old friends, as well as Henrietta and Lysander. At the graveside we drank the last of his schnapps and when it was over I went back to his apartment and wept.

The next day, as the movers were taking out the mahogany bookcases, I found a letter addressed to me taped inside the cover of his balalaika. "Dearest Penny Joe," it said. I had never told him my real name. "In those early years when you would bring up the matter of your lost Marcel, I professed not to know where he was. I am sorry. Here is an address where you can find him if you so choose. Think carefully about whether you want to do so. Regardless, know that I have loved you deeply ever since I first laid eyes on you. Your dearest Isaac." I looked at the address. Marcel was in Chicago, the city where I had left him seven years before. I looked up to see the last of Siggy's furniture being carried out the door. I had decisions to make. Where to live. What to do about Marcel. How to feel about Siggy's keeping his whereabouts from me.

CHAPTER 34

I had no furniture, no place to live, but Siggy had left me a good bit of money in the envelope inside the balalaika case. I took it he intended me to be able to travel to Chicago if I so chose. Siggy had known my real name all along, though how he found out I never knew. Perhaps he had contacted Marcel. But why had he not told me?

Of the three places I could imagine going to live— Washington, Chicago, or Seattle—common sense required that I arrive as the person I had left. I knew nothing of what had happened to Harry Ault, had not once contacted my mother. But perhaps becoming Penny Joe once again was not so dangerous. While I was living a snug life in Baltimore, the country had been caught up in the jazz age. No one, I hoped, was any longer paying attention to enemy aliens or Bolsheviks. People were buying bootleg gin, stocks on margin and voting Republican. Penny Joe Copper was no longer of interest to the Justice Department or the Communist Party. So I thought about writing my mother a letter, but decided to put it off until I had a better sense of where I was headed. In the end I picked Chicago, but put off the question of whether to contact Marcel.

Once there, I decided to try my luck on the north side, and found a one-room apartment, with a shared kitchen. I got a job keeping books for a restaurant supply company and enrolled in night school at the University of Illinois. As winter set in, sadness overwhelmed me. The loss of Siggy, his companionship, the sheltered life he provided. I began to wonder if I'd made a mistake, coming to Chicago, resuming my old solitary existence. Of course I had, I decided, as I spent yet another weekend waiting for Monday to come around so that I could be in the company of others. But did I have a choice? I couldn't go back to live with Henrietta and Lysander, not the least reason being that Lysander had finally married his friend from church, the lady with the lovely hats. I had no one, no friend or occupation or family to draw me back to Baltimore. What I did have was a Faberge egg and the address of a man in Chicago I had once loved. So, one Sunday afternoon in the early winter of 1928, with much trepidation, I bought a ticket for the Chicago Symphony and, from the far balcony, watched Marcel perform in a program of Berlioz and Schumann from his position of second violinist.

Each Sunday afternoon that winter I bought my ticket for the balcony. From reading the music listings in the Tribune I discovered he also played in a quartet that gave free concerts around town. One Friday evening I went to Hull House and listened to a short program of Vivaldi. I tried to slip in late in the back, but the room was small, and within seconds Marcel looked up and saw me. After that he kept his gaze on the window curtains, and when the time came for applause, stood but kept his head down, face blank as he briefly acknowledged the applause from the first few rows.

I was ashamed of interrupting his life, of stalking him in my loneliness. On the other hand, I needed to know. That evening I left without speaking to him, but went back to my room and wrote him a letter, then mailed it before I had a chance to read it over and destroy it. My memory of that letter is that I told him I still cared deeply for him, that I had been living on the East coast for a number of years but that my employer and mentor had died. I mentioned Siggy, a name I knew Marcel would recognize, and said I had often spoken of Marcel, had wondered what became of his life and career. When Siggy died, I told him, he had left me an address, and, in a weak moment, I was now writing this letter. I begged Marcel to meet with me just once, to talk of old times, to put behind us what had been. That is not what I hoped, of course, but that is what I wrote. And it was in that vein that Marcel wrote back a brief note, thanking me for my letter, inviting me to his apartment one Sunday afternoon to meet his roommate. I understood what the term *roommate* meant, and it was with heavy heart and much dread that I wrote back thanking him for his invitation.

It was now April, but April in Chicago is not as lovely as April in Seattle. There were no rhododendrons in bloom, the air was not fresh and vivid after rain. Slush coated the sidewalks as I made my way to the "L" and took the nearly empty train two stops closer to downtown. There were some new apartment buildings by the lake, quite fashionable, and Marcel lived in one of those. I wondered how he could afford it on what I knew to be the meager earnings of a second violinist, but didn't dwell on that puzzle, so concerned was I with keeping up my courage and making sure that the hothouse tulips I had brought didn't flop out of their paper and drop petals.

Marcel met me at the door. He had on a velvet jacket, loosely tied and wine purple, a costume that made him look like an English peer. I told him so, and complimented him on the color, which set off his complexion. Then, before I could stop myself, I reached up and kissed his cheek. "I missed you," I said. "You were my best friend."

That softened him, put him more at ease. I took the moment to shove the tulips at him, saying they matched his smoking jacket. He unwrapped them and tried the purple black against his jacket, and this bit of business made us both laugh and allowed us to enter the living room more or less relaxed in each other's company. A young man was sitting in a big chair by a fireplace, the glow of the flames against the darkening sky casting his blond hair into sharp relief. This is the roommate, I realized. Everything, the whole of my circumstances, fell into place. I understood, finally, what had happened, and not happened, between us, the beautiful, almost unearthly, gentleness of his caresses. "Gilbert," Marcel said, guiding me toward the young man. "This is Penny Joe. From Seattle. My oldest friend."

"His mother hated me," I said, trying to smile.

Gilbert tried his best to smile as well. "Me, too," he said. "Still does." It was on that basis that the three of us spent a careful hour, generous in our exploration of both present and past.

I saw the two of them occasionally after that, as I set about mending what was left of my heart. I renewed my correspondence with my mother, taking a week that summer to go out to Everett and see how Rudy and the boys were doing. My mother was the same. She had put on a few pounds, become a Methodist, but otherwise showed no sign her life was any different. I think she was mostly content that Rudy made a decent living and didn't drink.

A year or two later, when the depression hit, Rudy took his loss of livelihood hard—he had mortgaged heavily on a bigger store—but mother took it in stride. Like my time with Siggy, she looked upon that interlude of relative calm as a blessing, and felt no injustice in its coming to an end. She went back to working in a factory while Rudy became more and more morose, but she never let on that she was unhappy with this turn of events. Toward the end of the thirties Rudy got a job with the New Deal, through me, actually. I was by then a minor government functionary and had enough clout to steer Rudy to the man who did the hiring in Seattle, and life got a little better for them after that. Rudy died of thrombosis in 1943, and left my mother the house, which they had managed to keep, and by then there was Social Security, so she was well enough off until she died in 1957. I made a point to visit her once a year and we exchanged cards at Christmas. She met both my first husband and my second husband and never said anything about either of them, one way or the other.

A couple of times I took a trip down to Seattle after my annual Everett visit, to find out what had happened to Harry Ault. He stayed on with the *Union Record* until 1923, then threw in the towel after the well-publicized trial of Sam Rabinowitz. (Well publicized in Seattle, that is, it made no impression in Baltimore.) He moved back to his wife's hometown outside Tacoma and took up truck farming with his brother- in-law. Anna Mae did what she said she would, joined the Quakers in Poland, then slipped across the boarder to the Ukraine, and became a confidant of Trotsky and then, when that became politically unfashionable, deleted all reference to him in her voluminous outpouring of bad books and signed on instead with the rising star, Stalin. Her father continued as a minister at the church on Queen Anne Hill, but I never went back there to visit. Nor did I ever make any attempt to look up Marcel's mother or Sam Rabinowitz.

I ran into Anna Mae once, in the mid 1930s, when she was in Seattle attending to some business regarding her father's health. I met them at the zoo, and it was clear that her father was well along in his dotage, and that she was at wits end as to how to properly care for him.

"I have my career," she wailed. "I am a well-known personage in Russia."

I watched as her father tried to unlock the secret of opening a peanut. It turned out she was editing a newspaper, an English language one, with my old friend from Mexico, Mikhail Borodin. I resisted the impulse to let on that I once knew him. She said that she was married, to a Russian, and I allowed as how I was married too. She said she had run into Sam Rabinowitz, that he and his wife Etta were still living in the same house near the port. That was when she told me that Sam, for some mysterious reason, held her poor father responsible for certain damning evidence at his trial.

I said nothing, merely watching the Reverend Sloan turn his peanut over and over.

She asked about my husband, and I told her that he was a teacher in Chicago. I did not want to get into a discussion of politics, or tell her that I took up with Ashton not long after my painful reunion with Marcel. I had signed up for a course on the history of the American labor movement, which I should have had the good sense to stay out of. In my weakness I let slip my connection to the Everett massacre, and that was enough to attract the attentions of Ashton.

I suppose I was still licking my wounds because I fell for him, the kind of man that, in a stronger frame of mind, I would have passed by. I may have mentioned that Ashton was both a drinker and a hopeless romantic. A Marxist and probably a member of the Communist Party. I never asked, but his interest in me swelled when he found out I was Joe Copper's daughter.

We were married in the fall of 1932. He went off to Moscow not long after. The whole time I was with Ashton I was afraid Gabe would somehow appear, that Ashton would invite him home to dinner, and begged my husband not to tell his friends anything about me. Ashton was a ladies' man as well, something I found out near the end of our marriage. By then that news came as something of a relief. Truth was, I never liked him much, and couldn't, for the life of me, figure out what had attracted me in the first place. Very little, I finally decided. By 1936, I was about to tell Ashton it was time to end this unfortunate experiment, but then the Spanish Civil War intervened and Ashton upped and joined the Lincoln Brigade. Two months later he was dead in the mountains near Barcelona. Thus I became a widow before I became a divorcee.

Once again my life became solitary. By then I had a college degree, in botany, and a profession, in plant genetics, and a steady job with the U.S. Department of Agriculture. I spent one summer in Washington D.C. teaching a course at the

Department's night school, but did not contact J. Edgar Hoover or ask him to join me for dinner.

After the war, a short assignment took me to Detroit, where I met my second husband, Vernon, who worked for the Auto Workers and later got involved in the investigation into the shootings of the Reuther brothers. As it happened, Rosa was also in Detroit and I tried to rekindle that friendship but it failed. My years of marriage to Vernon, however, were happy ones and, like my time with Siggy, an interval I count as blessed. When I moved back to Snoqualmie in 1958 with my widow's pension, I thought my life pretty much over. I had had enough twists and turns for any one person and was content to live what remained of my life with my seed catalogs and my Faberge egg. I thought of it by then, with Siggy's bogus provenance papers, as mine. After all, Siggy had willed it to me, along with his wife's jewelry and his balalaika. I never told anyone a different story.

Then, about ten years later, I saw an article in the paper. About a violinist, a minor hometown celebrity, Marcel Freid, who was destitute, crippled with multiple sclerosis, and living in a Musicians' Home in Evanston, Illinois. The next day I took my egg to an appraiser in Seattle and went from there to a jewelry shop and sold the egg for $47,000. I could have gotten more if I had bothered to establish its Romanov pedigree, but $47,000 seemed enough for my purpose. I flew to Chicago and arrived in the middle of the tumultuous 1968 Democratic convention. Shaggy imitation Gabes were everywhere, prowling the streets, pasting up broadsides, provoking furious Chicago policemen to violence.

That evening was the famous riot. I was not there. I had taken the train to Evanston and was visiting Marcel, who was so crippled he had to be strapped to a bed board and fed with a straw. I kissed his forehead and smoothed down the last of his once beautiful hair and showed him the cashier's check for $47,000. I told him it was his. That he could use it to buy himself the best medical care he could find or, what I hoped he would do, come back with me to Snoqualmie and let me nurse him for the remainder of his days. I said I wouldn't beg, but I could hear the begging in my voice. I asked him to grant me this one wish—told him that I loved him, had always loved him, and couldn't think of how I could go back to my life in Snoqualmie knowing that he was alone. He was silent for a while and then offered the thinnest of smiles. "As a favor," he croaked. "Not because I want to." I hugged him and then wept all over his bed sheet and soon after set about making the arrangements.

It took over a month to sort through the paperwork. The Musicians' Home did not want to relinquish his health benefit. Marcel came to live with me in my Snoqualmie cottage in October of 1968 and I cared for him until two years ago, when he died. I buried him in the Mount Pleasant cemetery near where Horace lies. Each Saturday, in the summer, when I bring my cut flowers and seed packets into town to sell at Pikes Place Market, I take the bus up to the cemetery and get a ride in the little electric cart over to the section where their two graves are. I regret I was not able to have buried them side-by-side. But then, I remind myself, I was a different person to each of them, they never knew each other, and I should not try to make them best of friends. And so I visit each separately, each wrapped in their mysteries, each a different deeply loved person.

I have lived a wonderful life. To have known, and loved, so many—my pa, Horace, Marcel, Harry Ault, Siggy, Henrietta, Lysander, my dear husband Vernon, and then again Marcel. A full life. A blessed life.

A NOTE ABOUT SOURCES

This is a work of fiction, but I have hewn fairly closely to historical events and have incorporated within the story some historical figures. For those who wish to keep track of such things:

Penny Joe and her family are fictional characters, as are Marcel and his mother, Gabe and Sam Rabinowitz, and all the people Penny Joe met in Washington D.C. and Baltimore. Anne Mae Sloan and her father, the Reverend Sloan, bear passing resemblance to Anna Louise Strong and her father, although most of the incidents I've written about them are fictional. Likewise there was a Harry Ault who was editor of the *Union Record,* but his relationship with Penny Joe is just part of my story.

On the other hand, Mikhail Borodin, Mike Gold and Manny Gomez, M.N. Roy and his girlfriend all lived together in Mexico City in 1917-18, and there was a failed effort to smuggle jewels. Fanya Borodin lived in Chicago until she joined her husband in Moscow in 1921. J. Edgar Hoover was starting out in the Justice Department at the end of the war and later become head of the Alien Radical Division in the summer of 1919. There was a mysterious stranger named Leon Green who arrived in Seattle just in time for the general strike but he wasn't Gabe Rabinowitz.

For those who wish to read more on the history of the times I can suggest some of the sources I consulted:

Detailed accounts of the Everett Massacre are found in

Mill Town, by Norman H. Clark, and *The Everett Massacre,* by Walker C. Smith. On the Mexican interlude, Dan N. Jacobs's biography, *Borodin, Stalin's Man in China* provides a full description, as does *It Had to Be Revolution,* Charles Shipman's memoir of his time living as Manny Gomez. For information about the Seattle General Strike, I relied on a book by Robert L. Friedman, *The Seattle General Strike,* as well as the biography of Anna Louise Strong, *Right in Her Soul,* by Tracy B. Strong and Helene Keyssar.

About Jan Shapin

Jan Shapin has been writing plays and screenplays for nearly thirty years, in the last decade concentrating on fiction. Shapin has studied playwriting at Catholic University in Washington, DC, screenwriting at the Film and Television Workshop and University of Southern California, and fiction writing at a variety of locations including Barnard College's Writers on Writing seminar, the Sewanee Writers' Conference and Bread Loaf Writers' Conference.

Her plays have been produced in the Northeast and Mid-Atlantic states. She has received grants from the RI Council for the Humanities and has served as a juror for the Rhode Island State Council for the Arts screenplay fellowship awards.

She lives in North Kingstown, RI with her photographer husband.

Made in the USA
Charleston, SC
18 February 2014